CECILIA EKBÄCK was born in the north of Sweden; her parents come from Lapland. During her teens, she worked as a journalist and after university specialised in marketing. Over twenty years her work for a multinational took her to Russia, Germany, France, Portugal, the Middle East and the UK.

In 2010, she finished a Masters in Creative Writing at Royal Holloway. She now lives in Calgary with her husband and twin daughters, 'returning home' to the landscape and the characters of her childhood in her writing. *Wolf Winter* is her first novel and she is at work on her second. You can find out more about Cecilia via her website www.ceciliaekback.com and you can follow her @KarinCecilia on Twitter.

Acclaim for WOLF WINTER

'Like a silent fall of snow; suddenly, **the reader is enveloped . . . visually acute, skilfully written**; it won't easily erase its tracks in the reader's mind.'
Hilary Mantel, author of *Wolf Hall*

'*Wolf Winter* eminently repays reading for the **beauty of its prose, its strange, compelling atmosphere** and its tremendous evocation of the stark, dangerous, threatening place, which exists in the far north and in the hearts of all of us.'
Guardian

'Swedish Lapland of 1717 is evoked so vividly that it **seeps into your bones . . .** A **highly intelligent** piece of historical Scandi-noir.'
The Times

'A **compelling, suspenseful** story.'
Sunday Times

'**Rich in history** and authentic detail, *Wolf Winter* is a **deeply satisfying read. I highly recommend it.**'
Rene Denfeld, author of The Enchanted

'A Scandi novel to leave your **spine tingling** with fear.'
Essentials Magazine

'An **icy mystery** unfolds.'
Esquire

'Cecilia Ekbäck's debut *Wolf Winter* is **an absorbing tale** about fear, death and a cursed land.'
The National, UAE

'Just when we thought *Fortitude* might have marked "peak Scandi", along came *Wolf Winter*. And it's **bloody brilliant . . . Chilling in every sense of the word**, it has a mystery with the same tug that *The Miniaturist* did, as well as a comparably **unique sense of place**.'
The Debrief

'An **absorbing** read.'
Historical Novels Society

'The main storyline itself was **brilliant** as the murder mystery unfolds through the eyes of both Frederika and her mother, Maija, down two very different routes. One of them embracing the "sorcery" of the old religion and trusting in something primal, the other looking at the cold facts.'
Mabismab

'Peopled with finely drawn characters, this is a **powerful murder mystery** with a supernatural twist and some unexpected turns, but it is the setting and the **brilliantly evoked atmosphere** that really draws the reader in.'
Choice Magazine

WOLF WINTER

CECILIA EKBÄCK

HODDER

First published in Great Britain in 2015 by Hodder & Stoughton

An Hachette UK company

First published in paperback in 2015

3

Copyright © Cecilia Ekbäck 2015

A CIP catalogue record for this title is available
from the British Library

Paperback ISBN 978 1 444 78955 3
eBook ISBN 978 1 444 78953 9

Typeset in Plantin Light by Palimpsest Book Production Ltd,
Falkirk, Stirlingshire

Printed and bound by Clays Ltd, St Ives plc

Hodder & Stoughton policy is to use papers that are
natural, renewable and recyclable products and made from
wood grown in sustainable forests. The logging and manufacturing
processes are expected to conform to the environmental
regulations of the country of origin.

Hodder & Stoughton Ltd
Carmelite House
50 Victoria Embankment
London EC4Y ODZ

www.hodder.co.uk

For the women in my family who don't sleep

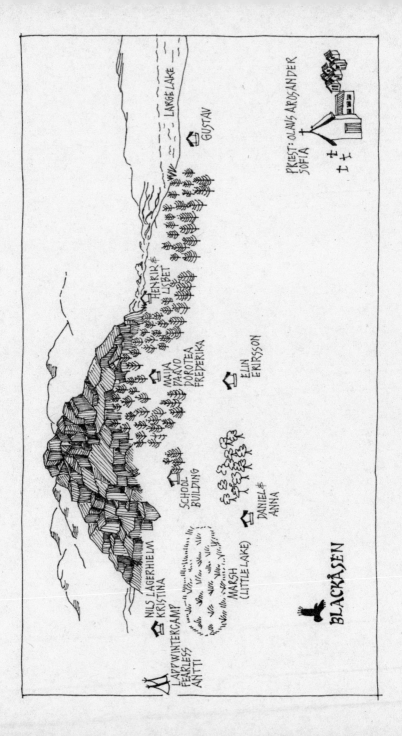

INTRODUCTORY NOTES

The Swedish King, Charles XII, spent almost his whole adult life abroad on military campaigns. When he finally returned to Sweden in 1714, it was to a country on the brink of rebellion, torn apart by the consequences of his foreign policy and by poverty. Nonetheless, in 1716 and in 1718 Charles launched new strikes against Norway, and in 1717, the year in which *Wolf Winter* is set, Sweden found itself at war with Denmark, Poland, Saxony, Hanover, Prussia and Russia.

Links between the Church and the King were strong and the King used the Church as a means of propaganda to explain the necessity of his wars to its parishioners and ensure their continued support.

As part of Sweden's nation building, land previously used by the indigenous people, the Sami (referred to as 'Lapps' throughout *Wolf Winter*, as they would have been at the time), was distributed to Swedish settlers during this period. As a result the Sami way of life, largely nomadic, came increasingly under attack.

As in much of Europe at this time, fear of 'sorcery' was still rife.

CAST OF CHARACTERS

On Blackåsen Mountain

Paavo Ranta, arriving from Ostrobothnia, Finland
Maija, his wife
Frederika, their daughter
Dorotea, their daughter
Jutta, Maija's grandmother, now deceased

'Eriksson,' born on Blackåsen Mountain
Elin Eriksson, his wife, said to have 'gifts'
Their children

Gustav, a former soldier

Henrik, arrived from Stockholm some twenty years
before the book opens
Lisbet, his ill wife
Their children

Daniel Eriksson, Eriksson's brother, also born on
Blackåsen Mountain
Anna, his wife
Their children

Nils Lagerhielm, a nobleman from Stockholm
Kristina, his wife
Their children

In town

Olaus Arosander, priest, former court priest
Johan Lundgren, verger and teacher
Anvar, the former priest, now deceased
Sofia, the former priest's widow
A Night Man
The priest's staff and their families

In the Lapp winter camp

Fearless, leader of the community
Antti

By the coast

Karl-Erik, bishop

PART ONE

Swedish Lapland, June 1717

'But how far is it?'

Frederika wanted to scream. Dorotea was slowing them down. She dragged behind her the branch she ought to be using as a whip, and Frederika had to work twice as hard to keep the goats moving. The morning was bright; white daylight sliced the spruce tops and stirred up too much colour. Frederika was growing hot. There were prickles on her back beneath the dress. She hadn't wanted to go, and now the goats didn't want to, either. They leapt to the left or right in among the trees and tried to run past them back towards the cottage. The only sounds were those of a tree shifting, of a hoof striking stone and the constant bleating of the stupid goats.

'Only poor people have goats,' she had said to her mother that same morning.

They were sitting on the wooden porch of their new home on the side of Blackåsen Mountain. In front of them, bugs flitted above the grassy slope. There was a small stream at the base of the hill and beyond that, a field. Enclosing all this was forest – jagged black spears against pink morning sky.

'We'll sow turnips up there.' Frederika's mother, Maija, nodded towards the barn. 'That's a good place with sun.'

'At least cows and sheep manage on their own in the forest. Goats are a lot of work for nothing.'

'It's just until your father and I have built a fence around the field. Take them to that glade we saw on our way here. It's not far.'

The barn door opened and Dorotea hopped out. The door clapped shut behind her.

'It will be fine,' her mother said in a low voice as Dorotea ran down the slope.

Frederika wanted to say that here, nothing could be fine. The forest was too dark. There was spidery mould among the twigs and on the ground beneath the lowest branches there were still patches of snow, hollow blue. She wanted to say that this cottage was smaller than the one they had lived in, in Ostrobothnia. It was lopsided and the land unkempt. Here was no sea, no other people. They shouldn't have left. Things hadn't been that bad. Hadn't they always managed? But the wrinkle between her mother's eyes was deeper than usual. As though she might want to say those things, too, and so Frederika had said nothing.

'But how far is it?

Frederika looked at the blonde child in the hand-me-down dress that billowed around her like a sheet on a clothes-line in wind. Dorotea was still little. Frederika was fourteen, Dorotea only six. Dorotea stumbled on the trailing hem.

'Lift your feet when you walk and hurry,' Frederika said.

'But I am tired,' Dorotea said. 'I'm tired, I'm tired, I'm tired.'

It was going to be an awful, awful day.

They climbed higher, and the forest below them turned into a sea of deep greens and stark blues that rolled and fell until the end of the world. Frederika thought of grey lakes; of a watery sky. She thought of flat earth with sparse growth that

4

didn't demand much and missed Ostrobothnia so badly that her chest twisted.

The path narrowed and dipped, with many loose stones. To the left, the mountain plunged all the way into the valley far beneath.

'Walk after me,' she said to Dorotea. 'Watch where you put your feet.'

Along the base of the rock, star-shaped purple saxifrage peeked through the stones. There was a small mound of brown pellets sweating in the sunshine, spilling; a deer of some sort. Above them, growing straight out of the stone, was a small, twisted birch.

The path veered right. Frederika hadn't seen this when they came, but here the side of the mountain had burst. There was a fracture cutting deep into the rock. Lynx lived in crevices like this. Trolls also.

'Hurry,' she said to Dorotea and lengthened her steps.

There was a large boulder and another bend in the path. The trail broadened. They were back in the forest.

'I stepped on something prickly.' Her sister lifted her leg and pointed at the sole of her dusty foot.

Then Frederika sensed rather than saw it. The goats sensed it too. They hesitated and stared at her, bleating large question marks.

It was the smell, she thought. It was the same stench that lay over the yard when they slaughtered to have meat for winter. Earth, rot, faeces.

A fly buzzed into her ear and she hit at it. Further away, between tree trunks, there was light. The glade. She put her finger to her mouth. 'Shhh,' she whispered to Dorotea.

Watching where she put each foot among blueberry sprigs and moss, she walked towards the brightening. At the edge of the glade she stopped.

5

Tall grass sprouted in tufts. A bouquet of hawthorn butterflies skipped and danced in the air like a handful of pale flowers thrown to the wind. At the further end of the glade was a large rock. The pine trees behind grew close into a wooden wall. There was a shape beside the boulder. Yes, something had died. A deer. Or perhaps a reindeer.

Dorotea took her hand and stepped close. Frederika looked around as their mother had taught them, scanned the evenness of tree trunks for a movement or a shape. In the forest there was plenty of bear and wolf. Whatever had attacked could still be about, still be hungry after winter.

She concentrated. A woodpecker tapped. The sun burned on her scalp. Dorotea's hand was sticky, twitching in hers. Nothing else. She looked back towards the carcass.

It was blue.

She let go of her sister's hand and stepped forward.

It was a dead man there in the glade.

He stared at Frederika with cloudy eyes. He lay bent. Broken. His stomach was torn open, his insides on the grass violently red, stringy. Flies strutted on the gleaming surfaces. One flew into the black hole that was his mouth.

Dorotea screamed and at once it was upon her: the stench, the flies, the man's gaping mouth.

O Jesus, please help, she thought.

They had to get their mother. *Jesus – the goats*. They couldn't leave the goats.

She grabbed her sister's shoulders and turned her around. Dorotea's eyes were round, her mouth wide open, strings of saliva that became a bubble, then popped. She lost her breath and her mouth gawped in silence.

'Dorotea,' Frederika said. 'We must fetch Mother.'

6

Dorotea wrapped her arms around her, clambered up her like a cat up a tree, clawing. Frederika tried to loosen her arms. 'Shhh.'

The forest was quiet. There was no rustling; no tapping, murmuring, or chirping. No movement, either. The forest held its breath.

Her sister bent her knees as if to sit down. Frederika grabbed her hand and yanked her to her feet. 'Run,' she hissed. Dorotea didn't move. '*Run!*' Frederika yelled, and raised her hand as if to hit her.

Dorotea gasped and set off down the trail. Frederika spread her arms wide and ran towards the goats.

They flew through the forest, hooves and bare feet drumming against the ground.

Faster.

Frederika whipped the back of the last goat. She fell, knees stinging, hands scraping. *Up-up-don't-stop.* One of the goats jumped off the trail. She screamed and slapped its rear.

When they reached the pass, Frederika grabbed her sister's arm. 'We must go slow. Be careful.' Dorotea hiccuped and dry-sobbed. Frederika pinched her and Dorotea stared at her, her mouth wide open.

'I'm sorry, please, a little bit longer.' Frederika stretched out her hand. Her sister took it and they followed the goats into the pass. One step, two, three.

The rupture into the mountain seemed larger. There was a sound. It might have been breathing.

Oh, don't look. Frederika kept her eyes on her feet. Four, five, six. In the corner of her eye she saw Dorotea's naked feet on the trail beside hers, half walking, half running. Seven, eight, nine. The goats' hoofs were loud against the rocks. *Please*, she thought. *Pleasepleaseplease.*

The path slackened, twisted a little and then flattened and fell downwards and outwards and they began to run – slowly at first, then faster. Downhill now, sighting their house between the trees. Dorotea ahead of her, screaming, '*Mamma, Mamma!*'

And at last, safe in their yard. Her parents came running, her father with long strides, her mother just behind him. It was then that Frederika vomited.

Her father reached her, hauled her up by her arm. 'What is going on? What happened?'

'A man,' Frederika said and wiped her mouth, 'in the glade and he is dead.'

And then her mother swept her into her long skirts as if she would never have to emerge again.

'We need to do something,' Maija said.

Frederika had let go of her. Now it was Dorotea who was on her hip, fingertips on Maija's shoulders, face in her collarbone. Holding this child was like holding no weight at all. She clung on. Like a little spider.

'Your uncle said there were other settlers on the mountain. We need to find them,' Maija said.

Her husband, Paavo, rubbed his forehead with his knuckle, pushed at his hat with the back of his hand, pulled it down again with two fingers. Maija's chest tightened.

'He belongs somewhere,' she said. 'This man. He belongs to someone.'

'But which glade are you talking about? I don't know where it is,' Paavo said.

Maija put her nose in her younger daughter's thin hair. Inhaled sunshine and salt. 'I'll go,' she said into the hair. 'I'll see if I can find anyone.'

The sun doesn't help, she thought, as if that excused him. Its glower made them seem brittle, beige quaking grass anticipating a storm.

They hadn't seen anyone during the three days they'd been on Blackåsen, but surely, eastwards there must be others who, like them, had come from the coast. People who had been there longer than they had. Maija walked fast. Blueberry sprigs nipped at her skirt. The sun was high; her body left no shape on the ground. She noticed her nostrils were flared. That little pull of dislike that was more and more often on her face. She wrinkled her nose, relaxed her features and slowed her pace.

'It's not his fault,' she said to herself.

She imagined her dead grandmother, Jutta, walking beside her: the snub nose, the forward-slanting forehead and the underbite, elbows lifted, as if she were wading through water. 'It's not his fault,' Jutta agreed. 'He's going through hard times.'

Hard times for everyone, Maija couldn't help thinking.

The men in Paavo's lineage were of a weaker make-up. Faint-hearted, it was often whispered back in the village. When Paavo proposed to Maija, he'd told her himself. Told her some among his family were prone to fear. It didn't bother her. She didn't believe in such a thing as destiny. And she had known the man in front of her ever since he was a long-haired boy pulling her braid.

'You are solid,' she said, and touched his temple.

Neither of them expected what was to come.

As soon as they were married, they started. The terrors. As if being wedded brought damnation down on him. At night, Paavo threw himself back and forth. He moaned. He woke up soaking wet, smelling salty of seaweed and rank like fish.

Paavo began to avoid the edge of his boat when they pulled up the nets. She tried to warn him, said, 'Don't.' But soon her husband no longer took the boat out in the brackish bay, where herring swam in big silver clouds and the backs of grey seals were oily slicks of joy. Then he decided he did not need to accompany the other men at all. His hair darkened and he cut it short. His skin became pale. He thickened. Little by little, his world shrank until he could no longer bear the sight of water in the washbasins in the house, or the sound of someone slurping soup.

And that was when Paavo's uncle, Teppo Eronen, came to visit from Sweden last spring and said, 'Swap you your boat for my land.' Teppo sang of a country with ore in every mountain and rivers full of pearls, and it awoke in Paavo a desperate longing to leave the waters of Finland for the forests of Sweden.

Yes, Uncle Teppo wasn't the shrewdest. And he told tall stories, everybody knew that, but might there still not be some truth to what he said? After all, the Swedes had tried to possess the north for centuries. Besides, Finland was being destroyed by the war. And it might do them both good, a fresh start?

Maija's heart felt heavy. If it wasn't the Tsar's soldiers hounding their coasts, burning their villages and looting, it was the Swedes, and that's where her husband wanted to move.

'It is not easy to leave something behind, you know,' she said.

'I know that.'

'It is possible though,' she had to admit.

She put her hand to his cheek, forced him to look at her. 'Then if we go, you must promise you will not take this with you.'

His face told her what he felt. He wasn't sure a promise like that could be made. The fear might be braided in with his very fibre.

'People hang on to their past way beyond what's necessary,' she said. 'Swear you won't take it with you.'

In a burst, he promised. And she trusted him.

The walk over the ice on the throat of the Baltic Sea ought to have taken them a few days, a week at most with the snow, but wind pressed down between the two landmasses. It lashed at their eyes with grains of ice until they couldn't continue.

They dug a hole in the drifts and lay down with their daughters, as the wind ripped layer after layer of snow off them, until all that was left was the reindeer skin they clung on to. Paavo shouted in her ear. The wind cut out his words.

'What?'

'Forgive me.' He shouted again. '. . . lied . . . There was a boat . . . I couldn't go by boat.'

And then, as fast as it had angered, the wind mellowed, leaving behind blue sky, deep green ice.

But inside Maija, the wind still screamed. All those things they had left behind, and yet her husband had chosen to bring his fear.

Maija stopped to wipe her forehead with her sleeve. June warmed spruce and pine trees all the way to their cores, worked on their frozen centres until they loosened and gave and the heat could reach into the ground along their roots, to break the frost at the deep. But for June, this was hot. It was a good beginning. If it continued like this, nature would provide. Above her, a high wind tugged at the crowns. At ground level, all was still, a golden-green smell of resin and warm wood.

And then, instead of silence, there was the murmur of water. She began to walk again, head tilted, following the only timbres that were familiar in the midst of the woodland. And as the rumble of rapids became louder, she lengthened her steps, anticipated the opening; the air. She came out on to a large rock on the shore above a river and stopped. The water in front of her churned, screamed against stones and gushed down. She knew this, had seen it before, and yet she had never come across anything like it in her whole life. Once, he would have loved this, she thought. No, she could almost hear her husband say. I never liked anything like that.

She turned right, walked alongside the river torrents until they fell into a lake, faint swells on a blank surface the only signs of the violent struggle beneath. And on the south shore, about a kilometre away, there was a cottage.

The settlement lay on a grassy hill overlooking the lake. Behind the house, the forest was lofty pine, not the craggy spruce of the mountain. Maija came out in a yard surrounded by four small buildings, sheds to store wood and food for winter. There were the rhythmic whacks of an axe and she followed them towards the back of the barn. Along the wall, scythes, rakes, shovels and levers stood in a well-ordered row. She passed cages where meat must be kept to dry in early spring before the flies. Four fat graylings hung on a hook, a string through their gills, bodies still glistening, their mouths agape. This was what a homestead should look like. She hadn't said it to the others, but she'd been shocked at the poor state in which Uncle Teppo had kept his. She walked around the corner and a man looked up. His dark hair was cropped close to his skull. There was a glitter of beard on his cheeks and a scar on his upper lip that pulled his mouth aslant. He steadied the piece of wood on the chopping block and split it in one blow. He reached for another log on the ground.

'My name is Maija,' she said. 'We've taken over Eronen's land. We arrived a few days ago.'

He remained silent. His eyes lay so deep that they were like black holes under his eyebrows.

'This morning, my daughters found something – someone – dead in a glade on the top of the mountain. Frederika, my elder, said his stomach was slit.'

He stared at her.

'We don't know who he is,' she said.

The man spat on the ground and drove the axe into the block. As he walked away, his hips were stiff, as if he had to will each leg to lift. Maija took a few steps until she was standing by the chopping block. A personal thing, a chopping block. A man needed to pick one with care. This man's was long used. You could no longer see the year-rings of the tree, so destroyed was its surface with gashes. It resembled their own back home. Their new one here was still clean and white.

He returned, holding a pack. In his other hand was a rifle. He began to walk, and she assumed she was supposed to follow.

'Has something like this happened before?' she asked his back, breath in her throat.

He didn't respond. She kept her distance. He ought to have asked about her, her husband, their origins, but he didn't. Above them, the head of Blackåsen Mountain was round and soft – a loaf of bread on a tray in the sunshine.

The yard they came to at the mountain's north base was as disordered as the first man's had been tidy. Tools were scattered over the ground, a mound of planks lay along one side of the cottage, and laundry hung on a sagging clothes-line. A sheep was in the garden patch eating the weeds. There was a lethargy to it all that didn't fit with long-term survival.

A blond man came out on the porch. He was thin and his shoulders narrow. His hair grew in a crest like a fowl's.

The man beside Maija tensed. They don't know each other, Maija thought. Or they know each other and they don't like each other. He tilted his head towards her and the scar pulled his mouth large and diagonal as he spoke. 'A body on the mountain.'

'What? Who?'

'Don't know. Perhaps bring your eldest.'

14

The blond man opened the cottage door and said something into the opening. He was joined on the porch by a younger version of himself: the same blond wave of hair, the same bony figure, hands like large lids by his thighs.

'What did you see?' the man said. There was a greyness to his skin even though he couldn't have been more than ten years her senior. His son had a surly look on his face. Older than Frederika, perhaps sixteen–seventeen.

'I didn't,' she said. 'My daughters found him.'

The man was still looking at her.

'I am Maija,' she said.

'Henrik,' he said.

'And who did I come here with?'

'That,' he said, staring at the back of the man who had already begun to walk away, 'is Gustav.'

Henrik nodded for Maija to pass ahead of him.

'How are your daughters doing?' he asked.

'They'll be fine.'

Dorotea was still little. She would forget. And Frederika was strong.

'Where are you staying?'

'Teppo Eronen is my husband's uncle. He traded us his homestead for ours.'

'Oh,' Henrik said, with a tone that made her want to turn around to see his face.

'Well, Eronen's land is good,' he added after a while. 'It's better on the south side of the mountain than here. You'll have more sun.'

The shadow side of the mountain was full of thicket underneath the spruce trees. The ground was cool and the grass, wet. Maija pressed each foot down hard so as not to slip. Her breathing was rapid. Beneath them, the river trailed all of the north side of the mountain and beyond, flexed through the green like a black muscle, or a snake. A snake shooting for the blue mountain chain at the horizon.

She didn't know what they might find at the top of the mountain. Frederika hadn't made much sense. But she had cried. Frederika didn't often cry.

'I thought the girls could take the goats to that glade close to the summit,' she said, as if to explain.

'There is the marsh, too,' Henrik's son said. 'But she's treacherous. Better not send girls there.'

When they reached the summit, she hesitated. Henrik passed her. His son made as if to pass her as well, but she shook her head and walked ahead of him, in.

The glade was basking in colour and light. And then, she saw the man for herself.

He was ripped from throat to genitals, the body split apart, turned inside out, shaken until what was within had collapsed and fallen out on the ground.

Behind her, Henrik's son moaned.

'Eriksson,' Henrik said.

Gustav walked to the body and knelt down.

Maija took a step to the side, her hand searching in the air for a tree trunk, something, anything.

When she looked back, Gustav's hand was on the body. 'Bear,' he said. 'Or wolf.'

'Bear?' Maija asked.

But what kind of a monster would it take to do this?

'We'll take the body to the widow,' Gustav said.

Maija thought of Dorotea, her bony chest and pouting belly, her shape still that of a baby. She thought of Frederika, the bulging vein at the base of her neck where the skin was so thin it was clear, the blue tick making her feel both joyful and frightened. Half an hour, she thought. Half an hour's walk at most to their cottage.

'We need to track it,' she said.

The men turned to her.

'We can't have a killer bear on the loose.'

Henrik looked to Gustav.

Gustav rose. 'Fine,' he said, his mouth a twisted, black hole. But he had shrugged.

'I'll come with you,' Maija said.

'There is no need.'

'I'll come.'

'Fine.'

'Eriksson,' Henrik's son said. 'The mountain took him.'

'What do you mean?' Maija asked.

There was a sheen on his upper lip as his blue eyes jumped from his father to her. 'The mountain is bad,' he said.

Gustav bent to open his leather satchel and took out a piece of canvas and ropes. He spread the sheet on the ground beside the body and sat on his heels. Henrik squatted beside him. After a brief hesitation, she did the same. The boy remained standing.

The three of them rolled the body on to the cloth. Heavy and spumy, it crawled and came undone in their hands. Behind her, the boy dry-heaved. Maija focused on the rim of Gustav's hat, let her hands work without looking.

'We'll wait for you at Eronen's old homestead,' Henrik said. A quick glance at Maija. 'At your homestead,' he corrected himself.

He pushed his son to get him moving and the two of them wired the ropes around their wrists and lifted. They became a flicker between tree trunks before they vanished.

Gustav hunched down. He poked with a twig in the

squashed grass. Then he rose and walked over to some mountain carnations at the side of the glade. He moved the tiny purple flowers with their black stems and emerald blades aside to look at the silvery moss beneath. At once their strong perfume was in the air, tangled with the smell of rot.

The tracks led them west down Blackåsen Mountain. At the foot of the mountain was marshland, black water, green spongy tufts.

Maija stepped on it and water welled up around her shoe, and – she waited – yes, there it was through the leather, cool between her toes, filtering up and down, becoming warm. She tried to put her feet in Gustav's footsteps. The ground smacked each time she lifted a foot. This was the kind of land that didn't know how to let go.

'Walk close to the trees,' Gustav said, without turning around.

She did as he said. Kept so close her side scraped the bark. Felt their roots under her feet in all the other that yielded. The marsh water was not always black. Sometimes it wore a large sheet of silver. Sometimes it mirrored what was above. Then the sun came out and it pretended to be blue.

On the other side of the swamp, the ground was dry, rosy with Lapp heather.

'Why did the boy say the mountain took him?' she asked.

Gustav bent down to study the twigs on the ground.

The sun edged over the sky. The heat changed and the air became tight. It pressed two thumbs against her temples. She would get a headache. At this time of year, light won over time. Only the change in sounds and the detachment of the sun told her that evening had fallen, and then when night had come.

'Are the tracks easy to follow?' she asked.

Gustav stopped. He waited so long before answering she assumed he wouldn't.

'Yes,' he said at last. 'He's not trying to hide.'

'How long ago?'

'The tracks are a few days old.'

He rubbed his chin. 'We'll stop here,' he said. 'The beast is long gone.'

Yet they stood for a while and stared in among the trees before them.

When they turned around, clouds were building a stack at the horizon. There would be a storm. Milk-blue and sickly yellow, the clouds swelled and stirred, like unfinished business.

'I hate this,' the priest said out loud.

He kicked at a tree, and a branch swung and smacked him on his bare leg under the cloak. 'Good Lord in heaven,' he said.

He didn't say anything more. It was his one chance that God or the bishop would have mercy on him and return him south. He had to be careful.

Here he was, roaming the forests to make sure the settlers' names and those of their spawn were registered in the Church Book. The region had a town, at least in name. Surely newcomers ought to think to go there before they set out to make their mark on the wilderness. And thinking you could make a mark on these wastelands – preposterous.

He was overcome by a yawn and felt how tired he was. It was most likely evening – impossible to tell time with all this light. He chose a large spruce tree and crawled on all fours in beneath it, wrapped his cloak closer, listened to the ticking and croaking in the forest and didn't like it. He should have known to dress better. Summer here was summer only in name. Though the cool weather meant fewer mosquitoes. He could pretend he had not heard of the new settler family on their way to Eronen's old homestead, he thought. There was an owl's call, and he tensed. Nothing more.

Better to think of singing stone towers. Of natives in bright wide trousers and turbans shuffling around them in pointed shoes. Of dinner conversations with the young King that could at any point end with their horses racing down roads gleaming in the moonlight. 'I dare you.' 'You dare me?' As the court priest, he had been invincible, or so he'd thought. But he had paid for thinking thus. The Church had seen to that.

There was a violent cracking of branches. The priest sat up, his back pressed against the tree. Something tore through the forest before him. There was a rumbling growl and a black shape between the trunks, then silence.

An animal.

He must have fallen asleep.

Elk?

No, it ran too fast.

When all had been silent for a long time, he stood up. He wasn't going to be able to sleep more, so he might as well continue his journey. He glanced over his shoulder twice as he walked, but there were only trees.

At a bend in the river, he became uncertain of the way and slowed down. He had been at Blackåsen one time only for the Catechetical meeting – pointless affair – the peasants dressed in their best rags, hair combed with sugar water, ears scrubbed hot and red. Him noting in the Church Book while focusing on producing beautiful handwriting: *Some reasoning, Lazy, Weak intelligence*. He couldn't remember having passed this place. Here, the river had slowed. It more resembled a tarn than something that was alive and flowing. There was an islet just by the shore, covered with shrubs. The water was murky, yet the outline of the islet seemed to descend and descend. He hadn't realised the river was this deep. The base of the atoll appeared made out of leaves.

One single leaf drifted in the water, just underneath the surface. It orbited around itself in the dark, as if ensnared.

He stepped backwards.

But the lake was behind him, the mountain was still ahead. It must be this way, he thought; it couldn't be far.

The small house the settlers called Eronen's lay dark in the middle of the empty yard. For all the priest knew, it might still be night. The air smelled of mud, nettles, and . . . He couldn't remember the name of the tall crimson flowers, but he could see the sticky milk inside their stems tarnishing his cloak. Then there were voices, strands of words in the air, coming from up by the outbuilding.

On stones, their outlines dark blocks in the faint light, sat three men. A fourth man was standing up and beside him, a woman. At first they didn't hear him. Then, at once, the five lifted their heads. The men got to their feet and removed their hats. Henrik, one of his sons, and the other one, the one who kept to himself, who had a limp – Gustav. The new settler was thick and slow. The woman stood without moving.

'What's this?' the priest said. 'A little parish meeting?'

'No, no,' Henrik said. 'Not without you.'

'I am the priest,' he said to the newcomers, 'your priest, Olaus Arosander. I have come to register you.' He found he was speaking to the woman. She was small, but her chin was lifted. Though young, her hair was a blonde grey or white, but that could have been the light. Beside her, the new man's hat was going round in his hands. Round and round.

'Eriksson is dead,' Henrik said.

The priest stopped sharp. 'Eriksson?'

'We found him on top of the mountain,' Henrik said. 'By the Goat's Pass.'

The priest felt his insides fall, fall from the top of the mountain and all the way down. He felt giddy. Then unwell.

'What happened?' he asked.

'Bear,' Gustav said. 'Perhaps wolf. Tracks were old. We have been out all night.'

The woman was staring at Gustav. 'It's unusual,' she said, 'for bear or wolf to attack. Especially during summer.'

'Land isn't giving,' Gustav said. 'Predators, too, are starved.'

'What did you do?' the priest asked. 'I mean, where is he now?'

'We took him to Elin,' Henrik said.

'She was in the yard waiting for us,' his son said.

The new settler stirred. 'What do you mean? She knew?'

'There have been problems with Elin,' the boy said.

'That's your mother talking,' Henrik said.

Father and son stared at each other.

'What do we do now?' the woman asked.

'Whatever you used to do,' Gustav said. Without saying goodbye, he set off down the yard.

As the priest followed the newcomers towards the house, he heard things insist and stir in the tall grass and from the barn. Morning was coming.

He sat down on the bench inside the kitchen, took his black book from his satchel and put it on the table in front of him. He found the ink and the pen, wet his fingers and touched its tip. They stood in a half-circle before him. Both daughters had their mother's large grey eyes and blonde hair. They had their father's round cheeks, though, and the same solemnity – something knotted about their mouths.

'I will need your names. You are all baptised, of course?'

The man nodded.

23

'My name is Maija,' the woman said. 'My father's name was Harmaajärvi. This is my husband, Paavo Ranta. And this is Frederika and Dorotea.' She touched each daughter's shoulder in turn.

The priest wrote the names with large letters.

'Dates of birth?'

Again it was the woman who answered: 'Me, January 1680, Paavo in August the same year. Frederika was fourteen this March and Dorotea, six in April.'

'From?'

'Ostrobothnia. In Finland. All of us.'

Finns. Of course. He saw it now – the pale complexion, the profusion of moles. 'F-i-n-n-s,' he spelled aloud. 'These are your offspring?'

'Yes,' she said – the Finn woman.

'And you will farm this land?'

'Yes,' she said again. 'Though I am earth-woman by training – midwife. I might be able to help the women here in their difficult times.'

The priest noted it down, closed the Church Book and placed it on the table in front of him. The Finn woman nodded and her older daughter put a pan on the fire. The man handed the priest a ladle filled with water.

He drank until it was empty.

So Eriksson was dead.

The first time the priest had met Eriksson was on Blackåsen's marsh, the autumn after the priest's arrival. The pine forest south was on fire, crackling with a smell of burning wood, millions of angry orange sparks in black smoke hurtling towards the sky. The priest had turned to run, and Eriksson was in front of him. 'I'm clearing land,' he said.

'It's forbidden,' the priest said.

'Don't get close then.'

That was what he had been like, Eriksson. No respect. Sometimes God did take the right people.

The kitchen sizzled and smelled of fried butter and grayling. The priest's stomach rumbled.

And at once, he remembered his sudden awakening, the animal tearing through the forest. How did a bear kill a man? Strike him? Bite him? He found himself shuddering. He didn't really want to know.

The Finn woman put a plate in front of him. Fish. She cut a thick piece of bread and covered it with yellow butter and gave it to him. He nodded to her, thank you.

He grabbed the fish with both hands, bit into its side and tasted salt and charcoal. The bread was proper bread with no additions of bark or haulm.

When he had finished, he leaned back. They had rinsed the walls, scrubbed the floor with birch twigs so its wood was white. There were fresh rags around the windows.

'What will happen now?' the Finn woman asked.

She sat down opposite him. The mounting light that came in through the window turned her blonde tendrils into the gold Crown of the Righteous. 'Will you go and see her now? The widow?'

He took a cloth from his pocket and wiped his mouth. 'Of course,' he said biting down around the words.

'Then I'll come with you,' she said. 'She might need the company of another woman.'

The air was cold, but the priest was soaked with sweat. His cloak caught on twigs and branches. Elin would bury the body of her husband in a temporary grave. The coffin would be dug up and sent to him for its proper burial in the graveyard in town in October or November, when the snow allowed for transport. This whole venture was unwarranted. He should have just said no. He stepped wrong and imagined the Finn woman sneering behind him. He slowed down until they were level and they continued in silence on the trail.

'Did you know him?' she asked.

'Eriksson? Why do you ask?'

She looked at him.

'Of course, I did,' he said, annoyed. 'Member of the congregation.'

'It's interesting, he's called by his last name.'

The priest shrugged. Eriksson was the kind of man from whom others kept their distance.

'Who was he?'

'I don't know. All of you come here fleeing someone or something, and so you avoid talking of the past.'

'We didn't,' she said after a while.

'Didn't what?'

'Flee.'

The priest looked to the sky. I like them better broken, he thought. Broken, humbled, ready to face the cross.

'How many people live here?'

'There are five settlements on and around Blackåsen Mountain. Six now, with yours.'

Six other mountains in his parish. And in the middle, an empty town.

'And the Lapps,' he added.

'The Lapps?' She sounded hesitant.

'They spend winter on Blackåsen,' he said and felt almost fatherly. 'Bring the reindeer down from the high mountains so the animals can eat. You'll meet them in church at Christmas, if not before.'

26

'Henrik's son seemed frightened,' she said.

The children on Blackåsen were.

'And Gustav is . . .' she hesitated.

Well, yes. The priest, too, didn't know what to call it. She nodded, as if he'd said something out loud.

'Uncle Teppo didn't tell us much about what to expect,' she said with a little smile, as if they were sharing a joke.

'I didn't know your uncle. I've only been here a year.'

Not even. Two hundred and thirty-three days.

She was staring at him. 'But when did our uncle leave?' she asked.

'If I remember rightly from the Church Books, four, five years ago.'

The priest stopped to wipe his forehead. By the side of the path a small mound of stones were built into a pyramid. In their midst, a fat stick pointed to the sky. A signpost of some sort. He wiped his hands. There were black dots in the lines of sweat on his palms. He wiped them again, put the kerchief back, and flattened his collar with two fingers.

'What will happen to them?' the Finn woman asked.

'To whom?'

'Eriksson's wife and children.'

'Oh. That, I don't know,' he said.

A lone woman with four children couldn't manage a homestead. It would either be the poorhouse by the coast, or they'd have to go on the pauper list, the rota, spend a few days on each farm. The peasants would protest, though. Say there were already so many. He wasn't going to talk to the widow about it now. She'd still have hope, he told himself, but knew he was procrastinating. Come winter, when they took the body down, he'd have to arrange for them to take the widow and her offspring as well.

27

There was a woman in among the spruce trees ahead of them. She was pale and thin. Her hair was frizzy reddish brown – it almost didn't look human. She stood with her head lifted high and waited for them to reach her.

'Elin,' the priest said.

'Please see him, before we bury him.'

He shook his head.

'I really want you to see his body,' she said.

The priest shook his head again before he realised Elin wasn't looking at him. She was looking at the Finn woman.

The long skirt of the woman in front of her brushed the trail. Henrik's son had said there had been problems with Elin. Maija thought about his father silencing him. The words had been harsh, but it hadn't been a rebuke, she thought. No, Henrik had pleaded.

Elin made a sound and said, 'It's good that you're not from here.'

'Oh,' Maija startled. 'Yes?'

Behind her, the priest stumbled.

On the porch sat four thin children, side pressed against side. Maija's breath slowed. The priest's face was indifferent. Here, man is nothing, she thought. In these lands, we will pass unnoticed.

Elin turned to her. 'Henrik said it was bear.'

'Elin,' Maija said. 'I was there. I've seen the body of your husband.'

'But did you see?' the other woman asked. She stressed the word 'see'. Pointed out there were more ways to see than one.

The priest was shifting his weight on his feet, back and forth. 'The dead must be given their rest,' he said.

'Please,' Elin said.

As they followed her towards the barn, the children on the porch still had not moved. Maija felt their eyes chill her back.

There were no animals in the barn. The silence was so present, it felt loud. The roof was full of openings through which daylight floated to blend with dust in white, still ducts. Elin lifted the lantern off its nail on the wall. She lit it, and Maija could no longer avoid looking at the shape on the table, wrapped in canvas and tied with mucky ropes. 'Be bigger than yourself,' she had said to her daughter the other morning when her fourteen-year-old's lip trembled as she woke from a bad dream. 'For your little sister's sake, for the sake of all of us. Be bigger.'

What stupid advice. She would never give it again.

Elin handed her the lantern and turned to loosen the ropes and fold the canvas aside. Its insides were stained brown and the smell of decay struck Maija again, filled her mouth with a coppery tang – as if she tasted the man's blood. The priest covered his face with his arm. Elin tucked the canvas underneath the edges of the body. Holding together. She was trying to hold together what had once been a husband and a father, a life.

A wave of nausea or sorrow flooded Maija and she had to open her mouth wide. She handed the lantern back to Elin, took off her kerchief and tied it around her nose and mouth. The skin on the dead man's face hung loose. There was a bundled-up rag under his chin to keep his mouth closed, a stone on each eyelid. Death came in many shapes. Though bad, this was not the worst Maija had seen it.

She sensed the woman on the other side of the table. I don't know what you want me to do, she thought. Wolf attacked and . . . She stopped. Elin nodded. Maija stepped closer. With her finger, she picked Eriksson's frayed shirt out of the wound and bent to look.

'Do you have water?' she asked. 'And a cloth.'

Elin put the lantern on the table and disappeared from its circle of light. She came back with a bowl and a rag. Maija washed the dry blood off the skin on both sides of the open cavity. She paused. She lifted Eriksson's heavy hands, first one and then the other, looked in the coarse palms. There was a small red mark, like a burn, on the side of his right index finger; otherwise nothing. She pushed what was left of his shirt up to see his shoulders and his throat. She removed the stones from his eyelids, signalled to Elin, and they pushed the body on to its side. The back of his neck was black from the blood that had settled there. But the shirt on his back was whole.

They lowered the body down. Maija lifted his right hand again to see the mark on his finger. She looked at Elin. Elin shook her head; she didn't know. No, it was an everyday wound. The kind that normally wasn't noticed. Some seeds had caught on Eriksson's shirtsleeve. Maija scraped them down into her hand. They looked almost like dry pine needles, but denser and with a greyish tint. She smelled them, and even amid the odour of death, these managed a scent fragrant enough to prickle her nose. Herbs? She took one between her front teeth and bit it. Its taste was sharp, bitter.

Elin bent to see. She took a couple of the seeds, rubbed them and smelled her fingers, then shook her head again. 'Not from here around,' she said.

Over Elin's shoulder, Maija's eyes met the priest's blue ones. She nodded to Elin and stepped away. Elin handed her the lantern and folded the canvas back over the body.

Once, back in Ostrobothnia, Maija had seen grey-legs attack. It was winter, in the middle of the day. She'd been fishing for pike through a hole in the lake ice. She tugged at the fishing line with small jerks, willed the fish to bite. There was sun. It was quiet. On the other side of the lake, a deer skipped across the ice. Maija dropped the line and stepped on it before it slipped down the hole. When she squatted to pick it up, they came. Five of them, a leaden streak over snow. Yellow teeth, footsteps within footsteps, total silence. Then one of them dived in, head low. The deer staggered. The others leapt in. She remembered her surprise when the sound of flesh being torn was no louder than that of cloth being ripped.

And as for bear . . .

Elin bound the ropes around the remains of her husband and Maija stood there and knew that although she had never seen a man dead from a bear attack before, she wasn't looking at one now, either. This body lacked the marks of a man protecting himself. There were no tears from claws or teeth, only this clean, vertical rip. Even to her untrained eye, this was not a bear's kill.

They were sitting on the porch. The priest had gone to wash his hands. Elin's face was pale. Maija could not see the children. Towards the right side of the yard, birch trees grew in a group. Too close together; they ought to have cleared them out. With the grown ones taking up that much space, there wasn't going to be enough light for the saplings.

'Bear didn't do this,' she said.

Elin stared ahead. Her face was vacant. It was as if she herself had gone somewhere else, now that Maija had seen what she wanted her to see.

'How would the seeds have ended up on his sleeve if they are not from here?' Maija asked.

Elin moved her head a little. 'I don't know,' she said.

'When did he go missing?'

'He was going to the marsh. He'd talked to Gustav about trying to harvest it further out in the wet areas this year. Three days ago. Perhaps it was three days ago.'

'Weren't you worried?'

Elin lifted her shoulders a fraction, let them fall again. 'He was often gone for long periods.'

'Doing what?'

'He travelled to the coast to trade. When he was here, he did whatever it is our men do. Hunting, fishing.'

The wound had not been the hacking gash made by an axe. It had been lengthy, narrow. The kind made by knife. No, not knife. Not stabs. Something swung by force. Rapier. The others would have known, too. As soon as they saw the body.

'Did anything happen before he left?' Maija asked. 'Anything unusual?'

'No. Nothing unusual.' Elin met her gaze and her voice became sharp. 'He was going to the marsh.' The moment of strength was gone and her shoulders sank.

A faint wind drew over the yard. High grass bent as in prayer. The priest returned, wiping his mouth with a cloth. His tall figure and the long strides were too decided for the stillness; his profile too sharp. He tugged with his hand at his brown hair. He is young, Maija thought. Younger than you might think at first.

'His brother . . .' Elin's voice waned.

The priest had reached them. In the corner of her eye, Maija saw him shaking his head.

'If you tell me where he lives, I can speak with him on my way home,' she said. She hesitated. 'What will you do now?'

Elin didn't answer.

As they left, Maija turned around once and now she saw the children. They were in the cluster of birch trees, flitting between the pale tree trunks like ghosts.

Nothing, she thought. We are nothing.

Frederika sat on the porch, her legs stretched out in front of her. The wood was warm against her palms, the earth damp under the soles of her feet. She stuck the top of her index finger in a knag in the dull timber that probably had been there for ever.

Dorotea was squatting by the barn, digging underneath it with a twig. Her father was in the woodshed restacking wood, organising it according to type. The kind of work that doesn't need doing, but with which a man could fill many odd days if he liked. She imagined him, felt hat pushed low, hand hovering in the air, face grim. Birch, could he see any more birch? Yes, two pieces. He'd pull out two – one with each hand, throw them on top of his new birch section. *Chink, chink.*

Her mother had not yet returned. Frederika shivered and put her feet up on the step beneath her, pressed her toes flat against the wood.

Her father wasn't going to be good with the forest; that was clear already. The forest watched him, but didn't warm to him. Her mother had said once that her father's element was water. That her father had been a fisherman, the best there was – fearless of any height of wave or beast of the sea. 'He only laughed,' her mother said, and smiled at the images inside. 'His hair was long and bleached, his skin battered, and still he laughed.'

Frederika tried to imagine her father with long hair, laughing on top of the bow of a ship, but it was difficult.

The smile was gone from her mother's eyes before her lips followed.

'What happened?' Frederika asked.

Her mother shook her head. 'It isn't my story to tell,' she said. 'Maybe one day he'll tell you himself.'

Her story or not, Jutta told it anyway.

'It's the Ranta great-great-great-grandfather,' Jutta said. 'He visits.'

Jutta and Frederika were sitting on a fallen birch by the lake, mending fishing nets. Nature around them was a flouncy green, but she gave nothing. The earth remained black no matter what they put into it. Their fingers working the nets were thin, like birds' bones.

'Oh,' Frederika said. 'But he is dead?'

Jutta looked as if she were sucking on something. 'Not really,' she said. 'Not enough,' she corrected herself.

Jutta picked at the net. 'Poor people . . . Forced to provide for the King's men, though they hadn't enough for themselves. When peace came, they still fed the soldiers, still clothed them and housed them. Then they rebelled. Fought with what they had: clubs and iron rods. Lost, of course.'

'What happened?'

'The army set fire to their farms and killed them. Men they had cared for in their own homes, attacking them.' She threw her head and the tiny white braid on her back skipped. 'As for Ranta's great-great-great-grandfather, they made his sons cut a hole in the ice. Then they bundled him together with other farmers and drowned them in the hole. And ever since, he haunts the adult Ranta men, generation after generation.

'Happens close to water. They see this thin man, long hair

35

like a horse's mane. Eyes bluer than the sky in summer. He is tied at the waist with thick ropes to other men, and he wrestles to break out. The noises are the worst, they say. The same as by the rubble fields in the forest where the ice forced rocks and stones together. Grating. Screaming.

'Mustn't try to free him.' The braid skipped again. 'Must let him be. He can't hear them; that's how scared he is. Whoever tries to help gets dragged down with him.'

Frederika thought of her mother's cool eyes, the way she stepped past her father, her movements brisk.

'Does my mother know this?' she asked.

Jutta nodded.

'It doesn't seem that way.'

'Your mother knows.'

Jutta had looked as if she might say more, but then she pressed her lips together and bent her head over the nets.

A house-martin flew in and out from under a roof ridge above her. *Sirr, Sirr*, it cried. From far away on the mountain came the lone chiming of a bell. Perhaps Mirkka's, their cow.

'Frederika,' Dorotea called from beside the barn.

'Yes?'

'Does Lapland have snakes?'

'Yes,' she called back. 'Be careful.'

'Careful, careful. Always careful,' Dorotea muttered.

Did Lapland have snakes? Of course it did. It wasn't far from Ostrobothnia. Yet it was worlds apart. When they arrived in Sweden, they had stayed by the coast for three long months awaiting spring. It was so close to their old home that, if Frederika climbed the stone outside the cottage where they had stayed, if the weather was clear, she saw their past life across the empty white: another Frederika walking down to the pen to collect eggs, a Dorotea swinging the door open and yelling that she wanted to come, a father on the porch, wringing his hands, a mother passing with her back towards him, milk steaming in her pail. Then, too, sometimes the fires lit up, one, one, one – until the coast was a necklace of burning pearls. And if the wind held its breath, there it was – *thump, thump, thump* – the stomping of a thousand feet, growing stronger, making the earth spasm. Then the eggs were on the ground, broken, precious yellows on soil. Blue milk dripped from one stair down on to the next. She saw the family flee.

Her mother said it was no good, fantasising. Her father didn't want to talk. He worked cutting logs, left before dawn and returned after nightfall. Said they needed that money to buy seeds and goats. Was certain they wouldn't have enough to buy a cow. Lucky then that her mother convinced a merchant to give them one in exchange for their reindeer skins.

'Barren.' The merchant had eyed her mother. 'Every calf she has dies as soon as it is touched by light. There's no milk to be had from her.'

'Then we'll name her Mirkka,' her mother had said, '"Sea of bitterness", because that is surely what she must carry inside.'

Spring came. The snow began to melt, the other Frederika paled, home blurred, and Ostrobothnia shrank until it was so small, it slipped into the sea.

That's when they set out into the Swedish forest. They had arrived here at Uncle Teppo's abandoned cottage four days ago.

Frederika stuck her nose in her lap. She wasn't sad. Not sad, more like . . . empty. The niggling kind of emptiness you feel

37

when summer is over, before winter tops you up, or alone in the evening when everyone else has gone to bed.

The wool in her dress smelled white. Her feet were dirty, though, her toes a dusty black. She was older now; she ought to wear her shoes, but she liked feeling the path under her feet, coarse and soft at the same time, springy, perhaps like walking on bread.

Then, of course, she saw in front of her what she had tried to push away all this time: a dead man's mushy body. She sat up, tried to drive the image away, but when that didn't work she forced herself instead to keep looking, to see all of him in sharp detail.

Inside a man there was nothing. She had thought a dead man would be different compared to a dead animal – she didn't know in what way – but man was empty. Now, when she wrapped her arms around herself and bent forward, she could almost touch the void inside.

She didn't think anything had been eaten. Perhaps the predator had been scared off. It was a large wound, though. Needlessly violent. Men died from smaller ones than that.

Her father came out of the woodshed and stopped, eyelids batting against the light.

'And why are you sitting doing nothing?' he asked.

Frederika shrugged.

'Don't sit for too long. It's your turn to make dinner today.'

'Mine? Today?'

No, but hadn't she cooked yesterday? And the day before?

'Especially today. Come on.'

They sprawled on the grass. Stomachs full, chores completed, a short rest before bedtime. Swallows hunted evening bugs. They dived, shrieked with joy or annoyance, looped and scaled, then dived again. Her mother had not returned and they didn't mention it out loud, but every now and then, one of them stole a glance towards the yard. Dorotea lay beside Frederika, feet straight up in the air. She flexed them as if walking the sky. Frederika scratched her head, twirled her hair, made a face – it smelled of the goats. She turned on to her side.

Her father's black felt hat was covering his face. His arm was flung over it, but he wasn't sleeping, she was certain.

And then, all by themselves, her eyes slipped again to the empty yard. Never before had she felt her mother's absence in this way. Like the cow must have felt the loss of her dead calves – the absence in itself physical enough to grate and nag against her flank.

The forest in the valley was messy: birch, aspen, grey alder, their offspring and good-for-nothing weeds. The leaves shouted brighter than the green of the spruce. The birds were noisier. Invisible things bit, and Maija slapped and itched. 'Go due south,' Elin had said. 'One hour's walk. Eriksson's brother is the only settler in the valley.'

Maija slapped her calf again.

And the priest. Olaus Arosander, *pfha!* Olof, more like it. An Olof who, perhaps, had lived or studied in a town called Aros or similar. He'd told her as soon as they left Elin's yard that he wasn't coming. Couldn't wait to leave, stepping from one foot to the other, that ridiculous cloak of his hovering above the ground.

'Eriksson wasn't killed by any animal,' Maija said. 'He was killed by another human being.'

'We don't know that.'

But she did.

'A passer-by, perhaps,' the priest relented. 'A tramp.'

The incision had been strong enough to cut bone, deep enough to slice the heart. 'No,' Maija said. 'Not a passer-by. Not a stranger.'

'We don't know that,' the priest repeated. 'But I'll send a message to the authorities at the coast.'

40

'Someone took his life. And who knows what will come of Elin and her children now.'

The priest left anyway. Maija shook her head. This was not a priest who cared.

Beside her, Jutta scoffed. 'Name me a priest who does,' she said.

And if anyone knew, it was Jutta. After all, she had been married to one.

A dog barked, once, then several times. There was the breaking of branches, the ripping of bushes, and the dog emerged through the thicket in front of her, ears tight against its skull, strings of saliva hanging from its jaw. It bent its head towards the ground, not letting go of her with its yellow eyes. Growled. She didn't mind dogs, but this one was different. More wolf than dog. She took a step forward and the dog rose up, barked, held her where she was. She waited. Her heart pounded.

A name was called: 'Karo'? The dog hesitated, ears erect now, listening. Then it slipped back into the thicket. Maija paused before continuing to walk, heart still loud in her ears.

A man waited for her in the yard. His face was thin and his eyelashes colourless. His ears stood out from his head. Lying down on the ground, pressed against his leg, was the dog. It pulled its face back into a snarl, but there was no sound. Not now, submitted as it was to its master.

'Daniel? My name is Maija. Maija Harmaajärvi.'

By the house, a woman was watching them, kerchief low, arms crossed.

'I am afraid I am coming with bad news,' Maija said. 'It's about your brother, Eriksson. Your brother is dead.'

She didn't know if he heard, if he understood. Then he took

a step out to the side and stood broader-legged, seemed taller. He stroked his chin.

'Your brother is dead,' she said again.

And then he laughed.

They sat behind Daniel's cottage. The air smelled fruity, of turned earth. By the garden patch were picks and a sack of seeds. They had been planting when she came. There was a field beyond the garden. Over a hundred square metres they had opened up amid the broad-leaf trees. Maija could not begin to imagine the work involved. Four children, two boys and two girls, were in the field digging up stones. They cleared and cleared, but the earth this far north was evil. Stones emerged when you thought you were down to the bare bone of the land; brushwood shot forward on ground already liberated. If she listened hard at night, she heard it – faintly – but it was there, the chewing up of land.

'So he's dead.'

Each time Daniel said it, his voice was full of something: wonder, thoughtfulness, something else she could have sworn was glee.

His wife was making a fire, her back to them. There was a copper pot beside her. Her dress was taut over her shoulders, her shoes muddy. 'Anna,' Daniel had said, and nodded towards her when Anna half turned to lift the pot. The woman broke off in her movement and pressed the heel of her hand into her side.

'Elin says the funeral will be in winter,' Maija said.

Anna put the copper pot down on the stones, hard. Maija waited, but there was nothing more. The woman turned towards them and her eyes were light, brown or green – seawater through the slats of a dock. She had a plump nose and the hair that stuck out from under the kerchief was brown. There were a couple of tiny pockmarks on her cheek – not pox scars, they were too small.

Daniel sat on an overturned bucket, elbows on his knees, feet steady on the ground.

'You were born here?' Maija asked him.

'Yes. Me and my brother grew up further north, by the river.' Daniel indicated with his head. 'Only us and the Lapps were here at that time.'

Anna was studying her husband. Perhaps he was one of those men who discovered words in the presence of outsiders.

'I can imagine it must have been very different,' Maija said, but thought to herself it must have been the same.

Daniel turned to spit at the ground.

'And you have just arrived now?' he asked.

'A few days ago. We've taken Teppo Eronen's land.'

She hesitated, but she had to ask. 'Do you know when Teppo left Blackåsen?' She tried to make the question sound ordinary.

'Four years ago,' Daniel said. 'Right, Anna?'

'Yes.'

Four years . . . How could Uncle Teppo not have told them this? The homestead could have been taken by somebody else in the meantime and then what would they have done?

'How did Eriksson die?' Anna asked.

'I don't know,' Maija said.

Daniel's look grazed hers and moved away.

'There was a large slit in his stomach,' she said.

'Some animal then,' Daniel said.

'It was as if he hadn't tried to defend himself.'

Daniel shrugged.

His wife had turned again and was hunched over the fire. Secrets, Maija thought. Shielding secrets.

'Don't just stand about,' Daniel called out. The small figures in the field rotated at the sound of his voice.

'We can't get this stone up, Father,' one child shouted.

Daniel muttered something. He rose and headed towards them with long steps in the mud.

'I'll have to leave,' Maija said.

Anna stood up, too.

'How far along are you?' Maija asked.

In sunlight, Anna's eyes were a clear green. 'One month or two. He doesn't even know.' She tilted her head towards the man.

'I am an earth-woman, so it's easy for me to tell.'

'It's not going well this time. I'm sick.'

'May I feel?'

Anna nodded and Maija stepped closer, her back to the others. She put her hand on the rounding and felt the usual pinch inside of longing. She herself had wanted more. At least one or two. They had tried, but it wasn't to be. She focused on the small bulge underneath her hand. It was too early. She couldn't feel anything. She shook her head.

'Many women are sick during this period,' she said.

'Never been with the others.'

When Maija walked back home, she felt how tired she was. I will have to sit down, she thought, and I might have to sit here until they come for me. But she didn't. Instead, she caught sight of Blackåsen's mountain-top and tried not to think about feet that ached and pained. Tall grass wisped against her legs under her skirt. She stopped to look at a strange oak tree whose mighty trunk swirled, and then came out on top as four separate trees. 'So what are you?' she asked. 'One tree that had enough and split into four, or four trees that decided to grow up together for support?'

The tree didn't answer. She reached out to touch its side and ended up leaning against it. A wife who doesn't care that her husband is gone for three days; a man who laughs when he finds out his brother is dead; and a priest who doesn't want to know.

She thought of Henrik's son saying the mountain was bad, and remembered the piece of wood set up to point to the sky, that she had passed with the priest. She had seen similar things before, a long time ago. Before it was forbidden to worship anything else but the Church's one God.

And Uncle Teppo. She tried to remember what he had been like when he came to see them. He had been all large gestures, blustering and joking. But his eyes . . . She remembered them staring at her mouth, not meeting her own eyes. Had he been frightened?

She became aware of the cold from underneath the pine trees against her legs.

'Well, now you have overdone it,' she scolded herself, 'if you let yourself get scared. Uncle Teppo might have decided to travel for a while. Perhaps he set up a settlement somewhere else. And as for Eriksson's death, apart from Henrik's son, none of the others were upset. The priest was certainly not disturbed.'

But beside her, Jutta pursed her lips.

Just as if they had discussed it and agreed, which Frederika doubted, as she was always with them, neither her mother nor her father talked about the dead man in the days that followed. Her father chopped wood and worked on filling the woodshed until late each day. Her mother fished and gave the girls their chores to do around the homestead. The evenings were light and warm. On the little field, the grass grew a strong green and the water in the stream rippled clear, topped up by the melting snow from the high mountains.

Midsummer's Eve occurred at the end of June. The evening before the birthday of John the Baptist. Six months before that of King Jesus. And the most magical time of the year.

'Seven different flowers under the pillow,' Jutta used to say every Midsummer's Eve. 'Put seven different kinds of flowers under the pillow tonight and you'll dream of the one you'll marry.'

Maija's face would become hard. Jutta's face, too, but from fear, not anger. Jutta had said it wasn't solely good magic that was about on midsummer. The coming night was when the trolls were at their worst.

Today they were going to the river. All that was fabric had to be washed. Whites, blacks, blues. *Dresses-shirts-carpets-curtains*. It was the day to rid yourself of the old. Middle of summer. Before winter turned around and started his journey back to them.

'Wait,' Frederika said. She pointed. 'You're putting the clothes in with the bed sheets.'

'Oh.' Her mother pulled up a blouse, put it in a new sack. She pushed her hair away from her forehead with the back of her hand, pulled up another piece of clothing, then shoved it back and got up. 'We'll sort it at the river,' she said. 'When it's all out in the open.'

Her mother was like that: everything at once and in the open.

The river was dark blue, its surface dotted and streaked. It ran fast, although it was still a long way to the rapids.

They lit a fire, filled the large wooden barrel with water and placed it over the embers. When it boiled, Maija emptied into it the sack containing the birch ashes they had brought to make lye-water. And then she began to put in the laundry. She let it simmer for a while before she swirled the hot fabrics around with a wooden stick, heaved them up and threw them down on the flat stone in the river. Frederika and Dorotea beat the washing with sticks. *Clap. Clap. Clap.* Out with the old.

The day was brisk and airy. Frederika's hands were cold. Still, better than washing clothes in winter when they had to melt snow for water, boil the clothes in the big iron pot in the barn and carry the wet laundry to rinse it in a hole cut in the ice. And each piece of clothing had to be rinsed three times. By the time they finished, their skirts were frozen solid to the ground and they had to break them loose.

'The water is dirty,' their mother called.

Frederika poked at her knees. They were white and lumpy, bitten by grit.

'Stand beside me,' Maija said. 'Watch your feet.'

They pushed the barrel until it toppled. The frothing water

47

pierced the earth in hot rivulets, striving to join the larger body below.

They waited for new water to boil. The river smelled of mud and angry stone.

Mid-morning, Frederika showed Dorotea how to make a small fire. Their mother sat down beside them. Her hair twirled around her forehead. When she closed her eyes, her eyelids looked like the blue-pink petals of chicory that shut overnight. Across her mother's top lip was a wrinkle, fine, like a hair. Frederika had never seen it before, but in the daylight it was as clear as a scar. Was her mother getting old? Jutta had been old, her head stooping further and further until she came to resemble a little iron hook. Towards the end, they had been the same height, Frederika and her, and Jutta had had to turn her head sideways and up to see her when they spoke.

I don't want you to die, she thought, without knowing that notion had been inside her and she felt a pain cut so deep, it was almost good. She held on to the thought of her mother dying until it didn't feel good at all any longer.

'Dorotea can boil water.' She found her mother watching her. 'And you can make bread.'

Frederika leaned forward and poked at the embers with a stick. They were still unreliable: thin, skipping all over.

'It wasn't wolf, was it?' she asked.

Her mother glanced at Dorotea. Her sister was filling a pot with water, tongue steering. 'No,' she said.

'What happens now?'

'It's with the priest now. He'll find out what happened.'

Frederika divided the dough into pieces and patted them straight on to the embers: *Glödhoppor*, emberjumpers.

'I know it was awful to find him, but this has nothing to do with us,' her mother said.

Frederika picked at the breads, flipped them over with her fingers.

'We must not become frightened,' her mother continued. 'In Ostrobothnia, you used to know the village and the forests around as if they were part of you. Don't you think you can make Blackåsen your own, too? When you are ready?'

They snapped the breads off the embers and covered them with a thick layer of bright yellow butter. Their fingers became black from the charcoal. On the opposite shore, Blackåsen Mountain was a muted block of grey. Frederika licked each finger and tasted the fat.

Mirkka mooched when they returned. Frederika sat down on the stool in the barn. She pulled on the firm teats. She was wet and cold and wanted it done and then of course, the cow couldn't. The cow turned her head and looked at her. Her watery nostrils trembled.

'It's like when you're in a rush to wee,' Jutta had explained. 'You want it too much and then it doesn't work. Think about winter calm, how the snow falls.'

Frederika did what her mother had done when she taught the cow to milk. She leaned her forehead against the animal's flank and hummed a song and felt like a fool, but both she and the cow relaxed and the warm milk squirted down into the bucket.

She carried the trough to the cottage. Further down the slope, Dorotea and their mother were hanging clothes on the line. The kitchen was silent. They had removed the moss between the logs for the cottage to breathe in summer air, and the light that seeped through the whitened wood made her

49

feel as if she were in a dream. The room smelled irritated from the lye. Her mother and Dorotea had hung their dresses on the iron rack in the roof to dry. Water dripped from them on to the floor below. Frederika didn't like the look of them empty.

The timber was cool and smooth against her feet. She pulled off her dress and let it slap down on the floor. She examined the sores on her hands made by the lye-water. But now all the old was out. And Midsummer's Eve was soon over. The day had passed, and all was still well.

She grabbed her dress and stepped on a chair to hang it over the drying rack beside the others. She tried to flatten it out. Otherwise it wouldn't dry, and you'd be sorry tomorrow.

There was a knocking. She covered herself, but nobody entered.

There it was again.

A black crow sat on the window ledge. The bird tapped on the pane with its beak. A second crow flew and sat beside the first. Then they both pecked on the glass. *Tock-tock-tock.* As if they wanted to come in.

'Birds carry the souls of the unborn and the dead,' her father had told her once. They were watching a large flock of starlings, a black cloud on the sky that changed shape, twisted, fell, picked up. There was a tic by the side of her father's mouth. 'A person has to know how to read the signs.'

'What signs?'

'Oh, there are so many.' He hit out with his hand. 'Hundreds. Maybe thousands.'

She didn't ask more. She had thought that, later, she would ask Jutta.

Frederika stepped down from the chair. The crows didn't move as she approached the window.

At first she didn't register. And then she realised what she was seeing and gasped. In among the trees, there was a brown bear on his hind legs, his paws in the air.

Her eyes leapt: barn, field, woodshed. Where was her mother? Where was Dorotea?

Before she found her wits, the bear fell down on all fours and lumbered away.

Frederika ran to the field. The sun was hot on the crown of her head. The space between the straight pine trunks in the forest was empty, and she went more slowly. By the barn, she ran into a spider web and had to stop to brush her face with her fingers to remove it. And then, from inside the woodshed, something so unusual: her father chuckling. Through a slit between two wood planks, she saw him embrace her mother. She hesitated and then tiptoed backwards. She wanted this moment for her father. And anyway, the danger was gone.

But later, at night, she thought about what she'd seen. She didn't know what it meant, but one thing was clear: her mother was wrong. In some way, Eriksson's death had to do with all of them.

And they had not found him. He had found them.

'Has everything been done?' The priest slapped the back of a psalm book protruding from the low bookshelf by the entrance to the church hall.

'It's ready,' the verger said. Underneath his straight fringe, the thick, lifted brows gave his face a startled look that always managed to worry the priest, even though by now he knew the verger was unflappable.

'The silver is clean?'

'Of course.'

'You'll make sure the graveyard and the church green remain clear.'

'Yes.'

'No trade, no drinking.'

'No.'

The priest took one final look. The gold on the pulpit gleamed. There were new tallow candles in the holders underneath the cross. He sniffed the air. No odour from the cadavers under the floor. Good. Even if you'd grown up with the smell, you never got used to it.

'And there will be no ringing of the bell,' he said.

'No ringing of the bell.'

The priest took the stairs up to the first floor two steps at a time. The stairway curved to the right. Pale wood shone through the dark brown paint on the places where people trod the most. There were no candles in the stairwell, and a dark corner loomed at the far end of each step. The church was already old. The once-black roof had oxidised and turned green. Nothing he could do about that – not without funds, not without a favourable King. And the church bell. Built during his short tenure, but what a problem. Three times already he'd sent for the bell-founder at the coast to come and rectify the issue. The first time the bell-founder came, he had the verger ring the bell for a whole morning as he stood underneath the tower, his hands elevated and facing outwards, his head bent – an image of a portly Jesus Christ in their empty square – to then declare the timbre of the bell 'pleasant'.

'It's not,' the priest had said.

The heavy man had nodded until his head almost reached his chest. 'What is the problem?' he asked.

'I don't know. The ringing is awful. Bleating. Not elegant.'

The bell-founder kept on nodding.

'It's broken,' the priest said. 'That's it. Broken.'

Then the bell-founder had taken his horse and disappeared for two days. On the third day he returned and declared that he had listened to the bell from all over the region, and its sound was harmonious and whole.

But the bell jarred and jarred with the priest, and he sent for the bell-founder again. This time, the founder spent time in the bell tower. He chipped away at the metal with a chisel. But the first Sunday after the bell-founder had left, it sounded the same.

The priest sent a message again, but the messenger returned saying maybe it wasn't the bell that was the problem, but something else. Something perhaps to do with the priest.

In the room on the first floor, the Church Books were laid

out on his desk. Two rapid steps, then he pinched the fall of the green velvet curtain so it fell straight. A glimpse of his own face in the window: drawn cheeks, sharp nose. Then, through it, horses and carriages on the church green. The bishop had arrived.

The priest had met the bishop twice before: once when he himself was a rising star in the court and then, much later, when the bishop came to remove him. The priest couldn't remember the bishop from their first meeting. The second time, it was the bishop who had been acclaimed, raised to nobility by the King, instated as a member of the Privy Council. Then they had spent two weeks together travelling north, but on that occasion neither had anything to say. Nothing they were disposed to share with each other, that was.

The priest took a deep breath, touched the edges of the ribbons to make sure they lay flat on his chest, then turned the iron handle. The wind swept his collar to one side, like a flag in a breeze.

The bishop was standing beside his carriage, looking up at the bell tower.

'Olaus,' he said. He had aged: the thin hair wafting in the wind was whiter, his stomach in the black robe larger.

The priest bowed. 'Welcome.'

'It turned out well, the tower.' The bishop spoke as a man who could afford to be unhurried by wind, untroubled by his ageing.

'Yes.' The priest turned his back on the structure. 'We have prepared a meal for you.'

The bishop waved with his hand. 'Hungry wolves hunt the best. Let's look at the inventories before we sit down.'

*　　*　　*

It was late evening when they at long last sat down for their meal, though still as light as day. The windows were wide open, curtains floating in an indiscernible flow of air.

'I have no real observations to make on the building itself.' The bishop reached for more bread.

The priest caught the eye of the verger at the back of the room. This needed to be written down in the Church Book.

'Upkeep has been good, the interiors are orderly,' the bishop said, mouth full. 'What is attendance like?'

'Four households live in the town all year round: mine, the former priest's, the night man's and an old couple, but everyone else comes to stay as prescribed during the period between Christmas and *Missa Candelarum*, and again to the sermon on Lady Day.'

For those few weeks, the town was a town. The settlers, the tradesmen and the Lapps came and settled into the purpose-built houses and, by God, for that period, the Church owned them limb and soul. They were preached to, taxed and judged if necessary, all in the space of those weeks. Then they departed again, leaving behind them the priest and his verger, holding forth in this ghostly place of dark timber.

The bishop leaned back and cleaned his teeth with his tongue. 'No problems with the Lapps?'

'No.'

He nodded. 'Anvar, the previous priest, did good work with the Lapps. And no issues with any . . . private sermons?'

'Is that still on-going?'

'Even some of the priests are now in favour. The King takes every offence personally.'

He would. The King had forbidden it – any self-made

prayers, any attempts by common man to explain the scriptures, or to proclaim some personal connection with God, was a delusion and an affront to the one true relationship between the King and the Almighty.

The bishop moved, and his chair groaned.

'We have made much progress in the Catechetical hearings,' the priest said, forcing his mind back to the matters at hand. 'You'll see it in the records. When I arrived, the lack of reading skills was the problem, but we have managed to increase school attendance.'

The bishop burped.

The priest nodded in the verger's direction. 'Tomorrow our verger, Johan Lundgren, will tell you about his work teaching the children on the mountains. We'll show you the finances, too.'

'Yes, and the poor relief and your administration of the royal proclamations.'

The ubiquitous King.

'How is he?' the priest asked, though he had promised himself he wouldn't. He wondered if the bishop would tell the monarch they had met.

He looked up and found the bishop studying him. 'Our ruler is well,' the bishop said. 'He seems resigned to staying in Sweden after all those years away. He's down south. Untiringly making new plans, of course.'

With his inner eye, the priest saw the royal, the tall muddy boots, his curly hair white from dust, his blue coat smelling of smoke and gunpowder.

'There are rumours,' he said. 'About how the new wars are going for us.'

The bishop rose.

'I'll show you to your room,' the priest said.

'I'm certain your maid can do that.'

The bishop swept his black cloak around himself and left the room.

The priest sat on the bench outside his house, his fingertips on the soft leather cover of the Bible in his lap. Across the green, the door to the verger's cottage was open. There was movement in the kitchen of the vicarage where the widow of the former priest still resided. A child ran from one of the further cottages to another.

The roof ridges of the empty houses in each district – Settler Town, Trade Town and, further away, Lapp Town – were dark towards the light blue sky. There was a smell of grass in the air. And here he sat, priest of nothing.

The stone wall of the tall church was a compact white. By its entrance, the iron bell hung still in its wooden structure. It seemed brooding. Foreign.

'No bell,' the priest said to the verger in the morning.

'Of course not,' the verger said.

The priest didn't have time to deal with the potential insubordination. Where was his Bible? He hadn't slept well, and had a headache. 'Are the books out?'

'Yes,' the verger said. 'The bishop asked to see them.'

'The bishop is already in the church?'

'He said he always rises at dawn.'

'God in heaven.'

The priest pushed past the verger down the stairs. The verger should have woken him. Surely, that was obvious. He had forgotten his Bible. Had he brushed his hair? He couldn't remember. He dragged his fingers through it and felt dirty.

As he entered, the bishop was sitting in the priest's own

chair facing him, his large hands flat on the desk's leather top, his index finger tapping.

'Good morning,' the priest said. He lifted out the wooden chair opposite the bishop and slid on to it sideways.

'You have not asked for any grain from the parishioners to support you over the past year,' the bishop said.

Nothing like a surprise attack. The bishop would have made the King himself proud.

'No.' The priest pulled his fingers through his hair again. The bishop was looking at him. 'I am alone. I cleared land behind the provisional vicarage to sow barley.'

'I was worried that, with the widow still remaining, the demand on the congregation would double,' the bishop said.

'No, there was no need.'

'Her year of grace will soon be over.'

The priest nodded. The widow would have to abandon the vicarage and its lands.

'It's a shame they did not have any children.'

The bishop flipped a few pages. 'I see you managed to solve a dispute among the women about their seating arrangements.'

'Oh, that.' The priest crossed one leg over the other. He nipped at his cloak to make it fall straight.

'No, but how did you do that?' The bishop's oval eyes did not blink.

'I preached about why all Jesus' disciples were men.'

The bishop burst out laughing, a deep laughter that made his stomach hop. The priest hadn't heard one of those for a long while. The bishop shook his head. 'We have such a problem. All over Sweden. The country is being torn asunder, and the women fight against their status, striving to sit underneath the pulpit. God help us.'

The bishop looked up to the roof as if he expected God to lift it off and intervene at this precise moment. 'Very well,' he said. 'What about the parishioners?'

'Twenty-two new children since last year – all baptised. Ten of them are Lapp children who were given new, Swedish names. Last winter there were twenty-eight funerals, this spring eight. There are four bodies buried at different locations that will be transported to the church when there is snow: two from the area of Storberg, one from Vanberg and one from Blackåsen.'

'From Blackåsen?'

'A settler. Eriksson,' the priest said. 'Wolf,' he added.

'Eriksson is dead?'

The priest nodded.

'Wolf had him?'

The priest hesitated. 'One or two people seem to think otherwise.'

The bishop got to his feet with astounding agility for a man of his age. He walked to the window. His large frame blocked out the light. 'What do you mean "otherwise"?'

'A new settler woman, a Finn. She thinks Eriksson was killed by someone. Everyone else says wolf.'

The priest wasn't certain why he said so much. It was a fine balance between not neglecting to tell anything you'd later be blamed for concealing, and giving your senior too much say in how to manage your congregation. It was one of the predicaments with being in such a remote place: you lost your astuteness.

'Where on Blackåsen was he found?' the bishop asked.

'On the top.'

'Close to what they call the Goat's Pass?'

'I believe so.' The priest hadn't realised the bishop knew

Blackåsen that well. The bishop had been in the district much longer than himself, but still, to know such detail . . .

The bishop turned around. 'Your judgement worries me,' he said, with early thunder in his voice, a low rumbling the priest felt rather than heard.

'Anything, anything at all regarding Blackåsen and in particular regarding the Goat's Pass, is of highest priority.'

'I don't understand,' the priest said.

'I know your predecessor died before you arrived, but you ought to have familiarised yourself with your parish by now.'

'I have read the Church Books.'

'Not everything is in the Books. Especially not what concerns the Prince of Darkness and those who are with him *in pactum*.'

The Prince of . . .

'What do you mean?'

'There was a hearing against Eriksson's wife, Elin.'

'That, I know. For acts of sorcery. You resided over the enquiry. She was found guiltless, fortuitously.'

'Guiltless.' The bishop swung his large head. 'She didn't deny anything – claimed to have received her sagacity from God. No, I deemed we couldn't afford rumours of sorcery on Blackåsen, and so I closed the hearing down.'

The priest looked away, to give himself time to arrange his features. It was as if the bishop were telling him he believed in magic. But they knew that the trials of the previous century had been misguided. The bishop had turned back to face the window.

'Blackåsen is full of the old,' he said. 'The old and the ugly. The Lapps used the mountain for their worshipping. In one of the missionary's stories, he tells how he came upon them after they had raised a pillar towards the sun – I have

60

read the account myself. What isn't written down, but what people believe, is that during the tumult that followed, one of the old Lapp women pushed the pillar so it fell. It hit the mountainside and the mountain split open. She reached down and pulled the Devil out by his tail, tied it around one of the boulders inside the crack and put a spell on him so he couldn't leave the mountain. "You think your god has all powers?" she is supposed to have said. "Let's see then how strong he is." They burned her at the stake.' The bishop turned to face him. 'That's how the name the Goat's Pass arose. And now, whenever something happens on the mountain, people claim it is the Devil. They say that on that mountain, God does not rule. They say that whatever is said on the mountain will echo for generations.'

'There is talk of some . . . disappearances? I've heard it said that children disappear?' The priest tried a chuckle.

The bishop tossed his head. 'I looked into that when I first came to the district. Two children have gone missing over ten years. It's no more than anywhere else. Most likely they got lost, or there was some accident their parents want to hide, but it's enough to keep the fear alive.'

The bishop interrupted himself. 'I want to know with certainty what happened to Eriksson,' he said.

'I will send a message to the law enforcement officers by the coast.'

The bishop hit the desk with his fist. It was so sudden, the priest jumped. The bishop remained so, leaning on his knuckles on the desk.

'No,' he said. 'I don't want fear to spread. I want you to find out what happened, but discreetly. You report back to me.' He rose. 'Anvar's widow, Sofia, could have told you things like this. She was her husband's right hand. Nowhere else have I seen a woman contribute as much to the service of the Lord. Have you made her acquaintance?'

'Yes, of course.' The vicarage was just across the green.

'I mean really made her acquaintance,' the bishop said. 'It is not normal for a priest your age not to be married. It would make it easier on the funds of the Church as well, if there was one vicarage instead of two.'

And then, above them, the old church bell started swaying. The priest rose in disbelief. The dry clang bellowed from the bell tower, hammered body and soul. The priest opened his mouth, but his voice drowned in the sound.

Maija was by the edge of the marsh. Ducks flitted in and out of the reeds. Uncle Teppo had said their part of the swamp was the part furthest east, the one that clung on to the mountain. But the sedge was not ready to harvest; the green shoots barely broke water. Seven rack wagons of sedge equalled one cow and one sheep surviving winter, that's what Uncle Teppo had said. They hadn't harvested sedge before. Paavo believed that once they took the barley, the grass from their field ought to be enough to feed Mirkka and the goats through winter. 'If we can avoid the wet . . .' he'd said.

A crane stepped broad-legged in between tufts, head pecking in a large arc. Beyond the bird, the water was black. Apparently, Eriksson had said he'd like to see if they could harvest further out in the wet areas. She wondered how far out they reaped sedge now.

She leaned down and scratched her leg. An insect bite that she couldn't stop itching. A branch snapped behind her. Gustav's face tightened as he saw her. He sat down not far from her and unlaced his shoes. His lips were moving as if he were talking with no sound.

His feet. Red stumps, scarred and torn.

Maija looked away. When she looked back, Gustav was already on his way out into the marsh, stepping like the crane, legs lifting high. He headed for some planks of wood. He pulled at them and put them in between tufts, making what could have been a path.

So Gustav had been a soldier. So many of them had lost limbs to the frost in similar ways. There had been winters so cold, birds fell dead to the ground, frozen in mid-flight.

A brisk voice said, 'This marsh used to be a lake.'

She swirled around.

The newcomer was clean-shaven and his grey hair short. There were deep wrinkles on his forehead and by the sides of his mouth. What might have been a smile turned his face into a different kind of frown. He was tall and straight. His eyes were streaked red. He's been drinking, she thought. Although sun on water could burn eyes like that, too.

'Nils Lagerhielm,' he said.

'Maija,' she said, and curtsied before she could stop herself.

The skin on his hand was soft, not used to hard work. But then, he'd told her as much already. He had a nobleman's last name.

'The peasants called her Little Lake,' the nobleman continued. 'She wasn't strong enough. The forest seized her and she became swamp. A part of her turned bottomless. The moss keeps growing upwards, feeding off itself. It is impossible to say from the surface where there is firm ground and where there isn't. The planks are put out so nobody goes past them and drowns.'

Nils was watching Gustav, upper lip curled. 'Sometimes the spring floods move them. I came to inspect them before people came to harvest, but it seems Gustav has already tasked himself with correcting the matter.'

'There isn't much to harvest,' Maija said. She was still annoyed with herself for having curtsied.

He turned towards her. 'It's been a cold summer. Where is your husband?'

'He's at the homestead.'

'I will go and introduce myself to him. I understand it was your daughters who found Eriksson.'

She lifted her head.

'I need to talk to your husband about that,' he said.

Paavo sat on a wooden bench by the barn and sharpened the scythes. He wielded the stone against the edge with long slow strokes and the blade sang. Through the laundry on the clothes-line, Maija glimpsed Frederika trying to shift a boulder with an iron rod.

Paavo rose.

Nils nodded to him. 'My name is Nils Lagerhielm,' he said.

Her husband stroked his shirted chest with his hand and mumbled something, impossible to tell what. Nils looked at Maija as if to tell her she could leave now. When she didn't, his lips narrowed, but he turned back to Paavo.

'I heard your daughters found the body of Eriksson,' he said.

Her husband nodded.

'I came to see they are well.'

'They're doing better,' Paavo said.

Maija looked for Frederika. Are you, she thought, doing better? The stone was large and her daughter leaned her weight on the rod. Careful, Maija thought. You put that kind of pressure on and something will have to give. As if she had heard her, her daughter released the rod, and inserted it from another angle.

Nils cleared his throat. 'I was wondering if there was . . . Was there anything strange about it?'

'He was dead,' Maija said. 'That was rather strange.'

Both men frowned.

'There wasn't anything that appeared . . . mystic?' Nils asked.

'Mystic?' Paavo repeated.

'It's not the first time there has been trouble on the mountain.'

Trouble again. But for some reason Maija was certain that Nils would tell them what had happened.

'What do you mean?' Paavo asked.

When Nils spoke again, he'd lowered his voice. 'Two children have gone missing on the mountain,' he said. 'One, ten years ago. She was going to pick lingonberries and didn't return. The second, five or six years ago, during the harvest. It's not strange in itself. We are in the wilderness. But the siblings of both children raved of having seen things in the forest. And then last year, a whole family disappeared overnight, the Janssons. One day they were here; the next day they weren't.'

'People don't just disappear,' Maija said.

'Precisely,' Nils replied.

Paavo blinked.

'Before they were Christianised, Lapps from far away used to travel to this mountain to see the shaman here. It was said he had uncommon powers. I am an educated man, but out there, on this mountain is . . . something. And that something isn't good.'

Sunlight twinkled in the crowns of the spruce trees. A fly landed on Maija's arm, and she brushed it away.

'Back home we had the village,' her husband said, and she knew he was looking at her.

'A village,' the nobleman said.

He said it slowly.

'We were safe,' Paavo said.

'Perhaps we do need to come together,' the nobleman said. 'If we lived in a village, we'd have each other to rely on. Just as long as we didn't bring the trouble with us in our midst.'

The nobleman creased his forehead and nodded to himself. He's thinking of someone in particular, Maija thought. Someone he doesn't want to live close to.

'Let's think about this,' Nils said. 'I'll talk to the others about it, too.'

He nodded curtly and left.

Frederika was by her side. Maija didn't know how long she had been there. Her daughter waited one breath to see if she would be told anything more, then sauntered off.

Paavo juggled the sharpening stone in his hand a couple of times.

'Don't tell me,' Maija said.

'We shouldn't have come here,' he said.

'Paavo . . .'

'Things in the forest? I don't like it.'

Oh Paavo, she thought. She put her hand on his sleeve. 'The other day she – the widow – asked me to look at Eriksson's body . . .'

The muscles in his arm tensed. He stared at her, his nose wrinkled, mouth open.

'Together with the priest,' she added.

'You looked at the body?'

'Yes.'

'But why would you do such a thing, Maija? Why?'

'It wasn't bear or wolf that killed Eriksson.'

'That's not what he suggested, either.' He indicated with his head the direction of Nils's leaving.

'I can assure you that Eriksson was not killed by sorcery or

67

by evil, either,' Maija continued. 'He was killed by a man, by flesh and blood.'

Her husband shook his head. 'Leave this,' he warned. It sounded like a growl.

'Paavo, listen to me. People like Nils don't care about people like us. For some reason, he wanted to tell us about Blackåsen's past. And he said that some people oughtn't to be welcome in any village, if it was to be built. Could you hear that? Don't you see what that ought to remind us of?'

'I know exactly what this reminds me of. Leave it. Think of your children.'

Maija laughed, but it didn't come out like one.

'As if that were the reason,' she said, before she could stop herself.

There was a pause, then: 'What do you mean?'

'Nothing.'

'No, say it. For once, say it out loud.' Her husband's voice rose. 'Do you think I don't know what you're thinking?'

'Paavo.'

But she spoke too late. He was walking away.

The ground in the glade was yellow. Autumn had begun to blanket the top of Blackåsen Mountain without letting anybody else know. The sun was out, small and white like one in winter. Maija stood over the brown patches left by Eriksson's body. Death worn down and forgotten. Nature not impressed. She squatted and pulled her fingers through the grass, felt the spongy ground beneath.

The watching eyes of a village. Villages were good things, but not if built on the wrong grounds. Those eyes could fast turn from watching what was outside, to inside, and then there was no saying where they might take things.

We must find out what happened before this gets out of hand, she thought. Never again will our family stand by while fear spreads.

She glanced at Jutta. They were done talking about it. Many people had something like that in their past. A grief, a time when they had fallen short. But Jutta didn't meet her gaze.

Maija got down on her knees. Inch by inch she crawled the glade, studied the ground, fingers prodding. Nothing out of the ordinary. No trace of the strange herbs either. The sun leaned on her shoulders. Her knees ached. She sat back on her heels. Who brings a rapier to the forest? Someone who always carries it, or someone who, this time, has brought it with a purpose.

She looked around. The glade wasn't close to anything in particular; it was on the way. On the way from the valley to the river, or the other way around. Passing from one side of the mountain to the other.

She got to her feet. So: Eriksson had been lying with his head south and his feet north. He hadn't defended himself. The man who killed him – for the length of that wound would have had to be done by a man – must have been standing . . . She took two long steps. Somewhere here, she thought. In the middle of the glade – same blue above him, same sun. Her eyes followed the tree trunks all the way to the sky. They waved and waved as if it didn't concern them.

She turned around. Whoever killed Eriksson might have come from this direction. She walked into the forest and in a loop around the glade: passed the trail down to the river, then the one leading to the valley through the pass. There was a whirl of birdsong coming from the glade, bells and trills. Bluethroat. Maija stretched her neck to see. She stilled. Right here, there was a scarcity of branches on the low larch beside her. One step forward and she had a view over the whole glade. Underneath the lowest branches, something gleamed blue. She bent down. A piece of blue glass, with colour, like the windows in church, its edges round. Now they told her. The larch said, yes, there had been an infringement. The crowns of the pine trees whispered that the view from there was almost as good as their own. Yes, someone had stood here.

Someone might have stood here just before, during, or after, the kill.

Henrik's derelict yard lay empty. A damp cough came from inside the house. Leaning against the porch railing, beside a shovel and an old meat grinder, its rusty crank pointing straight up to the sky, there was a broken fishing rod. Maija followed the trail in the grass towards the river.

A blond head moved among the reeds. As she came closer, she saw Henrik and the knife in his hand. He shot forward, stabbed into the water, scooped the knife up and swung it.

The pike slapped to the ground in front of her, flailing, soil sullying its green fins, its large mouth with the underbite snapping. Maija grabbed a rock and struck the fish on its head. It shook and stilled. She rose, threw the rock away.

He waded towards her, his hand raised. 'Sorry.'

He squatted by the fish, laid it on its back on the grass and gutted it with one slit of his knife. He threw the guts into the water. Then he leaned back on his heels, one hand covering his eyes against the sun. 'What brings you here?'

'Someone called Nils came to see us.'

Henrik stroked the sides of his knife against the grass. He stood up, walked to the water and washed the inside of the fish with his fingers. A glimpse of sallow red.

'He's a nobleman?' she asked.

Henrik nodded. He rose, the fish hanging from one hand, his fingers in its gills.

'They are settlers?'

Henrik nodded again.

'I am surprised,' she said. 'Nobles are no settlers.'

Henrik chuckled. 'That family can fend for themselves,' he said. 'I'll tell you a story. When Kristina and Nils first arrived here, one of the merchants saw his chance. He sold them rat meat, called it pheasant. Someone told on him, and it's said that when this same merchant arrived back to the coast after a long journey and unpacked, he found his cases full of the vermin. Under the cover of night, someone had replaced all his furs with dead rats.'

That would have done it, she thought. Nils was certain never to have been bothered again.

'I went back to see where Eriksson was killed,' she said. 'I found this.'

She took out the piece of glass from her dress pocket. In her hand it looked dull.

He took the piece from her. 'In the glade?'

'At its edge.'

'Where?'

'Underneath some bushes. South, towards the pass.'

He turned it around in his hand, then handed it back to her and shook his head. He began to walk and she followed him.

'It wasn't wolf that killed Eriksson,' she said to his back.

'No,' he agreed.

'Then why did Gustav say it was?' she asked, meaning, 'Why did you?'

'Henrik?' A woman's voice, calling from the yard. 'Henrik?'

Henrik lengthened his steps.

There was a thin woman in a long white dress on the porch. 'I told you not to go far. The children are out, and I am all alone.' She began to cough and supported herself with her hand against the doorframe. Then she noticed Maija.

'And who are you?'

The air in the cottage smelled of wood fire and fever.

'We don't get many visitors.' The woman had introduced herself as Lisbet. She had long dark hair and blue eyes framed by bowed eyebrows. Her skin was pale and fine over her bones. Maija removed her own arms from the table where she had crossed them, freckled and rough-skinned.

'I forget my manners.' Lisbet put her hands on the table to rise.

'Don't,' Maija said, as Henrik stepped forward to wrap his arm around the waist of the woman. Lisbet coughed and coughed until her thin frame hung as a coating on Henrik's. When he lowered her, the skin around her mouth looked green.

'Have you been sick for long?' Maija asked.

'A long time. Poor Henrik. He takes such good care of me.'

Henrik took the pike and put it in a bucket of water. He didn't look at his wife.

It was hard to see the two of them together. There was nothing unexpected about finding a man like Henrik on Blackåsen, but Maija could imagine Lisbet younger, dancing in a frilly dress, chatting. She must have been beautiful and, at some point, Henrik must have doubted his luck. Now his wife was marked. Not by one of the obvious diseases, Maija thought. Crayfish, perhaps. Crayfish was like hatred. It ate away at a person from the inside, and nothing was seen until they crumbled.

'I am sorry,' Maija said.

Lisbet shook her head.

'Where are you from?' Maija asked.

'We've been here so long now,' Henrik said. 'This is home.'

'Twenty years,' Lisbet said. 'We were among the first to arrive.'

She sounded proud. Maija thought about the cluttered yard. To think that people could live somewhere for such a long time without getting better organised. But Lisbet was sick. Not so easy to manage, then.

'What about the others?' Maija asked.

Henrik raised his brows to her.

'It's just interesting,' Maija said. 'All of you from such different backgrounds.'

Lisbet counted on her fingers. 'Daniel and Eriksson were

born here,' she said. 'Nils and Kristina arrived some years ago from Stockholm.' She smiled and small dimples appeared by her nose, a reminder of the beauty she'd once had. 'They had so much luggage you wouldn't have believed it.'

'Why would they come here?'

Lisbet shrugged. She didn't seem to find it strange.

'And Gustav? He was in the army?' Maija asked.

'Gustav doesn't get involved with the rest of us,' Henrik said. 'He keeps to himself.'

'Oh, I heard Eriksson saying he was a soldier – he would have known,' Lisbet said.

'What was he like, Eriksson?' Maija asked.

Lisbet giggled. 'Unafraid. He knew Blackåsen inside out, and he made living here seem so easy. He was gallant, pleasant—' She interrupted herself and looked to her husband. 'I don't want to be left alone,' she said, remembering her earlier grievance. 'People disappear here.'

'Nils told us,' Maija said.

Lisbet was still looking at her husband. 'And now she's killed Eriksson, too.'

'She?' Maija shook her head.

Lisbet's eyes fixed on Maija. 'Elin,' she said.

'His wife . . . Why?'

'She's a sorceress.'

'She was under investigation for sorcery a long time ago, but she was declared innocent,' Henrik said, correcting his wife.

But the trials had all stopped. Oh, what was wrong with people? Maija was glad she hadn't told anyone about the seeds she had found on Eriksson's clothes. Everyone used herbs for medical purposes, but some people were quick to point out that sages had faculties beyond the simple restoration of health.

'Even her husband wanted her trial to go ahead,' Lisbet answered her husband.

'To get her officially exonerated,' Henrik said.

This wasn't a new discussion.

'The bishop didn't listen to us,' Lisbet said. Her face was gaunt. 'She was let go, and now we will all pay for this decision. She'll get us one by one . . .'

Henrik was looking out the window. 'Are you managing for food?' he asked Maija.

Maija could see what he was doing. She tried to follow him on to ordinary matters such as the graylings they had caught and salted, the partridges and the hares that were hanging from the roof beams of the food store, the turnips growing in the earth and the field, full of barley.

'Yes,' she said. 'So far, it's been good.'

'The month of rot will soon be over,' he said.

Before coming to the mountain, Maija hadn't known the rot of July – the smell of death that hovered over everything. You couldn't finish your dinner; you thought you'd save it for breakfast, and in the morning it was unrecognisable. Made your stomach quiver to think you had ever eaten that. Yes, month of rot, harvest, and then winter.

'Be careful,' Lisbet said when she left, her eyes large. 'Don't let your children out on their own.'

As she came home, Mirkka was there although it was only afternoon. Maija walked close to her. She hung her arms across the back of the cow, felt the soft hair and warm skin against her cheek, smelled grass and animal, a trace of manure.

'There was a hearing for sorcery here, too,' she told the cow. 'Would you have believed it?'

Perhaps that was why the others had said it was wolf that

killed Eriksson. Wise people were afraid of fear. Maija thought of Lisbet's warning and felt her heart shrink. It was hard not to get caught in the webs of other people's fears, especially if it concerned your children. But that's when you had to remain level-headed and remind yourself you knew otherwise. Protect and preserve, she thought, as always when something concerning her children was too difficult even to contemplate. She sent the thought, perhaps to a God. Protect my children and preserve them the way they are now, unspoiled by the rest of us.

'Lucky, lucky we found you,' she said and patted the cow's flank. 'Little Mirkka.'

And she thought of milk and butter all winter long.

Sometimes when you had a thought, it refused to leave. You rejected it, disowned it, sent it away, to find, moments later, that you were still spending time with it. It might have a different shape or use different words, but there was no mistaking: it was the same one. It happened to her mother all the time and her mother grew distracted and ill-tempered. Then her father noticed and worry lines grew deep on his face. Now Frederika knew how her mother must feel. As soon as she relaxed the slightest, Eriksson's body was before her, the image jolting her like a penknife prick in her chest.

Frederika was standing by the edge of their homestead. Her mother had said they now needed bark to make their flour go further. She'd asked her to get it. Above Frederika, the spruce trees pointed into blue sky, thirty, forty, fifty metres – she didn't know – enough to dwarf everything else. She had a feeling the trees had both thinned and blackened. Their massive branches drooped almost vertically. The spaces between made them seem lost, although they stood together. She turned. Their cottage was a light brown block between the tree trunks. There was still time to go home. She didn't have to say she was frightened – oh no, she could see her mother's brows stitch up. She could say that she'd forgotten.

Use the speed of the wind, she thought, you'll be back here in no time. A memory skidded through her mind. It had been autumn. Hiding with Jutta in the forest. Fear making her ears pulsate, her mouth dry. Soldiers so near they had to feel them – how could they not? Insane impulse to stand up and scream, 'I'm here', unable to bear the tension. Meanwhile, Jutta, clasping her, whispering litanies. 'The shrewdness of the fox, the wisdom of the owl, the strength of the bear . . .'

And then, on the ground, behind the squatting Jutta, dead Eriksson again.

Frederika sighed.

Bark. Birch bark. She liked it better. The bread tasted more of bread and less of tree. She had seen birch by the river. She began to run.

Frederika reached the river at a spot not far from where they had washed their clothes. The river moved fast. Further downstream, pale trunks leaned over the water, small green hands twirled in the air. Red-veined grass grew in a pinkish fog.

Once, when she was small, Frederika had been allowed on to water. It had been back home, when her father still went fishing. He had showed her how to angle for grayling from the edge of the boat. She was impatient, but her father's hands were jittery and she held back, worried that if he thought she wasn't listening, he would not let her come. They had got in the boat and floated. As they drifted, her father closed his eyes. His face softened and its angles disappeared. He seemed different from the man she knew. When he relaxed, her father looked old. The river poured from his lifted oars with the sound of waterfalls.

Now there was another water sound. There was someone in the river. A woman, swimming. Red frizzy hair – elf hair – the waxen arcs of her body glimmered beneath the surface. She took a couple of strokes upstream, then turned over and

78

floated down on her back. Frederika had never seen the woman before, and yet she knew her. She was certain she did.

'Can I come?' she shouted, knowing full well that her mother would not allow this and would never forgive it, yet all of a sudden feeling she could not stand it if this woman said no.

But the woman called out, 'Yes. Come!'

Frederika stripped off, taking care to fold her dress on a stone. The water was freezing and its force so strong that for one moment she thought that this was too much – it was a mistake. At first the panic and later the sensation of wickedness made her scream with what she would remember as joy. The woman laughed at her with her mouth wide open, and then she screamed. Together, they howled with all their might with the fear and the happiness in being alive.

Spent, they sat on the stones to dry.

The woman's breasts unfolded into pink suns, her flesh splayed over the stone. She had spider webs of blue on her thighs. A breeze rippled the water, swept up over the shore and made the tiny hairs on Frederika's legs and arms stand up straight. She reached for her dress, and pulled it over her head.

The woman rose and put on her white blouse and fastened its hooks. She put a pin in her mouth, tried to untangle her hair with her fingers, but gave up and swirled it together at the crown of her head. She stepped into her skirt and tied the wide ribbons around her waist. She bent at her hips and reached down to smooth away the creases with firm strokes.

'I saw honey-paw this morning – bear,' she said. 'He came almost all the way up to the cottage.' Her eyes widened as if she'd seen something on Frederika's face. 'You've seen him, too.' She nodded to herself. 'You know the meaning of seeing bear, don't you? Ancestor, coming with a warning. I am now thinking it might have been for you.'

'For me? Why?'

'Oh, I'm not that good.'

'Then how do you know he didn't come to warn you?'

'Clever . . .' The woman laughed. 'I don't. Though I do think that whatever was supposed to happen to me has already happened. Signs are like that. You half make things up, half know. Most often you are right.'

'I saw black crows; what does that mean?'

'Whatever you think it means.'

The woman turned to look out at the river. She stood for a long time and watched it, eyes narrow. She sighed. Sometimes Frederika, too, felt she loved a place so much she could eat it with her eyes.

'And what brought you here?' the woman asked.

Frederika had forgotten. She scrambled to get up. 'I have to get bark for the bread. I wanted birch.'

'You're in the wrong place. Go to the valley. I am going that way. I can show you.'

The woman began to walk upriver and Frederika followed her. She took the path that led to the top of the mountain. Frederika hadn't realised they would have to pass the glade. She wondered if the woman knew what had happened, but she didn't know what to say and so she said nothing. When they reached the summit, the woman stopped to look out over the valley, shading her eyes with her hand. There were erratic bursts of fierce colour in the landscape, which otherwise seemed to have dulled since Frederika was last there.

'This place is holy,' the woman said. 'At least that is what they used to say, the people who lived here first. One can understand why.' She pointed to a flat boulder some metres away. 'We call this "the King's Throne",' she said and laughed.

'This is where our men come to sit and look at the world as if they owned it.'

Frederika couldn't concentrate. The glade insisted behind her. She stepped sideways to keep it in the corner of her eye.

'Something happened here,' she said.

'Lots of things have happened here. It is that kind of a place – it attracts things. Maybe it is the view.'

'Is it evil?'

'The place? Whatever evil you find here is not of the worst kind. The obvious things rarely are.'

'My mother says I should try to make Blackåsen my own,' Frederika said. 'There is an awful lot to Blackåsen, isn't there? If a person wanted to try to make it their own.'

'And then, perhaps it's not up to you to choose,' the woman said. 'Come. I'll show you something.'

She walked towards the pass. As the path narrowed, she dragged her hand along the rock wall. At the crevice she paused, glanced at Frederika and then walked straight into it. Frederika stopped.

'Come on,' the woman said.

Frederika followed her into the mountain. There was a thread of blue far above her in between the rock walls. At the end of the path, there was a boulder and there the fracture cut to the right. There had been a landslip. Large rocks and small stones made a hill against the rock, all the way up into the blue.

The woman stepped up on one of the larger stones and reached with her hands to climb further.

Frederika touched the rock. She began to climb.

They reached the summit and there was a level part. Around them, the mountain fell away. Frederika gasped. The woman was watching her, eyes small slits.

'The men on the King's Throne don't know about this,' she said. 'It makes me laugh that they sit there pondering a sliver of land, while just a bit further up, there is the whole world.'

The woman pointed. 'West – our marsh, forest, Norway and then the oceans.'

Blue forest became blue mountains and then blue sky.

'South, lies the valley.'

The valley was a vibrant green, sprawling fingers of silver waterways. 'The town lies beyond the hill.'

The woman put her hands on Frederika's shoulders and turned her around.

'East,' she said. 'Our lake, forest, the sea. Finland.'

At the horizon, a mere haze. Air.

'North: our river, more forest, the mountains. Up there, where green turns brown, they say we are all one: Norway, Sweden, Finland and Russia.

'You can see the homesteads,' the woman said and turned around in a circle, pointing out small patches of cleared ground at regular intervals in the forest. 'Henrik by the river, Nils by the marsh, Daniel in the valley, me in the deep forest, you by the field, Gustav by the lake. All of us close to the mountain. None of us on the mountain itself.'

'Trees, trees, trees,' her father had muttered on the porch this morning.

And yes. The land was old spruce leaning in over them with shaggy branches, pine trees, no more than a hand high, jabbing at their ankles. There were hollow trees, tree stumps and fallen trees flaunting snarled clods of roots and earth . . .

But more than that, most of all, this land was sky.

The forest in the valley dozed in the heat. She stirred when they came, as if rising from some dream before sinking back into slumber. Through the spruce trees, the marsh sparkled: green moss with yellow star shoots, and, further out, black water. If she turned left now, Frederika would come home.

The fir trees stopped behind them and gave way to bright, young trees.

'There was a fire here once,' the woman said. 'That is why this bit of forest is leafy. It will take a long time before the spruce grows back. Bishop's weed, polypody, nettles – you'll find it all here. In late autumn, there are a lot of rowanberries.'

'There was a fire?'

'It was the driest summer anyone can remember. One morning, there was a white pillar rising to the sky. And it was off. A blazing line dividing healthy from charred. There were yellow explosions, smoke bubbled among the trees like clouds rising from the ground . . .' She wrinkled her nose. 'Westwards, the fire drowned in the marsh. The pine trees on the mountain, of course, managed on their own. But the valley . . . It was vulnerable, open flat, and full of spruce.

'They tried to create a fire-break – they chopped down trees . . .' The woman swirled around, 'in this direction.' She made a path with straight arms. 'But the fire caught both bush and crown. There was a brown fog before the sun, fragments swirling all around it like black moths against a light. And they had to let the fire take the valley.

'The day after, seen from the mountain, the valley was still glowing – a thousand devils looking out from inside the black ground.'

Frederika shivered. 'Weren't you scared?'

The woman's pose slumped and she smiled. 'I hadn't arrived yet,' she said. 'We all talk about this as if we were here when it happened. It's the one joint memory we pretend we have. That and the disappearances.'

'The disappearances?'

'I have to go now. You'll find plenty of bark here. The sort you like.'

'Thank you for helping me,' Frederika said.

'Somehow, I think you'll return the favour.'

'Wait,' Frederika said as the woman turned away, 'what is your name?'

'Elin,' the woman said. 'I am Elin.'

'They're already there.' Paavo opened the barn door. Maija blinked against the light. The scrawny body of the goat wriggled under her arm. It had been limping and she'd put a leather strap around its neck to take a closer look at its foot. It could be a rock or a thorn. As long as it wasn't rot. The goat kicked and Maija let go of its body, but held on to the strap.

'They being who, exactly? There being where?' she said.

'I saw them from the mountain. The marsh is full of people,' Paavo said. It sounded like an accusation. 'They're harvesting the sedge.'

'I guess we'd better go too, then.' There was hostility in her voice now, too.

As he slammed the door behind him, the goat jumped and pulled the strap with it. *Ouch.* Maija lifted her hand and looked at her index finger. There was a red mark where the leather had burned the skin. Not blood. Just . . . a burn.

Perhaps, not long before he died, Eriksson held something made of leather in his hand, she thought, and it was snatched from him. Maybe that something had contained herbs, some of which caught on to his sleeve.

They weren't prepared, and she wasn't certain what they'd need to take with them.

'You have the scythes?' she asked Paavo, although she saw them on his shoulder.

'Yes.'

'And the rakes?'

What was she doing? It wasn't far to the marsh; they could send the girls home if something was missing. Paavo muttered and she felt her stomach pinch.

Breathe, she told herself. She remembered Daniel's pregnant wife, Anna, and took the pouch of fennel seeds she had dried.

'Do you think the others all talked about it and agreed to harvest?' her husband asked.

'Of course not,' she said, though she couldn't know. 'They've just been here longer than us, that's all. They knew what to look for. We'll ask them, so that next time we know, too.'

They walked the whole way in silence.

'Mamma,' Dorotea whispered.

The figures on the marsh seemed to have risen from the mud. Their skin was black. The metal flashed in the sun as they lifted the scythes. There was a humming of blades cutting air. It was loud, like the wings of a hundred dragonflies.

Then one of them lifted his hat to wipe his forehead and underneath was a blond tuft of hair. Henrik.

'They've put something on their skin,' Maija said, with a calmness she didn't feel.

'Tar.' Her husband gave a strange laugh. 'I've heard of it being done. Against the mosquitoes.'

'Goodness,' Maija said.

Now it was easy: there were Henrik and five children, Daniel and Anna with four children, and further away, Nils and what must be his family. The man in the middle, where the marsh seemed to be more lake than swamp and the tufts

86

of grass were few and far between, was Gustav. One part of the marsh lay empty. That's theirs, Maija thought. Eriksson's and Elin's.

Maija watched for a while.

'I guess you and I will scythe,' she said to Paavo. 'Frederika and Dorotea can rake and carry the sedge on to dry ground.' She turned to her daughters. 'Pile it in heaps. We'll let it dry a bit and then we'll all help lift the grass on to the racks – you see them? Those are drying racks.'

It was difficult to get started. The water slowed the scythe down and made it heavy to lift up again. The blade didn't seem to bite on the sedge. The mosquitoes were bad, but even worse were *sviarn*, the small black midges that tore a piece of flesh each time they bit. Maija bent down to pull at the wet grass with her fingers. It was slimy and thick and didn't break. As she walked, her dress squelched against her legs, and chafed the skin on her ankles. Beside her, Frederika struggled with the rake. Dorotea shrieked and slapped her legs, then her arms.

'You need to put this on.' Nils came wading towards them. He held a vessel in his hand containing what seemed like black grime. 'Come here,' he said to Dorotea. He began patting the filth on to her cheeks and nose. 'Fold your sleeves down,' he commanded. 'You'll get eaten alive.'

Nils turned to the marsh, vessel in one hand, the tar dripping from his other. 'Time for a break,' he called. 'Make a fire!'

Far out, two figures lowered their scythes and began to walk. They were followed by others.

Nils focused on Dorotea again. 'Tie your kerchief lower. Cover your forehead.'

He turned to Frederika, hand raised, then cleared his throat.

'Your mother can help you,' he said and pushed the bowl into Maija's hand.

Maija dabbed the tar on to Frederika's forehead and nose. Its smell was pungent and made her eyes water. Once Frederika was covered, she continued with Paavo, and then herself. She looked to the edge of the forest where the settlers had gathered and shrugged to Paavo.

'We'd better join them,' she said.

The fire was vigorous and its flames were a bright orange with sooty ends. It was unnecessarily large. Wasteful. Nils was standing beside it. The others had gathered in a loose circle around him. Gustav stood to one side and looked at the marsh rather than the people. His face was twitching. Maija looked from Gustav's curved back over to Daniel with his protruding ears, on to blond Henrik, and back to nobleman Nils. If I am right and Eriksson was killed by someone he knew, then it was most likely one of you four, she thought.

Why 'if'? It had certainly not been evil powers.

Nils turned to throw another log on to the fire.

They have to talk about Eriksson's death, she thought. A man had just been killed among them. They will have to have the words out.

'What you need is a blacksmith,' Daniel said. 'I know a good one. He comes to town at market time.'

This was all too ordinary. But perhaps they had spoken about Eriksson before she and her family arrived?

Maija tried to picture Eriksson here among them, sitting on one of the stones, or standing beside Nils. Tall and muscular. The bald head. The features slackened in death, that must once have been sharp. It was hard. The problem was Nils. She couldn't imagine Eriksson and Nils in the same place at the same time. She tried to imagine Elin with them, instead, and could almost see the air growing darker. They wouldn't have had this break, she thought, if Elin had been at the marsh.

Anna sat down on a rock. Her face was grey.

'Still poorly?' Maija asked.

Anna grimaced and spat at the ground.

Maija moved the tar bowl over to the other hand and dug in her pocket. She handed Anna the leather pouch with fennel. 'Put a few seeds in hot water and drink it as often as you like. It will calm the vomiting.'

A blonde woman came towards them. Though tall and large, she moved with the agility and precision of someone small. Maija got an image in her head of the clock she'd seen once in Ostrobothnia, *tick-tock, tick-tock*, metering out her time. She had to bite her lip not to giggle.

'I am Kristina,' she said. 'Nils's wife.'

'Maija.' Maija gave her the bowl of tar, nodded a 'thank you'.

The bowl looked small in Kristina's hand. 'We make it out of birch bark,' she said.

'It's a useful tree, birch.'

Kristina was not like Maija imagined noblewomen to be. There was nothing fragile about her. Her face was broad, her lips full. The tip of her nose was turned downwards. She, too, looked at Maija, as if appraising her.

'You've never harvested sedge before,' Kristina said.

'No. My husband, Paavo, used to be a fisherman. I'm an earth-woman by training. If ever . . .'

Kristina's eyes glinted. 'Oh, I am beyond childbearing days now. But I am pleased to hear it. It will be good for the younger women to have you here.'

'How far away is the town?' Paavo's voice cut through the air.

'One day's walk.' Nils indicated the direction with his hand.

Paavo and Daniel had walked closer to him.

Alongside Maija, Anna put her head between her knees. Poor woman. Some women were sick all their childbearing time, and meanwhile, inside, the child clawed at them for nourishment.

'You're lucky still to have a grown daughter with you.' Kristina was looking at Frederika.

'I didn't get any sons, and so I don't want her to leave just yet.' Maija looked to the square boys who stood behind their father. 'And you have three sons?'

'I have daughters too, but I send them south as soon as they can walk.'

'You send them away?'

'It takes time to insert someone into a certain place in society. They'll be growing up with my sister in Stockholm.'

Maija imagined a row of blonde girls in white dresses and hats, holding parasols. She looked at her own daughters with their faces smeared black, kerchiefs low and in the thick dresses she herself had woven, standing on a land that smelled of the piss of mating elks. But you get a lot of love, she reminded her daughters in her mind.

'Why would you stay here?' Maija asked. 'I mean . . . with your options.'

'Fifteen years of tax relief for settling here.'

Maija was surprised. But perhaps in Sweden nobles, too, were in need of funds. Kristina's nostrils flared. She didn't like talking about it.

'And you, why did you come?' she asked.

'My husband traded the house with his uncle.' Maija was pretty certain that, by now, her nostrils were flaring, too.

'And what do you think, Maija? Are you here to stay?'

As if they could move from one place to another on a whim.

'Yes. Though I am not certain we would join you in any village if you decide to build it.'

Kristina raised her brows.

'I'm not against villages as such,' Maija said, 'but I am against people allowing fear to make important decisions.'

'A village?' Kristina asked.

Didn't she know?

'That's right,' Nils said, interrupting them. 'The more I think about it, the more I believe it's what we need to do. Come winter, we could start felling trees for houses. We'll set ourselves up somewhere close to the lake. We wouldn't have to be frightened any longer. We'd be safe.'

Kristina was looking at her husband.

'You don't agree?' Maija asked.

'Why? I think it's an excellent idea,' Kristina said.

Kristina had the kind of smile that didn't grow on to a face, but appeared already formed. But there was something else in her face, too, when she looked at her husband. Caution?

'Did I hear right?' Nils asked. 'You're an earth-woman? Do you have any suggestions on how to rid yourself of toothache?' He grimaced and pointed.

'I normally advise just to pull the tooth out,' Maija said.

The former priest's widow opened the door to the vicarage herself. The corners of her mouth rose, as if amused.

The priest saw her in church every Sunday, but then she was sitting down – linen bonnet over bent head. Here at home, her head was high, her hair light on her shoulders. Golden. Young. Her straight bearing, the merriment in her voice – she reminded him of the women you'd meet at court. For a moment, he imagined the King behind her, winking at him.

The widow pointed to one of the armchairs. As he took off his coat, she stood without talking. It made a nice change. Most people blathered when they met him – pattered through his mind with their dirty feet: stupid questions, petty quandaries.

She poured both of them some liquid from a flask, handed one of the cups to him and sat down opposite him. He noticed her eyes were blue. The drink in his hand smelled sweet and tart by turns. Elderflower?

'I thought,' the priest said, 'that it's been a long time since we spoke.'

When the widow smiled, dimples appeared at the sides of her mouth. The priest wasn't sure they had ever spoken. Knowing well the practice of new priests marrying the widow of the former one, he had not hurried to make her acquaintance.

'So . . . How are things?' the priest asked.

'We are busy with the preparations for winter.'

The priest noted the 'we'.

'With any luck, the harvest will come good this year,' he said.

'Let's pray.'

Yes, let's pray. The previous year, the peasants were so famished when they came to the Lady Day sermon, their eyes were like craters in their skeletal faces. They had stared at him as if they were about to eat the words off his lips, or worse. He'd been told some among them had had to slaughter their cattle. The settlers he'd seen this summer looked better. He guessed they ate mushrooms and things. And now the crop was growing anew. The previous day, as he passed the field, he'd bent down and touched the emerging green hard sprouts – their promise rasping the flat of his hand.

'The bishop's visitation was a few days ago,' the priest said.

'Yes. Karl-Erik called in to say hello.'

Karl-Erik? It was difficult to think of the bishop as a man who had a first name.

'He said there were things you wanted to ask me about Blackåsen.'

'That's right.'

The widow put her cup down on the table and tilted her head. The priest crossed one leg over the other. This was stupid. He couldn't know what he didn't know.

'Has something happened?' she asked instead.

He didn't see why he wouldn't tell her. 'One of the settlers on Blackåsen died.'

'Died by what means?'

'There is a difference of opinion about that.'

'Then that's why Karl-Erik is worried. My husband used to say that the settlers on Blackåsen were like wild dogs that ought to be kept chained.'

This stunned him. He'd heard the former priest was lettered; firm, but mild.

'The bishop seems to be concerned about some supposed curse,' he said.

'Oh.' Her surprise seemed genuine. 'Perhaps it worries him because it worries the peasants? They are prone to overreaction. Who died?'

'Eriksson.'

Her right hand flew up and tugged at her earlobe.

'Well, you know about his wife Elin, I'm certain,' she said.

'I read about the hearing in the Books. What did your husband think about the outcome?'

'He said that Karl-Erik . . . the bishop, had told him it was better to try to heal wounds rather than open them.' She shook her head. 'Anvar didn't like declaring her innocent without a trial. He felt it was trying to put a lid on a pot where the water already boiled. While in the beginning Karl-Erik seemed to share his view, once the hearing was under way, he changed his mind and closed it down.'

The priest wondered about the relationship between the bishop and the former priest. One severe, the other mild-mannered. Yet when it came to Blackåsen, they both appeared to have behaved counter to nature.

He wasn't certain what the bishop wanted him to do. The widow changed position. The skin on her neck was a bluish white. Almost a year had passed since her husband's death, and still she was here.

'Anvar was an old man,' she said with a rapid smile. 'His methods were sometimes . . . archaic. But in similar circumstances, he would have worried about hysteria spreading. About people blaming the Devil, the curse, engaging in old superstitions to protect themselves.'

'And he would have done . . .?'

'He would have called for parish meetings. Or an extra sermon. He would have aimed to restore order.'

The priest nodded. She was right. Calm was vital. God telling the subjects to fear Him, their ruler, and nothing else.

They both lifted their cups to drink at the same time. The beverage tasted of summer blossoms.

'I understand you were at the court?' the widow asked and sent the priest back to the battlefield at once. He put his cup down.

'I was a priest there.'

'Have you met the King?'

'Of course.'

'What is he like?'

The priest pictured him now: the King galloping in the lead on a horse drenched with sweat, throwing himself off without warning – Was he all right? – rolling around, his rapier, still in its sheath, thrust forward. The horse next after his, stumbling. Falling. Breaking its neck. Total silence. Its rider rising from the dust. The King slapping his back a few times. 'Now you attack me.'

Later that evening, their King, dancing with one of the many eager women – some princess or duchess or other – coolness so palpable that watching him chilled your heart.

Vicarius Dei.

'God. God's representative on earth,' he said, and ached. 'He has this habit. He twists your coat button around when he speaks with you, until it comes off in his hand.'

Then walks off with it like some prize, he thought.

'How amusing,' she said.

The priest rose.

'There is another matter,' the widow said and made him sit

95

down again. 'It seems like Lena Rolfsdotter, the night man's daughter, has started a relationship with my farmhand Joel.'

He couldn't help but sigh. She nodded.

'But in this region, the harsher you are seen to be, the better. Order,' she reminded him, and squeezed her lips into a decisive line.

Yes, order.

Before he left, the widow decided to tell him. 'Just before he died, my husband visited Blackåsen. When he came back, he was unlike himself. He was . . .'

She shook her head. 'When I asked him, he said that he had never before come across such evil as on that journey. It was as if he were shocked.'

The light in the vicarage flickered.

'Did it have to do with the curse?' The priest surprised himself by asking.

'No, I think he was talking about a person. Anvar told me most things, but he was perturbed. And the next day, as he was about to mend the barn roof, he fell off the ladder. I didn't get another chance to ask him.'

The priest walked from one window to the other in the temporary vicarage and looked out at the bright squares of other windows. He realised that to anyone else who did the same, he must appear like an animal pacing in its cage. He sat down.

The first time he met the King had been in the field. The army was preparing for the next day's battle. In the afternoon, the priest had an inspiration. Together with the other priests, they made the men stand in formations – squares of thousands – and they sang a psalm. '*Wår Gudh är oss en wäldig borg. Han är wår sköld och wärja.*'

Through the corner of his eye, he saw the King arrive on

his horse, the skirts of his blue jacket flailing. With him were Stenbock and the Little Prince – legends in their own rights. And the priest stretched out his arms, bade the men sing louder. The King was watching him. That evening, the call came for the priest to join the King at dinner.

Vicarius Dei.

The priest rubbed his hand on his heart in slow circles.

He thought of the widow.

A person evil enough to shock a priest? Eriksson would have known who – he knew everything about everyone. It might indeed have been Eriksson himself. The man had been vile. Though it wouldn't have taken his predecessor that long to discover Eriksson's nature. It had taken the priest that one meeting, and the man had revealed himself to him.

The widow was right. He needed to close the matter down in a forceful manner. He would have the verger send out the call to sermon.

And he would have to see Lena and Joel.

'Does he realise what he is asking?' Maija said. 'The barley will soon be ready for harvesting, and he is calling us to church.'

The man who'd come to deliver the message had known to shrug as if apologetic. Even he had grasped the extent of the priest's demand.

Frederika and Dorotea looked at her, but her husband made as if he hadn't heard her.

Fog had descended during the night and it still lingered. It was a fog without veils, a low sluggish paleness wrapping the trees and them in nothingness. Further away, the clouds were frayed. Rain on its way. Maija wrapped her scarf tighter. It had been darker when she woke up this morning. Not much, a feeble amber tinge hanging in the air, vanished before the others woke up. She wouldn't tell them. Let them think summer has not yet come and gone, but that it is on its way: strong and bright.

Below them on the plain, surrounded by a timber town, the church stood tall. Its lines were proud and white, broken by the roof displaying its dents for heaven to see. Despite herself, Maija was moved. The church had been there for over two hundred years, seen all that humans had to offer: births, deaths, laughter, tears, even wars – and remained there, silent, unmoved, its sanctuary facing the light of grace from the east. It wasn't about religion. It was their past. The church held their past.

Frederika puckered her nose.

'You don't find it beautiful?'

'It's too big,' her daughter said, and Maija felt a sudden urge to prove her daughter wrong. 'Look at the rest of the houses,' her daughter said. 'The church is too white. It doesn't belong here with us.'

People descended from all the hills. They came together in one stream flowing in the direction of the church. In town, the windows gaped empty. Weeds sprouted along the house walls. There were no children playing in the streets, no dogs looking for scraps, no smells of food, of sewage – of habitation. Uncle Teppo had told them: during a few weeks each year, they were to live in the area called Settler Town to give the Church and the state its dues, sharing a house with one or two other families. The rest of the year, the town was empty but for the keepers of the church. On the green in front of the church, the grass grew tall. There was one single tree, a large oak.

Maija had to stop. It was one of the most beautiful trees she'd ever seen. It was old. Its branches reached so high it seemed to touch the sky, while the lowest ones stroked the ground. Its crown was broad and the winding branches thick. It was one of those trees that at some point would have to be cordoned off from fear of falling branches as, in age, it began to lose control of its limbs. Maija wondered who'd made the decision to let it remain. It gave you hope. That someone had seen beauty. In the bell tower, the bell hung motionless. But perhaps they didn't ring it because this was not an ordinary sermon.

Entering the church hall, the men removed their hats. The women touched their kerchiefs. Their footsteps echoed against

99

the stone walls. It smelled of prayers, perhaps of mildew. There were dark brown benches in two rows from back to front. There were scraping noises as people sat down, mumbling as they greeted others they hadn't seen for many months, and turning to see if anyone was absent. On the arched roof high above them, were painted scenes in frames that made them look like medallions. Maija recognised Jesus teaching his disciples, Jesus waking Lazarus from the dead. One of the pictures seemed to be from a torture chamber. Naked people in flames speared by brown devils; the eternal threat of hell. She scoffed to herself. Hanging at the front, in the air high above them, its body clad in gold and its roof and curtains of red velvet, surrounded by lit candles in massive candlesticks, was an enormous pulpit. Like a chariot already halfway to heaven.

Then Maija felt cold.

A young woman knelt on a stool in the middle of the aisle, her hands clasped to her chest, her head with the white linen bonnet lowered. People parted around her. A man spat on her dress.

Dorotea pulled her sleeve: 'What's going on?'

'That, Dorotea, is called a whore stool,' Maija said aloud.

'Shhh,' Paavo hissed.

'The priest puts people there to punish them and to scare us others.'

'But what has she done?'

'Something the priest considers a sin. Notice, Dorotea, that she is alone. There is no man being punished together with her.'

Paavo pulled her with him into one of the aisles and down on a bench.

'Stop it. Stop it right now.'

'This.' Maija pointed at the woman. 'This is insane.'

'Do you want to join her?'

In her lap, her hands, their chapped skin and square nails. Ugly hands. Honest hands. Working hands. She opened them. Shut them again. Paavo still stared at her. She ignored him. Her cheeks burned. She remembered a Paavo shouting at the village priest over the practices of the Church. He'd only been a boy. Four days in the stocks, he had got. She had walked past him again and again, full of admiration. She had thought about it so often, used him as her beacon. And instead, now, his fear maimed her.

She thought of Henrik and Lisbet and recognised herself and her husband. Only there it was the woman who was frightened and the man who was trying to soothe. It was like what Nils had said, about the little lake on the mountain that had turned into marsh and the large one that had remained a lake. A being was either strong enough to hold their ground, or they became small and bottomless and started feeding on themselves. They turned into something they never saw coming. Something they never intended.

She must not begin to hate, she told herself.

'What your mother isn't telling you,' Paavo said to Dorotea, his voice pointy, 'is that the priest could have given a much harsher punishment to this woman. She could have paid with her life.'

Towards the front, Nils stood with Kristina. Daniel entered with Anna a step behind him, and Nils smiled and greeted them as if welcoming them to his church. Henrik and Lisbet were already sitting in the sea of balding heads and kerchiefs. Maija didn't know how Lisbet had managed the journey. Then Elin walked by with her children.

Nils was looking at Elin. There was no greeting. Not for her. Elin sat down in the same bench as Henrik and Lisbet. Lisbet pushed on her husband and they stood up and walked to some benches further back. Elin's children stirred, hovered around her, jostled to sit close to their mother. One of the children put a thin hand on her shoulder, but Elin didn't react.

The door at the front opened and the priest strode in. He held a Bible in his hand. He mounted the golden stairway up to the pulpit and bent his head. There was a cool draught from behind her and Maija turned around to see Gustav enter. The great hall fell quiet and then the priest looked out over them without seeing any one of them.

'Repent,' he whispered. 'Repent,' he whispered again.

'Eve in the Garden of Eden, oh, you despondent, can you see her? God's creation, perfect in every way. Everything has been given to her – the animals and the plants bow to her, she is never cold, never hungry. She is allowed all things in a universe of pleasure, all things apart from one, the fruit from the tree of the knowledge of good and evil.

'"And why can't you eat from this tree?" the snake asks her, amazed.

'She looks at the tree. She thinks it's beautiful.

'"Dazzling, isn't it?" the snake whispers. "None of the others looks like this."

'Eve finds she likes to keep the tree in her line of sight wherever she is. Soon, she sits in its shadow – for a short while. Then she lies beneath it, looks up through its foliage to the sky and it is fine. Its fruits are red and plump. If one falls beside her, she touches it.

'"What harm could it do?" the snake whispers.

'And it isn't long before the woman lifts one of the fruits up, looks at it, smells it, and she and her stock are doomed.'

At this moment, there was an interference in the sermon. It was the flame of one of the large candles beneath the pulpit.

First it shivered, as if to attract attention. Then its yellow flame swelled to a height that threatened the fringes of the velvet of the pulpit itself. And so it died. There was a sound in the church hall – a wind sweeping through shrubs and whipping up dry leaves.

The priest lifted his chin and pulled his shoulders back, seeming content with the effect of his words.

'And the punishment: condemnation for all of us. And eternal condemnation it shall be if we do not hear the voice of God.'

His voice sounded normal now. A man speaking with fellow men. Maija's arm hurt. Dorotea's hand with the dirty nails that dug into Maija's skin looked older than her years. But the comfort sought was still that of a child.

'There have been events in our midst,' the priest said. 'A settler died on Blackåsen Mountain, a tragic mishap. And then, here in town, people sinned and risked bringing God's wrath upon all of us. The Church is dealing with both matters. Your duty is to conduct your chores and your service to the kingdom eagerly, diligently and to the best of your abilities.'

He paused.

'Repent.' With his voice, he lashed at the people in the benches below him. 'Remove the filthiness of the flesh from your heart. Cast temptation far away from you. If your hand or your foot causes you to sin, cut it off and throw it away, for it is better for you to enter life maimed or crippled than to have two hands or two feet and be thrown into eternal fire. If your eye causes you to sin, gouge it out and throw it away, for it is better for you to enter life with one eye than to have two eyes and be thrown into the fire of hell.

'But if you do not give yourself to Him, if you hold back from Him, if you put anything before Him, if you are rebellious to Him, if there is sin in your heart, then He will tear you in pieces and all that awaits you is an eternity away from Him.

'*Kyrie eleison*, have mercy on us, O God.'

It was over. Maija detached Dorotea's fingers from her arm, gave her hand a squeeze and rose. 'I need to speak with him,' she said.

'No.' Paavo stretched for her, but she moved away.

She made her way forward, side-stepping people walking in the opposite direction. She didn't look at the girl on the stool in the aisle. Above the crowd, the priest's eyes met hers. He turned from those around him to meet her alone.

'A mishap?' she asked.

They eyed each other in silence.

Careful, Maija thought. You don't know what he's capable of. 'I wanted to ask you to look at this.' The piece of glass resembled a pool of blue water in her hand. The priest came closer. He bent to look, then straightened his back.

'Yes?' he said.

'Do you know what it is?'

'Stained glass.' He shrugged.

'I found it where Eriksson died. I wondered if you knew where it came from?'

'One of the merchants, perhaps.'

A woman with blonde hair scarcely tucked under a bonnet swept past them, eyes lowered as if she didn't notice them, yet so close she brushed against the priest's arm. It distracted him. He followed her with his gaze. Maija put the glass back in her pocket and nodded to leave.

'The sermon will calm things down,' the priest said.

Maija snorted. 'Then you didn't see the candle? One of the candles went out during the sermon.'

He still didn't react. The imbecile.

'A candle goes out and somebody close to it will die,' she said. 'That's one of the most obvious signs there is – at least where we come from. I think the settlers now believe someone else will die.'

There was some pleasure in seeing his chin fall down.

Maija walked with long strides, stretching her legs out at each one.

'What did you think about the sermon?' Paavo asked, as they started up the hillside. He had the round black eyes of a robin redbreast.

She slowed to look at the tracks of animal in the mud. 'Maybe lynx,' she said and pointed. Then shrugged. 'He's the Church's man, but preaches like a pietist,' she said.

She could have laughed at herself: as if she knew. She had met one pietist, at a marketplace. She'd seen him later, too, being led away, still shouting that the Kingdom of God was near.

Yet, there was something to what she had said. The priest was conceited, but when he preached there was more than arrogance and contempt: fervour? Hunger.

'It's not how I imagine God,' she said.

Paavo nodded. 'Did you see the candle?' he asked.

Above them a flight of black migrant birds flew south in a 'v'. People didn't think it, but grey could be the most violent colour of all. Things bred too well in grey.

Spatter against her face. It began to rain.

Heaven opened. A wall of water poured out and down. The world dissolved into bleary blocks of colour. The rain drummed against the roof of the house. On the green, someone ran for cover.

'Anything more?' the verger asked.

The priest waved him away. He stood for a while by the window and watched the rain dig in the soil, making hopeless rivers and lakes. The winter he'd spent with the army in Sachsen, for months, it had rained every day. Even the King who, it was rumoured in enemies' camps, had magical protection, had fallen ill – their own, of course, foreseeing the end of the world and the coming of *Christos*.

The Finn woman had said a candle had gone out during the sermon.

He had asked the widow about it.

'I didn't see it,' she said.

'Are you certain?' Not that he worried.

'Yes. Why do you ask?'

'You don't know if people think it's a sign? A candle going out?'

The widow laughed. Her blue eyes glimmered. 'No, I don't. I can ask my maid, if you like?'

'No, no, no.' He'd smiled.

He ought to take the Finn woman in hand. But something

about her made him uncomfortable – he couldn't tell what. Here, he was closing the matter out, and yet she had pressed on, showed him the piece of glass she'd found. At the place where Eriksson's body had lain, she'd said? Well, he had recognised it, but the matter was closed.

Despite the fire, the room felt dark. Sometimes this house croaked and moaned as if it were alive. The rain was still thundering on the roof. It was time to go to bed.

The priest woke with a start. He had dreamed of earth. Of trying to find something to hold on to, feeling the ground turn to phlegm between his fingers. The room smelled of dead fire. His nose was cold and he touched its tip with his hand. Freezing. He pulled at the blankets, pushed his hands deep down inside the cover and closed his eyes. But then his mind started to wander. It reverted to the candle in the church.

He wouldn't be able to go back to sleep. He was wide awake.

He sat up on the edge of the bed. The room was cold. The maid needed to put more wood on the fire at night. He patted with his feet on the floor to find his shoes and grabbed his cloak from the wooden chair and pulled it over his head on top of the nightshirt. He walked to the window. Put his hands on his back and leaned backwards. Shivered and then yawned. The window had fogged up; he wiped it with his hand.

The sky was low and closed. The black earth and the yellow grass glittered. He leaned back and stretched again.

Then he realised what he was seeing.

Oh no.

The priest ran down the stairs. He flew through the hallway, flung the door open and jumped off the porch.

At the other side of the field the verger came running, coat flapping.

The priest slipped on the grass, caught himself before falling, continued running. At the white-rimmed field, he plummeted to his knees. With shaky fingers, he pulled the thin seeds off a straw. They were frozen into small stones. Many of the heads were already empty.

The sky was a white lid above them and he was gripped by a senseless urge to laugh. There would be no harvest.

'What do we have?' the priest asked.

A fire boomed in the fireplace. The verger sat with the books before him.

'The woodshed is full.' The verger followed the accounts line by line with his finger. 'Three barrels of grain remain since last year. The barn is full of hay for the animals. There will be milk.'

'More?'

'There is salted fish, meat. The turnips ought to survive the frost. You have four cows and five sheep. Worst case, you can slaughter. You'll manage well,' he said.

The priest remembered the local people – in Rawicz? – attacking the King's army one winter when the famine grew unbearable. He saw before his inner eye flocks welling down the hills. 'Do not kill,' the King had shouted. The soldiers had used the flat sides of their swords. But the aggressors came ready to kill with stones and sticks or their bare hands. They were mostly women and children. The images of their distorted faces – the face of hunger – would remain with the priest for ever. 'We are God's envoys,' the King had said to the subdued company that evening. 'If we don't have food, we cannot do our duty. And these people need us to succeed. It's hard, but we mustn't forget this. From now on, we put guards around the supplies.'

'Are there locks on the barns?' the priest asked.

'No.'

'Arrange it. On the house, too.' He walked to the end of the room again. 'What about the vicarage? How is their position?'

'You'll have to ask the widow about that.'

He would go over and see her. They might need to request backing from the peasants this year for both households to manage through winter.

From outside came the neighing of a horse and the rustling of carriages. The priest turned to the window. The verger walked close and peered from over his shoulder. 'But the bishop was just here,' he said.

The bishop stared out over the frozen field.

'I wanted to see you again before winter, and now this.' He put his hand to the back of his head and held it there. 'Third year in a row,' he said. 'How will things be?'

'I'll manage,' the priest said.

The bishop stared at him. He opened his mouth, then shut it.

'I was thinking about your congregation, Olaus Arosander,' he said. 'The settlers, the peasants. Do you think they will be fine, too? Your herd? All those who already have bled from the wars, the scarcity, the diseases?'

The priest wanted to tell the bishop about Rawicz. He wanted to tell him what the King had said, but, even in his head, the words now sounded peculiar.

'Have you found out what happened to Eriksson?' the bishop demanded.

'We had a sermon yesterday where I addressed it.'

'You had a sermon.' The bishop's voice was full of scorn. 'I must not have made myself clear. I want to know what happened. I want a name, and you shall give that to me.'

The bishop grabbed the priest's collar and stepped so close, the priest smelled the dung of his breath. 'When I come back the next time, you shall tell me, or, so help me, God, you shall rot here and never leave.'

His hand on the priest's chest was trembling.

The priest hit the bishop's hand away. 'You never liked me. You and the other bishops. From the beginning, you were against me.'

The bishop sneered. 'Why would we have been?'

'Because I was close to the King. You couldn't wait to ruin it. I don't know how you did it, but you did.'

The bishop shook his head.

'You made me fall out of favour. You had me removed,' the priest said.

The bishop was still shaking his head. 'We didn't remove you from the King,' he said, coolly now. 'The King asked for it to be so. I said we'd take you, offer you a new position here.'

The words struck the priest harder than if he'd been slapped.

'That's not true,' he said.

'Olaus, you knew him,' the bishop said and now there was something different in his voice. Pity? 'Why wouldn't it be true?'

Late autumn this year had violence in her hair, angry crimson, orange and yellow. The trees wrestled to free themselves of their cloaks, crumpled up their old leaves and threw them straight out into the strong wind rather than just let them fall to the ground. Dry leaves ran across the yard with the crackle of fire.

Frederika's mother held some frozen grains in her palm. Her hand seemed blue.

'I'll have to go to the coast,' Frederika's father said, 'and find paid work. Come spring, I'll bring back food and seeds for next summer.'

Her mother tipped her hand, and the grains fell to the ground.

'We have no money left to pay for lodging this time.' She was looking at the icy field.

'You're right,' she said after a while. 'The girls and I can manage with what we have gathered, and with Mirkka's milk.'

'I am not certain this is wise.'

Already her father didn't like it. To separate: what a stupid idea.

'It's the only way,' Maija said.

'There is still war,' Paavo said.

'There's always war,' her mother said. She sounded tired.

Frederika's shoes were scuffed and muddy. They looked like they belonged to someone else.

'Perhaps some of the others are going,' Maija said.

Her father looked up. Maybe he wouldn't have to go it alone. Her mother throwing him a titbit of hope, like you brush crumbs off a table pretending you are leaving a decent meal for the dogs.

The barn smelled of pelt and sawdust. There was a bucket by the pen. Frederika kicked it, and it hit the wood with a *clank*.

She remembered another time, kicking a tree stump, Jutta watching.

'But she's horrible,' Frederika had yelled. 'She's so . . . cold.'

Jutta sat down on the tree stump. She put her hands on its top beside her thighs, as if to appease what was hurt. The skin on her hands was wrinkled and see-through, the blue veins on her hand large and bubbly.

'Before your mother came to live with me, she lived with her father inland in a hamlet,' she said.

Stories. As if all that was ever needed was another story.

'Outside the hamlet, there was Näkki, who pulled you down if you looked too deep; Hiisi, in crevasses and by boulders who attacked you if you came too close; and Ajatar, who made you sick if you ventured too far into the forest.

'But inside the hamlet was Maija's father, Ari, and her four older brothers, who took turns to carry her around in a haversack they'd braided out of thin strips of bark.

'Now you wonder: why were they carrying her? You see, Frederika, your mother was born with thin legs, twisted like ropes, of no use at all.

'Your mother's father had a brother who was travelling the seas. Whenever he came to visit, Uncle Erkki brought gifts. Once, there was a roaster grid from Turkey and small black beans in a leather pouch. They roasted the beans, made juice of them and the hot black liquid banished sleep for several days. Another time, there was a piece of cloth from Bengal, with sallow stars so delicate and beautiful, not even night did better. Then it was a yellow root from China. This was an important gift. They boiled the root and mashed it and put it on Maija's stick legs and they stared and there was stirring and pricking, but that was all. Maija's father forced her to eat what was left of the root and Maija vomited beside the porch.

'The last time Uncle Erkki visited, he brought a disease from Calcutta.

'Ten days after Erkki's departure, Maija's brothers got a rash: small red dots on their foreheads. Maija and her father watched with fascination and then fear as the boys grew thin, as if drained from the inside, and the bumps grew larger, until her brothers' skin was covered by shining jellyfish. The jellyfish puffed up and puffed up and then they breathed out and deflated into dried sheets of skin. Pale fluid began to seep out. Her father lifted Maija up and shushed her on to the porch.

'Your mother sat on the porch night and day. At first, the villagers came to ask how things were. Then, they bent their heads when they passed. Towards the end, nobody walked the road by their house at all. Sometimes Maija put her hands on the wooden railing above her and pulled herself up. She looked in through their window, but her father put his hands up: 'no' – the disease whirling around him like a small storm. Later, jellyfish had her father, also.

'One morning, her father came out. His face was covered with so much dried skin it looked like thick bark. Maija saw eyes in there, round, blinking, but her father had turned into a tree. He fell off the porch. And that's when I came to take your mother with me.'

Frederika took a step forward, close enough for Jutta to

reach her. Her great-grandmother smelled of sweat, of love, perhaps of spring onion.

'She's walking now though, my mother,' she said to the wool on the chest.

Jutta leaned back to look at Frederika. 'And you know what? She did that all on her own.

'One day, I found your mother staring at her legs. "As far as I can tell, there are two legs," she said.

'Well, undeniably, there were.

'I would watch through the window as your mother pulled herself up with the help of the porch railing and tried to move those shrimp legs of hers. Your mother would fall over and I'd leave the window sill. Then I'd come across her in the barn, kneading her legs like sour dough with her hands; knead and pull and twist.

'And your mother's legs grew, thicker and straighter. Towards the end of that summer, your mother stood up. Before the snow fell, she walked.

'I asked her about it once. How she had known. She said that the most frightening part had been believing. Many people would have been happier not trying. Most people never try.'

Jutta patted the sides of Frederika's legs with her hands.

'I don't know any other way to describe it than to say that your mother healed herself. This is why she sometimes becomes . . . impatient with other people. She wants them to fight.'

'Hmm,' Frederika said, still unwilling to let go. 'Not everyone is as strong as her.'

'That's true. And your mother used to be more tolerant of others, but—'

Jutta interrupted herself and patted the sides of Frederika's legs again – this time to tell her to stand up. Frederika rose.

Jutta bent over the tree stump and stroked its top. Her lips were moving as if she were praying.

There was a dull clang of bells, dogs barking, voices. Frederika ran out from the barn and across the yard at the same time as her mother opened the cottage door.

'Winter,' her mother said when Frederika reached her. She was squinting towards the forest. 'This is winter coming.'

Men and women came walking out of the forest. Frederika counted five men, four women, children, and with them a herd of reindeer with tall antlers. The dogs yapped. The reindeer slowed and came to a halt. They moved to drink from the stream.

Two men left the others and mounted the slope towards them. The older had silver hair and a silver beard. His face was wrinkled and darkened by the sun. His coat was of leather patches sewn together with large tendon stitches. The younger was quite young. He couldn't have been much older than her. His black hair almost reached his waist. He looked at them down a straight nose.

Lapps.

'Greetings,' the older one said.

His voice surprised her. It was soft.

'So you are here,' Maija said.

There was this look on her mother's face. Not fear, nor shock. Happiness, Frederika realised. Her mother was pleased to find the Lapps here in their yard.

'The dark time is approaching, *čakčadálvi* is already here.'

'Ssakca . . .?' her mother mumbled.

'Early winter,' he said.

The Lapps had eight seasons, Frederika thought. Someone had told her. Jutta?

'I am Maija,' her mother said.

He bent his head. 'I am Fearless,' he said. 'This is Antti.'

They looked each other over.

'Will you keep a few goats for us for the winter?' Fearless asked. 'They don't fare well at our winter site.'

Her mother was still silent. She was counting, Frederika thought. Thinking if they had enough fodder.

'What's there in return?' Maija asked.

'A reindeer to slaughter.'

'When?'

'Before the snow melts.'

Her mother nodded. 'We'll take them.'

Antti turned and ran down the slope. Fearless stood without talking until the younger man came back towards them, leading two black goats by rope. He touched one of the goats' head as if stroking it, and it seemed to calm.

'Frederika, take them to the barn,' her mother said.

Frederika reached out ànd Antti unwound the ropes from his hand. She took them and tried to avoid touching his skin.

'This year there is more in the air than snow,' Fearless said behind her. 'This year, better to be careful.'

'Wolf winter,' Antti said.

Frederika didn't meet his gaze.

'We'll spend the night by the stream,' Fearless said. 'We leave tomorrow.'

Dorotea was standing so close to the window, she fogged it with her breath. She drew a line in the whiteness with her finger. There was a strange light in the air outside: pink and dark at the same time. The sort of dusk that floated in and out of a house.

'How long did they say they were staying?' her father asked with a low voice, as if the Lapps might otherwise hear.

'One night,' her mother said.

'I am not sure we should have agreed.'

'I'm not sure we were asked. Besides, all of Lapland – it is their land.'

Frederika sensed rather than saw her father frown.

'What is a wolf winter?' Frederika asked.

'A cold winter,' her mother said.

It had sounded worse. Like a threat. She was about to ask again, but her mother made a small movement with her head and caught her eye.

'Henrik said the Lapps pass through here a few days before the first snow,' her father said. 'As if they can smell it in the air.' He took a few steps backwards. 'I'll have to pack up. Get ready.'

'Are any of the others going?'

'None of them.'

He looked at her mother, wanting. But her mother's eyes were fixed on the figures in their field.

The autumn gale threw itself against the wall of the cottage with thuds and muffled screams. A branch spanked at the rear. Frederika lay on her side in her nightgown her mother had dyed red.

She turned on to her back. The sheet beneath her was damp, the hay in the mattress lumpy.

Wolf winter. She tasted the words in her mouth. Wolf. Winter. She bit on a hangnail until it was salty and hurt. She bent her legs to squeeze her warm toes and stretched out again. If a person didn't have sleep in them, they shouldn't be made to stay in bed.

I don't have to, she realised.

His father's chest rose and sank. Frederika supported

herself on her elbow and looked over him. Her mother had turned her back. Frederika sat up. Sat still and waited. Nothing. She pulled her dress off the chair beside her and stuck her head and arms into its openings. She stood up. Held her breath. Tiptoed on naked feet across the floor. *One. Two. Three.*

The door to the hallway squeaked. She bent down, found her shoes with her hand, opened the front door and sneaked out.

She stood for a while on the porch and waited, but no one came. She sat and put on her shoes. The wind was cool against her bare legs, the hay in the shoes rough. Around her, the sky was a black pink and the crowns of the trees swayed. The air was full of their murmurs.

Frederika ran across the yard. The wind pulled at her, filled her lungs with new air.

Behind the tree line, she slowed. There was the light from a fire down by the stream, and she made her way towards it in protection of the trees. As she came closer there was a low, rhythmic chant.

Her great-grandmother had told her about it. How the Lapps' songs captured the very core of an object – no, more: captured the object itself. But they weren't allowed to sing them any longer. Devilry, the priests said.

She crouched and made her way forward on all fours.

'Stop now,' a man said and she froze. She recognised the voice of Fearless.

The chant ceased.

'Do you remember when you taught it to me?' another man's voice said after a while. 'I was small. It was my first hunt. I was frightened.'

'Stop now,' Fearless repeated.

The other man's voice rose in anger: 'We've all seen the signs. You could protect us if you wanted it.'

The voices moved away until she couldn't make out what they said any longer. She sat still for a long time. The ground was bitter against her legs. She shivered and stood, began to tiptoe back up towards the cottage.

She glanced to her right. A figure. Motionless. It took a step forward and she almost screamed.

She swallowed. 'I was going to . . .'

Antti was silent. She couldn't see his eyes, only the straight line of his nose.

'I just wanted to ask . . .'

He still didn't say anything.

'Wolf winter,' she said, her voice small. 'I wanted to ask about it. You know, what it is.'

He was silent for a long time. 'It's the kind of winter that will remind us we are mortal,' he said. 'Mortal and alone.'

Maija walked towards the lake. She paused to look at an old oak tree with a scarred trunk, broken and hollow. Lightning. The stump was still sprouting the green leaves of summer, as if it didn't know it no longer had a centre; as if it didn't understand it no longer had a future.

But the wind pushed at her. It had a cold heart, this wind. Snow was not far away. Maybe that was how the reindeer smelled it. She was pleased the Lapps had chosen to leave the goats with them. When they come to pick up the animals this spring, she thought, I'll try to get to know them. She thought about snow again. Paavo had to leave before the first snowfall. The land would be difficult to traverse after.

It would be good if he left, she thought. That was awful. She shouldn't be thinking like that. But it was hard enough, without somebody else spreading fear.

'Mirkka,' she called and listened, but couldn't hear the cow's bell. She wasn't certain when she had last heard it. It was always there, melded with the birdsong, the stir of the grass and the hum of the forest. Surely, she would have noticed if it had been long absent?

The wind whipped up froth on the lake's dark surface. The sky above was bruised. Further away, smoke pushed out of the vent of Gustav's cottage and was forced back down again towards its spine by the gusts. But the cow was nowhere. She called anyway.

'Mirkka!'

She turned and walked back into the forest. She stopped by a stream and squatted to drink. The water was so cold it had no taste. She had already been up on the mountain, in the glade and by the pass. The one place left to look was the marsh. Or the valley. But she wouldn't have gone as far as the valley; cows stayed close to relief. Unless somebody else had milked her. It wasn't unheard of – people who stole from each other by milking each other's cattle. But the time milk would be needed was this winter and by then, the cow would be tucked in, in her pen.

The birds were gone from the marsh. They had left its surface a sullen black.

'Mirkka!'

This time there was a cry. Not Mirkka, but it was animal.

Maija began to run. She stepped sideways, head tilted, listening, calling the cow's name.

Again. That horrid sound. Not crying – screaming. Animal screaming. Maija had to make a large loop around thick reeds.

The cow was lying dead on the ground. And this – this was wolf. Wolf at its worst. They had come from behind. Mirkka's head and chest were whole, but her flank had bite marks and her anus was torn wide open. The bowels had been pulled out through the rift and eaten – probably while Mirkka was still alive.

Maija put both her hands before her mouth.

And then Mirkka lifted her head.

Oh no.

She didn't have anything with which to kill her. There were no stones anywhere nearby. Maija ran to one of the trees, kicked at one of its branches. But the tree held on to its limbs.

She ran back to the cow and fell to the ground to cradle the large head in her arms, rock it back and forth. She cried into her muzzle and the cow's uneven breaths were hot against her ear.

Maija got to her feet again. She ran all along the marsh, tried to find something, anything, but in vain.

When she came back, the cow was dead.

At the homestead, she saw the blood on her arms and the filth on her skirt. She limped to the barn. She must have hurt her foot trying to break the branch. In the empty pen, she took the cow's water, found a rag, wet it and rubbed it against her skirt. The rag tore and her knuckles scraped against the wood of the pen. She watched as tiny red and blue streaks appeared on her knuckles. She put them to her mouth and sat down, forehead against her knees. She smelled of sweat. Of urine. Her ankle was pulsating. What now? Without barley? Without milk?

They would have to go with Paavo to the coast. Maybe someone would take pity on them and help them with lodging until they earned some money.

There was a twinkling in the corner of her eye and she lifted her head. It came from one of the Lapp goats.

She limped towards the goat, grabbed it by its pelt. Around its neck on an animal tendon, pieces of blue glass chimed empty tunes.

Paavo was wearing his black wool hat with the floppy rim. His rucksack sagged on the floor. Maija went to wash her hands.

'I can't find anything,' he said, and laughed out loud. It was so long since she'd heard it, she'd almost forgotten the sound. 'My winter hat. My mittens. I need your help to pack.'

The water dripping into the bucket was pink. She dried her hands.

'Paavo,' she said.

He reached out and grabbed her hand. 'I need this,' he said. 'You're right. The past is the past. We said we would leave it behind us. All this fear . . . I have begun to feel as if I am no longer a man.'

He squeezed her fingers until they began to hurt.

And then, before her, stood a long-haired, spirited boy; a boy who had used to pull her braids, and she couldn't tell him about Mirkka or about the piece of glass, but set him free.

She watched as he crossed the yard. Waved and smiled and wished him safe journey. When she let go of the porch railing, her hand ached and she didn't know whether it was because of his grip, or because of hers.

That same night, it began to snow.

At first, there are only single flakes falling from a solid sky on to Blackåsen — one, then a couple more. The mountain parries them. As if considering not allowing things to proceed. With spruce and pine, it blocks the snowflakes from reaching the ground. By the river, it swallows them with water. Over the lake, they are so moist, they seem like sheer mist.

Beyond the hill, in town, God's soldier has gone to see his verger.

'I am going to have to travel to Blackåsen,' he says.

The verger is sitting down. He's sewing on an altar cloth, head tilted, legs and scrotum hidden underneath sacred fabric. 'That won't happen now,' he says. 'We call this period the time of decay. The first snowfalls. The frost needs to go into the deep of the ground before the snow becomes hard enough to carry the weight of a man. Until then, the mountains are unreachable. We'll have to stay here.'

God's soldier looks out. All he can see is his own reflection in the window.

North: a settler stands by his window. He watches the snow fall. Behind him the woman he used to find so beautiful; a gift to him from the gods, asleep in their bed. Her breathing grates.

'Half a metre,' he says to himself. 'Before tomorrow morning, at least half.'

The woman coughs and he stiffens. So die then, he thinks. Die.

He waits without turning around. No. Sleeping. Still sleeping.

By late afternoon, the snowflakes that float in the air above the mountain are as big as Lapp mittens, as soft as the wool closest to the sheep's heart. Snow settles on the trees' branches. It covers the rocks by the river. By the lake, you can no longer see across to the other side.

A few perennials shed their last leaves. Life twines itself downwards along roots and bulbs. The annual plants prepare to die, knowing their seeds are buried in the earth, thinking thus they shall return. The animals are still. All is quiet.

By the lake, a man stands on a porch, hands flat by his thighs. He stares at the sky falling down around him. He leans his head against the cold of the house, lifts his hands and places them on the timber, and breathes. Then he whacks his forehead against the wall as hard as he can. He grabs new snow off the railing and presses it against his forehead. Feels pain turn to water in his hand.

Day after day the snow falls – to reach a metre on day three. The snow floats and drifts with the wind. Restless, but not light. The branches have to give under its weight. One after another, they squeal, fold, snap, and let the snow fall to the mountain's surface with a dull, achy sound. On the river, crystal sticks to crystal, making floating islands. The ice by the lake shore creeps further out on the open water. The marsh is white.

On the roofs of the few houses, snow lies in thick bulges. In the windows, there are lit candles. Lit, for the light has mellowed. A small change, but darkness is on its way. Inside, there is already dimness in the corners of each room.

Here, someone is telling tales. His wife is baking knäckebröd – *crispbread. She's learned this and more since they came. With the help of her sons, she has hung a pole in the roof on which the bread will dry.*

'To turn wild reindeer into a herd, the Lapps first need to castrate one reindeer.'

He speaks as if he knows this by experience. Let him, his wife thinks. Whatever keeps him occupied.

'They put a cloth around its testicles and bite them off with their teeth.'

Their children are too old for this kind of story, yet they moan.

'That reindeer becomes for ever calm. He can be led by a rope. But the most important one is that which follows the first. He is still wild, a leader, and he brings with him a large following.'

'Why does the second one follow?' *one son asks.*

'That depends on its character,' *he invents.* 'Perhaps it is out of loyalty to the castrated one. Perhaps it feels forced.'

His wife is making porridge. Her steps are heavy. It's the child inside slowing her down. He remembers his mother saying that porridge calmed the nerves. He's not certain it calmed hers, his father a drinker and with sons like the two of them.

His woman hangs the iron pot on its hook. She stirs in it. She lifts the vessel off the fire. While the meal cools, she sits down to wait. There is the whine of the spinning wheel. Never resting. She's a good woman, this one, stoic. At once, his whole chest stitches up and makes it impossible for him to breathe.

It is like that, missing. It comes in waves

*   *   *

Warmer, colder, warmer again. The snow thaws and refreezes and mellows and turns grainy. The floating islands on the river catch each other. Across the lake there is a thin sheet of ice, clear as glass. The marsh is asleep now under metres of snow. The trees have doubled in size. At dawn, the crystals on the branches catch the remaining light and shine like a million tiny stars.

A woman sits by a table. She is folding clothes. How strange, she thinks. All this time, all these struggles, you think you have a new beginning and it proves to be an end.

The children are running around, chasing each other, shouting. They are too young. Too small. Too old, too large, too fast. They'll do her no good.

The days become shorter. The dark from nightfall lingers on right through the day. Underneath the lowest branches of the spruce trees, it lurks and watches. By the river and the lake, it hangs in the air like a tinted haze.

The real cold arrives. The houses come alive. There is ticking and creaking. Wind and snow work on any painted area and what is left will be a sheer memory of the original colour: small, flaking squares in some places; minute, almost coloured droplets in others. When the settlers come inside after feeding their animals, their curls are silvered. You can break off hair that's frozen like that, feel the tress come loose between your fingers, and not hear a sound.

Her daughters have rubbed the last traces of food off the plates with their fingers. More poor or less poor, she tells herself. That's all it's ever been. She refuses to feel anything. As if not feeling would make a difference.

127

Her elder daughter is clearing the room, sorting laundry, folding clothes.

Find it now, come on. There you go: feel. What is that in your mother's skirt pocket?

The girl hesitates, then her fingers close around it. She takes it out and holds it towards the light: a piece of coarse blue glass in her hand.

PART TWO

Maija didn't hear the first shot; heard something perhaps, but didn't make sense of the sound. She was in the barn seeing to the animals. The goats bleated, complained to her of the new cold.

The second shot could have been anything – a shutter slamming, ice rupturing, a tree breaking . . .

It was with the third, that Maija recognised the sound. She ran out. Five shots in total echoed out, rolled against the mountain with the sound of a whip.

Southwards from.

Elin, she thought. Or Daniel and Anna.

Maija ran as fast as she could, whispering with each step, *please* let me be wrong. The night was black, but the snow glowed and gave off light. Her shoes scraped as they struck the crust. When she came to the open area that was the marsh, she slowed down and made her way around it in a jagged half-moon.

At the edge of Elin's homestead, she stopped. Her nose and forehead ached. She was panting. The cottage lay dark in the middle of the empty yard. Nothing roused. All was silent. She abandoned the shelter of the trees and walked out into the open, her gait slow and careful. There was a thick drift of snow on the porch. She knocked and tried the handle, but the door was frozen shut. 'Elin?' she said.

There was no response.

In the sparse light, she couldn't see a pick. She began stamping on the snow to break it into pieces. The sound echoed out over the yard and hit against the trees. She kicked the slabs down on the ground and tugged at the handle, but it didn't move.

'Elin!' she called.

She fell down on all fours and dug in the snow with her hands. She rid herself of her mittens and edged her bare fingers underneath the door, pulled them under its frame, squeezing her fingertips a few times against the palms of her hands every now and then to numb the pain. She tried the handle again.

'Elin?' she whispered into the hallway and took a few steps forward.

The kitchen was silent. Packed snow pressed against the window and threw a blue tint on to the sill and into the room.

It took time for her to be able to see. And then she could.

Spots, snaky traces, smears, rivers gleaming black.

She walked towards the bedroom. On the threshold, she stopped.

They were clad in their nicest clothes, as if ready for a visit to the market in town – the boys in round-necked linen shirts, the girls in white, embroidered dresses – had it not been for those stains, those large brown cornflowers withering on chests and on arms. Their faces were already grey with frost, their vacant eyes shining light blue. They lay side by side on the bed. They must have been dragged there.

And their hands – oh God, their hands, positioned on each tiny breast in the symbol of prayer, arranged with the love and precision with which you fold a newborn's shirt.

Elin herself lay on the floor across an overturned chair, her back in an impossible arc, her neck undone, the rifle beside her. She was no larger than the children on the bed.

Maija covered her mouth with her hand. Why didn't you come to us? she thought and her eyes filled. Why? Surely, there must have been another way!

The front door opened behind her and she turned. A cloud of white whirled in and down through the dark like a glittering mesh.

'Don't,' Maija called. 'Don't come in.'

But the heaving sound told her it was too late.

Elin's brother-in-law Daniel rested his head against his arm on the wall. He had vomited on the floor. Now he was still. Except his hand, which touched the doorframe as if caressing it, again and again. The gesture made Maija think of Dorotea, the way she was after she had cried for something, when the emotion was gone and yet the tears kept coming because she was caught in it and didn't know how to stop.

Maija stood just behind him, each of her breaths like a puff of ash falling through the dark.

Daniel cleared his throat, inhaled and stood up straight. He wiped his face on the back of his sleeve, and without acknowledging her, he left. She felt his presence by the window and then he was gone.

Maija thought she saw their souls beneath the roof: thin, restive veils. Her guts churned. She opened the two windows in the bedroom and the one in the kitchen. She didn't want to think about where they would go. From this point onward, this part of the forest would be considered haunted.

Her legs were at once so weak they could not hold her weight. She sank down on a chair. How could a mother kill herself and the offspring she had carried beneath her heart for nine months, and in her heart ever since?

Her stomach wouldn't settle and she focused on the small

things. On the bed, the blanket and the sheet beneath were folded down in a neat invitation. Small, tidy flowers were embroidered on the pillowcases in red. The sheets had gauzy patches where the cloth was worn thin. Around the window someone had painted a red, leafy pattern on the pallid logs. The window lacked curtains. Outside, across a cast-off snowdrift, the branches of a black tree scratched the sky. She couldn't see what this home might have been like while there was still life. She thought about two brothers. About a man and his wife. She stared at the timber walls as if they might open and tell her the stories smouldering inside, but they were silent.

What could make a mother kill her children?

Only madness. Not the enduring, dull, weakness of mind; no – an abrupt plunge into unspeakable darkness.

Night began to close. The windows ought to be left open for many days, but there were the wild animals and so Maija shut them.

As she walked back, daylight broke. The small things that moved at dawn had already been. There were tiny footsteps and traces of joy in the sparkling snow, but they didn't move her. I guess people will be happy now that Elin is dead, she thought.

Gustav was on the marsh testing the ice with a wooden stick. She wished it was someone she could have talked to; anybody but him. Most of all, she wished it would have been her husband.

The priest was in his study. The room was cold. His bones ached. All appropriate. He would write about the frost in the Church Book:

The killer frost of 1717. We knew we had to be brave.

He tapped with his pen against the desk.

The killer frost of 1717. God's wrath on our province for the third consecutive year. We knew we had to be brave.

His hand holding the pen, with every passing year, ever more like that of his father: the long back of the hand, the softness prompted by the flat knuckles, the tilted ring finger. He was even getting the same ridged nails.

He threw the pen on the desk, rose and walked to the window.

It had stopped snowing. For three weeks they had been unable to go any further than the green. All the space in the north, yet cramped in the prison of a church green. He had imagined confinement would come easily to him. He remembered preaching once about Paul the Apostle's imprisonment as a blessing: a time to still himself in prayer and meditation before the Lord. But while the housekeeper and the maid – even the verger – settled down and picked up chores such as spinning and knitting, the priest found himself pacing the hallway, feeling as if the wooden walls were about to topple him. The verger said that the snow was hard enough now to carry the weight of a man. Thank God, it was over. What a miserable parish. What a castigation.

The King couldn't have asked for him to be removed. The priest had belonged in this little group of men who stood shoulder to shoulder around the King. He could feel the weight of the King's hand on his arm, as it had been that time the priest and his horse had fallen into a river and he didn't change his clothes when they fished them out, even though it was on the brink of freezing. 'Just like me,' the King had said.

Another recollection: wintertime. Stuck in a camp outside Minsk in whitest Russia. Waiting to war. Sluggish soldiers with thin faces. No food. No water. Just the eternal wait, while thinking about the fact that you had no food and no water.

One night, the priest was lying awake when footsteps drew near the tent. There was a moment's silence, then the fabric parted and a shadow sneaked in. The silhouette squatted by their clothes. There was a grating noise as their belongings were being elevated and searched. As if there were a rat with them in the tent.

No – the priest remembered thinking this. I'm wrong – this is a rat.

Enough.

He shot up and gripped his rapier. Whoever steals from our King, steals from God. He stretched to his full length and with the weapon still in its holder, he whacked the thief on the side of his head. The man fell backwards. The priest struck him again.

'More soldier than the soldiers themselves,' the King will say about the priest, later, when they bury the traitor.

And the priest knows it is true. Any lingering trace of the dead has been purged in the marches with the Swedish army.

He is a new being; one of them. No, the King wouldn't have asked for him to be removed.

The priest remembered the bishop's hand trembling on his breast. He couldn't stay here; he had to go somewhere he'd be seen by the King. The King had so much on his mind, but if he just saw the priest, he would intervene and restore him; he was certain of it.

The bishop had not visited the parish one single time for almost a whole year, and then he had come twice in a row. He's worried, the priest thought. Eriksson's death matters to him. Perhaps, if the priest did find Eriksson's killer, the bishop would become more generous. Perhaps even support his request for a new post down south.

The priest walked to get the old Church Books. He put them on his desk. The thick leather was cold against his fingers. He threw two more logs on the fire and sat down.

The previous priest had filled four volumes during his tenure. The priest opened each to look at the dates. He placed them in chronological order. He had skimmed the books upon arrival, considering what then seemed of significance. He pulled the first tome towards him and opened it, feeling the dryness of dust on his fingers.

His predecessor had not been wordy. *Spring 1705. Arrived. Recruited verger. 1706. Child lost on B.å. mountain.*

Blackåsen's forest fire the following year had, in the eyes of the Church's man, become: *Fire on B.å. mountain.* Nothing about the extent of the damage, although the priest had heard it was vast. Later: *Vera Fearless and child missing.* A few lines down: *VF and child not found.* Yes, this, too, the priest had heard about. Someone had said that for months, Fearless was seen wandering around Blackåsen, searching for his wife and child, before finding solace and reason in God.

1710. Reports of plague in the south. Many dead. Well, that was an understatement. A third of the population had perished.

The priest pondered his predecessor. Coming here was one thing, but staying – he calculated on his fingers – ten years? What drove the man? Priests in locations like this – it was either the adventure or a sense of righteousness, a feeling of being called. He suspected that with the old priest, it had been the latter.

In 1710, Eriksson had married Elin. Three years later, another child disappeared on Blackåsen, and soon thereafter Elin's hearing took place. There were no more details. *Elin Eriksson. Examined for acts of sorcery.* The next entry was the arrival of Nils Lagerhielm, wife: Kristina, sons: Petrus, Erik and Jacob. Then, written with different ink and in large letters – as if to exclaim or, perhaps, complain: *ELIN – INNOCENT.*

The priest had been astounded when he first saw the entry. There were still the sporadic accusations of sorcery, and the Church took them seriously – had to take them seriously – but he couldn't even remember the last time that allegations had led to an actual hearing.

The same year as Elin's hearing, in the autumn, a complaint had been lodged against Eriksson by the Lapps. They accused him of burning more forest than he was able to cultivate, and not leaving them enough winter fodder for the reindeer. It didn't say who had made the grievance. The priest flipped forward a few pages – births, deaths, births, deaths. The following year, the same dispute around the same time. And this time the accuser was mentioned by name: Antti. The priest saw before him black brows, a young long-haired Lapp staring at him in church with scorn on his face. Fearless unwavering in the bench beside him, balancing out the young firebrand.

The Finn woman had said the glass piece was found at the

spot where Eriksson was killed. The priest had seen one of the Lapps with coloured glass like that; he couldn't remember who or in what situation. But Fearless was in control of his kinfolk.

Although Fearless was getting on in years.

The year after, Antti had again complained. This time another grievance was also listed. *K against the church.* This was not clarified. Only marked: *Investigated. Dismissed.*

The last line in the Church Book was *Janssons gone?*

The widow was sitting with a piece of charcoal in her hand. She put it down and rose. She was wearing a pale, snug dress and her hair was braided down one side.

'I think I might have to go up to Blackåsen to try to understand what happened to Eriksson,' the priest said.

'Really?'

'The bishop wants to know what happened.'

She raised her eyebrows.

'Anyway,' he said, 'before I go, I wanted to ask you about some of the entries in the Church Books. A few years ago, there was a complaint against the church? The initial of the other party was K?'

She frowned. 'That doesn't tell me anything. When was it?'

'Two years ago. The plaint was dismissed.'

She shook her head. 'That's strange. I don't know anything about it.'

'And the Janssons? Who were they?'

'A family that used to live on Blackåsen. They left without telling anyone they were going.'

She gathered up her papers and bounced the stack against the desk a few times.

'What are you doing?' the priest asked.

'Indulging in a rather extravagant pastime.'

'May I?'

He extended his hand and she gave him the uppermost page. It was a sketch of the verger sitting in what might have been one of the chairs in the priest's place of work: the straight fringe, the lifted brows – captured in a few simple strokes.

'But this is excellent,' the priest said. 'Have you done many portraits?'

'I must admit, over the years, to having sketched most of the congregation.' She made a face, as if to mock herself for her own folly. 'How long will you be gone? If you do go, I mean.'

'No longer than I have to.'

'Be safe.' She dropped her papers in a drawer in the desk and shut it.

'There was no birthdate or birthplace in the books for Elin?' he asked.

'That's because we don't know them. Anvar had a good relationship with all the others, but Elin – she wouldn't even tell him when she was born.'

Indeed, Elin had deflected the priest's questions, too. How could he not have noticed? Her knowledge at the Catechetical meeting had been flawless, though. Impossible to fault her there.

'She didn't let me adorn her for her wedding, either – she said that before God, she was fine the way she was.' The widow gave a small toss of her head.

'And Eriksson; what did your husband say about him?'

'There was always noise around Eriksson. He fought with everyone. His own brother hadn't spoken to him for years.'

'Why?'

She shrugged to indicate she didn't know. Well, he wasn't

surprised. Daniel had seemed to him like a sensible man, and Eriksson . . . Eriksson had been Eriksson.

In the doorway, he hesitated. 'How are you for food?' he asked, and his face felt hot.

She smiled at him, a warm smile now. 'I am well provided for. Thank you.'

'Good. Well. Goodbye.'

As the priest walked down the steps of the porch, he thought again about the glass piece. It could have been the Lapps who killed Eriksson, taking the law into their own hands. There were so few settlers on Blackåsen. He would much rather Eriksson's death involved the Lapps. As long as it was a contained matter and Fearless remained sensible, it would be a good thing.

Something had caught his eyes. He slowed down. A movement in the stillness down at the base of the mountain. The priest shielded his eyes. He waited as the dots grew into four skiers. Each man was pulling a sleigh behind him.

'It's Elin,' one of men called as they skied into the square. 'She has done away with herself and her children.'

Nils was in the priest's office. The priest couldn't breathe. The bundles that were the children had been so small. As if in death, they had shrunk back to infants. He walked to the window, but in the square below, Daniel, Gustav and Henrik were standing by the toboggans and their loads. Destroying herself and her offspring. By God, what had driven the woman to this? The priest focused on the horizon.

'All her children?' he asked.

'Yes,' Nils answered. 'We brought them to you, them and the body of Eriksson.'

'Why would she do such a thing? The Church would have taken care of them.'

'Things aren't right on Blackåsen. Not right.'

The words were carefully put. The priest turned to face him.

'I'm not certain that her death has anything to do with that of her husband,' Nils said. 'Perhaps Elin was so frightened, she saw no other way out.'

'Frightened of what? Nils, we need to remain sensible.'

'Of course. And men like you and I are. But this is about them and about what they believe.' Nils nodded to the people in the square. His voice was calm.

'What are you saying?'

'A village. I want your permission to build a village on the mountain together with the other settlers. That way, we could control things and ensure the calm.'

'The others agree?'

'Yes.'

For a fleeting moment, the priest was tempted to say yes without further thought. When he'd heard that the children on Blackåsen had no school building, it had been Nils and his sons who restored an abandoned homestead and presented it to the Church for that purpose. The priest could just hand all responsibility over to Nils, tell him about the piece of glass and the Lapps, and ask him to look into it. Nils would handle the matter in a similar way – efficiently, quietly.

'I'll think about it,' he said instead.

Nils bent his head, but not before the priest saw him scowl.

'Well, I can't bury Elin in the graveyard,' the priest said, after a while.

Eriksson and the children in the cemetery. Elin not. No murderers or self-murderers in the graveyard; the rules were clear. Had Elin realised he would not give her a Christian burial? Of course she had. It was the difference between eternal life and damnation.

Nils put on his hat. The large, furred earflaps made his head seem wanting.

'We'll take the bodies to the night man for you,' he said, subservient now.

'Ask the night man to bury Elin in the forest when the frost in the ground allows it,' the priest said. 'Have him do it quietly. Tell him not to carve up the body.' There was no need to make this more gruesome than it already was. 'And that if I discover that there are any transactions in parts – bones, teeth, grease or blood – I shall, myself, see to the dismemberment of the precise same segment of his own body.'

The whole world was silent.

Frederika stood by the kitchen window. The blizzard was so heavy, their yard was swallowed in fog. But if you stared straight into it, you realised the haze was made up of thousands, maybe millions, of small white dots.

She hadn't been inside for long and her cheeks were burning. It had been her turn to shake the rag mats. They did it every day during winter. Put them on the snow and beat the dust out of them. Her mother had gone to the woodshed. Dorotea was feeding the goats.

Frederika leaned on the glass and stared at the snowflakes until her right side became so cold, it didn't belong to her any longer. Then she sat down on a chair and pulled her scarf over her head and face. This is what it is like to be dead, she thought. She imagined her face withering and falling off, big sheets of snow released off a tin roof, a *snap* and then *whoooosh*. Like Eriksson down in the ground. And now Elin.

Her mother had told her and Dorotea about Elin and her children. 'I prefer you hear it from me and not from anybody else,' she'd said. As if there were a lot of people around to tell them things. Then her mother had hugged them until Frederika couldn't breathe, and had struggled to get free.

Frederika didn't feel well. She felt her forehead with her hand, but couldn't tell if it was hotter than usual. She'd had the strangest dream the previous night; although the images had paled, the emotions they had unearthed remained intact. In her dream, she'd seen a man dressed in a blue jacket with large skirts, boots that reached his thighs, and a triangular hat on his head. He was striding forward in what seemed like a grave. There were shots – it was a trench. The man seemed unfazed by the sound. He passed another man who stood up to attention, patted him on his shoulder, said, 'Tomorrow, in the daylight, we'll have them,' then continued walking. At that moment Frederika noticed the shadows following him. The faceless shapes were gaining on him. They were so fast, and they were many. The walls of the trench began to crumble, but the man didn't notice. He just walked on and on, and soon he was moving in mud up to his ankles. Still he didn't notice. And then the mounds of earth on each side of him began to grow; she knew that soon they would collapse and bury him. Frederika had woken up screaming, scaring both her mother and her sister awake.

All this was the fault of the sound, she was certain. It had followed her since before the snow. *Dum. Tataradum.* From inside the mountain itself. As if there were a giant heart beating in its chest.

Sometimes, when Frederika spoke with her mother or with Dorotea, the sound was less present, a quiet tick. Other times it was so loud that, as she walked, she felt the pulsations around her in the air.

And then the snow fell, and things got worse. They woke up. It was hard to explain. But she knew – not just felt – knew, with the same certainty that she knew she was Frederika and she was fourteen years old, that the trees, the stones and the snowflakes had come alive. They watched her. Not in a threatening way, but not in a caring way, either. Just watching, as if waiting to see what would happen next.

'Settle down,' her mother would have said, voice sharp, eyes unwavering. 'Remember what you know.'

And Frederika knew that trees and stone and snow were not alive; not in that way.

'Say hello to the sea,' Jutta used to say whenever they went fishing. 'Say hello to the field, to the hill, to the plants.'

Settle down; they are not alive. But the way they shimmered. And she heard them. They whispered. They wanted.

Most of all, they hurt.

Somebody was on the porch. Frederika removed her scarf and sat up straight. The door opened. It was a man she didn't know. His brown hair was covered by a hat of snow. His brows were wide, and underneath them, his eyes a bluish grey. The flat kind that was difficult to see through.

'You must be Frederika?' he said.

She waited.

'I am the verger from the church in town. Where is your mother?'

'She's getting wood.'

'Well, I really came to meet your sister. I'll be teaching her and the other children this winter – reading and writing.'

Frederika had used to love school. Like all children, she'd had to leave when she was eleven.

He was watching her. His eyes had softened. 'If you ever have time, you can join us. One more or less . . .'

He was being kind. Frederika remembered her manners. 'Dorotea will be back any time. Please sit down. I'll make something to drink.'

'That would be nice.'

The verger walked to sit by the table. Frederika filled a pot with water and carried it with both hands to the fire.

'How old is your sister?'

'She's six.'

'Can she read and write?'

'Yes.' Frederika nodded. Their mother had taught them.

'We'll have our school in the abandoned homestead . . . Do you know it? It lies westwards.'

'I don't think I know it,' she said.

When she turned around, he was looking out the window like she had earlier. He turned as if he'd felt her gaze, and smiled.

'It's beautiful, isn't it?' he said. 'Snow. It turns the world flawless.'

'I guess.' She shrugged. Mostly hard work, if he asked her.

'Shame we can't hold on to it. But things advance, a new season arrives and with it the thaw of the snow, and there they are again – the imperfections.' He almost sounded bitter.

Dorotea was on the porch. Rather than kicking her shoes to remove the snow, she hopped about. The door handle rattled. She stopped when she saw the stranger, mouth open.

'This is your teacher,' Frederika said. 'This is . . .'

'Johan Lundgren,' he said. 'In class, you will call me Mr Lundgren, but outside class, Johan will do fine. You must be Dorotea.'

There were more sounds from outside. Kicking this time. Their mother came in. She unwound her scarf from her face.

'This is my teacher,' Dorotea said, in a haughty voice. 'In class, he is Mr Lundgren, but outside, Johan will do fine.'

Their mother gave Dorotea a stern look, but Johan laughed. The kitchen was full of sounds, as if he had brought them with him. Water underneath the pot fizzed on the iron plate in the fireplace. The fire crackled, and even her mother laughed.

★　★　★

'You found her?' Johan said with a low voice.

'Yes,' her mother said.

They were talking about Elin. Dorotea sat beside Frederika. She stared into the fire and her forehead was creased. Dorotea took off her socks, spread her toes wide and winked with her feet.

Johan shook his head. 'I can't get over it. What a tragedy. To think . . .' He fell silent.

Her mother glanced at her daughters. There were things she wanted to ask him, but not now, with them listening.

'The school,' she said instead, 'I assume there is a fee to pay?'

'The families take turns feeding the teacher. Will that be difficult for you?'

'We'll manage.'

'Don't be shy to tell me otherwise. It's a mean year.'

'We'll manage,' her mother repeated, and rose.

Johan met Frederika's gaze behind her mother's back. He smiled at her and shook his head. It would be a long time before it was their turn to feed the teacher. He, too, stood up.

'Perhaps Dorotea can walk with me?' he said. 'So she knows where we'll be when we start class? I'll bring her back, too. So she won't have to walk the mountain on her own.'

Her mother was about to say something, but nodded.

'I almost forgot the most important thing,' he said. 'One of the travelling merchants brought word from your husband. They met as the tradesman was leaving for our province and, as Paavo heard where he was going, he asked to tell you he has found a job by the coast.'

'There was no . . . letter?' her mother asked.

'No, but he said all was well.'

The goats bleated as Frederika entered. There was a lantern on a hook by the door, but she did not take it. She stepped into the mild darkness and inhaled the scent of straw and pelt. The animals were lying down in their pen. She couldn't make out their individual shapes; just a large, breathing bump.

'Only me,' she said in a low voice. Her mother had given a silly excuse for wanting to be alone. Of course Dorotea knew how to feed the goats.

Her mother had been sad, she thought. She wanted a letter from their father. He would write soon, though, Frederika was certain. You could depend on her father.

There was a movement in the dimmest corner of the barn and then a man took a step forward. Tall, bald, broad-shouldered, with bearing like an army man on watch. His mouth was slightly open. Last time she saw him, there had been flies flying in and out of that black hole.

Jesus!

She turned and her feet became snared by the hay. She fell, and scrambled rearward until she sat with her back against the wood of the pen. You're dead, she thought. Dead.

His eyes were fixed on her. They were small and set widely apart.

'A child,' he said with a scowl.

Frederika couldn't move. Her heart was beating in her ears.

He sighed and shook his head.

'How many times did you see Elin?' he asked.

She couldn't breathe.

'How many times did you see Elin?' he asked again, slowly this time. 'Answer!' he yelled.

Frederika gasped. 'Twice,' she whispered. 'Once in the forest, once in church.'

Eriksson smiled. It wasn't a real smile, but a showing of teeth. 'So you do speak,' he said. 'That's better. So what did you see?'

'I don't understand.'

'You must have thought something when you met her. People did.'

Frederika had to clear her throat. 'She was wise,' she whispered.

With his finger, he motioned for her to continue.

'She knew the mountain well.'

Eriksson rolled his eyes.

'I don't know what you want me to say,' she said.

'Compare the two sightings.'

Frederika remembered Elin in church. She had tried to catch her eye, but Elin hadn't seen her.

'She was different,' she said. 'The second time, she was different.'

His eyes gleamed. 'Different how?'

'She seemed . . . sad. No, more. It was as if she wasn't really there. She seemed far away.'

'So what changed her?'

'She missed you?' Frederika said. Her voice sounded doubtful.

He laughed. It was sudden and hearty, a very loud sound. When he laughed he wasn't beautiful, but . . . striking. The kind of person you'd want to please, and not only out of fear. You'd never have forgotten meeting Eriksson, she thought, even when he was alive.

'I don't have any illusions there,' he said. He fell serious. 'The second time you saw her, Elin wasn't just changed. She was destroyed. What destroys a person?'

Frederika shook her head.

He moaned and tapped his head with the heel of his hand. 'Think.'

She frowned. Lots of things could destroy someone.

'She'd found something out,' Eriksson said, and then he was gone.

Hopeless, the priest thought, late that afternoon. He tried to get his strides to hook into one another like he'd seen others do, but his skis refused. The strides came separately and in spurts. He focused. *One-Two. One-Two.*

No. No matter how he tried, this wasn't one smooth act, but several at once. Flakes poured through the air; small, but peppery. The priest bent his head and shuffled forward. The verger had told him that the Lapp winter camp was close by, somewhere beyond the marshlands west of Blackåsen. The priest had never before visited the Lapps during winter. He'd have to stay in one of those cots they lived in – thick branches standing in the snow, forked together at the top and clad with reindeer skins.

He must have taken a wrong turn for before him lay the river, the frozen waterway a white ribbon tied around blue land. The verger had told him not to venture out on any stretches of ice. 'They are not yet solid,' he'd said. Further down, steam rose from open black water. The priest's legs felt weak. It had been a long time since he'd had any strenuous physical exercise. He admired the view until the cold of his frozen clothes clutched at his body and he became aware of the sound of his breath inside his hat. He had to get going again.

It stopped snowing. The flush of the sky waned to grey. The

priest kept looking up to the mountain, making sure he was travelling close to it. Darkness drew in, and soon he could not tell the mountain's shape. He stopped. The swamp ought to be right here, but there were no sounds of people talking, or animals moving. It was now so dark that the priest couldn't make out his own feet strapped to the skis. Maybe he should head back. If he did, he would in due time come to the river. He could follow it to one of the settler homesteads.

If he missed the Lapp camp, there was nothing beyond it.

He stepped around with his skis in a large fan and started back towards where he had come from, his exhalations pumping inside his hat.

There was a howl.

The priest stopped moving. He held his breath. Above him, the sky had turned Bible-black. A shadow drew under one of the trees. Changed shape. He took a rapid step to the side, lost his balance and then his breath, as his hip hit the ground. His cheek burned. His foot was caught in the ski. He tried to kick it free; tried to get up.

Then the shadows grew into a shape and as the priest yelled, a woman's voice said, 'You're so loud, anyone on the mountain can hear you.'

It was the Finn woman, a dead bird hanging from her belt. She skied up to him, squatted down and loosened his foot from the fastening with a quick twist. She stretched her hand forward and hauled him up. All needlessly violent.

'What are you doing here?' she asked.

'I'm on my way to the Lapps.' He brushed the snow off his side.

They stood for a moment without speaking.

'It's late,' the priest said. 'I'll have to stay the night with you.'

'Paavo is not at home.'

'Nevertheless, it will have to be.'

She smiled, but it was not a pleasant smile. Scorn, he realised. As if he had misbehaved and she had expected nothing but, from him.

They continued in silence until there it was before them: a candle in a cottage window.

They had eaten, the priest ignoring the two children staring at him, the woman seemingly ignoring him. Heated by the fire, his hurt cheek throbbed. His frozen hair thawed and became wet; the skin on the back of his hands stung. He opened and closed his hands a few times. The skin was red. He breathed hot air on them.

'Crow pecks,' the younger girl said. 'No point blowing. That doesn't make it go away.'

'How are your feet?' the woman asked.

'No worse than my hands.'

'Then you're fine.' She began to clear the table. 'You can take the bed. We'll put up a cover so you can have some privacy.'

He watched as she and the daughters moved the bedding to the floor and laid new bedclothes in the bed. They hung a large blanket from the hooks in the roof. He rose – but the woman dismissed him with a movement of her hand. She nodded to him when his bed was ready.

He lay down and listened as the noises of every day on the other side of the blanket ceased – the blowing out of a candle, clothes being removed or folded, the clearing of a throat. The light from the fire faded to a glow. The priest lay with his clothes on and his eyes wide open, his insides twisting.

He hadn't prayed. Lost in the forest, plummeting, the most

frightened he had ever been, he had not called the name of Jesus.

There hadn't been time, he said to himself. It had happened so fast.

If he was honest, he knew that wasn't true. No, he hadn't called on Jesus because at that moment, he had felt that Jesus was powerless on the mountain. As if on Blackåsen, there was no God. As if Blackåsen belonged to someone else.

He turned his head sideways to look at the blanket. It hung immovable from the roof. Behind it, nothing stirred.

He sat up and bent down to open his pack. He took out the Church Book and turned the pages until he came to their names. Maija. The woman's name was Maija. Her daughters were called Frederika and Dorotea.

'You'll have to come with me,' the priest said. 'Maija.'

'What?' She stopped cutting the bread. Her name sounded strange pronounced by him. Clumsy. As if he were tasting a new vegetable or root, and didn't want it to touch the inside of his mouth. It was just before morning. The priest ought to be on his way, not sitting here and talking nonsense about her going with him.

Dorotea and Frederika had stopped eating and watched them.

'To the Lapp winter camp. I need you to show me the way.'

Maija resumed her cutting. 'Oh no. I don't know where it is. Besides, I can't leave my daughters.'

'Remember the piece of glass you showed me? I've seen them with similar pieces. And in the Church Books it was written that the Lapps complained about Eriksson. Year after year.'

Between his eyebrows, the skin was coming off. Dry and white. Someone ought to tell him to put butter on that.

'What kind of complaints?' she asked, although she didn't want to.

'Land,' he said and his blue eyes gleamed. 'The Lapps said Eriksson burned too much of it.'

'Bah,' she said. 'They wouldn't kill for land. The one thing of which we have plenty.' But, all by itself, her voice had risen at the end and become a question.

'We need to discover what happened.'

She wanted to ask if that meant he no longer called Eriksson's death 'a tragic mishap'. And there is no 'we', she wanted to say. Then she thought of what Nils had looked like when he spoke of something bad on the mountain.

'Do you still have the piece of glass?' the priest asked.

She took it out from her dress pocket, held it up for him to see.

'I don't know where their site is,' she said.

'But you would find it. I know you would.'

He looked at her two daughters. 'And Frederika and Dorotea ski, don't they? They can come with us.'

She wound the woollen scarves around the mouth and nose of each daughter several times, pulled down the hat on Frederika, pulled up the scarf on Dorotea. She hoped the Lapps would let them spend the night with them. She didn't think the camp was far away, but it was far enough not to make it there and back in one day. The priest was tramping beside them on the porch. She ignored him and waited until she got used to the darkness.

In the barn, the goats stirred and asked as she felt with her hands along the wall until she came upon their skis.

'Hush, hush,' she hissed. 'Go back to sleep. It's barely morning. And yet here I am already engaged in idiocies,' she muttered to herself.

She carried their skis outside and took off her mittens to help insert the peak of first Frederika's shoes into the leather loops, then Dorotea's. Her fingers touched snow – there was a pricking pain. She breathed hot air on them and dried them on her jumper before going back into the barn and getting her own skis.

The priest came struggling towards them. Frederika and Dorotea were standing still, watching her. She set off into the forest. She was stiff and cold, but her body soon warmed up and she lengthened her strides. She slowed and waited for her girls to draw alongside her.

'Glide on each ski,' she said. 'Rest on it as it goes forward, lean on it, use it. You'll get less tired.'

The priest was quiet, listening.

Maija skied across the open area of the marsh. She slowed down to look at the position of the waning stars as the dawn approached, and then adjusted her direction. Henrik had told her that the Lapps stayed one day's journey west of the marsh and Nils's homestead.

'You can't force a big herd to stay in one place.' Jutta's voice in her head. 'They follow their own instinct, and it ends up being the owner who has to follow them. If you want to find a herdsman, you, too, need to follow your instinct; not a path.'

Maija wasn't going to follow any instinct. One day's journey west, and then they would see the traces of beasts, of habitation. She didn't feel good about why they were going to see the Lapps, but the matter was better off closed.

It was long after the midday meal by the time they drew near. Maija was glad. Frederika and Dorotea were tired. Their movements were clumsier. The priest muttered and grumbled. But there was more.

She stopped. Hushed the priest. Listened.

There were sounds in the forest: nasal screams, like babies in pain. No louder than the faint echoes of nightmares. Maija began to ski again, faster, following that sound which turned real, ground through snow and tree trunks, pierced her bones, turned her inside out.

She emerged from between the spruce trees into a dell, by the first shelters of the Lapp winter village.

In front of her was a landscape of war. People were running, men calling. The snow was red from steaming blood, spotted by big lumps of white and black fur. The smell of sweat and iron churned in the air. Reindeer, torn reindeer everywhere. Some of them weighty with calves. Some still alive. A stab at the neck. A stab at the heart. The Lapps were killing.

Frederika's eyes were large, and Dorotea had clasped her hands before her mouth. The priest's face was a pale fleck in the dark.

Nothing to do but watch. Fearless came towards them.

'Twenty-two,' he said and gave a mirthless laughter. 'The wolves got twenty-two of them before we could drive them away. Had it been wolverine . . . But wolf? Wolf doesn't kill what's healthy. They don't take what they don't need. And the raven didn't warn us. He always warns.'

He rubbed his forehead with his knuckle. His bloody fingers left a smear. 'It was as if they killed for lust,' he said with disbelief.

'I am so sorry,' Maija said. 'Go back to the others. We've come at the wrong time.'

He shrugged without looking at her. 'There is nothing that can be done now, anyway.'

'We've come at the wrong time,' she repeated.

'Yes.' The Lapp sounded tired. 'And with accusations.'

He began to walk towards one of the lodgings and motioned for them to follow. By the *Lapp kåta*, he held the hide away from the opening.

It was dark inside, despite the fire in the middle and the smoke hole up high. Fearless didn't sit down, and so they all remained standing. Heads high, they were too close to the smoke. Maija squinted. Beside her, the priest coughed. Fearless didn't seem to notice. His hair was the colour of pewter. In the shadows, the smudge of blood on his forehead looked like the war paint on the Cossacks.

'You are coming to ask about grey-reaper,' he said. 'That's what we called him, that grower of yours, south mountain. Every year, as we visited the land we lent him, we found he'd burned more forest. He did not leave enough for the reindeer to eat. Four small children and a wife, he had. Yet he took land as if he were cultivating food for a whole village. Every year we tried to talk to him. We asked him to give back the land that was ours. Every year we complained to the priest in vain. But we left it at that. Our people do not kill settlers.'

'There was also a piece of glass,' the priest said and looked at Maija.

She clenched her teeth, but opened her satchel.

Fearless took one glance at it. 'We give them away with our word whenever we make a promise.'

There was nothing but blankness in his gaze.

Maija realised she might have deceived herself into thinking she was a bit like them, the Lapps. In her mind, they had become the real nobles, and she had wanted them to like her. And at once, she was disgusted with herself.

Fearless folded a corner of the opening aside. 'You may stay here until you are ready to return.'

'I am sorry,' she said to his back.

Frederika was awake. Her mother's side was rigid. Had she been on her own, her mother would have left and travelled through the night. She was still here because of her, Frederika, and because of Dorotea. Her mother wouldn't sleep. No, she was going to lie there and stare up into the small hole in the roof and smell of anger. This time there was no blanket to hang between them and the priest, only the fire. And her mother was angry with the priest.

Frederika closed her eyes. The insides of her lids glowed orange from the light of the flames.

When the priest's snores trilled over to their side, her mother's breathing quietened. She turned over on to her knees. Still kneeling, her mother pulled her jumper over her head, grabbed her hat and mittens, and sneaked out.

The reindeer skin was warm. Frederika didn't want to get up. She wanted to creep further down into her spot. Her body was heavy after the day's skiing. Her mind was busy with the dead animals. But there was duty and so she sat up, searched with her hands on the floor for her jumper and her hat and then crept out of the tent, after her mother.

She waited until she could see. She shivered. When her mother was upset, she left. Just like the animals did when they were injured: the cats crept underneath the barn, the sheep hid beneath a bush, and her mother went and sat on her own, staring at something or nothing. Separate. Until she felt whole again.

Only if the animals were really hurt, they didn't come back. They died there. You wouldn't know, for nothing seemed different. They left, but it was final. And that was why Frederika had to watch her mother. Just in case. Her mother was more frail than she seemed.

Frederika began to walk. The cold stung her skin as if pricking it with small needles. The Lapp-cots were faint blobs in the dark, aglow from the fires within. There was the clicking noise of the reindeers' tendons as they moved.

In a snowdrift, where her mother had dropped it or thrown it, she found the blue piece of glass. She bent to pick it up. She continued walking on the snow at the fringes of the camp, clasping the shard in her hand. The snow was dry, and squeaked under the soles of her shoes. The skin on her face was becoming numb. Difficult to move, but better than when it hurt.

Then somebody stepped out right in front of her and two hands pressed her arms to her sides.

She was tilted upward and found herself looking into the face of Antti. Even though she recognised him, she cried out. He put her straight back down into the snow.

'I am sorry,' he said. 'I thought you were . . .'

Her heart was hammering. Her mouth felt dry.

'I thought . . .' he began again. 'Do you want to eat?' he asked.

'Is this your home?'

The ground was covered by reindeer skins. At one side of the shelter, he had put his tools: fishing rods, snowshoes, a rifle. Alongside another wall were bundles of what looked like clothes rolled up in skins. It smelt smoky. Her hands clasped a cup of hot drink. It was clear, but tasted salty with meat. She thought of the reindeer dying. But she was hungry.

Antti was squatting by the fire. His long hair fell forward and covered his face. His leather trousers were filthy and stiff: there was black grime, perhaps blood, on the thighs. He was staring into the flames.

'Is this your home?' she asked again.

'The forest is our home,' he said. 'Only settlers have the need to own. As if humans can ever own.'

'I am sorry about your reindeer,' Frederika said.

Antti was silent.

'I thought wolf attacked the animals that were weak?'

Antti got to his feet so fast, Frederika spilled her cup. The hot drink burned her thigh. She stared at him, but he didn't move further. The spillage turned cold. She rubbed at the wet patch, picked at her trousers.

He squatted down again. He held out his hand without looking at her, and she gave him her empty cup. He filled it from the pot over the fire and handed it back.

'We're no longer protected by the spirits,' he said. 'That's why.'

'The spirits?'

He made a clicking noise with his tongue. 'Fearless used to travel between their world and ours to ensure our safety. The spirits knew him. But he doesn't practise since his wife and child went missing. Nobody else has come forward.'

Fearless had lost his wife and child. Poor Fearless; no wonder he no longer practised. Grief ate away at people until they had a different shape from before. Her mother had said many bad emotions could do the same: grief, hatred, fear . . .

'It is forbidden. You pay a high price for continuing with the practices of old,' she said without thinking. Her father's words in her mouth tasted stale.

'Forbidden by your priests, not ours. We don't care about your laws.'

Antti poked in the fire. 'Eriksson,' he muttered. 'He was killed in a sacred place. That kind of blood needs vengeance. The spirits will seek someone to avenge.'

Frederika thought of the tall, erect man in their barn. She tried to swallow. 'Why?' she asked.

'It's the way it is. Spirits need an instrument, a human being.'

'How do they pick someone?'

'They call. Some people hear.'

Dum. Tataradum.

The drumming had returned. It was low, but insistent. Could he hear it? How could he not hear it?

'Then why don't you do it?' she asked. It came out sounding angry. 'Become their instrument, or whatever it is?'

He was silent for a while before making a face. 'I don't have the gift,' he said.

She lowered her head and thought of her father. It was hard, desiring something and not having the faculties for it.

'And the welcoming way Fearless receives you, although you are coming to accuse us,' he said.

'I think we just wanted to ask.'

Antti spat in the fire.

'It was you who complained about Eriksson. And this' – she took out the blue glass piece from her pocket – 'was right by where he lay dead . . . Where I found him,' she added, stressing the 'I'.

He looked at the glass in her hand and pressed his lips together. 'Eriksson was a bad man,' he said. 'He sought out evil.'

'Elin liked him, though.' Frederika had thought about it as they travelled. Elin had been married to him. She assumed

163

Elin had loved him like her father loved her mother; borne him children. Eriksson couldn't have been all bad.

'She came here with the other one, the brother, Daniel. Eriksson stole her, like he did with all other things.'

She hadn't known you could steal a person.

Antti was still looking at the fragment of glass in her hand. 'Besides, it isn't our glass piece, but that of whoever we've given it to.'

Frederika was still thinking about Elin being stolen.

'And that one, I gave to Nils,' he said.

The priest had woken up early. Maija lay watching the dark of his back behind the fire, knowing his eyes would be open. She stared at him until she couldn't breathe.

A little longer, she admonished herself. We'll travel back today. Then he'll be on his way and we won't have anything more to do with him. It wasn't fair. Whatever she was feeling, it wasn't his fault.

'Are you awake?' He rolled over.

'Our women don't sleep.'

'What did you think about what Fearless said about the glass piece?' he asked.

She sat up, pulled on her woollens and pushed her feet into her shoes.

'It means it could have been anyone watching when Eriksson was killed.'

She opened the canvas. It was snowing. A light, sparse sprinkle dancing in the air. The Lapps had hung the flayed reindeer skins to dry. Grey-white squares, like small sails, navigating a red wave spatter. Someone had left wood for them beneath the opening. She brushed the snow off the pieces with her sleeve and lifted them inside. There was still a glow among the embers. She found her knife, pulled bark off the wood and put the strips close to that glow, blew on it to encourage flame, careful not to suffocate the sparks.

'Makes it impossible to know what to do next,' the priest droned on.

Beside Maija, Frederika sat up. She wrapped her arms around her legs and shuffled closer. She smelled funny; almost of meat.

'I guess I ought to speak to the settlers on Blackåsen next,' the priest said. 'Though it might still have been a passer-by.'

'Eriksson was evil,' Frederika said. She gave a shiver and then yawned. 'He stole Elin.'

Frederika stood up.

'Sit down,' Maija said. 'What did you say?'

'That he stole Elin. From his brother.'

'How do you know that?'

Her daughter was pondering how much to tell her. 'One of the Lapps said it,' she said. 'I heard it.'

Maija turned to the priest. 'Did you know this?'

'No.' He shook his head so his hair bounced.

'We could have gone to see Daniel, before we travelled all this way to blame the Lapps,' Maija said.

'Don't you think I would have preferred that, too?'

'Frederika,' Maija said with a stern voice. 'If you know anything more, you need to tell us.'

Her daughter made herself blank until there was stillness and calm water.

'That was all,' her daughter said.

As Maija bent down to tighten the ski loop around her foot, the young, long-haired Lapp who had accompanied Fearless when they left their goats, arrived.

'A storm is coming,' he said.

There was no sun. An eerie white sheen filled the morning, but the sky was high.

'Perhaps,' she said.

'The first storm of the winter. And it will be big.'

Frederika gave him a long look as he left.

So he was the one who had spoken with her daughter about Elin and Daniel. Maija looked towards the sky again. In the mountains, the weather changed faster than you turned a hand. They could stay, but she wanted to go home. The feeling was stronger, she had to go home. But now that she knew where the camp was, they would take a shorter route, one straight across the large hill that lay between the camp and the marsh. And if the weather deteriorated, it wasn't as if she and her daughters hadn't skied in snowfalls before.

There was less forest on the hill. The snow had drifted unhindered by trunks of trees and frozen in spiky waves. Like a sea caught in time. It was harder to cross than she had expected.

'I am surprised nobody told me about Daniel and Elin,' the priest said from behind her.

Maija thought about what Frederika had said. Daniel might still have loved Elin. After God knows how many years. And his poor wife – poor Anna. Had she known all that time that her husband loved another woman? Would Maija have known, if it had been Paavo? Oh yes. At least before. They'd been so close. The idea that he might love somebody else now felt strangely absurd.

'I spoke to a few individuals before coming here,' the priest said. 'They said the two brothers weren't speaking, but they didn't say why. Then again, these individuals I am talking about might have arrived after this happened and not known. Though it is the kind of event that people would talk about for a long time. Yes, I am surprised.'

There was wind now. Currents from the east, bringing with

them a cooling of the air. The sun showed itself, but it was colourless behind a layer of white. This high up, they were visible at the horizon: dark clouds building fast, consuming the land as they advanced.

It wasn't far back to the Lapp site. Maija clenched her teeth.

No, she decided. It was downhill from now on, the journey would go faster. Besides, it would take them almost as long to return there as to continue on home.

'Can we have a break?' Dorotea asked.

'No.'

Above Dorotea's head, Frederika's eyes were serious. She, too, had seen the clouds.

However, going downhill wasn't any easier. The hill was icy. Maija created a flat zigzag trail. The sky came upon them and it began to snow. The flakes were large and wet. Soon, they came in such abundance, her eyes were full of water. She blinked and blinked.

'Wet,' she shouted.

'Awful,' the priest shouted back. Then there was only the hushing of their skis.

The wind grew. It was icy. The limp flakes froze and began to insist. They drove in fierce waves and smattered at her front.

'We need to press on,' she called, but her voice was stolen by the wind. She stopped, shuffled with her back against it, and made signs for her children and the priest to come near.

'We're not far from the marsh, but it will be hard. Ski close to each other, so you don't get lost.'

They looked at her to see if there was more, but the wind shoved flakes in her mouth. She shook her head, turned, gestured for them to follow.

She skied head down, but the gusts still hit her face with ice. Every couple of strides, she half turned to make certain

Dorotea was behind her. Dig a shelter, a voice inside her said. Dig it now. They ought to, but she hadn't brought a spade. She half turned again. Dorotea was still there.

For hours, they skied straight into a wind that drove so strongly, she felt it might wipe them off the mountain. Maija leaned into its force and pressed her legs forward one after the other, and still she was not certain she had moved. It was too late for shelters – they were sweaty and their clothes were frozen.

It was night by the time they reached the homestead. Maija fell on her knees to help Dorotea and Frederika take off their skis. She pushed on them and they flung themselves towards the porch.

'Hurry. Undress in the hallway.' She called the words, but didn't think there had been any sound.

She crept on her knees until she found the priest's skis and undid his. He tried to speak, but she waved. Go in. Go inside.

Dorotea stumbled against the table as she tried to sit. Frederika was building a fire. The priest had bent beside her and was handing her wood. Maija grabbed the stones. Her eyes were burning. Her fingers shook so she had to let go of the flint stones and shake her hands to try to get some mobility into them. Try again. *Knock, knock, knock.* Fire. She bent forward and blew on the dried grass. Her lips quivered. With trembling fingers, she put splinters of wood close to it. Careful. Don't ruin it.

'Get all the skins and blankets,' she said and didn't recognise her own voice. 'Put them here.'

She put a blanket over Dorotea. The girl was shaking. Frederika pushed her sister backwards and lay down beside her and hugged her.

We could have died, Maija thought. Her head felt muddled and thick.

We didn't die, she thought.

She removed her woollens – the clothes were wet and her movements slow. She lay down beside her daughters in front of the flames that were licking the stone of the fireplace.

Snow whirled up and with the sound of a handful of pebbles it threw itself against the window panes.

'We are going to have to shovel the porch tonight,' Maija said. 'Take turns.' She made as if to sit up, but beside the fireplace, the priest shook his head.

'I'll start.'

'Look at the window. An inch on the window sill and you'll have to shovel. Wake me up when you're tired.'

She lay down again.

'What is it with you and the Church?' he asked.

'What?'

'For some reason you hate the Church. Or priests. It isn't just me.'

At once Jutta was there. By the fire. Her back towards Maija, erect. Listening.

'I mean . . .' he said.

'I know what you mean,' she snapped. That she had the strength surprised her.

Beside her, Dorotea stirred. 'I know what you mean,' Maija repeated, more quietly. 'I don't want to talk about it.'

'I am a priest,' he said after a while. 'You can talk to me.'

Though we don't do confessions any longer, she thought.

We could have died, her head insisted.

But we didn't.

Their toes. Get up, she thought. Get up. She forced herself. She reached for Frederika and removed her socks. Lifted them off. Pink toes. Five. Ten. Pink.

She would never have forgiven herself.

She pulled the blanket over Frederika's feet and found Dorotea's. Dorotea's legs were hopping underneath the blanket. Maija put both her hands on her daughter's legs as if to try to still them, then removed her hands and pulled off Dorotea's socks.

Her baby's feet looked unreal, as if made of yellow wax. Her middle toe still a little bit above the others in an imitation of the foot it had once been, for now the foot was hard.

The priest met her eyes. He did not turn away.

'Dorotea,' she said, and pressed her nail down deep into the flesh of her daughter's foot. 'How do your feet feel?'

'Fine, Mamma,' Dorotea mumbled.

Maija closed her eyes, opened them again. 'Snow.' She rose. 'We'll rub the skin with snow.'

The priest grabbed her arm. 'No. I've seen it in the war. It makes it worse.'

He bent to cover Dorotea's feet.

'We wait,' he said.

Maija lay down again. She pressed with her fingers and thumb into her eyelids. As she held herself so, she became aware of the silence. All this time, it had been concealed beneath the chores, the changing seasons and weathers; beneath all words, all thoughts, it was there.

Like a block of ice, it pressed against the window, waiting to break in.

They alternated. Took turns to sit by the kitchen table and, as the snow climbed another inch up the pane, to dress, force themselves outside and shovel the white hell away, and then wake the other one up. Sleep like the dead.

'We have to keep the porch clear,' Maija repeated.

At first the priest didn't know why, but then, on one occasion, when he waited that little too long – oh God, he was so tired, just one more minute – he wasn't able to open the door and then with a jolt, he understood. He was certain he had seen more winter than she. Nothing could be worse than what they'd had in Russia. But this she had foreseen, and he had not.

Frederika appeared by his side. She began to throw her shoulder against the wood at rhythmic intervals. He joined her and together, they edged the door open.

'Thank you,' he said, although 'Don't tell your mother' was what he wanted to say.

The light from inside turned the snowfall into a wall in front of him, a wall crawling with life. He stepped out, the door shut behind him and he was inside that life. All was dark. He was totally alone.

Towards morning, the little one began to moan. It was her flesh thawing. Muscles, ligaments, blood vessels and nerves, waking up to discover the damage. The next time he and Maija looked, Dorotea's feet were swollen and purple. The blisters weren't far away.

He must have been sleeping, because the sound of breaking glass made him sit bolt upright. The little girl had been lying so close against him, she rolled into his space.

'Sorry.' Maija lifted her hand with the ladle. 'The drinking water has frozen.'

His heart beat fast.

'Is it still snowing?' he asked, although the winds pounded the cottage so hard he had to raise his voice.

She nodded. Her eyes seemed large.

'We don't have much firewood,' she said. 'It's in the wood-shed. I didn't bring enough in. I didn't think . . .'

He rose and walked to the window. The floor was glacial. He shifted from one foot to the other as he bent to peer out. It was black outside. Impossible to see anything.

'We'll wait until there's some light,' he said, 'and then we'll get it.'

She nodded. In the circumstances and for the moment, there was some sort of truce between them.

Her mouth was a thin line in her face. 'Her feet are not black,' she said about her daughter and nodded several times, as if she had decided something for herself.

The priest didn't say anything. He had no solace to give. They wouldn't know the extent of the damage done to the girl's feet for many weeks, perhaps months.

At daybreak, they saw the face of the storm: the snow battering down, the rush of flakes driven sideward by the squall. He could not see the trees or the outbuildings, although he knew they were right there.

'Well, the longer we wait, the worse it will be,' he said.

'Frederika, see to your sister,' Maija said.

When the priest opened the door, the wind snatched it and threw it against the wall. He grabbed it and pressed it shut behind them.

They pushed across the yard, leaning against the wind. With each step he took, he sank to his knees. She was there, beside him, behind him, a shape, a shadow. Yet he'd never felt more lonely.

She leaned forward and pointed: the woodshed. When he reached it, he supported himself with his hand against its wall, until he found the door. It was already half covered. He began to shovel. For every spadeful of snow he removed, the storm seemed to throw two back at him. Rather than seeing the whole, he centred himself on that one scoop, then the next. He found there was silence in the midst of tempest. She took the shovel from him and he rubbed his fingers against the heels of his hands inside his mittens and wriggled his toes inside his shoes to keep hot blood flowing.

After a while, he took the shovel from her.

He didn't know how long they worked like this. It might have been hours but then, it might not. When they could open the door, he continued shovelling, knowing now it wasn't only about getting inside, but about keeping ahead of the snowfall.

Inside, the mound of wood reached the roof. He exhaled in relief. Someone had done good work.

As they left, Maija looked further away. They had to do the same for the food storage. He touched her shoulder, nodded, but then shook his head. Later. They'd do it later.

They came inside and the little girl was screaming.

Once upon a time, there was a small bird . . .

'What kind of a bird?'

The priest stroked the younger daughter's head. It was clammy. 'Think of something different,' Maija had shouted at her in frustration when she kept screaming. Not so easy. He stroked it again, combed the blonde locks stuck to her forehead away with his fingers.

'I don't know,' he said. 'One of the usual ones. Small, grey . . .'

The bird was ravenous. It rummaged in the soil for worms, but found none. In the sky, high above it, a hawk floated an airstream. Oh, if I had eyesight like the hawk, the little bird thought. Then I would see to find worms when they hid from me.

God heard and gave it the eyesight of the hawk.

Now the little bird saw each separate blade of grass, the grains of the moss on the stones, the veins on the leaves. The world was so plentiful and its colours so sharp, it had to shut its eyes. Oh, if I could fly as high as the hawk, the little bird thought. Then I would be at the right distance to the earth to watch it.

God heard and gave it the ability to fly as high as the hawk.

The little bird glided in the sky. Below it, far down on the ground, it discerned many worms and insects, but the little bird shivered. This high up, it was cold. Oh, if I had the thick feathers of the hawk, it thought. Then I'd be warm here in the sky.

God heard and gave it the plumage of the hawk.

But the feathers were not fit for such a small bird. It beat its wings as fast as it could, with all its might, but before long it had to surrender and it plummeted through the air and down to the ground.

As the little bird lay dying, in the soil beside it was a worm. The little bird saw it. But now it no longer cared.

Who had told him this story? It was obvious: his father. Who else would tell tales like that?

Dum. Tataradum. Dum. Dum. Dum.

Frederika

Answer me

Frederika tried to breathe as usual. In. Out. They'd lived through so many storms. Perhaps more than a hundred. Ostrobothnia's tempests came the sea way. They were wet and tasted of salt.

But the way this wind tore at the house. As if it might rip the walls down for something to reach in and seize her.

She was being stupid. Storms did not speak. They did not live. Storms happened when there were too many clouds and winds in the same place. It was her mind playing with her because she had pictured it so many times, she knew it: that split second of nothing and then the violence of being grabbed. The Russians stole children. They did much worse to the adults, but the children, they took with them. They hauled you away and you knew you'd never again see the ones you loved. And your pain would be so great, you'd die. Though you wouldn't. No, you'd live for ever with a black hole inside you that grew until the hole had swallowed all of you. And then you'd become just like them. Everybody had heard about the mother and father who, ten years after he'd been snatched, had seen their own son among the killers. He had not recognised them. His eyes had been dead.

Focus on your sister, Frederika told herself. Hold your sister. She's screaming. She's hurt.

Dum. Dum. Dum. Dum.

You can't hide

Her mother's profile, grim in the light of the fire. The priest sat with his head bent. Neither of them moved or spoke. They might as well be dead, she thought, and then she'd be all alone with her sister and this time there was no Jutta and they wouldn't stand a chance against what was outside. It would float through the walls, and there would be nothing but this swelling darkness until you realised you sat in it and that it had a face and when you looked, it would be your own face and . . .

Snow rose in a violent twister and beat at the pane. Frederika cried out. There was a new smell inside. One that didn't belong. Earth, she thought. The air was damp and cold despite the fire. It was like when they'd finished excavating the underground food storage and she'd crept into it for the first time, soil still crumbling down its walls. The roots in the roof had looked like small worms. They'd been cut off by the digging and their small ends were a naked white. The plants reached out for their amputated limbs, knowing that without the rest of them, they were certain to die . . .

Open

Dum. Dum. Dum.

Open to me

In the Bible, Jonah had been on a boat. There had been a gale and the others had to throw him in, for the sea to quieten. If she walked out into the storm, it might settle. It might take her and leave the others in peace. Her sister was so hurt. And her mother. How Frederika loved her mother.

Stop this. Stop this. Stop. This.

Frederika sat up straight. She wasn't a small child any longer. She was older, and she knew what she knew: there were storms. Things might seem alive – they might make noises, but as long as you were with adults, as long as you were with your mother, you were safe. Her mother always knew what to do. She . . .

Their world exploded—

Jesus.

The storm was inside. The screams of wind and darkness were all around them.

The priest grabbed the metal sheet they cooked on. He and her mother pressed it to the open hole that had once been a window. She held it while he put a chair on top of the table to block it there.

Dum. Dum. Dum.

Maija lay awake and listened. The tiny house squeaked and groaned. She wondered if the roof would hold the weight of the snow.

It's built for this kind of weather, she told herself.

The blizzard gave no sign of abating. In the barn, the goats weren't tethered; they'd be able to get to the dried grass. Water might become a problem. But goats didn't need much.

Slowly, so as not to make a sound, she turned her head and looked towards the pile of wood. Wood for two more days, perhaps three. They had to go and get more, but more importantly, they needed food. There wasn't anything left to eat now.

Dorotea was lying close to her side. She was burning hot. The hairs by her temples had curled themselves. Maija wanted to put her hand on her daughter's forehead, knowing she would find it both hot and cold at the same time. Frederika lay on the other side of Dorotea, her blonde hair on the pillow a bird's nest. This was all her fault. Why had she taken them on the journey? Why . . .

'We need to go and get food.'

She startled. In the dark, on the other side of Frederika, the priest was just a shape.

'Yes.' She whispered so as not to wake her daughters.

'We might as well go now. We're both awake.'

'It's still dark.'

'The longer we wait, the weaker we'll be.'

She wanted to stay with her daughters, but he was right. They put on their outerwear in silence. Maija tied her shoes and pulled the end of her trousers down over them. She bound a piece of string around the ankles. Hopefully that would hold the snow out. The priest nodded.

As she opened the door, the cold and the wind rushed in. Her heart flipped over and she was wide awake. The priest stepped out beside her and they pressed the door shut behind them, the wind forcing them to move slowly. Maija stared into the dark. The snowflakes hurt and she bent her head. She tried to judge in which direction the food storage would be and took the shovel. Luckily they'd taken it inside. She had to make sure they never left it outside, or they wouldn't find it again in the snow. She put out her hand, feeling for the porch railing. Once she had found it and located the top of the staircase, she took a step down and sank to her waist in snow. The priest reached for her, but she shook her head and pointed. They had to continue.

But the snow was too deep. It was impossible to move forward. She needed to get out of the snow, get on top of it somehow and so she leaned to crawl, using the shovel to support her, but her other hand sank straight down and she caught a mouth full of snow.

This wasn't going to work.

The skis, she thought, before remembering they had left them on the ground on returning from the Lapps. They were gone now. She tried to get on top of the snow again.

The priest had squatted down on the porch. He was waving to her. She turned and stretched out her arm. He grabbed it and pulled her up with him on the porch.

'Snowshoes,' he yelled in her ear. 'We need snowshoes.'

Snowshoes. Of course. The branches, she thought. They had a big pile of spruce branches they had gathered to use to wipe the floor. Perhaps they were still not dry and some of them might be big enough for them to construct something. She pointed to the door. They pulled it open and tumbled inside.

She removed her scarf and wiped her nose. She took off her woollens. The silence inside hurt her ears after all the noise.

'We gathered spruce branches before you came,' she said and opened the door to the wall cupboard. She squatted down and selected the largest and greenest ones.

'We'll need string,' he said.

'Take a lot,' the priest said then. 'We should make two pair of shoes each.'

He was right. If the shoes broke or got ruined on the way, they needed a reserve.

They sat down by the kitchen table. She had seen snowshoes used many times and couldn't believe they hadn't thought to make some when they had had the time. The broadest part should be towards the front, she thought. And we'll weave with the string.

They worked in silence by the light of the tallow candles, looking every now and then at each other's efforts, and adapting their own. Maija tried not to hear the howling of the wind outside. If only Paavo had been here. He would have known how to do this.

'That's not a knot,' Paavo said once, laughing as he watched her attempt to tie two cords together to make a longer clothesline. They had just moved into the house in Ostrobothnia. He took the strings from her, made a knot on one of them and then stuck the second one into the knot of the first and made a second knot that sat above it.

'This is a knot,' he said. 'A real fisherman's knot.'

She snorted. When she looked up, he was watching her, his eyes on her lips. He came closer.

'Then there is the water knot,' he said in a low voice. He tied the two strings together with just a normal overhand knot, but followed it by feeding the ends through in the opposite direction.

She felt the warmth of her man against her stomach and held her breath.

'There is the true lover's knot,' he said in her ear. She watched his hands as they moved to tie an overhand knot and then a second overhand knot inside the first. As they worked, his hands bumped against her chest. 'This knot is supple,' he said, 'but the strings don't ever come apart.'

'We'll tie them to our feet with strips of fabric,' the priest said. He held up what looked like a sweeper.

Maija looked down at the thing in her hands. He was right. It might just do it. The priest looked out of the window at the storm, visible now in the morning light.

'Don't look,' Maija said. 'Focus on this.'

'Is that how you do it?' he asked, and he wasn't talking about now or about the storm.

She rose and pulled her woollen jumper over her head.

'We'll go now,' she said.

She bent down to tie the brushes of spruce to her shoes. When she looked up, the priest's face was taut and he was staring at the door, steeling himself.

She opened it.

It was as if the wind screamed at them, mouth open wide. Maija turned the side of her face. She found the shovel, took a deep breath and stepped off the porch. She sank down to her knees and at first she thought the snowshoes were a failure, but then she realised that they would do. It was good enough to allow her to walk. She took a step and fell forward, snow entering her sleeves, her mouth and nose. It took some time for her to struggle upright again. She spat. She was going to pull off her mitten to wipe her face, but thought better of it.

Exaggerate, she thought, as the wind tore at her front. She lifted her foot up high and put it down. Keep your balance, she thought. That was it. Large, high steps. She glanced over her shoulder. The priest was coming. Concentrate, she thought, but she felt joy and raised her hand to hit in the air for him to see. They were moving forward.

A few days later and the storm was abating. The beats of the shutter that had been banging in the wind came slower.

Maija met his gaze. She had noticed it, too. By the fire, her daughters were asleep.

The priest listened for the noise.

And, there it was: stillness. One more faint wind push. Silence.

And silence.

Was it really over? The priest almost didn't dare to believe it. But everything was indeed still.

Maija exhaled. She pushed back her hair, and he thought her hand might have been trembling. The priest realised he was holding his breath. He wasn't certain for how long they could have managed. They were physically worn out from shovelling and not eating properly. Things had become some-what better once they'd been able to enter the food store, but as they didn't know when the storm would end, they had had to ration the food.

What day was it? He didn't know. Monday, Wednesday. In hell, every day is the same. He could preach about that at some point.

In town, they must be wondering what had happened to him.

'Why you live here, I don't know,' he said.

She began to laugh. He stared at her, angered. Then he saw and joined her. What else was there to do on a Monday or a Wednesday evening in hell? They laughed and laughed.

She laughed with her mouth open wide and her eyes in small slits. The locks of her hair shook. She had a small dimple high up on one cheek, or it might have been a scar.

'I imagined Blackåsen wasn't much different from home,' she said when they had quietened, and that set them off again. Maija hit the table with the flat of her hand. The priest laughed so much, he had to lean forward and hold his stomach.

He wiped his tears. He'd seen it many times in the war: the extraordinary giddiness ensuing from a battle. Your mind needed it, you felt strong and wild, ready to embrace any insanity, set to try anything, before rationality returned and you realised who you were and where you were and why you were . . .

Both of them sat up straighter at the same time. They sat for a while in silence. She sniffed.

'Well, I guess I'll better get some sleep,' he said.

'Yes,' she said.

'Goodnight.'

She didn't respond.

He slept better than he had done any night since he first set out on his journey.

When Maija and Paavo were children, there was once a great storm. This was still how it was referred to back in the village in Ostrobothnia: 'The Great Storm', voices low, as if the mere mention of the tempest might bring it back. The odd thing was that there had been no signs. In the morning, when the men set out to hunt grey seal, the sky was blue and there was a delightful summer sun. Much too wonderful – they should have known, some said later, but they were just trying to be clever. The truth was, it was the perfect day to hunt; if anything, there was not enough wind. The boat's sails were limp and the vessel was only jolted forward by the occasional breeze, and so there were no large conversations that morning and nobody turned up to wave goodbye, or embrace the departing men. 'Bring us silver fur,' was all they said. 'Hey ho, bring us silver fur.'

At the beginning, the men sailed well. They were aiming for the rocks far out in the young sea where they knew the greys were sunning themselves, shedding, pups in the water, playing.

And then, at once, the storm was over them. It was so sudden, it might as well have stepped right out of heaven and on to their boat.

At first they attempted to outride it – brawny – the skipper was a young man, but it was faster than them. Then they tried to ride it, but soon that ship was tossed about like a piece of driftwood in the towering waves. It was only a matter of time before they would lose control and the water break the boat.

It was Pekka Sihvola who grasped the fact that this was no normal storm. He was standing mid-deck watching the wind, despite the others shouting at him that they needed his help. Rather than blowing at them from the side, the wind seemed to be bending. Was it blowing around itself in a loop? Wind needed room to keep up speed. In the centre, Pekka thus reasoned, it might be different. Perhaps there, the wind was less powerful. But to get to that place, they had to sail into the tempest rather than away from it.

Pekka Sihvola pushed the skipper aside and gripped the rudder, and then he sailed that ship straight into the eye of the storm. And when they were all certain the end had come and they would die – they found a vacuum. They navigated that nothingness until, around them, the storm died.

As the men told their story to the elders that night, still trembling from the power of their journey, the villagers were amazed. Thanks to one single man, the full crew of ten had survived: that was ten husbands renewing vows to their wives that evening, ten fathers holding their children close . . .

'Reason,' the elder said when they had finished. He nodded. 'What you had was an apparition.'

The skin on Jutta's arm which pressed against her own had been cold. Paavo had been on Maija's other side – even back then, he always seemed to be near her. At the time of the Great Storm, she still thought these men and women in the circle, all of them, to be of the same blood and marrow as her own. She thought she was one of them.

'The circular wind is life,' the elder said. 'What was yesterday comes again tomorrow. It runs from place to place and returns. But in the midst of disorder is reason. And if you can hold to reason, you shall be safe.'

'Are you then saying that there's no changing things? That we have no choice?'

It was Ari Sihvola speaking, Pekka's younger brother. Later, he'd be among those who died in the Great Northern War.

'There is little choice,' the elder said. 'And yet the acts we undertake have repercussions.'

For some, his words were a relief. Others found them disturbing. Maija didn't think the elder was right; she believed in man's ability to have an impact on things, but she took away with her the significance of reason.

And now, having survived her first storm on Blackåsen Mountain, she was appalled at herself. She had set out with two young children into the forest, without any preparation, without any further thought. What had she been thinking?

We could have died.

But we didn't.

Was it flattery in that the priest thought she was of this world? Was it the excitement of a potential answer to the question of Eriksson's death?

She had underestimated the mountain, seen its plump shape and in her head she'd likened it to one of the benign hills in Ostrobothnia. Blackåsen was nothing like home. She had been foolish and proud and now her daughter paid. Each of Dorotea's cries took a slice from her heart. Each scream vibrated in her mind until Maija had to grab her head with both her hands for it not to splinter. And the thought she'd had during their journey had taken root inside her: it was not given that they would survive this winter.

Had Paavo been here, this wouldn't have happened. He

would have known better. She should have known better. But she was reckless. She was dangerous.

'It's not your fault,' the priest said just then. As if he read her thoughts.

He was packing his bag. He pushed his black book down at one side. She walked to the window. Outside, the sky was an after-storm bright blue. Early that morning, they had removed the snow from in front of the barn door. The new snow had already frozen and it had been hard. When they finally got the door open, the goats had taken one look at them and gone back to sleep. They're like weeds, she thought. They'll always flourish.

'I was the one who convinced you to come,' the priest said. 'If anything, this is my doing.'

Her throat stitched up.

The priest pulled his bag shut and fastened the leather strap. The room looked empty without his belongings. She could perhaps ask him to leave his collar. The thought made her want to laugh amid all the misery.

'Maija.' The priest was looking at her. 'I know it's a lot to ask, but please come with me and see Daniel. Now that we know what we know about him and Elin . . .'

She shook her head. She had done enough damage already.

'The bishop demands that I find out what happened to Eriksson. I think . . . It might be easier for the settlers to talk to one of their own.'

She shook her head again. Then she thought of Anna. Hopefully, they had weathered the storm all right. It was hard giving birth on your own, or with only your husband for support. But Daniel would know what to do if things happened, wouldn't he? Of course he would.

She had taken a vow. She had pledged always to help women in their difficult times like she had been helped in hers.

Dorotea was sleeping. Beside her, Frederika met her eyes. Her elder daughter nodded.

'All right,' Maija said.

Daniel had already shovelled a path from the cottage to the barn. When they arrived, he was throwing snow against the walls of the house with the spade, as if he were trying to bury it. Strange. The sound of him scooping was muffled. They stood for a while before walking closer. The sunshine changed the landscape into one of fairy tales. The thick, white trees threw blue shadows on the glimmering snow. Hard to imagine this was the same Blackåsen of a few days ago.

As they approached, Daniel stood up straight, pulled off a mitten and wiped his nose on the back of his hand. His eyelashes and brows were white with frost. His eyes were bloodshot.

'Some storm,' the priest said.

Daniel nodded.

'Is this weather normal?' Maija couldn't help but ask.

'No,' Daniel said. 'Can't remember anything like it.'

She felt the priest's gaze. Told you, it said, you couldn't have known.

'Elin came to Blackåsen with you, not Eriksson,' Maija said, though that was not at all what she had come for.

Daniel stared at her. She was certain he was weighing his alternatives: speaking now, or risking her raising it again, with Anna present. Maija hardened her expression. Daniel clenched his teeth, his jaw turned rigid.

'We were promised to one another,' he said then.

'What happened?'

'My brother.'

They waited. He threw a glance towards their cottage, then continued.

'I left Blackåsen after the forest fire. The fire set something loose in my brother that might always have been there, but that he'd, so far, kept in check. He enjoyed it. There's no other way of putting it. He didn't care if anyone got hurt or died. He loved the way fire was uncontrollable, loved putting himself up against it, loved being a part of it. After that, it didn't feel safe to stay.

'I worked down by the coast. Thought I'd join the army . . . I did join the army, but just as I was supposed to depart, I met Elin.'

Daniel's nose was red and he wiped it.

'We had saved money to get married when my father came to find me. He was feeling his age, he said, and wanted me back on the mountain. He didn't want to leave Eriksson there on his own. I don't know what my father thought I could do about my brother. I don't know what I thought I could do. But it was an old man's last wish. Elin and I decided to get married later. I thought we could settle in the valley, where the ground would still be easy to clear after the fire.'

Daniel shook his head. 'It was in his gaze . . . It was in how he looked at her. But I trusted. Her, not him. And then she left.'

'Why?'

'Who knows why anyone does anything? Maybe he forced her the first time. Maybe she felt she had no choice. Maybe she loved. She never said. One day she was gone.'

'The Church could have helped,' the priest said. 'A promise like that is binding.'

Daniel shrugged, but Maija remembered the woman in the whore stool. You still loved Elin, she thought. You didn't want to see her punished.

'Was that why she killed herself?' she asked and made her voice soft. 'Because he died?'

'I can't imagine that being the reason for her killing her children,' Daniel said.

'She would lack means for them.'

'Poverty didn't scare Elin.'

'Then why?'

'I don't know why!' He hit out with his hands.

No, no despair for the future, no regret for the past, could be as strong as to drive a woman to the deed. Elin had not been right in the head when it happened.

'I ought to have killed my brother,' Daniel said, 'but I didn't.'

'Not many men would have let it pass – a brother stealing a woman,' the priest said.

'I am not going to become like him,' Daniel said, 'never. Besides, if I was to kill him, don't you think I would have done it then, rather than wait for seven years? No, no. I married Anna. Tried to get on.'

It's all we can do, Maija thought. Try to get on.

The priest, too, was nodding to himself.

'Where is she?' Maija asked. 'Anna?'

'She's emptying the traps,' Daniel said.

Emptying the traps? That work was too hard.

'The child was born dead during the storm.'

Oh no, Maija thought. Not that.

Daniel was looking at the priest. Maija's eyes filled.

'We didn't have time to baptise it,' Daniel said and his voice broke. He looked away, then he inhaled. 'It was a boy. His soul will be damned now.'

The muscles on the priest's cheeks were working. 'Perhaps God is more compassionate than we think,' he said.

When she came home, Frederika was pale. Maija looked towards the fire and the bundle on the floor in front of it.

'She is sleeping now,' Frederika said.

Maija walked close to her daughter and gathered her hair in one hand. 'How are you?' she asked.

'I can't bear her screaming,' Frederika whispered.

'I know,' Maija said.

'No, I can't bear her hurting, but I also can't stand the sound.'

'I know,' Maija said. 'The sound of pain is difficult to listen to.'

She looked at Dorotea. Lord, please let her keep her feet, she thought. What would they do if Dorotea lost her feet? She had to close her eyes. This was not good. We try to go on, she repeated to herself, took a deep breath, opened her eyes again, pushed her chin forward, as if she could take herself through the angst, through and out on the other side.

Frederika took out something from her pocket. It was the blue glass piece Maija had thrown away.

'Antti . . . One of the Lapps said he gave this one to Nils,' she said.

In the weeks after the storm, Frederika and her mother worked harder than ever. They'd seen the face of Blackåsen Mountain and both knew they'd misjudged it. Frederika hovered close to her mother, fretful about being on her own, anxious for things to be said out loud, but her mother was silent. Though that could have been because there was so much to do: they needed to bring in much more firewood and build a food store in the snow by the wall of the cottage. They had to make new skis. They would make more snowshoes. The shutter had to be mended, the broken window covered up.

The mountain was still. For now, it was silent. And the days passed. Frederika found she liked the cold. She liked what she became in it: her brain worked well. As she blew her breath out and watched the pillar of steam rise above her head, she felt the way she did after a nightmare: while the memory of the storm made her shiver, she also felt silly. But Dorotea's feet spoke of the gravity of what they'd been through. The tips of her toes blackened and dissolved. Her mother cleaned them, lips pressed together. She pulled skin off in strips, lifted off small pieces of tissue, dabbed away buttery slush.

Two weeks after the storm, it was time for Dorotea to start school. When Frederika came out, her sister held a large branch in her hand.

'A walking stick.' She grinned. She was wearing her mother's large shoes, unable to fit her wrapped feet into her own, and had acquired a rolling walk not to put weight on her toes. With both hands she dragged the stick after her in the snow.

'Much too heavy,' Frederika said.

Her sister scrunched her mouth up to one side.

'I'll find you another one when we come back,' Frederika promised. She took the branch from her sister and stuck it in the snowdrift close to the porch. Her sister sat down on the sledge they'd made and Frederika grabbed the rope and began to pull. It was harder than she'd thought and she had to lean forward.

'So are you excited about going to school?' she asked.

'So-so,' Dorotea said. 'They don't teach you much.'

'That's not true. You'll learn to read and write.'

'I can read. But there isn't anything to read.'

That was true.

'Why don't you go any longer?' Dorotea asked.

'I am too old.'

For a while, Frederika had dreamed of becoming a teacher. She'd tried to get noticed by her tutor, hoping he'd say she was unusually gifted and convince her parents to let her stay in school. But her mother needed her. At least she hadn't been sent away like most girls, to start working for some other family.

The roof of the schoolteacher's house sagged under the snow. But there was smoke coming out of the chimney and the porch was cleared.

She helped her sister off the sledge and up the steps. Mr Lundgren greeted them in the hallway. Four children sat by the kitchen table, three boys and one girl. The girl's braided hair was loosening, hair sticking up all over her head like a hedgehog. Two of the boys had red hair, the other one black. Their noses were snotty.

'Welcome,' Mr Lundgren said. 'What weather we've had.' He pointed to some hooks on the wall. 'You can hang your outerwear there. Will you be staying with us?'

The question was aimed at Frederika.

Frederika shook her head. 'I've got chores,' she said. 'I'll pick Dorotea up after school.'

Mr Lundgren watched as Dorotea limped to the table, but he didn't comment.

'We will begin with the basics,' he said as Frederika shut the door. 'I will question you on the Ten Commandments and Luther's explanations of them. We will do reading, too.'

'Not yet,' Eriksson said. 'The ice doesn't carry yet.'

Frederika inhaled. Eriksson had appeared by her side. He was looking out over the waterway. Her heart was pounding so loud, she was certain he could hear it.

'Please,' she said, 'please don't do that.'

Eriksson laughed and winked at her. 'Sorry,' he said.

After a while, she asked, 'So when will we be able to start fishing?'

'In a few more weeks. Three at the most.' He nodded to himself, and continued: 'Gustav once walked the ice too early. It was the year he came – that man didn't know anything when he arrived. He was way up there' – Eriksson nodded towards the bend in the river – 'took one step and he was gone. Current caught him. I was standing here. The ice gets stronger here quicker – there are fewer rocks. I ran out and cut a hole in the ice with my axe. Gustav managed to swim towards the light. I caught him like you catch a fish.' Eriksson laughed. 'He was lucky. Came up, though, and was insane. Couldn't get one clear word out of him. Seemed he was afraid of that – of being caught, unable to get out.'

Frederika thought of her own fear of being snatched, and shuddered.

'I need to go,' she said. 'I am to pick up my sister from school.'

'I'll walk you.'

Frederika thought about what Antti had said, that Eriksson's blood needed vengeance.

'Is it to find out who killed you?' she asked as they walked. 'Is that why you're coming to me?'

He shrugged. 'Seems to me that journey is as good as any other.'

'Can't you just tell me what happened?'

He shook his head. 'This is not my journey to make. It is yours.'

They had reached the bend of the river and he stopped. 'Look at these trees,' he said.

Two large oak trees grew there on the bank, side by side. The trunk of one of them was twisted, as if the tree had rotated while growing. The trunk of the other was bumpy, but straight. Their crowns were intertwined.

'The wind comes fast here around the bend of the river,' Eriksson said. 'It hits these trees straight on. Both of them have faced the same hardship, but they have responded in different ways.'

'Both of them are damaged, though.'

He bent towards her and looked her straight in the eyes. 'I am growing to quite like you. You are clever.'

Frederika felt her breathing become uneven. Eriksson stood up straight and began to walk again.

'I gave you a hint last time I saw you,' he said after a while. 'What did you do with it?'

Now she was embarrassed. 'Nothing,' she said.

'Nothing?'

'There was a storm.'

'You don't have to hurry for my sake. I have all the time in the world. This is for you. You hear them, don't you? How long do you think they'll wait for you? I am warning you, Frederika. I am not the most dangerous thing around.'

'So how am I supposed to find out what happened to you?'

'Those of your sort have gifts. Elin saw things in her mirror. She had dreams. Find your gifts. Practise. And learn fast.'

He bent under a branch and held some others to the side for her.

'They say you argued the trial against your wife for sorcery should go ahead,' Frederika said.

Eriksson spat in the snow. 'Nils told you,' he said.

Frederika didn't correct him. 'Why?'

'Oh, she was never at any risk. That wasn't about her. I was trying something out. An idea I had.'

'You were trying out an idea?'

They were arriving at the school. They stopped just short of the yard, in among the trees.

'Nils,' Eriksson said again. 'Those nobles think they're better than everybody else. But the only thing that's different about them is that they were pushed out from the private parts of some woman wearing silk. We bowed and scraped to him. My brother, too. Shunned me. Treated me like you treat a flea. You'd be horrified if I told you some of the things those people did to me . . .'

'You did things too.'

He fell silent.

'You stole Elin from your brother.'

There was a pause, then his arm shot out towards her. She

199

cried out, bending from the pain. Blood? That was blood dripping on the snow. Frederika hugged her arm to her chest.

Eriksson's eyes were as pale as the river ice. He wiped the knife blade against his trousers and put it back in its sheath.

'You can't touch me,' Frederika said. Her voice shook. 'You're dead. You can't.'

'Says who?'

Her arm was pulsating. She walked backwards, away from him. 'You can't,' she said again.

'Oh, trust me, I can do worse than this. Remember that, Frederika. Remember it well.'

'Frederika, could you come here please?' Mr Lundgren called.

The door to the teacher's house had opened and the children were coming out. Mr Lundgren was standing on the porch saying goodbye.

'Begin with what is damaged,' Eriksson hissed and, again, he was gone.

'Frederika?'

'Yes.'

There was blood on her front. She couldn't let Mr Lundgren see it. How would she explain it? She didn't know how bad the cut was. Frederika ripped off her scarf and wrapped it around the gash, crossed her arms and pressed them against her chest, as if cold.

In the yard, she passed Dorotea. Their eyes didn't meet. Dorotea hobbled to the sledge and sat down facing the forest.

Frederika stopped beneath the stairs. 'Yes?' she said to the teacher. Her arm hurt. Mr Lundgren was looking past her at Dorotea.

'I'll have to talk to your mother,' he said and shook his head. 'Or you could speak to her for me. Dorotea doesn't have enough Bible knowledge. She ought to be reading better, too.'

Dorotea sat motionless on the sledge. If she didn't move soon, she'd become cold.

'She's going to need more schooling than the rest of you.'

'I'll tell her,' Frederika said.

'Tell your mother not to worry about the cost,' the teacher said. 'Dorotea can stay behind after school once or twice a week, at no charge. I'll make sure she won't have problems with the priest, come the Catechetical hearing.'

'Thank you. I'll tell her,' she said again and half turned away from him.

'Frederika, is everything all right?'

She'd been too eager to leave.

'Yes,' she said. 'I don't want my sister to get cold.'

'Ah.' He nodded. 'I'll see you soon.'

Frederika grabbed the rope to the sledge and began to pull. As soon as they were in the forest, she stopped and rolled up her sleeve. It was too dark to see and she raised her arm towards the light of the moon. Mid-arm, the lesion gaped black. Her body was holding back the blood for now, but it would soon relax and then the bleeding would start again. It was a bad injury.

She felt tears rising and clenched her teeth. Eriksson was crazy. She needed help. She couldn't tell her mother. Her mother wouldn't listen. Besides, she had enough on her mind.

Perhaps she could speak with the teacher? She turned to look back towards the lights of his house. But what would she say? I was cut by a dead man?

'What's wrong?' Dorotea asked, a voice in the dark.

'Nothing,' Frederika said. 'I hurt my arm coming back from the river.'

She pulled her sleeve down and bent to pick up the rope tied to the sleigh.

The mountain was no longer silent. *Dum Tataradum.* The darkness around her seemed to pulsate in rhythm with the drumming in the air. Frederika had never felt more alone.

'Sofia is not at home,' the maid said. She curtsied so her linen bonnet fell over her eye. 'The missus.'

'I understand,' the priest said. 'I asked when she would return.'

'Oh, but I don't know. She's gone to the coast. Maybe she'll be back tomorrow, or the day after.' The maid curtsied again.

To the coast? That was a long journey.

'I saw her not long ago,' the priest said. 'She didn't mention she was going away.'

'It was sudden,' the maid said. 'Six days back. I had to pack at once.'

The priest walked down the steps of the vicarage porch. Winter was no time to travel if you could avoid it. And you didn't make long journeys on impulse. Purchases were planned long in advance. If you needed anything, you borrowed until the market time. Illness in the family, perhaps?

It was dark as he crossed the church green. It wasn't the sky, but more as if darkness hung in the air itself. The verger's lodging was without light. The priest wouldn't have minded speaking with him.

Back home, he resumed his place in front of the fire. Tomorrow, he'd confer with his farmhand, see how the animals were doing. He'd speak with his housekeeper, too, for an update.

The walls of the temporary vicarage creaked. He wondered

how Maija and her daughters were faring. If only their house had been better built. But the cold sneaked in through the slits and the gaps, and the window panes were thin. Thick glass, in his mind, was linked to wealth. He remembered it crunching underneath the soles of his borrowed shoes as a child. The whole of Stockholm knew that on a night out, the King and his friends used to throw stones through the windows of people they liked. Their idea of a joke.

One night, on his way home after work, he'd seen them. They'd come towards him, dressed in coloured silk jackets with wide sleeves of velvet. Two of them wore hats. The King seemed to have lost his. They were walking arm in arm. Pushing each other. Laughing. Yelling. He had stood there on the shards of glass. Covetous, he realised now. Already then, he had so wanted to be one of them. One of the King's friends had caught his eye and left the others. He stood swaying in front of him, before bending down to peer into his face. His coat had silver buttons. The man had stuck out his tongue.

The priest had run the whole way home.

Perhaps they never really saw him as one of them. He'd thought the others had accepted him, and not only for the sake of the King. What if it was the King that had asked to have him removed? No, he didn't believe that.

The room felt bigger this night. The fire didn't manage to light up the far corners. The bright chairs shouted about being vacant.

The housekeeper might still be up.

There was a smell of boiled cabbage in the dark corridor towards the kitchen and he wrinkled his nose. He pushed open the door. A woman screamed and recoiled. There was a loud crash—

'I am so sorry,' she said. It was the young maid. She was

blonde and small. Childlike. She bent down to pick up the pieces of a plate and put them in her apron. 'I didn't expect you here. Normally, you don't come to the kitchen . . .'

'Nothing to worry about,' he said. 'I just wanted . . .'

What – company?

'I need something to eat,' he said.

She curtsied. 'At once,' she said.

The rest of the evening, the priest walked from window to window, without being able to see a thing. Still, he didn't have the peace of mind to sit back down.

The widow returned the following day.

'I hear you've been looking for me,' she said. 'I came back late last night.'

The priest gestured for her to sit down. She did so and took off her fur. She was wearing a dark blue dress with a lace collar. Her hair was tied behind her neck. A fire blazed in the fireplace. The room felt small and warm this day, and the brightly coloured chairs welcoming. Funny how things seemed different in the daylight, he thought. Or perhaps it was having other people around.

'Did you have a good journey?' he asked.

'As good as journeys can be.'

They chuckled.

'So you were by the coast? Family matters?'

The widow smiled. 'And how was your journey?'

'Not fruitful. We travelled to the Lapps.'

'We?'

'Maija Harmaajärvi accompanied me. She and her daughters did. You know, the new settlers from Finland.'

The widow's smile was somewhat cooler now. 'I know of them.'

'Fearless claimed that none of his people had anything to do with Eriksson's death and I believe him. To think that they would go to such drastic measures for land doesn't seem plausible.' He paused. 'They did, however, tell us about Daniel and Elin. Did you know that Elin came here with the brother – with Daniel – not with Eriksson?'

Her lips parted and exposed small white teeth. 'I did,' she said.

'But . . . why didn't you tell me?'

'I worried it might have been spoken of in confession. Anvar was not always as careful with what he told me as he perhaps ought to have been. It was up to me to be cautious. You do understand, don't you?'

Some priests spoke too much. The priest could understand the loyalty of a woman towards her husband. Towards the Church. In actual fact, it was commendable.

She leaned forward and touched his arm. 'Elin belonging to Daniel was so long ago. If I thought I knew anything that might shed any light on Eriksson's death, I wouldn't keep it from you.'

Her hand was warm.

'Irrespective of the circumstances under which it was told.' She looked him in the eyes.

He nodded.

A delightful woman, he thought, when she left. A pleasure to be around. Distinguished, virtuous, able.

Someone cleared their throat. The housekeeper. Officious woman. Though nothing would work without her.

'Yes?'

'I understand there was some bother with Beatrice last night,' she said.

Beatrice?

'The maid,' she said.

He still didn't know . . .

'Clumsy, by nature,' the housekeeper said, 'drops things all the time.'

Oh, that. He waved it away with his hand.

'Beatrice needs her employment, see. Her father and mother are both poorly. They stayed here because she has her work.'

The priest nodded.

'Otherwise I would have let her go a long time ago. Not that there are any replacements.'

The priest felt a twinge of irritation. The housekeeper made to leave.

'Wait,' he said. 'How long have you been in the priest's service?'

'Fifteen years.'

'There can't be much you don't know about the parish after fifteen years.' He smiled. His face felt stiff.

'I guess not.' She nodded.

'Did you know that Daniel and Elin were . . . together?'

She was torn now, he could tell – struggling between some vague notion of the delicacy demanded by her employment and the chance to gossip with the priest. But she was not a delicate woman.

'They exchanged wives,' she said. 'Daniel and Eriksson.'

'I didn't think Eriksson had anyone,' he said, aghast.

She puckered her mouth. 'Maybe not,' she had to admit. 'But at least Elin came to town first with one, then with the other.'

'What did the old priest say about it?'

'I am not sure he noticed.'

Of course he would have noticed. The old priest had let it be. Perhaps he, too, had been afraid of Eriksson.

'There was a case in the Books many years ago. It was written down as *K against the church*. Do you know what that might have been about?'

The housekeeper shook her head. Her eyes flickered and she licked her lips. The priest could imagine her dismay at possibly having missed something. So whatever the claim against the church was, it hadn't been gossiped about, he thought. The old priest had kept that matter close to his chest, not even sharing it with his wife.

I don't know what I am looking for, he thought then. It's like fumbling in the dark. He remembered what the widow had said about her husband's state of mind just before he died.

'Do you remember the last time the old priest went to Blackåsen Mountain?'

She nodded. 'He and the verger went for the Catechetical hearing.'

'What was he like when he returned?'

'Sat in the same chair you are sitting in right now and cried,' the housekeeper said.

'Cried? Are you certain?'

She nodded again. '"Sweet priest, what's wrong?" I asked him. "Don't cry," I said. "Oh, my dearest Lydia," he said, "how can I do otherwise, after what I have learned."'

The priest didn't quite believe the exchange had happened that way, but waved for her to continue.

'"Tell my farmhand to prepare the horses and the carriage," he said, "I must travel south."'

'Did he tell you what had happened?'

The housekeeper shook her head. '"I wouldn't want to tarnish the purity of your mind, dear Lydia," he said when I asked him.'

Oh God.

The housekeeper sighed and looked to the ceiling. It was one of those sighs that shivers a little in the middle.

'Right. Thank you,' the priest said.

She curtsied, mouth reverting to its habitual pout.

'Now that the widow . . . Sofia . . . is back from visiting her family, I'd like to invite her over for a meal one day.'

'Of course.' She curtsied again. 'Though Sofia doesn't have any relatives.'

It was such a throwaway remark, he almost missed it.

'What do you mean?' he asked.

'She's an orphan. Old priest said she had no one but him, his Sofia.'

'Did you ever see the dead?' her elder daughter asked.

'Of course not,' Maija said.

Maija was sitting by the table. It was morning, but night still floated in and out of the window. Frederika was standing, looking out. There was something in her face that Maija neither recognised, nor liked.

'Don't stand in front of the window,' Maija said. 'I don't know what you think you can see.'

Her daughter sighed and moved to sit down opposite her.

'The Lapps see murdered souls in the Northern Lights,' Frederika said.

'Who told you that?'

'I think you said it.'

'Did I? I don't remember that at all.'

'Why did you say it if you didn't believe it?'

'Perhaps I needed to believe it then,' Maija said, irritated. 'I don't know.'

'The priest would say seeing them is wrong.'

Maija stood up. 'Frederika, we don't have time for this. We have a lot of work to do. You and your sister are going to spin wool, and I am going to set traps.'

The night had been bitterly cold, but it had been calm. Without the wind, the timber of the house squeaked and ticked.

It was hard to make yourself go outside. The body protested as if, this time, it might be allowed to have a say. But the conversation with her daughter drove her on. She found her skis where she'd placed them against the wall of the house, pushed them to the ground and placed her feet in the straps.

'Did you ever see the dead?' What a question. Maija didn't know when it had started, this . . . tendency of Frederika's. It might have been when she and her sister had found Eriksson's body. Maija needed to speak to her. She would put a stop to this right now, explain why it was so vital they stuck to reason. She might have to tell her what could happen when people didn't. Maija summoning up Jutta in her imagination was different. That was a bad habit. Jutta used to say that the older you got, the more present your past became and that might be true.

'Did you ever see the dead?' Pfha. She was her father's daughter all right.

That was terrible, and it wasn't true. Frederika was the one most like herself and she was strong. Even as a newborn, Frederika had known what she wanted, how much she was going to eat and when. She had never needed Maija in the same way as Dorotea did. It was strange. Frederika was the child Maija had expected she would have, the one that looked like her, and had her character. Dorotea didn't resemble Maija in the least. Her features were so neat and pure, they made Maija think of glass. Her bones were fine. Maija used to think of Dorotea as her hand-out child. She hadn't expected she would have a daughter like her – she was a gift. And yet, it was Frederika that Maija had never had. If Maija got close to Frederika at night, she woke up and moved away. Dorotea still liked to lie close to you, thin fingers twitching, touching your arm or your side. 'Wandering fingers,' Maija and Paavo used to joke, as they fought for the spot closest to Dorotea in bed. Her feet would move up yours to seek warmth, feeling like small, cold frogs.

Dorotea's feet . . . There was still blackening and blistering, but her daughter seemed better. She couldn't walk for long, but managed short stretches. She bore the agony well, apart from when Maija cleaned her feet. Then the pain took over, Dorotea cried, and there was nothing Maija could do to ease it for her. Nothing. Then Maija's helplessness turned to rage and she seethed with anger that they had to go through this on their own.

And not one letter had they received from Paavo.

They were supposed to be the weaker ones. He was supposed to worry about them – not the other way around. Before they married, it had been different. She'd had to pry anything about how he himself was out of him. They'd been equals. She assumed that at some stage she must have given him the permission to lean on her for strength. She knew women who wouldn't have taken it. Though she also knew women who'd had to take a lot more.

There was a slight wind now and some brightening of the sky. Snow drew in sleepy veils along the slope in front of the house. She would set a couple of snares by the river, some mid-forest and then a few more by the marsh. She'd gone through it in her head many times already: how much meat and fish they had in storage. It wasn't enough to take them through winter. There was plenty of hay for the goats; if necessary, they could slaughter, but she hoped it wouldn't come to that. Animals provided milk and clothes. Slaughtering them was the beginning of a downward spiral that was difficult to break. When the river froze solid they'd start fishing again. In the meantime, she'd try to catch a rabbit or a bird. It might have been this that drove Elin insane: the prospect of not having enough food.

The memory of the recent storm was a dark cloud in the corner of her mind, but you had to go on, keep moving, find new ways, look again. They'd manage. Though it had felt better when the priest was with them. Someone to share things with – even if it was despair.

The river ice looked thick. She imagined it working, thickening, underneath the snow. In a few more cold days, they'd be able to walk on it. She found rabbit tracks in the forest on her way to the marsh and set two traps close by. She tried to visualise the animal hopping along its habitual path, almost as if she could make it happen.

Did you ever see dead people? she thought again, as her hands pressed down the jagged iron mouth of the trap. She tore at the snow to remove enough of it.

She set one more trap south of the marsh and then skied onwards towards the bog itself.

Once again, he was in the middle of the otherwise empty field. She took a big step on her skis, bringing her closer to one of the fir trees so that he wouldn't see her. Gustav was poking with a large stick in the snow. But why? She didn't think there were any fish in the marsh, so what was he looking for?

He began to run. Maija sat down. He ran with heavy steps in the deep snow. As he came closer, she heard him wheeze and whimper. He fell down on his knees in the snow and howled to the sky until his voice broke.

She was shaking. A grown man's screams were awful to hear.

The war. It hadn't occurred to her that the soldiers, too, could become damaged. She'd only thought about the pain and agony they inflicted wherever they went. Perhaps before, Gustav had been normal.

She was tired when she got back to the homestead and stuck her skis in the snow by the porch. There was a thick branch, and she reached for it.

'Don't take it,' Frederika said. She was coming from the barn with a bucket in her hand.

'Why?'

'I'm going to use it later,' Frederika said.

Maija was tired and cold. She didn't ask.

When the priest arrived, the widow was cutting her maid's hair, her own blonde hair gathered into a knot at her neck. She was laughing, her cheeks were red.

'There.' She pulled the towel off the maid's shoulders. 'Like new.'

The girl touched her bare neck and curtsied.

The widow smiled at the priest. 'It had to be done. Now you.'

She nodded to the chair in front of her. 'Might as well, while I'm at it. Can't have a priest who looks dishevelled.'

The priest sat down. The widow dipped the comb in the bowl beside her and combed his hair. Cold water trickled along his throat and dripped on to his collarbone. The skin drew together in small bumps. He hated having his hair cut in winter. She took a strand of hair between her fingers and snipped it above his collar.

'Your journey to the coast,' he said.

'Mm-hm?'

The widow ran a finger down his scalp, gathered another lock.

'You said you visited family?'

She didn't respond.

He half turned his head, but couldn't see her. The *chtt, chtt* of the scissors made him sleepy.

'I thought you didn't have any relatives,' he said.

The widow stopped cutting. There was a pause and then she walked round in front of him. Behind her, the window was a black tablet framed by green cotton curtains. 'No.' She looked straight at him and crossed her arms. 'No, I don't.'

'Then why did you lie to me?'

Her mouth fell open. 'Lie? I didn't lie to you. You assumed I had gone to see family and I did not correct you.'

'I think that counts as a lie.'

She shook her head and walked to the back again. Her fingers tugged at his hair.

'In fact, I went there for you,' she said.

He tried to turn, but she pushed on his cheek. Not very gently.

'You are too young and too good to waste away here.' She let go of one tress and took the next. Efficient now. 'I couldn't understand why Karl-Erik wanted you to investigate Eriksson's death and not the authorities from the coast.'

'Maybe he wanted to avoid spreading fear,' the priest said.

'That may be so, but by not telling the authorities, he is, in fact, culpable of a crime. And a bishop who commits a crime can be replaced.'

Her voice was mild, as if to lessen the impact of her words. She still shocked him. Accusing somebody higher up in the order established by God was like accusing God Himself. Moreover, he had thought the widow and the bishop were close.

'Enquiries could be made by people in the right places, to see whether a younger priest, a former court priest, might be more suitable for the role.'

The priest turned around and this time she let him.

'Who? The King . . .?'

216

'Friends of my late husband,' Sofia said. 'Friends of mine.'

He had to admit to feeling disappointed.

'Close your eyes,' she said, and combed his fringe down. The cold edge of the scissors pressed hard against his skin as it moved across his forehead.

'My husband was here by choice,' she said. 'He felt he had a calling. But there was a time before, when he was more driven, and we made a lot of connections.'

Her voice was neutral, but the priest could imagine it would have been a real disappointment, this novel calling of her husband's.

'There is no need for you to stay here, but you do need new friends,' she said. 'The King is not the most . . . steadfast of men when it comes to his friendships.'

The priest remembered once, a new man in their midst, the King gushing over this novel acquaintance. The priest hadn't liked the newcomer. Ambition had shone brightly out of his eyes. At dinner, one of the others, Maximilian, had caught the priest's eye. 'Don't worry,' he'd said, smile on his lips. 'The King tires quickly. He'll be gone soon.'

Instead, it was the priest who was gone.

The widow tapped him on the shoulder and put the scissors on the kitchen table. As she walked across the room to pour the water bowl out, her purple dress flowed over the floor. Her hair had come undone and was falling over her shoulders. New allies, he thought. Allies who were certain to come with obligations.

'So what would you suggest we do?' he asked.

She looked over her shoulder at him and smiled.

'The markets at the coast are held a few weeks before ours – the coming one and the one around Lady Day,' Sofia said. They were sitting together on her settle. She was balancing on the edge, one leg crossed over the other. She had spread her drawings out on the table in front of them. 'People from the south come to trade with *birkkarlarna*, who then come to trade with us. This year, I decided to go, to meet up with old friends, and ask for the news.' She smiled at the priest. 'I talked about an amazing new priest in the Lappmark who ought to go far.'

He cleared his throat.

'I also took my drawings.'

Sofia's foot with its heeled shoe bounced in the air. The fire crackled. She shook her head. 'There was something about him, Eriksson,' she said. 'He was completely insolent. Even though I was a priest's wife, he'd hold my gaze just that little too long when we met.'

She scoffed and looked at him. The priest knew he was supposed to feel angry, but he didn't.

'The people on Blackåsen were afraid of him. I always wondered what hold he had on the others. I realised that a bit more knowledge of the settlers' pasts might do us good. And I must say, what I found out was rather amusing,'

She touched Gustav's drawing and lined it up straight with the others.

'So what did you learn?'

Sofia picked up the drawing. 'A lieutenant acquaintance of my husband's recognised Gustav as a soldier in his regiment. He was assumed dead in the Battle of Fraustadt.'

Fraustadt. Gustav and the priest would have been in the same place. One of Sweden's greatest victories. Yes, hundreds of fellow soldiers died, but, against that, thousands of Slavs from Sachsen, Poland and Russia. Gustav would have either deserted, or been captured.

'His widow and child were later forced to leave the croft. They died in the plague.'

Poor sod. The priest wondered how Gustav had found out about his family.

She picked up another drawing. Nils was glaring out at him from within it.

'Nils was a public official. His father was ennobled under the King's father. But what is interesting is Kristina . . .'

She searched among the drawings on the table and found it, a large, blonde woman with steely eyes.

'Kristina is from one of the oldest aristocratic families,' Sofia said. '*De la Gardie*', she mouthed.

'Magnus Gabriel de la Gardie?' he asked, incredulous.

Sofia laughed. 'Her grandfather.'

The priest chuckled. The de la Gardies had been the family most affected when the King's father reduced the nobles' privileges. Their fall from grace had been spectacular.

'And what about Nils?'

'Bribes,' she said.

Ah, the influences on the crown were many. Everybody wanted a piece. The priest had sometimes agreed with those who argued that while the King fought battles abroad, the real war was being lost at home. Treason, the King called that kind of talk. Believe in me, or you betray me.

'My friend said Nils went too far. At one stage, he seemed to be in charge of Stockholm, before the King put a stop to it.'

The priest thought about Nils having requested a village to be built on Blackåsen. An attempt, most likely, to create a new little kingdom for himself.

'Anything else?'

She shook her head. 'I asked them about the bishop. They

know of him, of course, as he is on the Privy Council, but nobody had much to tell. They said that in the Council he mostly keeps silent. The King seems neutral in his regard. Someone said others were impressed with him down south . . . said that not many men of the Church knew to show such mercy. Otherwise, nothing. Nothing about Henrik, or Daniel.'

'What circumstances?'

Sofia tilted her head. 'What?'

'The bishop having shown mercy – in what circumstances?'

She shook her head. 'I don't know,' she said.

'De la Gardie,' he said again and shook his head.

They sat in silence. The priest thought of Gustav. So the dead reappeared on Blackåsen. It didn't surprise him in the least.

'So what do we do?' he said, after a while.

'We make friends,' Sofia said. 'At our market, I will introduce you to some people – the taxman, Mårten Broman, most importantly. He knows everyone down south. In the meantime perhaps you go and see Nils and Kristina. The world of the nobility is so small. They are bound still to have connections.'

She put her hand on his arm. He stiffened and didn't look at her. Instead, he stared into the fire.

'I'll empty the traps,' Frederika said to her mother.

'I only set them yesterday.'

Frederika kicked her shoe against the doorpost. 'I want to see that they are still working. And who knows . . .'

'Fine,' her mother said. 'Dorotea stays here, though.'

'Ah.' Frederika tried to sound regretful.

Her mother was watching her. Frederika grabbed her hat and pushed it down to hide her eyes.

'Bye,' she breathed.

She walked across the yard, ears tense, half expecting her mother's voice to call for her to stop. When she reached the forest, she began to run. She didn't like to lie to her mother and before, if she ever tried, her mother had known. But lately, Frederika had discovered with a mixture of excitement and regret, she was getting away with it. Perhaps her mother was growing old, or perhaps her mother's mind was busy with other things, but she both saw and heard less than she used to.

Frederika was not far from Elin's homestead, but she had to slow down. Her arm was throbbing and she was worried that the wound would begin to bleed again. She had cleaned it and pressed the sides of the cut together while binding her arm tightly with a piece of cloth, but it was a large gash and she wasn't certain it would hold. Otherwise she would have to tell her mother and they'd have to sew the wound. She hoped it wouldn't come to that. She had to rid herself of Eriksson before something worse happened. She had to find out what happened to him. And it seemed Eriksson wanted her to begin with Elin.

Frederika stood for a long time looking at Elin's house, wondering if she dared. Then she thought of Eriksson and sighed. It had to be done. She crossed the yard and nothing moved. In fact, it was much too quiet. She steeled herself and walked faster. She ran up the stairs to the porch, not certain whether the worst evil was inside, or outside.

The cottage had frozen in time. The floorboards were a solid white and didn't squeak and moan as she walked on them. They were just mute. The walls glittered. There were ice roses on the windows. The fireplace gaped black. Frederika shivered. Elin had found something out; something that had destroyed her. Was it who had killed Eriksson? But then why hadn't she just told someone?

Frederika opened the cupboards in the kitchen and lifted the cutlery. Nothing. There was a wooden hamper on the floor by the kitchen settle with wool thread, a pair of scissors and needles. She lifted the flower pots with their shrivelled plants, with her fingers, she combed through the frozen shoe grass in its wooden chest, searched among the wood in the wood basket. She touched the settle, stroked its back with her fingers.

How did you find out whatever it was that shocked you? She sent the thought to Elin. It seemed like you and your children didn't leave your homestead much after that time I met you by the river. You didn't come to harvest the sedge. The only time anyone saw you was at church, and then nobody spoke with you.

She looked towards the bedroom. She didn't want to go in there. Her mother had said that was where it happened. What if something was still in there? She bit her teeth together hard and advanced towards the door. She looked in, heart beating, ready to run. But the room was so empty, it seemed quite possible nobody had ever lived there. There was no telling that this room had seen despair, and whatever blood there had once been had now faded to matted brown.

The bedding had been removed, but Frederika lifted the stained mattresses one by one to see underneath them. There was nothing. She opened the cupboards and took out the clothes and shook them. She did the same with the bed linen. Nothing. On a window sill were some stones and sticks that the children had probably played with.

Frederika thought about what Eriksson had said, about 'those of her sort' having gifts. She put her hands flat on the cold house wall. She breathed and closed her eyes. Who did Elin meet? she asked the timber. Did someone come to visit? The walls were silent.

Oh, this was silly. She pushed off the wall.

Besides, nobody would have come. People were afraid of Elin after her husband's death.

Apart from the killer, she thought then. He would have known there was nothing to be afraid of.

You found something out, Frederika thought again. It destroyed you, but still you didn't tell anybody. You must have been really frightened.

The light was going fast. The air was dusky when she knocked on the door. Eriksson had talked of that which was damaged, she thought. And there was one more person she thought of as damaged.

Gustav opened.

'Can I come in?' she asked.

The scar underneath his nose kept his mouth open. She took a step forward and he let her into his hallway.

She ought to have planned what she was going to say. 'I'd like to ask about Elin,' she said.

He stared at her.

'I didn't know Elin,' he said.

He could be lying, she thought. Frederika tried to catch his eye like Jutta had taught her, to see what was inside. 'Relax,' Jutta had said. 'Try to float into me and tell me what you see.'

Lake-summer. It was warm and the small flies droned above them.

Frederika had giggled.

'Serious, now,' Jutta said.

Frederika concentrated.

'No,' Jutta said. 'Not like that. Don't try so hard. Float. Relax.'

Frederika had tried and tried. Then she'd given up and lain down on her back. Jutta's head above her was covering the sun, her thin hair swaying around her head like the halo on Maria, in the painting in their church. Frederika smelled her hair – algae, chamomile. She wanted to put her nose in it. And then she just slipped into Jutta's eyes and there was red love and a little girl named Frederika.

She had laughed. Jutta smiled, but not for long.

'Use this gift with care,' she'd said. 'Secrets are most often awful.'

Now Frederika looked Gustav in the eye in that same way. She smiled at him. At first, Gustav's eyes were blue. A sea. The rings from a jumping fish.

Not rings. An opening. A hole in the earth. A den of an animal? Shackles attached to a stone wall. The iron soiled black.

Pain. Pain so huge she hadn't known it existed.

Frederika walked backwards. And then she ran.

She ran as fast as she could, along the lake, into the forest. Her throat ached. Her gasps for air sounded like sobs.

Not far from home, two hands grabbed her and she howled. It was Antti. She still screamed. He swirled her around and wrapped his arms round her.

'I see Eriksson,' she yelled.

His body stiffened, but he didn't let go of her.

'I see him,' she repeated. 'And I hear the mountain speak.'

He was silent.

'Eriksson isn't nice,' she said after a time.

He released his grip. No longer held, she felt cold.

'The dead are supposed to travel,' he said. 'If they stay, it brings problems.'

'But what's holding him?'

'You see him, so you are.'

That was an awful thing to say. He pushed her to start moving and kept pushing to make her go forward.

His voice, behind her: 'I couldn't stop thinking about you. You asked questions . . . If the spirits are calling you, Frederika, you have to respond.'

She tried to shut out his voice.

'It's about protection for all of us. The signs are so bad. You can help us.

'Fearless used to have a drum,' he continued. 'It helped him travel between worlds. It was his most important weapon. It kept him alive. But he burned it when he became a Christian.'

They reached her yard, and she kept walking because she knew he wouldn't follow. He remained in the shadows.

She turned once. 'Eriksson is mean. Why did Elin go with him?' she asked.

She imagined Antti shaking his head. When he spoke, his voice was hesitant. 'In summer, some of the reindeer don't want to leave when it's their time to roam. Perhaps Elin felt safer in captivity.'

Unable to see it, she knew the wound on her arm had begun to bleed.

In November, it became yet colder, though that had hardly seemed possible. The air was so cold that their nostrils stuck together when they inhaled. They had frost spots on cheeks and earlobes, and the hair on the goats' necks grew thick and long as a dog's. The days were still shortening. Every morning, night lingered, loitered by the steps of the porch, stuck to the icy branches of the spruce trees. Every evening, it returned earlier.

'How much more?' Frederika asked. 'I want it to end.'

'Night will take over,' Maija said. They were in the woodshed. Maija had been thinking that later, if need be, they could put sawdust on the kitchen floor to absorb damp, and place another layer of planks on top of that. 'Only for a few weeks. Then it turns and we creep towards summer.'

That creeping in itself would take several months. She didn't say that. What had she been thinking, telling Paavo to leave them here?

She whacked the ground. Just hold it together, she told herself. You're not doing too badly. The paths from the house to the sheds and the barns were cleared of snow. The animal bins were stuffed with dried grass. There was still frozen food in the storage place, enough for another couple of weeks, maybe three if they rationed. They had managed to snare two pheasants. And now, with the plates of frozen sawdust thawing in the kitchen, their home smelled of summer – chopped wood and cool water. No, not too badly. Apart from Dorotea's feet, that was. While her younger seemed in good spirits, the decay of her flesh continued. That thought crushed all the others.

Dorotea opened the door. 'Mamma,' she said. 'Someone is coming.'

Nils was waiting for her in the yard.

'Good morning, Maija,' he said.

'Good morning,' she said, and God damn her, it was still all she could do not to curtsy.

He was wearing a long-haired fur coat. He looked comfortable, warm and round. Her own hands beneath her jumper were scaly and red. Fisted.

'It got Elin,' Nils said.

'What?' She didn't follow.

'The mountain.'

'That's absurd. She killed herself.'

'Call it whatever you like, but this mountain is getting to us, one by one. It injures us in one way or another. And when we're weak, it takes us.'

'She had just lost a husband. She couldn't see a way. Stronger people than Elin have chosen that path.'

Nils shook his head. 'You remember we spoke of creating a village. If we come together, we'd have each other for help. We have to quell this.'

'But quell what?'

'I am calling the settlers to a meeting the day after tomorrow, mid-afternoon at my house. I heard Paavo did go to the coast, so I am inviting you to come.'

She wasn't going to have anything more to do with the quest for Eriksson's killer, but, as if by themselves, her fingers searched for her pocket, slid in and squeezed the glass fragment she kept there. The thought fluttered through her head that she had kept it with her, and so she had never thought of giving up, really. She took the blue glass piece out of her pocket.

Nils looked at the fragment.

'The Lapps say this is yours,' she said.

'The Lapps.' He paused. 'Well, then I guess it is.' He took off his mittens and stretched out his hand.

She held back. 'I found this where Eriksson was killed,' she said and looked him straight in the eye. 'Up by the glade.'

Nils gave a short laugh and shrugged. 'There is a place up there that we call the King's Throne. Have you heard about it? It has a lovely view. Everyone knows I sit there all the time. I must have dropped it.' He put his mittens back on. 'I'll see you at the meeting.'

Before leaving, he gestured towards their house. 'If you shovel the snow against the walls of the house, it acts as insulation.'

Maija remembered Daniel. That's what he'd been doing when they visited together with the priest. She sighed. She'd add it to the list of things she hadn't known.

The valley was much colder than the mountain. As if the cold had run off the slopes and settled into a pool of winter at the bottom. Just like the first time she went to Daniel's homestead, it was the dog who found Maija. This time with less bravado. It ran up to her side, barked twice, and then escorted her. The dog ran with its ears pointing forward. Maybe one could get used to you, she thought, and it looked up to her as if to say, *You think?*

Daniel and Anna were inside and as Maija opened the door,

the dog ran straight past her and lay down by the fire. Daniel stopped carving, followed the dog with his eyes and glowered.

'May I come in?' Maija asked.

Daniel returned to focus on the piece of wood and the knife in his hand. His back was stiff. She wanted to tell him she was not here to ask about Elin.

'I wanted to see how you were,' Maija said to Anna.

Anna shrugged. She was pale and had black shadows underneath her eyes. Her body still had the roundedness. Maija knew what it felt like carrying around bulk like that, feeling it whenever you took a step, or moved your arm; a constant reminder of what had come to nothing.

'Do you want me to see how you really are?' she asked.

There was an awkward pause.

Daniel rose. He turned in the doorway to tap his hand to his thigh and the dog followed him out.

Maija pointed to the bed and Anna sat down on its edge, pulled off her shoes and trousers and lay down. Maija poured some water into a bowl. She washed her hands and then rubbed them against one another to warm them.

'A clean cloth?' she asked.

Anna pointed to a wooden chest. Maija opened it and found what she needed. She pulled Anna's shirt up over her stomach. The woman was still swollen. But at least she was not torn.

'Winter is cold here,' Maija said, as she let her hands do her work.

'It is colder than usual.' Anna stared at the roof. 'I've never known it to be this cold before the New Year.'

'Did you get everything out?' Maija asked.

Anna nodded. One sole tear ran down her cheek, but she didn't say anything.

After that, they were silent. Maija pulled Anna's shirt down to cover her and went to wash her hands. When she turned back, Anna had dressed.

'Thank you,' Anna said.

Maija shook her head, there was no need.

'No,' Anna said. 'Thank you for caring.'

'As far as I can tell there is no damage,' Maija said. 'No physical damage.'

'It wasn't painful. It was as if the child had no hold in me.'

'Sometimes that happens. I wish we knew why.'

'No point thinking about it, I guess.' Anna walked to the kitchen table and sat down.

'Don't do too much,' Maija said. 'Try to rest when you can.'

'I was going to go to Nils's meeting tomorrow.'

Maija shrugged. 'If you feel ready for the walk . . .'

With her fingers, Anna combed the fringe of the tablecloth.

'Did he come to see you, too?' she asked.

Maija nodded. She sat down opposite Anna.

'Eriksson, Elin and our baby boy, too . . .' Anna's voice broke. She sniffed and rubbed her forehead with the heel of her hand. 'Nils might be right. Perhaps it is the mountain.'

'They are separate occurrences, Anna. Not one whole.'

'But there are too many of them.'

Maija hesitated. Anna had just lost a child.

'What was Eriksson like?' she asked, instead.

Anna's fingers had returned to playing with the border of the tablecloth. She sighed and held Maija's gaze as she gave in. 'He used to come here, from time to time. He'd stay for a few minutes. He'd talk, and I'd go about my usual chores.'

'Why?'

'His way of making right, perhaps. I think he wanted to convince me that he was not at fault for the rift with his brother. For some reason, I think it mattered to him.'

Anna's brown hair hung long and loose. Her sea-coloured eyes seemed larger. It was strange to discover that what you'd thought of as roughness in a person was resilience. What you thought was hostility was caution.

'Eriksson,' she said, 'he wasn't all bad. The way he thought, the stories he told, he was amusing.'

'I am assuming he and Nils didn't get on together.'

'Both of them were used to commanding. But Nils was the nobleman. He was in charge.'

'Eriksson must have been upset.'

Anna smiled. 'Not so. I think he waited for his time to come.'

Maija shook her head.

'Eriksson knew everything about each and every one of us. Made it his business to find out. Used it against people to get his way.'

'All of you come here fleeing something or someone,' the priest had said. But it wasn't easy, though, to uncover things people had decided to hide.

'How?' Maija asked.

'He travelled to the coast trade with *birkkarlarna*, the merchants, even off season. Perhaps he was told gossip. Though mostly, I think he was just very sharp-eyed. It was as if he smelled weakness in another person. He guessed and kept prodding. The last time I saw Eriksson, he'd just come back from another journey to the coast. He was smug, said he had found out a secret. Something big about someone big, he said. I assumed it had to do with Nils.'

'You have no idea what it was?'

Anna shook her head.

'Why on earth did Elin stay with him?'

'I am not so surprised that she did.' Anna hesitated. 'Eriksson . . . nobody else was like him. And then there was something skewed about their relationship. Whenever you saw them together, he acted as if she didn't exist. And she acted as if indeed she didn't exist.'

'What do you mean?'

Anna shook her head. 'I am not certain I know myself. You know how some people have so many bad experiences that in the end, that is the only thing they understand? I always assumed that there was something like that in Elin's past, and that that was why she stayed with him. She saw nobody but him. The nastier he was to her, the more she tried to please him. Yes,' Anna continued, 'Eriksson could be amusing. But then there was the other side to him, cruel. It was silly, but sometimes I thought to myself that the mountain lived in him. Or maybe through him.'

They sat silent for a while.

'If that something killed him, then we'll need the village,' Anna said.

Maija wanted to tell her that this particular kind of fear didn't die when people came together. It magnified, inflated. It took over and demanded sacrifice. It had in Ostrobothnia.

She got to her feet. 'It wasn't something that killed Eriksson,' she said. 'It was someone.'

One single slash, she thought as she walked home. Deep, without hesitation. Someone who killed like that, it was either because of lack of emotion, or too much of it.

Did Nils own a rapier? Of course he did. He would have been raised with one in his hand. But that didn't mean a thing. The wars had been so many and for such a long time. Most men had been in the army, and owned the same sort of weapon. Many had deserted. Paavo had, without ever seeing the battlefront. He and the other villagers had left in the morning and been back two days later. She ought to have been happy, but she had also felt something else. Disappointment, perhaps. Though with whom or with what, she wasn't certain. The rapier he'd brought home with him, she'd used to keep the barn door shut when the latch had broken.

Perhaps I just don't like the nobles, she thought. Although a big secret about someone big – could have been about Nils.

Their homestead was in between the trees, but she continued past it. There were two traps by the edge of the marsh. Please, she thought, and then scolded herself. You always do this: pray for good turns, when nothing is ever given. Hope so much, your chest feels in a knot. And then you tell Frederika to hold to reason, when you're no better yourself.

The south side of the mountain had been wind-free. The surface of the snow was flat and undisturbed. The snow itself was like layer upon layer of dust. As she walked, she sank down. She lifted her knees high for each step and breathed hard before she found a rhythm.

By the marsh, she had to search for a while. With new snow, the land was different, or rather, it all looked the same. She found the first trap and sighed when it was empty. The second held a bird. It was tiny and the little body was frozen white. She brushed the snow off it and held it up close to her face. 'Well, you're not anything to shout about,' she told it. In normal circumstances she would have left a prey this small for wild animals, but not this time. Soup. At least it would give the taste of meat. She turned and began her walk home.

Her legs ached. When she reached the base of the mountain, she continued walking further down, rather than cutting across.

It would make the journey longer, but much easier if she found her previous tracks and followed them home.

It took a while, but lower, between the pine trees, were her own footsteps. Potholes at regular intervals in the blue snow. She stopped.

Other tracks. Within hers.

She walked closer and bent down to look.

Wolf.

Still crouching, she scanned the forest.

The prints showed they were several, three or four. Adults. They had been following her tracks for as far back as she saw. Hunting. No. Wolf did not hunt people.

She rose and began to walk. Fast now. Fixating on her old footsteps. She glanced over her shoulder. Nothing. Not yet. Not far home now. The snow was less deep here. Her throat stung from the cold air. She slowed down her breathing and thought of the Lapp reindeer.

God. Mustn't think about that. No. Eriksson. Nils. She forced herself to be angry. Things must be dealt with, she argued, and let the anger drive her on, push her forward. We must find out and not let fear take over. Their cottage became visible between the trees.

An unhurried howl, and her heart was all the way up in her throat.

Grey-legs to her right. One was still, looking straight at her. Yellow eyes. Its pelt erect. The other three were tramping behind it, held back by the immobility of the leader.

Mustn't run. Wolf didn't attack people. *Oh God.*

She turned and began to walk backwards. Sing, she thought to herself. Sing.

Couldn't remember a thing.

'*EEn iungfru födde itt barn jdagh.*' Her voice broke. She

235

swallowed with a gasp. She swallowed again. And once more. Each time it sounded as if she were gulping for air. Mustn't panic. Not now.

'*thet skole wij prijsa och ära.*'

Careful. Foot by foot.

'*j thet haffuer gud itt gott begagh*'

She stumbled. Almost fell. It was the thick branch Frederika had told her to leave. She bent down, felt it solid in her hand, everything else weak and unsteady. She rose. The lead wolf curled its lips. White fangs, pink gums.

She continued walking backwards, the stick raised high.

'*han biudher oss höra hans lära*'

They went for her when she reached the porch. Came running. She swung with the piece of wood and hit the first one across its head. It fell on to its side. Then she dropped the branch. Two steps. Door.

A clapping by her back. Teeth closing on teeth.

She screamed. Slammed the door. A thick body hit it so hard that the door felt alive under her hands.

Cold had arrived in town, the wind adding to the chill. The priest wondered what the weather meant for Blackåsen. A light blizzard in town might mean severe weather up-mountain. The clean line of the church wall was broken by black dots. Visiting settlers. Or beggars. November, and already people were without food. He'd remind the verger about locks for the buildings.

He walked towards the church and avoided meeting the gazes, pushed his hands into his pockets, lengthened his steps.

In his room, he sat down by his desk without lighting the fire. It was so cold it was like being outside. He rose, took his mantle, and put it over his shoulders. 'Make new friends,' Sofia had said. It seemed so easy. It was easy. All his life, he'd desired a position like the court priest's. That hadn't changed. It was just that he had thought their friendship, his and the King's, was real.

He realised he was resigned to the thought that even if the King hadn't commanded his removal, he had agreed to it. He would have had to. The King was everywhere; he knew everything. For the priest to rise again, he would have to scheme; go behind the bishop's back, and win the King's heart once more. Somehow, he was certain he could do it. But it felt hollow. For him, their friendship could never be a personal one again. The priest would always have to remain clear-headed, detached. He'd have to be false. He'd been false before, but that had been different. He hadn't felt dishonest with the ones he loved.

He thought of Sofia; her blue eyes, the little nose, the dimples by her mouth, skin that looked soft as velvet. He'd have to marry her. He should marry her. She had everything a man could wish for. In his world, so much was about the woman. Why was he so reluctant?

It was too cold. He walked to the fireplace, bent down and began building a fire. Before his inner eye, he saw Maija: the precision with which she placed strips of bark, the way she sat back on her heels to judge which flame was strong enough to take more wood.

The verger was in the hall arranging the psalm books, bare-headed and mittenless.

'When are you leaving for Blackåsen?' the priest asked, his breath a white cloud.

'Tomorrow at daybreak,' he said, pastel fingers trawling the soft backs of the books. 'We will have classes Tuesday, Wednesday and Thursday. I will be back here before Mass on Sunday.'

The priest hesitated. 'Johan, you went with the priest to last year's Catechetical hearings . . .'

'Yes.'

'Did something happen? Something unusual?'

'Not that I can think of.'

'Did the priest seem upset or agitated?'

The verger shook his head.

'Was there anything that upset you?'

'Me? Like what?'

'Oh, I don't know. Anything.'

'No.'

Typical.

'There was a case in the books many years ago. It was written down as *K against the church.*'

'Most cases are trivial. Bickering, insults . . .'

'Apart from that of Elin,' the priest said.

'Yes, apart from that of Elin.' The verger nodded.

'And this one was against "the church".'

'Was it? That does sound strange.'

The priest frowned to show the verger he was not impressed. As verger, he ought to keep himself better informed about the church's affairs than this.

'I am coming with you tomorrow,' he said. 'There are some people I need to see.'

Maija and Jutta walked to Nils's homestead, the past between
them like a cloud.

'I am telling you to be careful,' Jutta said. 'People don't like
other people trying to tell them truths.'

Maija didn't answer. She kept listening for the pack of
wolves, but the forest was quiet.

'You can't undo bygones. My bygones.'

'I can prevent them from happening again.'

Jutta made a clicking noise with her tongue. She didn't
think so.

'I am not scared.'

'There are times when it is wise to be scared.'

Maija scoffed. She remembered Jutta – when it was clear
to both of them she was dying – refusing to undress in the
evening, as if that would stop night from coming. 'Hold my
hand,' she'd said. 'Hold Frederika's,' is what Maija had wanted
to answer, but it had to be her and so she had held it, felt
skin against skin, disgust for her grandmother's weakness and
then guilt for the disgust. She had wanted Jutta to be strong
enough to fend off any fear of dying. She had also known
that Jutta's 'bygones' were what made it so difficult for her to
leave. I'll never be like you, she thought. Never.

They stopped, shoulder by shoulder. There had been a
strong wind and it had blown a large part of the ice bare. The

ice would still swell and break. By the end of the winter it would be streaked white, scarred by ageing. But for now, although it was young, it was already a thick black.

'Frederika is growing up,' Jutta said.

Yes, she was. There was a new thoughtfulness to her daughter. A tiny pause before each act. The image that came to Maija was how in late summer, the sides of trees were sometimes coated by a mass of gore and marrow. Blood stopped flowing through the reindeer antlers as they hardened to bone and the animals rubbed against the trees to remove the beautiful velvety skin. Growth so often came like that, through pain.

'She's becoming like you,' Maija said. 'Though God knows, I've fought it.'

'No,' Jutta said. 'Frederika is nothing like me.'

Maija turned to her grandmother, but Jutta was still looking out over the ice.

The settlers gathered in Nils and Kristina's house, arriving alone or two by two. Some of the older children were there. They scuffled to squeeze in. There was a fire in the fireplace and a bear skin draped over a chair in front of it. A large carpet hung on the wall towards the back. Patterns shimmered in the blond of the sun, or the way churned milk gleamed before it turned to butter. Colours Maija had only ever seen in nature. The material, too, was different. It looked smooth, like water. It was the kind your hand flew up to touch. This might be silk. Maija lingered by it. But normal things took over. Soon, the room smelled of wet dog and sour wool. The light from the window fell in and painted a feeble cross over them. Then the window panes fogged up and they were on their own, hidden from the world.

Nils stepped up on to a chair. He was in his shirtsleeves. Kristina was standing behind him.

'I've called this meeting to discuss forming a village,' he said. 'Eriksson has died, his wife also, the harvest has yet again come to nothing, and now some among us have seen . . . things in the forest. The mountain is taking over. It is time we came together. Time for us to ensure that we are safe.'

Things? What things?

'What things?' Maija asked.

Nils looked to one of Henrik and Lisbet's sons.

The young man reddened. 'A shape. It was behind our cottage, in among the trees. It was black. It ran so fast.' His voice slipped into a high pitch and made him a boy. He cleared his throat.

'Wolf,' Maija said.

'No.' The boy shook his head. 'It was much larger.'

'It was the Devil,' his mother said. 'The mountain belongs to him.'

Beside her, her husband scowled.

'That's a fable.' Daniel pushed off from the wall he was leaning against. 'There are hundreds of similar stories all over Sweden, told by parents to stop their children from going into the forest alone.'

'Only we have, in fact, lost children,' Nils said.

Daniel turned white.

Nils's voice softened. 'I, too, came to Lapland to inhabit a piece of land of my own and farm it with my family, colonising this region for the crown. But something is going on here that isn't natural . . .' He held up his hands. 'I am not saying it is the Devil. I am just saying we'd be safer together, than apart.'

He was skilled. Maija felt the draw of being a part of the whole; of letting somebody else decide.

'I would like to understand why Maija says it was wolves our Hans saw?' Henrik said.

In a way, Henrik was like her, she thought. He, too, knew what it was like to live in the same house as fear.

Maija thought of the pitted claw marks in the wood on her door. The banging throughout the night as the animals threw themselves against the walls of the house. Her daughter's screams.

They were looking at her.

'Have you come across wolves?' Henrik asked.

'Wolves don't go near people,' Daniel said.

'They sometimes crave human flesh,' Lisbet said.

The room fell silent.

Maija could hear them again, the thumps against the walls, but the thought that remained was that had grey-legs wanted to, they would have had her. Yet she hesitated to speak. Things easily twisted and turned the wrong way.

'Perhaps the Lapps are still at their magic and they are bringing this on us,' Lisbet said.

'Someone should speak to the priest,' a voice said. Anna?

'The Church has never done anything for us. This is a Blackåsen matter.'

'If it's sorcery, it's a matter for the Church.'

Maija raised her voice. 'We had a cold summer and then a killer frost – yes, our harvest failed. I did see wolves. They were all adult males. I don't know what that means, but maybe there being no bitches among them changes their behaviour? And Eriksson . . . Eriksson was killed by man, by flesh and blood, like us.'

By one of us, she thought.

The room was silent again, but it was a better silence this time, less worrying. Maija met Henrik's gaze. Henrik nodded, perhaps encouraging her to go on. Maija turned to the boy.

243

'Tell us again,' she said, 'what you saw.'

'A . . . silhouette.'

'Running, you said?'

'More like . . . floating.' The boy looked her in the eyes. He was kneading his knuckles against his thighs. He's not making this up, she thought. He believes in what he's saying and is now realising that seeing something in the forest isn't exciting, but very frightening.

'It could have been a person,' Maija said in a kind voice.

The boy shook his head.

'Or the light playing tricks on you?'

The boy hesitated. He wrinkled his forehead. 'Maybe,' he said.

'It's an easy mistake.'

'Perhaps it was the light.' The boy nodded.

Maija turned to the others. 'Let's not get carried away,' she said.

After that, when all had been said, nothing had been said, and then people nodded to one another, departed, disappeared into the forest, to their own. Maija walked outside. The darkness was so dense, she had a feeling that if she reached out her hand, she would be able to touch it. It would leave her fingers smutty with something like burned rye. We're all going to start seeing things if we aren't careful, she thought. Gustav pushed past her. It surprised her that he'd been there.

The wind had picked up – her throat felt bare and she pulled at her scarf. The sky was thick. More snow on the way. A lot more. She'd cook pheasant for dinner. Then they would use the carcass for soup. The door opened behind her again. The snow squeaked under his weight as Nils stepped out. He looked towards the sky.

'Snow.' He turned to her and raised his brow. 'Belittling the fears of those who have been here much longer than you. Brave. Some might say imprudent.'

It wasn't a question, so she didn't answer.

'A woman trying to discuss important matters, questioning this and that, is both blasphemous and dangerous,' he said. 'Remember what you are, Maija. We forget that and we question the order of God Himself. Stay in your place unless you want to end up like Elin: secluded, separate.'

'You can't make that happen,' she said.

He turned to walk back inside, and now he looked almost amused. 'But I won't have to,' he said, good-naturedly. 'People don't like what is different.'

What was it Eriksson knew about you? she thought.

'Open the door!'

The priest sat up in his bed. There was banging on the door downstairs. A male voice, but light. A boy?

'Open!'

He searched for his cloak in the dark. There was the sound of running feet in the room beneath him, of the door being unbolted.

In his living room, he found the housekeeper in a white nightgown, grey hair sticking out from underneath her cap, and a young man. His cheeks were red. He smelled of frost.

'Message from the King,' the boy said and handed him a roll.

Message from . . .?

The priest took the roll. He felt parchment against his fingertips.

Message from my King.

His heart pounded in his chest. The maid arrived and squatted by the fireplace to build the fire. He turned away from her. He didn't want to share this moment with anyone.

He unrolled the parchment with shaking hands.

On Royal Command . . .

He read the few lines again. This was not a message from the King. It had his seal, but it had been dictated, or even written by somebody else without the King's contribution. His parish was requested to contribute twenty able men to the King's army in early spring, three from the town itself, seventeen from the surrounding mountains.

He turned the paper over but the back of the paper was empty.

Twenty men. That would be almost all men in his parish.

'They burned the whole town,' the boy was telling his housekeeper.

'What?' The priest turned towards the boy, paper roll still in his hand.

'The Russians,' the boy said. 'One week ago. They attacked the coastal town north of us. The people fled to the church. The Russians bolted it and set fire to it. They were fried to death.'

'What?' the priest said again. 'When?'

'A week ago,' the boy repeated.

'Where are they now? The Russians?'

'They left after the attack. They'll be back. They're always back. There were over a hundred people in that church.'

Stop, he thought. Stop. He raised his hand and walked out.

The priest lay down on his bed, parchment roll in hand. He had never known a world without war. But somehow, actually being in the army, the war had felt less real than it did now. They had fought terrible combats during the daytime, but at night, they dressed up for dinner with the King. He had seen things on the battlefield that he would never be able to forget. But at night, they had drunk wine and eaten roasted pig and conversed about politics and women. 'We know why we are doing this,' the King sometimes said. And yes, they knew.

Now, forced to tell twenty parishioners they would have to travel south to join the army – the peasant's war being very different from the one he had experienced – he felt that the wars were like thin fibres with thorny roots that had pushed down deep inside the country, tangled themselves with its very tissue and been allowed to take over.

They can't do it. He thought of the settlers. They are starved. They have nothing. They can't fight any more.

And an edict. Hundreds of them would have been sent out over the country. He crushed the paper roll in his hand.

But the King was God's representative. It was God's edict he had crumpled in his hand. What would happen if you started to question that?

Not the children, he thought. I won't take the young men.

But shall I take the fathers?

Perhaps I'll let each mountain choose their men, he thought. But then people like Nils, and Eriksson, had he still been alive, would never be considered.

The priest lay sleepless, squeezing the crumpled edict in his hand.

Snow rose to the level of their chests. The sun no longer mounted the horizon. Winter's midnight had begun.

Late that morning, Johan Lundgren came to see them. He sat by their table. Her mother was looking at him, as if expecting something. Then she seemed to conclude he wasn't going to give it, and she lowered her head.

'Did you speak to your mother?' he asked Frederika.

Frederika had forgotten. Her mother looked up.

'Dorotea needs more schooling than the others,' he said.

'She does?' her mother said.

'A few more hours every week would be good. Reading and Bible knowledge.'

'I am surprised. At home she reads well.'

Frederika thought of what the priests said happened if you didn't do well at the Catechetical hearing. Even small children burned in hell.

'It might be good,' she said to her mother.

Her mother turned to her and made large eyes, as if Frederika had said something important.

'Mr Lundgren says it won't have to cost us much,' Frederika said, annoyed with her mother. She wasn't paying attention.

The teacher nodded. 'We can begin today.'

'Fine. Frederika, you take her,' her mother said. 'I need to . . .

get more wood,' she said and nodded to herself. She grabbed her woollens.

The teacher rose and walked over to Dorotea.

Frederika edged herself forward so he wouldn't notice the firewood basket was full.

'And so the great darkness has arrived,' Mr Lundgren said.

Dorotea was sitting on the sledge and Frederika was pulling her. The runners sang in the snow.

'What do you think about Blackåsen, Dorotea?' Mr Lundgren asked.

'We're getting used to it,' Frederika said when her sister remained silent.

For a moment, she had almost thought she heard the sound of footsteps following them.

'The priest was planning to come and see you,' Mr Lundgren said, 'but he got a message from the King and couldn't leave.'

Frederika tried to pause between each step to listen.

There was a glimpse of a dark shape to their right. A man. He walked into a clearing between the trees and into the moonlight. It was Eriksson. The knife in his hand gleamed.

At once, her heart raced.

'I am surprised.' Mr Lundgren chuckled. 'So far, he hasn't paid attention to any of the parishioners. Why would he come to see you?'

'He and my mother talk about how Eriksson died,' Frederika said.

Eriksson was staring at her. He bared his teeth and made a low wheezing sound, '*Hnnh. Hnnh.*'

Could others see Eriksson, too? Suddenly, it was crucial that she did not tell the teacher, or make any sign. He wasn't going to be of any help. He would panic. He'd run, and Eriksson would attack. They needed to carry on as usual until . . . Well, until.

'So who do they think killed him?' the teacher said and smiled.

'They don't know.' She forced a steadiness on to her voice. 'They'll try to find out.'

'How on earth will they do that?'

She no longer liked him. He wanted too much.

'Here we are now,' the teacher said and walked into the yard.

Frederika moved so she was behind her sister. She put her hands on her sister's shoulders and pushed her so fast, she almost ran the sledge into the teacher's legs.

Hurry, she thought. Hurry. Eriksson stopped by the line of the trees. He held his arms up over his head stretching towards the moon.

Mr Lundgren walked up on the porch and kicked his shoes against the side of the door.

Eriksson left the forest and walked towards them with long steps. Frederika hauled her sister up the steps.

Open the door. Open it.

The teacher dropped his mitten and bent down to pick it up.

Eriksson stopped beneath the porch. Her teacher turned to face her. Now, she thought. He sees him and Eriksson goes for us.

'I am sure your mother needs you, Frederika,' he said. 'There's no need for you to wait. I can walk Dorotea home afterwards.'

Then Eriksson put his head back. He howled. A long, drawn-out wail. The teacher and Dorotea were looking at Frederika.

They can't hear him, she realised. They can't see him, either.

Eriksson began to laugh.

Frederika took a step to the side and at once Eriksson's knife shot out and cut the air just in front of her. He wasn't going to let her leave. He howled again and the sound sent a shiver down her whole spine.

'I'll wait,' she said.

'You don't have to,' their teacher said again.

'No,' she said. 'I'd like to.'

Frederika sat by the window. Eriksson was standing motionless in the yard. Behind her, Mr Lundgren read sentences, Dorotea repeated after him, he corrected her.

In the window-frame, many letters had been carved with a knife in the wood. There was a scraggly 'J', a 'U', and a long-legged 'K', an 'A', a 'B' . . . Was it children? Perhaps before leaving school for good. She wondered how they'd been able to do it without the teacher seeing. He must have been so angry when he discovered it. She traced the letters with her finger. She had to think of a way for her or Dorotea to be able to stay as long as possible. But if Mr Lundgren didn't see Eriksson, then it would be difficult.

'We're done,' Mr Lundgren said and his chair scraped.

Already? Outside, the yard lay empty.

'What are you doing?' Dorotea asked on the way home.

'What?'

'You keep turning around.'

There was no moon now, and so dark, Frederika couldn't see her. She barely saw to put her feet before her in the snow.

'After what happened to our mother with the wolves, I am just careful,' Frederika said.

'What wolves?'

Frederika tried to see Dorotea, but couldn't. She was struck by a thought. 'Dorotea, have you seen any animals since we came here?'

'Yes,' Dorotea's voice came from the sledge. 'Spiders and ants and—'

'No. Big animals. Like bear. Or wolf?'

'I saw a fox once,' Dorotea ventured. 'In Ostrobothnia.'

Frederika tried to think what Dorotea had been doing when the wolves attacked. Dorotea had been with her in bed. They had hugged and her sister's eyes were closed. Her body had been limp in her arms. Had Dorotea been sleeping? But her mother had seen the wolves? Yes, her mother had seen and heard them for sure.

It wasn't night, but the unending darkness made you conduct yourself as if it were. There was no strength for vigorous activity or loud noises. People moved slowly. The animals were quiet in their pens. The dogs kept their heads low as they crawled closer to the fires. By day, the priest tried to read, but ended up most often sitting with his head in his hand, a book open in his lap on no particular page. In the afternoon, he sometimes walked the paths of this ghost town the bishop had entrusted him with. So little time before he had to share the King's marching orders. A few weeks left to Christmas and the coming of the settlers for six weeks.

The priest tried to force himself into activity. A list, he thought. They needed a list. Winter froze the houses. Come spring, they would see the real damage when the ice supporting the walls melted and things began to sag and lean. But some things ought to be repaired before the settlers arrived and the verger would not have much time between schooling children and church duties.

He found broken windows in two of the houses in Settler Town and removed his mitten to sketch a map for the verger. His fingers began to burn, and he hurried. Somewhere, a door hinge squeaked. He should try to find it. An open door would allow the snow to move inside. He put his mitten back on and raised the lantern to try to spot the errant door. Unless he was right beside it, the lantern would not give enough light to see. His father used to have his lamp on a rod that he carried on his shoulder. Not a bad idea. As a boy walking behind his father, the mild swaying glow was sufficient to permit him to see where he put his feet, while his father murmured away, some story about the yarn of a man. 'We are what we are. We're what we're born. Be grateful, Olof. Be grateful.'

He'd told the King about his father. A clear warm night in Poland. Smell of grass. A lake shimmering in moonlight. The troops valiant. Augustus II yet to be deposed.

'He didn't think man was in charge of his own destiny,' the priest had said, heat in his voice. 'He never saw that man can change.'

'And you do?' the King had asked. It had been dark. The priest had not been able to see more than the other man's profile.

'It is what you do every day: shaping Sweden for generations to come.'

The King didn't answer at first. 'But can you say the two are the same?' he asked then. 'Is changing character as easy as enacting deeds?'

'Both are about making a decision and standing firm.'

Look at me and you, he had wanted to say. Here we sit together, you, the King, and me, your court priest. He'd been excited. He had been thinking about himself and his progress. He now wondered whether there was much more to that conversation than he had thought. Perhaps the King had had doubts and needed his priest.

The door hinge whined again in the wind.

Only, there was no wind.

The priest lifted his lantern high and held it left and then right to see. It was probably an animal that had made the noise.

In summer, he had gone in and out of the many houses and thought about those who built them on the crown's command. Christianise Lapland. Tax Lapland, rather. But now, in winter, the deserted houses were different. Their windows gleamed black, as if he were being watched.

A door slammed. The priest jumped. His heart scurried into his throat. He raised his lantern even higher, this time to hold the darkness away, rather than to see. He had spent most of his childhood in the dark and never minded it. And here he was, a grown man becoming afraid of it.

He began to walk. It was cold. He would go and sit down by his fire. He lengthened his steps. The walls of the houses shone, but he refused to look, focusing on his feet.

At the end of the street there was the same blackness, but the priest knew it as his church green. He walked into it and exhaled.

Not that it made any difference where he was, he thought, and lengthened his steps again.

The handle of the church glittered. Last winter, a boy had put his tongue against the iron and as they ripped it loose, the blood had been a violent red in the snow.

He pulled the heavy church door open and sneaked in. It shut behind him. In the hallway, he let out his breath.

There was a lit candle in the entrance. It couldn't be the verger; he wouldn't be back until the weekend. The priest's shoes made a dull sound as he ran up the steps to his office.

Sofia was waiting for him in his room on the first floor.

'There you are,' she said, voice purring. She was wearing a white fur hat and coat. Her blonde hair was braided. Her voice was soft. She was the kind of woman any man would be happy to come home to.

'I don't see you for a few days,' she said, the tone of her voice mocking, 'I begin to worry.'

'I had a message from the King,' he said.

'Really?' she said.

Her eyes were focused on his lips.

'Just another edict to add to the burden of my chores,' he said.

'Ah,' she said and smiled again. 'Come for dinner tonight.'

'I will,' he said.

When Sofia had left, the priest decided he might as well just get it over with.

It was the young maid who opened the door. Her hands by her sides were larger and redder than ever. She gasped when she saw the priest.

'Sire,' she said in a low voice and curtsied.

'I am here to see your father,' he said.

They were sitting by the table eating cabbage soup. The maid's old parents startled when he entered. The mother hesitated, and he knew she was wondering what she could offer him. He shook his head.

'I'm afraid I am coming with bad news,' he said.

The three of them exchanged glances.

'Bengt, you will be enlisted come spring. The King needs you in his army.'

How old was this man? Grey and small, hands shaking. But what could he do? The verger was in charge of the schooling. His own candidature wouldn't be accepted, nor that of the night man – their roles were considered indispensable in a town. All that remained were this man and the two farmhands.

None of them reacted at first.

Then the young maid said, 'My father is sick,' at the same time as her father said, 'How about the boys? The stable boys?'

'Them, too,' the priest said.

The old man coughed and wheezed, his whole frame labouring as if to squeeze the air out.

'Have mercy,' the mother said.

'There is no choice,' he said.

'I am so sorry,' he said, and left.

The fourth time Frederika met Eriksson, he was in their barn again. She opened the door and saw him, turned and ran, but he was faster than her. At once he was on her. She fell forward and hit the snow so hard, her air left her. The snow burned her cheeks and nose. He spun her over, straddled her and covered her mouth with his hand.

'Shhh,' he whispered just by her face. He smelled of morning breath. Of closed rooms and stale water.

Her eyes filled. She blinked and blinked.

'You are overreacting,' he said and looked her in the eyes.

After a while, she nodded and he let go of her mouth. She had to swallow several times. He rose and pulled her to her feet.

'You hurt me,' she said, after a while. 'My arm still won't heal.'

'Then you ought to have learned your lesson.'

They stood looking at each other.

'Elin had something in her past,' Frederika said. 'Something awful.'

'She did. The first time I saw her, I knew. She had a frailty in the midst of that strength of hers. You'd see it in her eyes when she first looked at you, before her features hardened. This beautiful kernel of dread. Once I knew that, it was easy. She was so infatuated with her fear, she would always choose it.'

Frederika thought about what she had seen inside Gustav. She thought about the trees Eriksson had shown her. Elin and Gustav had had similar experiences – not shared experiences; she believed Gustav had been telling the truth when he said he didn't know Elin – but similar ones. Gustav had been a prisoner at some point, she was pretty certain. The Russians stole children. Frederika's mind played it: the split second of nothingness and then the violence. Perhaps something similar had happened to Elin. She shuddered.

'Why didn't you leave her alone?' she asked Eriksson. 'Hadn't she suffered enough?'

'Don't you see that if it wasn't me, it would have been somebody else? It was what she sought. I loved Elin. Not that she ever knew or cared. She was too busy hating me.'

'But she didn't kill you.'

Eriksson squeezed his lips together. 'Of course she didn't. Now you disappoint me. You have to grow faster than this, Frederika. I've already told you. I am not the most dangerous thing around.'

He shook his head and walked away from her towards the tree line.

There was someone else beneath the pine trees. Eriksson brushed shoulders with him, but this second person didn't move. Straight shoulders. Silver hair. Silver beard. Fearless.

She half ran towards him. 'Eriksson,' she said as she reached him. 'He just passed you.'

Fearless didn't answer. She didn't have to say anything. He knew it all.

'I heard you talk,' he said then. 'This is not for a little girl. Alone outside in midwinter.'

'The mountain won't leave me alone.'

Fearless was silent for a long time.

'Antti told me about you,' he said then. 'Said I owed that much, to make certain you were safe.'

He turned towards her. She wanted him to see that her meanings were good. But his face was cold.

'That's the reason I came,' he said. 'Because Antti asked. We are Christian now. Talk to the priest. Beg God for mercy. Don't go looking in the shadows.'

Her cheeks became hot.

'But I am not looking,' she said. 'He is. They are. The spirits. You know this.'

'I don't know what you're talking about.' Then he seemed to change his mind and leaned towards her and said in a low voice, 'You have no idea what you are trying your hand at. Try to tame the spirits at your own risk. If you fail, they'll tear you apart.'

'But I'm not trying. They won't leave me alone.'

'Go on inside, Frederika.'

'What happened to your drum?' she whispered.

'It's long gone,' he said. 'I burned it myself.'

She watched him leave.

He couldn't have meant for her to pray.

When she was little, she had thought the stars were angels who had made holes in the sky to watch over her, and the light she saw was the glory of heaven. But now, after having called for help, after having reached up, she didn't think there was anyone there.

In the evening, Frederika and her mother sat by the kitchen table. Her mother was knitting a blue woollen sock. Frederika pulled the tallow candle on the table towards her. She thought about Fearless and about Eriksson. She pressed the hot wax close to the flame with her thumb. Turned the candle around. Pressed some more.

'Mamma.'

'Mm-hm?'

'Dorotea didn't hear the wolf.'

Her mother lifted her head.

'That day when you were attacked. She didn't hear it.'

They both glanced towards the bed where Dorotea was sleeping.

'Why do you say that?' Maija asked.

Frederika thought again about what Dorotea's body had felt like. The weight of her. And the smell had been that of a sleeping Dorotea. Sweet. Vinegary. 'I think she slept,' she said.

Her mother's forehead was wrinkled. 'Well, I don't know. Dorotea is still little. Perhaps the stress . . .'

'Don't you think it is strange that she didn't hear it?'

'Frederika, do you remember that wooden stick? The one you stuck in the snowdrift by the porch?'

'It's gone.'

'I know, but why did you want it there? Why did you say I couldn't move it?'

She didn't know. It had belonged there. 'I was going to use it,' she said, though she couldn't remember what for.

Her mother sat up straight. 'This is no good. The other settlers have seen the wolves, too. We talked about it at the settler meeting.'

Her mother's mouth became a thin line in her face.

'You have this trait, Frederika, of looking for the mysterious and letting yourself be overcome. I shouldn't have let you spend all that time with Jutta when you were growing up.'

Her mother shook her head. 'These kinds of thoughts, they spread rot.'

The yellow flame arced close to her fingertips. Frederika pushed the candle away.

In town, the merchants' calls vied with one another:
'Reindeer pelt.'
'Bear pelt.'
'Trade for salt?'
'This winter has been like no other.'
'I need shoes.'
'I have ptarmigans.'
'I can get those myself any time.'
'What about window glass?'

Maija sighed. The last time they had been here, in the wake of Eriksson's death, it had only been the settlers. The last time, her husband had been by her side. Paavo. She wondered where he was and what he was doing. He'll be back, she thought. Either just before the snow begins to thaw, or immediately after. But he could have written . . .

All along the verge of the church green, houses were alive. Shops. Outside, the merchants had built racks on which to hang the dead animals and thick furs that the settlers and the Lapps might bring to trade. Behind the church, further up on a hill, the night man had climbed the gallows and hung a new rope over its frame. By the frozen river, someone had set up a small brewery. She was glad they were here. The journey had been foul, but she imagined here in the valley the weather would be less fierce. And they would not be alone. People shuffled forward in the dark. The breaths from horses' nostrils were slow and large, the long hair on their hooves full of ice clumps and snow. The file passed the vicarage. The golden candle holders were visible through the tall windows, and people swerved so as not to walk on the light thrown on to the snow, as if, coming from inside the vicarage, even that were sacred.

Then she saw him, the priest, and fell back though he could not see her. He was standing by the window together with a blonde woman in a red dress. The woman turned towards him and touched his arm. The priest smiled. She had assumed he did not have anyone, though she didn't know why. After all, he was educated. Tall. Poised. She guessed you could say 'fine-looking'.

The woman's hair was tied back. She and the priest stood watching those outside, like royals on a balcony.

By the muted, light blue mass of the church, they turned right into Settler Town. On both sides of the street, yellow flames from tar torches flanked them. Then the church bell began to ring.

They were to share a house with Daniel and Anna and their children, and so they had travelled together; the two families and their animals.

'We used to share with the Janssons.' Anna interrupted herself.

The family that had disappeared. Maija wanted to tell her she was not superstitious, but saying the words would make it seem as if she were.

She helped Dorotea to sit down on the bed. She thought about the priest and his woman. The light in the house had been so yellow and seemed warm. This house was ice-cold. A few of the window panes were missing. Daniel squatted and there was the clinking sound of flint hitting flint.

Through the gaping hole in the window, the people who passed outside were dark shades. Their feet crunched on the snow. Their voices were muted.

'What about our neighbours?' Maija asked.

'All the settlers from Blackåsen are on the same street.'

There was a feeble fire now in the fireplace. Daniel nodded to Anna to care for it and walked out. He came back with a few planks of wood with which he covered the hole in the window.

'Can we go out?' Frederika pulled her sleeve. Dorotea was standing behind her.

Maija hesitated.

'Yes,' she said. 'See where your schooling will take place, and see what we need to do to register at Customs.'

She watched her younger daughter hobble to the door.

'Don't overdo it, Dorotea,' she said, 'and take good care to look where we live, so you find your way back.'

She pictured the two of them, walking hand in hand towards the marketplace, pictured them gaping at the size of the sugar lumps, sneezing at the smell of the spices, mouths watering at the sight of bread. She would have given them the world. She would have.

Lapp Town was the area furthest away from the church. The timber houses looked much like those built for the settlers, but there were also cone-shaped shacks, and the whole district was fenced in. The reindeer were already in their fold. The Lapps had hung large orange torches on the poles of the enclosure. Maija watched the animals for a while, hundreds of them, flank to flank, digging with their feet in the snow for lichen, locking antlers when they got too close. Every now and then, one of them took a few leaping steps, some others

265

would tag on and then snow smoke would draw over the herd in a glittering cloud. Maija raised her face towards the shimmer, and then had to lower it again when it descended on her and began to sting her face.

A woman approached. She wore a colourful dress with broad hem ribbons. There was a triangular shawl across her shoulders. She said something in a strange language.

Maija let go of the wooden railing. 'I was looking for Fearless.'

Fearless seemed both shorter and older than he'd been the last time she saw him. His skin was burned and the wrinkles by his eyes seemed carved. He made no sign of recognising her, but stepped to the side. There were two other men inside. One of them was stirring a pot over the fire. The other one was sitting down, legs crossed, sewing. It was the young Lapp with the black, long hair.

Fearless nodded to the settle. The table in front of it was covered by a reindeer skin. He picked up a knife. It disappeared in his hand as he cut through the pelt with small sawing movements. You could watch this for ever, she thought, a man good at his work.

'I wonder why you have come this time,' he said.

Yes, why had she come? It had been an impulse. Or, if she was honest with herself, she had known she would go and find him as soon as they arrived. Perhaps out of guilt at their last meeting.

'Things aren't too good on Blackåsen,' she said.

He held the leather up to look at its shape against the light.

'I worried in case some settlers might be quick to blame your people,' she said.

'Wouldn't be the first time.'

He began to cut anew through the pelt. When he had

finished, he walked across the room to give the pieces to the young Lapp who sat sewing on the floor. He came back, sighed and looked at Maija. 'So what's the grievance this time?'

'The harvest failing, Eriksson dying . . . Some settlers are claiming to have seen things in the forest and then they remember the children who disappeared.'

'All those are things that have befallen us, too,' Fearless said.

Maija nodded. The other men hadn't thrown one glance their way, but their movements had slowed down.

'They're just scared,' she said. 'It's the traditions of your past.'

'There are those among you who are more skilled in those practices nowadays than we are.'

'Among us?'

Surely, Fearless knew that Elin was dead?

He didn't continue.

'Well.' She rose. 'That's what I came to say.'

As she closed the door behind her, she saw the other men turn towards him.

The Christmas Mass began at dawn. It was tricky. Arriving early, but not by too much. The dead had their Mass before the living and that wasn't one you wanted to attend.

Frederika sighed with relief on seeing live people inside. At the entrance, the verger handed them the psalm book.

'He said I didn't need it now,' Dorotea whispered, as she limped beside her down the nave.

Frederika was watching the lit chandeliers in the roof. She didn't think she had ever seen that many candles burning at the same time. 'What?' she said.

'Mr Lundgren, yesterday at the market. He said I didn't need extra schooling. There's another girl who is worse than me.'

Her sister's voice was so full of joy that Frederika had to look at her. She hadn't realised her sister minded being thought a bad reader.

The church was cold. Their mother pointed to one of the pews and they sat down. Further towards the front was Henrik's blond hair. Beside him, the bonnet that must be Lisbet, and then a tall silver head: Nils. The priest arrived and walked towards the front. As he passed, there was a sound from the back and Frederika turned. The Lapps entered: Fearless in their midst, head high. She remembered their conversation and should have been angry. Instead, she felt ashamed: for her inexperience, her thankfulness when she thought he'd come to help, her failure to say the right things. Her eyes caught in Antti's. He raised his head ever so little, then he walked out.

The priest was climbing the pulpit.

'I need to go out,' Frederika whispered to her mother.

'Now?' Her mother looked at her, back towards the door, to the front towards the priest, back at her again.

'I have to go. I'll sneak in afterwards.'

Antti was waiting for her on the stairway leading up to the tower. He turned and walked upstairs. She tried to glide up the stairs as he did, but she was too heavy. Each of her steps creaked on wood. Antti walked into a room where a fire crackled. There were shelves lined with books from floor to ceiling.

Frederika hesitated.

'The priest doesn't need his room right now,' Antti said.

Still she dawdled.

'It's cold outside,' Antti said.

He squatted down in front of the fire. She hunched down beside him.

'Eriksson is still following me,' she said. 'Though not here.'

She realised as she said it, that it was true. Eriksson had not come to the town. Perhaps he needed to stay close to the mountain?

Antti was staring into the fire.

'Then there are wolves. They attacked my mother, but only my mother and I can see them. Though my mother says I mustn't talk like that.'

She wasn't used to squatting. She sank down on her bottom.

'I asked one of our elders,' Antti said. 'They don't want to talk about it. But she said two things were certain: when the spirits call, whoever they call needs to prove themselves worthy. The other thing that is certain is that there will be guidance.'

Frederika shook her head. 'Fearless doesn't want to help me. I tried. He said not to get involved.'

They sat in silence.

'These spirits . . . are they evil?' Frederika asked.

'No. Or, I guess, they can be. It depends on whose hands they are in. The elder said the gifts they bring can then be used to do either good or evil.'

'What gifts?'

'Justice, protection, answers.' He shrugged. 'Healing.'

Healing. Frederika thought of Dorotea's feet.

There was a scraping from over by the door. For one chilling moment, Frederika was certain the priest would walk in and find them there. There was someone, a shadow. But then, rather than move away, it faded. Antti was still staring into the fire.

'If you are found worthy, you'll be able to give more to humans around you than you ever imagined.'

He rose.

She wanted to tell him not to go, though she knew they had to leave before Mass was over. 'I have no idea how to speak with the spirits,' she said.

'I can't help you with that. Watch out for people, Frederika.' Now he looked at her. 'Make no mistakes. The hunts for sorcerers are recent, the fear still close, easy to resurrect. Speak with the wrong person and they will make you burn. Even people you never expected.'

It was the void after the sermon. Inside the church hall, her mother turned her head so that Frederika saw her profile. I am here, Mamma, Frederika thought.

Her mother nodded as if she'd heard, and turned back towards the front. The crown of Dorotea's head tilted and came to rest against her mother's shoulder.

Frederika looked to the profile of Fearless. Help me, she thought. Please help me.

But Fearless didn't move.

Back in Ostrobothnia, their Christmas celebrations had begun with Mass and were followed by a bath. Paavo would make a fire beneath the big iron tub in the barn and fill it with snow. They'd take turns to sit down in it, wash their hair, scrub their bodies, the girls squealing with horror that was really joy.

Maija had hung a blanket in the roof to give them some privacy, and she had filled the washbasin with snow. It wasn't Ostrobothnia, but they would be clean.

'Can I go first?' Dorotea asked.

'Ask your sister.'

Frederika nodded without looking at them. She had taken off her clothes and sat down on them, facing the fire.

Dorotea sat down in the washbasin with her legs over the edge. Maija scrubbed her younger daughter's hair with snow, scrubbed her face and neck. Her daughter shrieked.

'Rub your skin with cloth before you dress,' Maija said, 'so that you dry.'

Frederika rose. She had grown tall and her body was spindly. Maija hesitated. How strange. She no longer knew whether she should help her older daughter.

'Do you want me to wash your hair for you?' Maija asked.

'No. I'll do it myself.'

Frederika huddled over the basin, ribs protruding. Her long hair hid her face. It was no longer a child's body. Not quite a woman's yet, either, but the child was gone. She put snow in her hands and rubbed her chest and neck. Her skin pulled together in tiny bumps.

'What's that?' Maija asked.

'What?' Frederika said, but moved her left arm to her side, as if to hide it with her body.

Maija took a step forward. 'This.' She lifted Frederika's arm.

There was a two-inch-long rip on her daughter's arm. Half of it had healed, leaving behind a ruddy scar. Half of it was still crusty yellow.

'I hurt myself in early winter,' Frederika said.

'But this is a bad injury . . .'

Frederika stood up.

'No, let me look at it,' Maija said. 'Why didn't you tell me?'

'It's nothing.'

'What do you mean "nothing"?'

Frederika snatched her arm loose and bent for her clothes. She pulled her dress over her head and wriggled it down to cover her legs, moved the blanket to the side and disappeared.

Maija was staring after her. Her baby had wounds she didn't know about. When had Frederika stopped telling her things? I don't know her, she thought.

'She hurt herself in the forest,' Dorotea said, 'when I was in school.'

Maija lifted up each item of clothing beside her, folded it and stacked them on top of each other into a neat heap.

'If I didn't go to school, I could help look after her,' Dorotea said.

'We brought salted reindeer,' Anna said, when Maija removed the blanket she had hung up.

Maija was looking at Frederika.

'We have grayling,' Frederika said, without meeting her mother's gaze. 'I'll set the table.'

Frederika tied her hair up in a twist and nudged Anna's daughters to help her. As they put the plates on the table, Maija watched her elder daughter. Her wrists were fine, her movements smooth and precise. I don't know you, she thought again. She guessed there were things Maija ought to talk to Frederika about. Things that a mother told a daughter.

'What did you think of the sermon?' Anna asked as they sat down to eat. 'He's good, I think, our new priest.'

The candlelight made her eyes seem greener and her lips and cheeks tinted.

'I like hearing the Bible read at Christmas,' Maija said. 'It's the tradition, I guess.'

Daniel reached for bread.

'The Lapps were all there,' Anna said.

There was a pause in Daniel's movement.

'Why wouldn't they be?' Maija asked. She looked from Anna to Daniel.

Anna glanced at Daniel.

'Nils said he'd talk to settlers from other mountains and hear if any of them have had recent problems with the Lapps,' she said.

Maija wondered if this meant she was no longer invited to the settler meetings.

'You don't think Blackåsen's bad luck has anything to do with the Lapps, do you?' Maija asked.

'They have powers,' one of Anna's daughters piped up.

Her mother hushed her. Then she touched Maija's arm. 'Maija, you are new here. It's better we make enquiries now.'

'We might be new, but we know the Lapps,' Frederika said.

'Oh?' Anna said.

Daniel had raised his eyebrows.

'I wouldn't say we know them,' Maija said. 'Fearless left his goats with us for the winter.'

'He left them with you? He normally goes to Nils,' Anna said.

'My mother is good with the animals,' Dorotea said. 'She made our barren cow give milk.'

Now it was Maija who hushed her daughter. 'Our homestead might have been closer to their route this year,' she said.

'What happened to Fearless' family?' Frederika asked.

'They disappeared,' Daniel said.

Maija looked from her daughter to Daniel. No wonder Fearless had said that everything had befallen the Lapps, too. And this disappearance, Nils had forgotten to mention.

'Yes, but how?'

'His wife had taken their baby to town to be baptised – there was some problem with the reindeer, and Fearless stayed behind. That's when the big forest fire broke out. They were never found.'

'So they died in the fire,' Frederika said.

'Fearless spent months searching,' Daniel said, 'but found nothing. There ought to have been remains.'

'So what does he think happened?' Maija asked.

Daniel shook his head. 'The old priest said that Fearless found peace in Jesus and he stopped his search.'

Maija shivered. The worst farewell must be the no farewell, to have someone you loved vanish from your life without leave-taking. As if it hadn't meant anything. As if it never was. The image of Paavo came before her.

Dorotea caught her eyes. Her cheeks were red and her eyes gleamed.

Yes, Maija thought. Let's forget about this, for one night.

All of it. Let's pretend that all we have to worry about this night are the Christmas celebrations. She leaned forward and winked at her younger. Dorotea's face brightened. Maija rose and went to take out the parcel she had hidden underneath the bed.

In August, Maija had made wool thread, dyed it the clearest blue and wove cloth on the loom in the barn. The colour she'd created amazed her. It was like having a piece of the sky in their barn. She had sewn the dresses during the late autumn evenings.

'Ah!' Dorotea said when she saw it. 'Can I try it on? Please?'

Seeing her joy, Maija had to laugh. Frederika stroked the cloth of her dress with her hand.

'Don't you like yours, Frederika?' Maija asked.

The girl nodded, but left the dress without unfolding it.

Dorotea held out her hands and in them was a birch fungus so springy Maija would be able to use it as a pincushion.

'Frederika and I found it,' Dorotea said, 'when we searched for branches for new brooms. I hid it all autumn.'

Maija hugged her. 'Just what I needed.'

Frederika handed her some braids made from dried scent grass.

'That is so thoughtful,' Maija said. 'When we come home, we'll put it in our summer clothes and, come spring, we'll smell like the ladies from the south.'

Dorotea still had a parcel in her hand. 'This is for the priest,' she said when she saw Maija looking.

'The priest?' Maija said.

'It's his Christmas present,' she said.

Maija didn't dare to look at Daniel and Anna.

'So will you take me to him?' her daughter asked.

* * *

Maija and Dorotea walked to the priest's dwelling. The air was easy to breathe, high and clear. There were lights in the windows, music coming from somewhere. As they came to the church green, far away, the lines of the white mountains were clean, rolling together with the dark sky. Dorotea had stuck her hand in Maija's. She had a funny way of holding hands, keeping her own absolutely straight, which meant that Maija had to do the actual holding.

There was not much light in the priest's house.

'He's not home,' Maija said. She pictured the blonde woman she'd seen him with. They probably celebrated Christmas with friends or family.

Dorotea stepped up the stairs anyway, to knock on the door. It took a while, but then there was a sound and the priest opened.

'You're home,' Maija said. 'I mean . . . good,' she said.

He'd raised his chin, but lowered it again. He wasn't wearing a priest's clothes, but trousers and a shirt. He looked different without his attire. Seeing a man's throat made him appear more vulnerable. She wondered if he missed the collar when it wasn't there.

'Can we come in?' Dorotea asked.

The priest had been sitting in front of the fire on his own. On the table, there was a single plate and a glass of wine. He looked at it, too. She expected him to explain away his solitude – most people did, but when he didn't, she liked him for it.

'Would you like something to eat?' he asked.

'No,' she said. 'We've eaten. It was Dorotea . . . she has something for you.'

Her daughter stuck her hand in the priest's and pulled him with her. She handed him the little parcel and beckoned for him to bend down. She whispered something in his ear. Then she said, loud enough for her mother to hear: 'I would like something to eat. Pudding would be nice.'

'Dorotea!' Maija said.

'It would be my pleasure,' the priest said to her daughter and bowed. He wasn't making fun of her, she thought. His smile was tender.

He rang the bell on the wall. There were footsteps and a plump woman entered.

'Could we please have dessert,' the priest said. 'I have guests.'

The housekeeper had brought rice porridge and nuts, apples and gingerbread cookies. Dorotea talked and ate and asked for a napkin to take some food home to her sister. Then she fell asleep in her chair.

The priest and Maija sat in silence and watched the fire. I should go, she thought. I must wake Dorotea up so we can leave. Frederika will worry. Daniel and Anna will talk. But she remained where she was. Just a little bit longer.

'I am glad you came,' he said.

In the light of the fire, his eyes were a kind blue. Suddenly, she, too, wanted to give him something.

'The parishioners like you,' she said.

He began to laugh. She made a stern face, but then she joined him. What a thing to say.

The priest rose and covered her daughter with a blanket. He sat down again.

'Christmas,' he said. 'Christmas and then another year.'

'Yes. It gives you hope.'

'Hope? Myself, I always feel trepidation.'

That surprised her.

'It is clean. It is new,' she said. 'A chance to start over.'

'Precisely. One has to start it all over.'

She saw what he meant.

'I didn't think priests felt trepidation,' she said.

'Do you really think they are so different from you?'

Yes, she thought. No, she thought. How strange. She looked him over. He had narrowed his eyes towards the flames and was supporting his chin in his hand. Solitude at a time like Christmas was setting yourself up for melancholy, she thought and was about to say it. But she liked him for his frailty.

'Some people on Blackåsen are blaming the Lapps for Eriksson's death,' she said. 'I am worried I made it worse. I spoke with Fearless. I just wanted to warn him, but perhaps some things are best just left.'

She surprised herself. It's because he's a priest, she thought. There is this urge to confess, to tell him everything.

'Nils wants a village,' she added.

The priest glanced at her. 'He talked to me, too. He said you all wanted it for the sake of ensuring calm, but, I think, he probably just sees a chance to be in charge.'

Most likely, she thought. If only he didn't do it by encouraging fear. We are newcomers, the priest and I. We don't understand why the others are so fearful.

'Is there a record of Elin's hearing?' she asked.

'I haven't come across one, but we can talk to the old priest's widow. She was here at the time.'

She nodded.

'The King is requesting twenty men for the army from our parish this spring,' the priest said.

Twenty people. And why was he telling her? It was a while before she dared look at him.

'I know there is no choice.' The priest was still staring into the fire. He shrugged and looked tired and grey.

'There's been war for a long time,' she said.

He shrugged again.

'The kings did not always decide everything,' she said. 'There was a time when they listened to the people.'

Their eyes caught and neither of them moved for a long time. The skin underneath his eyes was thin. He had tiny wrinkles at the inner corners.

'We're on dangerous grounds,' he said with a quiet voice.

She found it was difficult to breathe.

'It's time for me to go,' she said and rose.

'I'll carry her home for you.'

He lifted Dorotea up with his hands under her arms and arranged her so that her head leaned towards his shoulder and wrapped his arms around her.

Maija took her scarf, covered her daughter and tucked the edges in towards the priest's chest. She saw his coat and lifted it from the back of the chair and hung it over his shoulders. She avoided meeting his eyes.

Outside, in wisps of unearthly greens and blues, Northern lights twirled around the stars. At places, they seemed to hang down to the earth, like fairies' curtains.

'What did my daughter give you?' she asked, and added, 'You don't have to answer.'

'Feathers,' he said. 'She said it was wings for the bird for whom the hawk's plumage was too heavy.'

Maija loved so much she hurt. What on this earth did I do to deserve this child? she thought.

As they came close to the house, Maija saw that Daniel had lit large tar torches by the four corners. They would burn the whole night long and, supposedly, keep them safe from evil. She didn't scoff or get annoyed. She didn't mind at all.

The crowd of people was folding away, creating a path for him to pass. The priest thought of Moses in the Red Sea. It could be lonely being a priest. He'd told Maija he'd meet her at the market. It would be better if people thought they had just bumped into each other, was what he'd thought. Why would he even be thinking about that?

He noticed her before she saw him, pausing by one of the stands, pointing at something, her hair glowing white in the darkness. Before he could catch it, his heart soared in his chest and then he felt a pang of pain. He stopped. He should go back home. But if he didn't keep his word, she'd probably come and find him.

'Good morning, priest,' the merchant said, but looked at Maija, eyes gleaming.

Maija didn't acknowledge the priest's arrival.

'The carpet,' she said and pointed.

'This one?' The merchant turned and lifted it up with both hands. Sunshine and shiny cream, flickering orange in the light of the torches. The merchant unfolded it but didn't offer it for her to feel. She might be attractive, but in the merchant's mind she was only a peasant, the priest thought, and felt a stitch of anger.

'It is valuable?' Maija asked.

The tradesman licked his lips. 'It comes from the trade routes of the East. Trust me, you cannot afford it.'

'Then I guess you are charging too much for your trinkets,' Maija said, and winked.

The merchant raised his hand and touched his heart. He was laughing.

Maija turned to the priest. She sparkled with cold.

'Are you ready?' he asked.

He walked ahead of her. He lengthened his steps, forcing her to hurry to keep up. Good, he thought. That should show her. Show her what? He didn't understand himself. They reached the vicarage at the side of the square opposite the church. He entered without knocking. A maid met them in the hallway. The priest handed her his fur. Maija shook her head.

'I'll tell her you are here,' the maid said, and showed them into one of the rooms.

Maija was looking around. The priest tried to see what she saw. The tall, iron-framed windows that stretched to the ceiling. The long brown silk curtains. The walls, stone, chalked crispy white. The two chairs by the fire, the settle, the small wooden table.

'Sofia is the widow of the former priest,' he said.

Maija glanced at him.

The door opened. Sofia smiled when she saw him, and then there was no more than a flutter, but it was there: a hesitation as she noticed Maija. Her dress hissed as she walked to stand by his side. Her blonde hair curled by her ears and fell in a thick torrent down her shoulders. The skin on the hand that touched his arm glowed, its nails pale and short. There was a summery smell of roses.

'I am Sofia,' she said to Maija.

'Maija.'

Maija nodded. Her mouth was knotted. This time, the priest knew what she was not looking at: her own grey jumper, frayed at the sleeves, the rough skin on the back of her hands, her black, thick woollen skirt, her stitched leather shoes.

Maija untied her scarf with one hand and pulled it off her head.

Sofia's hand was still holding on to his sleeve. It took all his willpower not to shake it off.

'Maija is from Blackåsen,' the priest said. 'We came to ask you to tell us more about Elin's hearing.'

'Why?'

'Just to be certain it didn't have anything to do with her husband's death.'

'Aha.' Sofia removed her hand. The priest exhaled. She walked away to open the door and say something to the maid, then returned to her guests. 'Please sit down,' she said and pointed to the fire.

Sofia took a seat on the settle. The priest sat down in one of the armchairs. Sofia gave him a quick glance, then spread her dress wider. Maija sat down at the edge of the other chair.

'Elin's enquiry . . .' Sofia said. She put her hands in her lap. 'What would you like to know?'

The priest shrugged. 'How it arose, what happened . . . all of it.'

'Hmm,' Sofia said and looked to the roof as if gathering her thoughts. 'Well, Elin always kept to herself, held herself apart. I don't think any one of us really knew her. I had heard she used herbs and read over wounds, but . . .' Sofia shrugged. 'She was first accused by a settler from Blackåsen. She helped to deliver his calf. They didn't see eye to eye about something and two days later, the calf died.'

A calf was valuable, the priest thought. It would have been hard to accept that it had just died.

'From there, it escalated. One of the night man's sons said

he'd seen Elin talk to her horse. He said the horse bent down for her to mount it. She was seen walking on water down by the Poor's Bridge . . .'

Oh God. The priest had heard similar stories a hundred times.

'There was no stopping things. Every day, there were new accusations. It was like people had waited for the opportunity of having someone to blame.'

'Who was the settler?' Maija asked.

'What?'

'The settler whose calf died?'

'His name was Eronen. He is long gone now.'

Maija exhaled and her face lightened.

Sofia looked at her and raised her brows.

'That explains things,' Maija said. 'Eronen is our uncle. He didn't tell us this. Didn't think we'd go through with trading our homestead for his if we knew there had been any problems, most likely. I am surprised he dared to accuse Eriksson's wife. How did Eriksson take it?'

'He stormed into my husband's office and demanded he annul the hearing. Luckily, Karl-Erik – the bishop – had already arrived, otherwise I don't know what Eriksson would have done.

'It was the strangest thing,' Sofia continued. 'The hearing went on for three days. It was very frightening. The first two days, as soon as anyone spoke against Elin, Eriksson counter-accused them . . . It was stated that Lisbet could identify sorceresses by seeing some sort of light, and she was adamant Elin was one of them. People told stories of all the things Elin had done . . . Yet on the morning of the third day, the bishop said what he'd heard was not enough to order a trial. He was closing the hearing down. And that's when Eriksson stood up and insisted the trial go ahead. He said he wanted Elin exonerated rather than always having suspicion surrounding her.'

'Really?' the priest asked. 'He was taking a big risk.'

'How did people react?' Maija asked.

'We were all stunned. Elin just stared at her husband.'

'And the bishop?' the priest asked.

'At first he turned white. He stumbled on his words. But from then on, the hearing was like a battle between the two of them, Eriksson arguing for a trial, the bishop against.'

'How did it end?' Maija asked.

'In the afternoon, Eriksson stood up and said that he had just ensured they looked into the issue properly. He said he didn't want to have Elin go through the ordeal again.' Sofia shook her head. 'The nerve. I would say he had become bored and wanted to go home.'

'And the bishop accepted that?'

'He immediately declared the hearing closed.'

The bishop had been relieved that it was over, the priest thought.

'Was Lisbet sick before this hearing?' Maija asked.

Sofia frowned. 'I don't think she was.'

Maija nodded to herself.

'What?' the priest asked her.

'I was just thinking that that's why she's so frightened now. She would have seen her illness as Elin's retribution.'

They were silent for a while.

'So did something happen that made Eriksson argue for a trial and the bishop against?' Maija asked.

Sofia shook her head. 'I don't know.'

Frederika was washing the dishes. The mound of plates was immense. She had to wipe each wooden plate as she cleaned it. If water sat in them too long, they swelled and then cracked when they dried. She was tired. There were more dreams. They were so vivid, she woke up feeling as if she had been up all night. She kept dreaming about the man in the trench. Those dreams frightened her. It was clear to her that the shapes that followed him were there with ill intent. But the moment that clasped her heart with terror was when the walls alongside him began to crumble. It was such a widespread collapse. Each time, she was left with the feeling that it was the whole world that was falling in on itself.

There were new dreams, too, about Eriksson. She would see his back as he walked up the mountain towards the glade. He, too, was being followed. But she never saw their faces.

She paused and rested her wrists on the edge of the handbasin. If only Jutta had still been around. She couldn't talk to Dorotea, she was too little. Antti only wanted his spirits for his people. Her mother could have understood, if she had wanted to. That thought made something stir in her chest.

Beneath her hands, the filthy water seemed to shimmer. Green-blue sunshine. Say hello to the sea, Frederika thought. 'Hello, water,' she whispered and spread her fingers wide, wide. The water shivered, hesitated, but then it folded away from her fingers. Frederika gasped. The water began to coo, as if she had caressed it.

Then the door behind her opened.

'Come,' her mother said to Dorotea.

Frederika kicked the leg of the chair on which the washbasin was standing. Some water spilled over the edge and on to her legs. The water screeched. She threw the rag on the floor.

And so it came about that she ended up going to the church.

The church was empty. Or so she thought. Then, too late, she realised he was sitting on one of the benches just by her side: Fearless, his arms crossed on the pew in front of him, leaning forward as if in prayer. She thought of leaving, but she, too, had the right to be there. They flashed before her, a myriad of days and nights, Fearless, alone on his knees on the hard floor under the cross, begging and crying to a silent God.

Fearless sat up, and she knew that somehow she had just walked through his head and he had felt it.

'Still at it then,' he said.

'Help me,' she said.

He didn't respond.

'I have no choice,' she said.

She felt a sudden pressure on her chest. As if someone had placed a hand against her heart. Warmth spread throughout her torso and opened her up. It made her think of the glimmering water. Then the pressure was gone. She felt cold.

'You like it too much,' Fearless said. She couldn't quite read the tone of his voice. It wasn't anger as much as sadness.

'There is still choice, Frederika,' he said, 'and I think you know this. But once you begin this journey, you leave choice behind. Then only something of immense importance can hurl you far enough from the path for you to leave it without being killed.'

'Are you free now?'

'Yes,' he said.

She wasn't certain he was telling the truth.

'Was it your family going missing that hurled you away?'

He turned to look at her and his eyes were black with anger. She shouldn't have mentioned them, but now she, too, was angry.

'You're being selfish,' she said. 'People who hear them have a . . .' – she was searching for words – 'a responsibility towards those who come after, and a duty towards all the others.'

'You are talking of things you don't understand,' Fearless said and rose. 'This is not some make-believe. It's not some childish game. This is for warriors.'

'Eriksson is visiting me,' she said. 'We need to find out who killed him.'

Fearless scoffed. 'Eriksson? Of all things.' He shook his head. 'If you let the spirits take the lead, you're making your first mistake.'

The spirits? No, she was talking about Eriksson.

She grabbed at his arm as he passed her. 'I dream,' she said. 'Something awful is about to happen. I don't understand my dreams.'

He shrugged her off. He didn't even look at her as he left.

Frederika could have screamed. Stupid Fearless. He had to help. And then she became angry with Jutta, too. Stupid Jutta. Jutta shouldn't have died. She had promised.

'Don't die until I have grown up,' Frederika would say.

'I won't,' Jutta would promise.

'I mean it.'

'Me, too. Because your mother doesn't teach you the old ways, it's my task to guide you.'

And still she had gone and died.

And then, of course, Frederika became angry with her mother.

The cold air hurt as Frederika walked from the church to the streets in Settler Town. She pushed her chin further into her scarf. The wetness of her breath on the wool came to rest against the bottom of her nose. There were candles in the windows. But here in the streets, the black sky had fallen and was lying face down and flat-handed on the earth itself.

She came to their house, just as her mother opened the door. She had the two rabbit skins they had brought to trade thrown over one shoulder.

'I am going to the market,' she said. 'Come with me.'

'I don't want to,' Frederika said.

'These tempers of yours,' her mother said, 'they don't suit you. I asked you to come – you come.' She stopped. 'Have you been crying?'

Her voice was efficient. The way she was asking, as if Frederika were just another chore.

'No,' Frederika said.

She turned and began to walk. Her mother paused, but then joined her.

'Salt and alcohol,' she said.

'Alcohol?'

'To clean Dorotea's feet.' Her mother glanced at her. 'She's brave, but this is not going well.'

'What do you mean? She is much better.'

Her mother sighed. 'The rot just continues. I have been thinking about how often in medical matters, there is like a rush in the body after injury. The hurt person feels better and you think all is healing. Then it is as if the damage catches up with them and that's when often it goes wrong.' Her mother pressed her lips together. 'I am worried.'

'Then why don't you do something?'

'I am.'

'No, you're not.'

Her mother grabbed her arm. 'You'd better explain yourself,' she said, eyes narrow.

'You could heal her.'

'I know some things, but I don't know everything.'

'That's not what I mean. Jutta said you healed your own legs.'

'God.' Her mother let go of Frederika's arm and began walking. 'Your great-grandmother brought misery on so many people with her superstitions, and yet she didn't know to stop. I did exercises, I stretched the muscles in my legs and worked to build them up. It had nothing to do with magic. This is why I decided to become an earth-woman. I wanted to know more about the body, its disorders and what can be done about them. As for Dorotea, we have to keep infection at bay.'

They had reached the market. The square was rolling, a dark mass of people, moving in between the stands lit by tar torches.

Maija headed down one row. Frederika followed her. The dry snow was squeaking underneath their shoes. Frederika was distracted for a moment by a booth displaying amber: rounded drops in ochre and brown.

'Take.' The tradesman's cheeks were fat, his eyes slits from squinting at his stones against the light. He leaned forward, took off his mitten and picked up one of the larger beads. His hand was broad with short fingers, and the back of it was hairy. She took off her mitten and received it, felt how light and warm it was despite its size, despite winter.

'They can heal,' he said. 'Both body and soul.'

She knew it. It was in the light twirling inside the stone.

Her mother's voice from behind her: 'We're after salt and alcohol—' She interrupted herself and stepped forward, beside Frederika. 'You have herbs,' she said.

'Of course.' The tradesman's voice had taken on chimes as he eyed her mother. 'What complaint are you seeking help for?'

Her mother pointed to one of the jars, glowing orange in the light of the torches.

'These?' The tradesman lifted it up.

The spices inside were as long as Frederika's thumbnail, green or grey, it was difficult to say in the light. The tradesman opened the lid. Her mother leaned forward to smell it. The merchant moved the jar in front of Frederika and she did the same. The herbs smelled like forest, but there was a different sweetness to them, sharper. They weren't from the woods, she was pretty certain.

'Can I taste?' her mother asked. She put her finger in the jar and then rubbed it against her gums and made a face. 'These ones,' she said. 'What are they?'

'Marjoram,' the tradesman said. 'From the south of Europe. You've picked a good herb.'

Her mother raised her brows.

'Marjoram does everything,' the tradesman said. 'She kills pain, cleans wounds. Whatever your ailment: phlegm, sneezing, bowel problems, toothache, she is your healer.'

'Toothache,' her mother repeated.

'Don't give her to your husband, though.' The tradesman winked at her mother. 'She kills lust.'

Her mother frowned. She looked the tradesman in the eye and lowered her voice. 'You don't know if she is thought to have any . . . magical powers?'

What? Frederika stared at her mother.

'The list is long.' The tradesman, too, spoke quietly. 'Happiness, love, money, protection.'

Her mother nodded and stood up straight. 'Oh well,' she said. 'Can't have it kill the lust.'

The tradesman had a real belly laugh, the kind that made you want to join him.

Frederika was still staring at her mother when they walked away.

'I found some of those on Eriksson's sleeve,' her mother said. 'I didn't know what they were.'

'You asked about their magical powers.'

'Eriksson also had a mark on his finger. You know, when leather skids through your fingers too fast, that kind of a burn. I was thinking perhaps he was holding an amulet and someone yanked it from him.'

'Or he pulled it off somebody's throat.'

Her mother's eyes gleamed, but then she shrugged. 'It doesn't tell us anything. Everyone wants happiness and love.'

'Or someone used it for health,' Frederika said.

They walked for a while in silence.

'Nils had toothache,' Frederika said.

'I know,' her mother said.

Harried times. Sermons to be held, parish meetings to be led, disputes to be solved. The priest took his evening meals with Mårten Broman, whom he found to be good company. Sofia had introduced the taxman and the priest to each other.

'I think the two of you will find much to talk about,' she'd said.

'Dispensing punishments is a task of the Church,' the priest said that evening. 'Or the state. It is not for the ordinary man to decide what is appropriate.'

Mårten leaned back and put one hand on his stomach. His thready cheeks and nose had turned bright red. The priest had contributed turnips, wine and bread to their meal. Mårten, the meat.

'The guilds have rules that are crucial to their survival. Yesterday at the market, I heard there was a tradesman who did not return the right amount after a purchase. His guild dealt with it. They have to – otherwise the confidence in their profession will be lost,' Mårten said.

'So they forced him to take down his trade sign.'

'Shame is a mighty deterrent – who better than the Church to know that? More so when you are humiliated by your own.'

'The removal of the sign seems a slight penalty, but if we allow groups to carry out their own justice, then where will it end? Do you know what the Lapps used to do – and this not

293

long ago? They buried murderers alive, face to face with their victims. Perhaps not worse than the punishment of the crown, but executed without proper trials.'

'The crown . . .' Mårten said.

They fell silent, each man in thought.

'The crown,' the priest repeated. Their eyes met.

'How are things?' the priest asked.

Mårten hesitated. 'Not good,' he said. 'He sees treachery everywhere. Now he has dismissed Arvid Horn from his Council.'

'But . . . the King respects Arvid.'

'Apparently, no longer. It seems the King now blames him for the dissent in the Council.'

The priest had first met the politician when he was still one of the King's generals, and again when he began undertaking diplomatic missions. Arvid had been one of the King's most loyal men, and he was sensible. Very sensible.

'And is he? Part of it?'

Mårten shook his head. 'Who knows?' he said. 'Rumours have it that some members of the Privy Council meet in secret to draft a new constitution.'

The priest gasped. Did the King know? No. The King's punishments were swift. If he thought the Council was scheming against him, it would soon be dissolved. He shouldn't have dismissed Arvid. Had the King begun to believe his army was enough? It wasn't. The King needed his politicians, too.

'Who knows,' Mårten said again.

There was a knock on the door and both men froze. It was the housekeeper, her cheeks red and her lips squeezed together. She wrung her hands.

'I am so sorry to interrupt,' she said, 'but he refuses to leave until he's spoken with you.'

'Who?' the priest asked.

'Bengt Svensson.'

'Excuse me,' he said to Mårten Broman.

The maid's father was standing in his hallway, hat in hand. The maid herself was nowhere to be seen. The housekeeper crossed her arms.

'You can leave us now,' the priest told her.

She stared at him, then turned on her heel.

The old man was grey. There was white stubble on his sunken cheeks.

'It's about the enlisting,' he said.

The priest nodded.

'What if I pay someone else to go?'

But who would you pay? the priest wondered. And by what means? The old man reminded him of his father. He put his hand on the man's shoulder, felt the bones under his fingers.

'I don't want to die out there,' the man said.

'I know,' the priest said. And this man would. Alone. Cold and hungry.

'I want to die here among those I love.'

'The King has demanded we send soldiers. We need to trust in him.'

'I look around me,' the old man said, 'and I don't see anything that makes me trust him.'

Treason.

The priest placed his fingers in front of the old man's mouth. Don't say a word. He half turned. The hallway behind him was empty, the door to the big room closed. He shook his head to the old man.

'Go now,' he said.

* * *

When he went back inside, Mårten Broman was standing looking at the books in the bookshelf beside the door, his wineglass between two fingers.

The priest hesitated. But the door had been closed. The taxman turned to him. He wavered slightly. He might have had more to drink than the priest had thought.

'I heard about Eriksson,' the taxman said. 'What happened to him?'

'Did you know him?'

'Of course. He often came to the coast.' The taxman snorted. The priest couldn't tell what was implied by this response.

'We don't yet know what happened. He was killed, but by whom or why . . . The bishop has demanded we find out, but I am at a complete loss. I just don't know how to go about it. He's sure to visit again at Candlemas and here I am, with no progress.'

'The bishop . . .' Mårten sipped at his wine.

'You know him?'

'I'm not sure you can ever know the Church's men. No offence.'

The priest waved his hand. 'None taken.'

The taxman took another mouthful of wine. The priest had a thought. 'Someone said that for a Church man, our bishop had shown himself to be unusually merciful . . .' he said.

'Hmm,' Mårten said.

The priest frowned. Now, he was affronted. He let his gaze speak for him: my table, my meal, my guest.

'He asked me to arrange something for him the year before you arrived,' Mårten said. 'A journey south for a family whose young daughter was in a problematic . . . situation.'

His hand drew a large belly in the air.

'What?'

'Like I said, I arranged it for him myself. The parents were so grateful that he did not sentence her, but helped them.'

The priest had to gasp. Refusing to enquire further into supposed sorcery was one thing, but not sentencing a whore was something different. What in God's name was the bishop playing at?

'What were their names?' the priest asked.

'I didn't ask,' Mårten said.

'Was the old priest aware?'

'I don't think so.'

If there was something about Paavo that you could trust, it was that he was loyal. In fact, he was the most loyal person Maija knew. She reminded herself of this again and again. Even during the five years when she was away, she had never doubted that he'd wait for her. And when she returned to the village, there he was, his hair a shade more ashen, a new wrinkle cutting up between his eyes and veering left. 'The lonely years' wrinkle,' they'd call that one later.

'You do go for a long time, when you go,' he'd said as he saw her. He'd been wiping the wood of the hull, though his boat had stood a long time on land and was already spotless.

She had begun to laugh. And he had thrown the rag on the ground and wrapped his arms around her. And then, behind him, a spindly girl who'd been a baby last time she saw her. And behind her, a grandmother whose hair had turned white.

Paavo would have written. She knew he would.

The thought of her visit to the priest at Christmas slithered through her mind, and she shook her head to rid herself of it. That was different. Paavo was different.

The merchants came from the coast. One of them might have met her husband. She began walking from stand to stand, asking: 'Paavo Ranta? From Ostrobothnia? Blond, large . . .'

She didn't know how to describe him. People shook their

heads, gave her pitying looks. Another woman abandoned, by a husband.

But one woman said, 'Finn-Paavo.' She was plump and grey, her hands moving fast over her goods. Flour, salt. Weighing it up on her scales. Not missing one beat.

'I can get ptarmigans any time,' she said to the man in front of her. 'Fur, to trade, bring me fur.'

'Yes,' Maija said.

'He works in the bishop's stables. Looking after the horses. Works with my husband.'

'Do you . . .' She didn't know what to say.

'Fox, I prefer fox fur.'

'Is he well?' Maija asked.

'Was well enough last time I saw him. He's got a hand with the beasts. And with people.' With her ladle, she hit a child. 'I said, don't touch.'

A hand with . . .

If he was well, why wouldn't he have written?

It occurred to her that she hadn't written, either, during the time when she was away. But Paavo was different. Not sending a message must mean something.

The woman was looking at her.

'Could you please tell him that his family wonders how he is?'

'Of course, of course.'

The woman waved with her ladle. Then, at once, she stopped. Her eyes became narrow. She was looking at someone by Maija's side.

'Come with me,' said Fearless.

The Lapp moved fast. He seemed to flow between people without them noticing. Maija tried to keep up, bumped into people and got angry stares. In the dark beside her, someone cursed. At moments, she lost sight of Fearless, but then she would catch a glimpse of the bright blue of his tunic, or his tasselled hat. Fearless took the path up towards the church, but didn't enter. Instead, he walked alongside the long white wall and she trailed him, half ran to catch up with him but couldn't. They came out behind the church.

The graveyard was a white meadow. They walked straight out into it. Close to the church, the gravestones were solemn blocks of stone. Further away, burial places were marked by simple crosses, or not at all. They passed holes in the ground; new graves dug up during milder weather, covered with planks during snowfalls and now waiting for their inhabitants to arrive. She shivered. A black shape skulked between the stones.

The Church Grim! she thought, her heart taking a giant bound in her chest.

Of course not. No. All those stories they were told as children sat rooted like in stone. She wondered if people still bricked up living animals inside the church walls when they built them. As if the church would need guardians.

Fearless stopped.

'What is going on?' he asked.

She shook her head.

He took a step to the side and pointed to the ground at a shrub with black, winter-sleeping branches stretching to the sky. Then she realised it was a set of antlers. There was a dark spatter criss-crossing the snow. Left to right. Up and down. Her heart began to beat hard.

'What is this?' she asked.

'That's what I want to ask you.'

'Me? Why? What is this?'

Fearless was staring at her. His face was in shadow, his breathing restrained.

'Eriksson is buried here,' he said. 'Last night, someone killed one of my reindeer. I found the body without its head this morning. I tracked the culprit to this.'

She took a step closer and now she saw the head of the reindeer, or the skull, for it wasn't a full head.

'It must be one of your people,' she mumbled. And, by the grace of God, she hoped it was.

'Slaughtering an animal for parts, leaving the body to waste? We would never do something like this. This is . . .' he struggled.

'. . . like a ritual,' she said.

'. . . lawless,' he said.

A ritual. Lawless. Yes.

'What have they done to its head?' she asked. 'Why is it black?'

'It's been burned,' Fearless said.

'Why would anyone do something like this?'

'Burned until only the skull was left.'

Blood, she thought. Sprinkling blood and leaving a sacrifice. You sacrificed to receive, or out of gratefulness for what had been given. Or to ask for protection. Appeasing something godly in the heavens – she stared at the antlers – or something vile in the ground.

Evil, she thought.

'Why are you showing me?' she asked.

'You are the one who came to see us,' Fearless said. 'You're the one saying the settlers are after the Lapps. I only have your words for that. And sorcery is in your family. The connection to Eriksson is with your blood.'

She shook her head. She had no idea what he meant.

'Do you realise,' he continued, 'what seeing this could mean to some of my people?

'A declaration of war,' he added, without awaiting her answer. 'You have no idea.'

'This has nothing to do with me,' she said. 'What do we do now?'

'We do nothing,' he said. 'I will take care of it.' He pointed his finger at her. 'You tell no one about this and you stay far, far away from us.'

'Go and see to the animals,' Frederika's mother said and banged her ladle in the pot. Her mouth was a twisted scratch in her face.

'Yes,' Frederika said. She had already been, but she might as well go again when her mother was like this.

She met Daniel in the doorway and made a face: don't talk to her. Daniel was already looking past Frederika.

Frederika walked down the street towards the square. There were lights in the houses. She liked it, walking outside, looking in. Alone, but not lonely. At the square, she lingered for a while underneath the one large tree. The frost on its branches made it look as if ashy moss grew straight on the sky. She stepped from one foot to the other. Gustav came out of the stables and walked towards Settler Town. There was no mistaking that walk. Though now Dorotea also walked like that. If I got gifts, she thought, the first thing I would do is heal Dorotea's feet. Then I would get us food.

Dum Tataradum.

The sound was faint, but clear. It came from Blackåsen, white in the light of the small full moon.

Funny, the mountain seemed so close, even though she knew it was a day's journey away.

There was . . . Was there something, on the side of the mountain?

303

She squinted and tried to see. Something had moved, she was certain.

A wolf's lone howl rang out.

The cry rolled down the mountain and became stronger. It bowled in over the square and hit her like a squall. Frederika fell backwards into the snow.

And now the pack of wolves was on the move, leaping down Blackåsen's sides, soaring, black scraggly shapes visible against the moon. Beasts hunting. Only these weren't after meat, but something immortal.

Frederika scrambled to get up. She ran across the square, towards the church. Her feet slid in the snow. She angled her feet, tried to dig the side of her shoes in. She was too slow.

She reached the church and fell against its door with flat hands, opened it, ran in and pushed as hard as she could from the other side for it to shut. It closed with a soft click. All was quiet. She walked backwards, staring at the door.

A scraping sound. Claws on wood. Then silence. Frederika waited. This was a church; she'd be safe here.

There was a howl so long and piercing it made her skin prickle. Frederika turned, ran into the hall and down the nave. The large candles in the chandeliers were lit, but the church was empty. Jesus hung on his cross above the altar and she ran towards him.

The door squeaked open. Wind swept in and blew out the candles. Frederika stopped sharp. There was panting, the patter of wet paws on stone. She turned around.

The wolves' eyes were yellow in the dark. One shape moved towards her and then waited as the others trotted down the aisles, circled her.

'Go away!' she shouted.

The lead wolf seemed to be laughing.

'Go away,' she said again. This time it was a plea.

A whimper. From her? From deep inside.

And then: a swell growing in that same place, building like the breakers of the sea, mounting.

Frederika put her knuckles to her temples and screamed the thought over the roof ridges, pushed it down past the houses on the streets of Settler Town. Shoved it through the timber of their cottage:

Mamma!

The wolf in the nave was thrust backwards and landed on its side. One of the others fell, too, claws rasping against stone floor as it clambered and whined.

Her mother turned around, forehead creased, ladle still in her hand. Soup dripping on the floor. *Drip. Drip.*

Mamma!

The lead wolf lifted its head and staggered on to all fours.

Leave me alone.

She threw the thought at the wolf, pushing it towards the animal, and through. It shrank back and growled. There was a shine in its eyes. Not excitement. Fear?

Leave me alone.

She was weakening now. She didn't have much left. The wolf sprinted down the nave and leapt at her. She landed on the stone floor, animal on top.

She tried to throw it off, to roll away, but it was too heavy. There was a sound of teeth tearing cloth. Frederika flailed, found the beast's throat, and pushed. Her arms buckled.

Above, God's son watched in silence.

She felt its nose on her cheek, then by her ear. Her last

305

thought was of Dorotea hobbling down a street alone. No one to protect her. No one to make sure she was safe.

Her mother was touching her shoulder. 'What on earth are you doing sleeping in the church?' she said.

Frederika sat up with a jolt. Her hands flew to her neck. She gasped. There was no one but her, her mother and Jesus on the cross.

'It wasn't a reproach,' her mother said and squatted beside her. 'At least, not much of one. Anyone can fall asleep.'

Frederika grabbed her mother and hugged her. She wept. Her mother patted her on the back. 'There, there,' she said.

'They tried to kill me,' she choked out.

Her mother moved back, held her at arm's length. 'What? Who?'

'Oh, Mamma. It was spirits.'

Even in the darkness, she could tell that her mother's eyes blackened. Her mother still held her away from her.

'Frederika,' she said, 'listen to me. People go mad from these kinds of fantasies. I have seen it happen. The fears take hold. They don't ever let go.'

'But look at my neck,' Frederika said.

Her mother put the lantern down and gathered Frederika's hair to lift it.

'There is nothing there,' she said.

That was impossible. Frederika didn't let go of her. Her mother bent again, not to wrap her arms around her, but to help her stand. She put her arm around Frederika's waist.

'I sent for you,' Frederika said as they walked through the nave. 'With my thoughts. And you came. You must have scared them off before they were done.'

'You dreamed,' her mother said and opened the door.

'I sent for you,' Frederika said, 'and I knew you would come—'

'Frederika.' It came out as a shout. They both stopped. In the darkness, her mother's breath was a white haze.

'Blackåsen's parish meeting is tonight,' her mother said. 'I came to tell you to go home and stay with Dorotea while I was out. That was all.'

If only Frederika had still been a child, Maija thought as she hastened down the streets in Settler Town; young enough to trust her mother to tell her what was and what was not. Then it would have been easy. But Frederika was a young woman, and to young adults the experience of others appeared archaic and redundant. Then, too late, as proper adults, they would lament, 'My mother knew what she was talking about,' or, 'My father used to say . . .'

Stupid.

Maija half ran across the church green. Calm down, she told herself. There will be plenty of time to talk to Frederika. She ran up the steps to the vicarage, paused to brush the snow off the hem of her skirt with her hand, and opened the door.

She was late. The hallway was empty, the large door at its end closed. She opened it and stepped inside. The room was warm and dim. At the far end was a blazing log fire. Nils was standing beside it, the flames lighting half of his face. He was talking as she entered. She tried to calm her breathing.

'The settlers on Dagsele Mountain have also had problems – not as bad as ours, but they, too, are worried.'

Maija unbuttoned her coat. She shrugged her shoulder to glide it down her arm. The priest was sitting on a chair on the other side of the fire, his head bent, chin supported by his hand. Daniel and Anna were standing beside Nils, and, further away, Henrik, Lisbet, Gustav. They were looking at Nils.

'That's why the settlers on Blackåsen ask the Church to be unyielding when confronting the Lapps,' Nils continued.

Confronting the Lapps? But what was Nils talking about?

The priest looked up. His eyes met Maija's and widened. He might have been shaking his head, but the movement was so small, she wasn't certain.

Maija thought of the antlers in the snow. Of what Fearless had said his people might do if they found out. Of Frederika raving about spirits. Of people acting under the banner of fear.

'I assume you are talking of this year's events on Blackåsen,' she said, 'and that you say the Lapps might have something to do with them.'

The priest lowered his head. The others turned towards her.

'I don't think the Lapps are responsible,' she said.

They were silent now, looking at her.

'How would you know?' Nils asked, and added before she could answer, 'Had you been here, you would have heard that the request was for a village to be built on our mountain. Disappearances, killings, misfortune . . . We have the right to protect ourselves. I was merely suggesting it might be worth the Church ensuring the Lapps are still on the right path.'

'How do you know the Lapps, Maija?' Lisbet asked.

Nils's voice gained edge. 'Maija doesn't want a village. As her husband is away, she must be allowed to speak and have her concerns heard, but I caution her to speak with wisdom and restraint so as not to raise any alarm.'

'It is not me who spreads fear,' she said.

'This is a community. We help each other. If we begin to suspect one another, then where will it end?'

309

Daniel nodded. Anna too. Maija thought about secrets. Bad secrets.

'Spoken by the one who'll go to any length to ensure his sins remain unknown,' she said.

'Maija?' The priest's voice, shocked.

Nils shook his head. 'You are accusing me,' he said. Something in his voice troubled her. 'A nobleman. In front of all these people. May I ask what I stand accused of?'

'I think you killed Eriksson,' she said.

Someone inhaled.

'Maija?' the priest said again.

A block of a man emerged from his place by the wall. Purple cloth swept the floor and filled up the room. A bishop? He raised his hand. They all stared as if spellbound.

'Speak,' he said to Maija.

Maija swallowed. She hadn't seen him. The others were avoiding her gaze. All but one.

'Eriksson knew things about them. Secrets.' She met Nils's gaze. 'But whatever he had found out about you was really bad.'

'Rubbish,' Nils said.

'Bad enough for you to kill him.'

Nils shook his head. 'This is senseless,' he said.

'In your home, on the wall, there is a carpet worth a fortune. You don't need tax exemption. Was that what Eriksson knew about you and your past? Did he blackmail you? Why did you leave the south, Nils?'

'You want to know about Eriksson. About which secret of ours he knew?'

Kristina's voice was calm. Maija swirled around. She searched for her in the dark, found her by one of the tall windows.

'As it seems that women are speaking out now, so shall I,'

Kristina said and took a step forward. 'Naturally, Eriksson knew why we left Stockholm. He did his homework about us, like he did with everybody else. My husband had many, shall I say, acquaintances among the foreign emissaries. The King decided my husband's allegiances were in question and forced us away.'

Kristina shrugged. 'Me, I don't know what the King imagines will happen when he doesn't recompense his men. And I don't know what you think it will do to us if people know.'

Maija's mind was buzzing. Secrets – the glade where they found the body – the body itself.

'There was a piece of blue glass where Eriksson was killed. The Lapps said they had given it to Nils.'

'I've already explained that to you,' Nils said.

'There were herbs on Eriksson's sleeve,' Maija said. 'Marjoram – it cleans wounds, removes pain. Nils had toothache.'

Kristina studied Maija.

Maija remembered giving her word to Fearless that she would not tell anyone, but still she continued, blazing straight forward on the path she had begun.

'And so, last night, someone killed one of Fearless' reindeer. Whoever did it, took only the skull. They placed it on Eriksson's grave. There was blood.'

'But that just proves the Lapps are up to something.' Lisbet's voice.

'Maija, I really don't know what you're talking about,' Nils said.

The village. Think, she told herself. How does the village link to Eriksson's death? She couldn't see it. Nils had grown to like the idea of the village after Eriksson's death, not before. What was she missing? There was something she was missing.

'Nils couldn't have killed Eriksson,' the bishop said. 'I know this for a fact. He and Kristina were my guests at the time I understand the murder occurred.'

Impossible. The air left her lungs.

The priest said nothing. Anna was staring down at the floor. Nils and Kristina were both looking at the bishop. The pores on the bishop's skin were large. In the light of the fire, they looked like black spots. Maija focused on those on the left side of his nose.

'The reindeer skull on Eriksson's grave,' she said, 'it was done to frighten us so that we would accuse the Lapps.'

'I would be worried indeed, if I didn't know this was a lie,' the bishop said.

'Why, Maija,' the priest said, hesitantly, 'I took the bishop to Eriksson's grave this morning. There was nothing amiss.'

Maija sat in the darkness, by the window. The moon rang on snow and echoed along the streets of Settler Town. Daniel and Anna had returned. Not a word was said and now they were asleep, thick sighs in the air.

Someone had once said to her that the able noble wife should know to speak Latin to the cultivated, and talk like a peasant to the peasants. Maija thought of Kristina's square chin, how the corners of her mouth were downturned, and the wrinkles between her eyes deep enough to bring the brows almost together. Kristina was Nils's equal. Or more. She thought of the story Henrik had told about the merchant who came home to find his load packed with vermin, and felt certain it wasn't Nils who had been behind that, but his wife.

The priest's face when he looked at Maija. Pity? He was right: she was pitiful.

Jutta was standing beside her, arms crossed. The stain that was their kin's past coloured them both.

'Nils needs to be stopped,' Maija said. 'It's people like him who start the hunts for sorceresses.'

Jutta didn't say a word.

Maija sat straight, without allowing her spine to touch the wood of the chair. If she relaxed now, she would surely die.

'How could you have allowed this to happen?'

The priest and Fearless stood at the centre of the room while the bishop paced before them, back and forth, his coat slithering behind him, purple flashes as he turned. By the wall, Sofia had lowered her head.

'And in the vicarage. God have mercy on you.'

He turned again. 'A peasant accusing nobles. A woman accusing a man. Do you not see what . . . what . . .' The bishop's face was red. He grasped for words. 'This is blasphemy: a questioning of God's order, a challenge of God Almighty Himself . . .'

He took out a kerchief and wiped his forehead, then his eyes fixed on the priest.

'I ordered you,' he said, 'to find out the truth. I told you to close this subject down. Discreetly, I said. Instead we have parishioners running amok. Control your flock, in the name of God.'

He raised his hand to stop the priest from speaking and moved on to Fearless. Fearless was motionless, no reaction showing on his face.

'You are part of this Church,' the bishop said. 'Do not think this does not concern you.' He remained standing staring at the Lapp as if to imprint his words on him. 'And if I find that your people have begun to root in their past again, you shall be made to pay, and pay dearly.

'I shall tell you what will happen,' the bishop said then. 'If there is no clarity in the matter of Eriksson's death by the time of the Lady Day sermon, I myself shall lead the investigation. And if I cannot find the answers, then, as the law has it, you, as Eriksson's fellow beings, will be forced to share the burden of the penalty.

'This . . . this Maija . . .' The bishop wiped his forehead again. 'She has to be punished, of course.'

The priest's eyes caught on Sofia. There was an expression on her face as she looked at the bishop – not a smile, but contentedness. A cat in sunshine licking its paw.

Let it run, the priest's father would have said. Bend your head, let it run. Welcome the castigation of those wiser than you. The priest had seen it a hundred times: how things ran and ran across his father.

'Is it really necessary?' the priest said. 'Her husband is absent for winter. She is frightened. It can be weeks before settlers see anyone, and that is not a good environment for anyone. People can get confused.'

'She falsely accused a nobleman, and this in public.'

'She is a simple peasant.'

'Thus more reason to lay down the law to her.'

'Maija may be impetuous, but she means well.'

The bishop's eyes narrowed, evaluating, perhaps, whether here was some other sin for him to discover. 'She may no longer attend Mass,' he said.

Leniency with a potential sorceress, mercy for a whore, but exclusion of a frightened settler woman?

'That is a severe punishment,' the priest said slowly. 'None of us is entirely without sin. I am certain God takes the motivations behind our actions into consideration.'

Careful, the bishop's face told him. I am but waiting to find faults with you. 'Tell her,' he said, 'that I shall personally pronounce the rest of her sentence at the sermon on Lady Day.'

It was his duty to tell her, but he would not do it in front of the other parishioners. The priest hoped the bishop's final penalty would be one of shaming her as opposed to doing her bodily harm – though he guessed Maija might favour it the other way.

When he entered, Maija was putting on her kerchief. She paused in her movement.

'Leave us,' she said to her daughters without looking at them.

She stood up straighter, waited for him to speak.

'You may no longer come to church,' he said, 'and the remainder of your penance will be declared at the Lady Day sermon. By the bishop.'

She barely opened her lips as she slowly let her breath out.

'And my daughters?' she asked.

'They are welcome to attend sermons. Should they so want.'

People were cruel. The parishioners would make them suffer on behalf of their errant mother.

'I promise you, I'll do my best to keep the peace if they come,' he said.

Maija nodded a few times to herself.

'What will you do?' he asked.

She was squeezing her fingers into her palms, as if to drive strength into herself. She stood up taller and inhaled. 'We shall pack up and leave.'

Still he remained standing.

'Accusing Nils was rash, Maija . . .' He shook his head. 'But something is wrong.'

316

She made a small movement of her head.

'It's just that . . .' she started, but then it was she who fell silent. 'Goodbye,' she said instead and avoided his gaze.

Candlemas, too, was a miserable affair.

It was their first night back home on Blackåsen Mountain. Maija sat up, her nightdress pasted to her breasts and lower back. She waited until her breathing returned to normal, then she rose, pulled the sweaty gown over her head, wiped her neck and stomach, and dropped it on the floor.

Just a dream. She felt in the dark for her trousers and her shirt, found them, and pulled them on. She stood for a moment beside the bed. From beneath her came the sound of Dorotea's snuffles. Maija wanted to lie down beside her daughter, put her arm around her – and inhale her dreams. She'd never been able to do that with Frederika, she thought then; not once had the girl relaxed and given herself over to her mother's cuddles. And the thought was back, unwelcome, but there nevertheless. I don't know her.

Maija shivered. It was just the nightmare, holding her bones. She'd had this one before, but not since they left Finland. The events in town had left their mark. She had the right to be frightened. She'd seen people broken in both body and mind. Never the same again after a Church penance, and now she would have to wait six weeks to hear hers.

On the table, there was a small covered plate containing leftovers from their evening meal. The fish was for the girls to have in the morning. Maija lifted the cloth. Her mouth watered. She'd had nothing today but tea. She wrapped the cloth around the plate again. She thought she had known hunger before this winter, but she had not. Real hunger did not just make you irritated and weak, or make your stomach grumble. Real hunger was pain.

Perhaps that was why she had dreamed.

In her dream, she was ill. The disease varied: sometimes she suffered from fevers, sometimes crayfish. Sometimes it was an illness with no name. What was the same was that when the dream began, she always found herself knowing that she would die within days.

She wasn't afraid of dying. She didn't know what to think about death – not that anyone on this side of life would ever get clarity in the matter. No, when the time came, she wanted to make up her own story about death and hold fast to it. The Church, of course, offered its own truth, but she didn't want to make that hers. Its truth demanded too much.

Jutta putting her hopes in Jesus had come late.

'Jesus, Jesus, forgive me, forgive me.'

Jutta's litanies on her death-bed hung in the air over the yard and penetrated every corner, every hollow in the house. Maija heard them wherever she was, whatever work she was doing, pounding in her head.

'Maija, hold my hand, hold it tight, don't leave me.'

I shall never become like you, Maija had whispered to herself, over and over. By then, she knew why Jutta was so afraid.

It wasn't Jutta who had told her. It was Paavo. Maija had been seventeen. They'd been sitting by his boat. They hadn't been lovers long. He'd squinted out towards the sea, aching to go, but stayed by her side.

'There is something I must tell you,' he'd said.

He'd told her about her grandfather: a tall, slim man with

fire in his eyes and in his heart and, later, fire wherever he went.

She laughed. But Paavo had dog eyes, and her face froze, silly smile still on her lips.

'I would have heard about it,' she said and her voice sounded stiff.

'It was better you didn't.'

'Says who?'

'The elderly. It happened long before you were born. Knowing could only do you harm.'

Then why are you telling me now? she wanted to scream. Instead, she looked out towards the sea, so far out that her eyes hurt.

'You kept this from me?'

He nodded. Admitted: yes, they had.

Why hadn't they told her?

The guilt, she thought. After all, it was villages that burned people, not single men. They were all at fault, and hadn't spoken about the events out of guilt.

But then why did the other children know?

Her head raced, trying to remember. Hadn't there been a hesitation in their dealings with her, a particular quickness to severity and to punishment? Had they been monitoring her for the qualities of her grandfather?

And Jutta . . . Where had Jutta been in all this?

She'd removed her hand from his.

'How many?'

'Maija . . .'

'How many?'

'Thirteen.'

And when he gripped her fingers again and squeezed hard to say he still loved her, expecting her to feel gratitude, she felt nothing but disgust. The same revulsion she later felt for Jutta.

'Jesus, Jesus, forgive me, forgive me.'

'Thirteen women!'

Maija screamed at Jutta when she found her by the lake.

'And you remained married to him?' Maija's heart had swelled so much in her chest, she was choking. 'Who were they?'

'Maija . . .' Jutta's face was grey.

'Who?'

'Aino and Eeva – Mielikki's mother and grandmother . . .' Jutta spoke with difficulty.

Mielikki had lived next door to them all Maija's life. Maija could smell when the woman baked bread, and she would run over for a taste.

'Helli – Katri's sister . . .'

Katri was Maija's teacher.

'Eira – Paavo's grandmother . . .'

Oh God.

'Anneli – my daughter . . . your mother.'

And with this, Paavo and Maija together opened gates to the past and to the future and nothing could ever be the same. They had unearthed what was buried in a much too shallow grave.

Jutta couldn't stop talking. As if absolution was in Maija's power to give: *the uncontrollable fear – the fervour – God, an evil force sweeping across the land. Her husband – old – she didn't take him seriously – he just prayed and prayed and prayed. The women had come to Jutta to have their futures read – laughed, perhaps they danced – midsummer – it was midsummer. Someone said something – someone talked – Devilry. One by one, the women were accused. Helli, Eira, Anneli . . . Anneli . . .* My daughter

Anneli. Jesus, Jesus, forgive me, forgive me. *Nobody stood up for the accused. You must understand: nobody.* My daughter! *Surely it would come to nothing – it would go away – they were sensible. They'd known each other* for ever. *Unless it was true – what if some among them belonged to the Other Side? What if some of them* copulated *with the Devil? The smell of cooked meat and burned hair as they sat on their porch in amber evening light – what screams of lives on fire sound like –* images spewed out of Jutta's mouth and were made Maija's, to carry for the rest of her life.

Then when Jutta lay dying, clinging to the last of life with skeletal fingers that ought to have let go already, Maija sat beside her and thought of the mother she could have had; the mother she had once had, but couldn't remember. It should have been you, she thought. Not her.

'Why not you?' she asked.

'I was accused,' Jutta said, 'but they retracted it. Perhaps my husband . . . Jesus, Jesus, forgive me, forgive me.'

I shall never become like you, Maija swore. I shall never lay my misery on anyone. I shall carry my burdens with dignity. No emotion. Not now. Not ever. I will get by, by getting on. I shall know to die alone. And never, never, ever again, shall I use the gifts.

Paavo's voice in her head: 'We don't know what we would have done in her situation.'

But they did. They did! You decided what was right. You held to it. You fought.

And then again: the dream.

Maija was dying. But even more frightening was the fact that this time and every other, in her dream, as the knowledge of her death dawned on her, the first thing she did was to reach out: for Frederika, for Dorotea. Sometimes for people

322

whose faces she didn't even recognise. She would cling on to them, screech and tell them she was soon to be gone.

This was how she knew she was still not strong enough.

Maija took the cloth off the plate and ate the fish. Then she ran out and was sick on the porch.

Frederika lay awake. Her throat hurt and it was hard to swallow.

In her mind's eye, she kept seeing the wolves. She heard them panting.

Her mother had got up and then gone out. The dampness she'd left on the sheet beside Frederika turned ice cold. Frederika didn't give any sign that she was awake. It wasn't a night for words. Under the cover, Dorotea pressed into her. *Dadum-Dadum-Dadum.* Her sister's heartbeats against her side.

Eriksson had come and left again while her mother was still indoors. Frederika didn't look at him, and her mother didn't react. Perhaps it was enough to deal with your own ghosts without having to take on anybody else's.

She shivered. The spirits weren't waiting any longer. They would come for her again and she wasn't ready for that fight. Though there had been something in her. When her mind had yelled at them, for a brief moment, she had been the stronger one. But then she had weakened.

She lay frozen on her back and didn't dare to move. There was a pressure on her chest. She worried that if she inhaled properly, she might make a gulping noise, and so her breaths were thin and ragged, not giving her enough air.

Jutta had been able to sense people without seeing them. Jutta had tried to teach her.

'Stand still and try to feel where I go, rather than see it.'

A June in Ostrobothnia. Frederika and Jutta were hanging laundry on the clothes-line. They had stretched the rope far between two pine trees. The spring winds were strong and the sheets snapped in the wind; large white sails shining in their yard, flapping over the boat that no longer had a purpose.

Frederika closed her eyes. *Flap, flap.* She could imagine the ropes hitting the masts of the boats, but there was no Jutta.

'No,' she said.

'Try again.' Jutta's voice came from her left.

'No.'

'Don't listen for me. Feel.'

A presence, to her right, an imprint in the air. Then again: the warm wind against her cheek.

'Perhaps,' Frederika said and tried again. Yes, a dent. A shape. 'Got you,' Frederika said and opened her eyes.

'Now try and hold me there,' Jutta had said.

'How?'

'Think of it as trying to put a ring around me. A ring of wind, or of fire. Something I won't be able to leave.'

Frederika had concentrated and tried to think a circle around her great-grandmother. But soon Jutta's arms were around her. 'Needs some work,' Jutta had said in her ear.

Jutta had known things. Could the same be done with spirits?

Frederika tried to see the wolves in front of her: the sinewy bodies, the matted pelt, the sharp teeth . . .

She shuddered.

Oh no. I am not afraid of you. She closed her eyes and tried again. She didn't know how long she'd been trying, when at once, she was overcome by a yawn.

And then she felt the shift.

It was as if the space around her, or time, something unforgivable and unbending, had risen on its end and let her feel through it, travel through it. There was a movement, far away, and she knew she had them. West of the mountain. A den. Or a passage? The lead wolf was standing tall, gazing ahead, the others foraging. It lifted its nose and its nostrils flared. It knows I'm here, Frederika thought. It can feel me, too. The other beasts became nervy. One of them came too close, and the leader brought it down, pinned it to the ground with its paws and bared its teeth. The other wolf whined, rolled over and bared its belly.

I can't put a ring around them, Frederika thought. I would never be strong enough to hold them.

Beside her Dorotea twitched. Frederika turned her head. Her sister swallowed and opened her mouth. Frederika smelled sour milk, sweetness. Sister.

Perhaps, she thought, if I cannot put a ring around them, I can put a ring around us. One of protection.

She closed her eyes. At first she tried to visualise their homestead, but she couldn't see all of it at one time. Then she pictured their cottage, but she couldn't hold that picture for long – other thoughts came in and broke it. Now she was tired. Finally, she put her arm over Dorotea and held her, and at once she saw the two of them in her mind's eye. She tried to imagine fire, but the cottage was too dark and cold. Then she thought of the storm they'd had. Wind, she thought. She pictured the snow outside and how the wind began to finger its surface, disturb its peace. Come on. Wake up. The wind blew harder, hard enough to lift the crystals. They rose. Faster, faster. Snow in a flurry. A thick whirl of white. And in the calm of its midst: Dorotea and Frederika.

Her mother ought to have been there with them, Frederika thought as she fell asleep.

The days passed and with them came reason and sisters squabbling and the nuisance of having to get dressed and go outside to perform chores. A week gone, and the other settlers would be back at the mountain too, but no one had come to visit.

'It's a school day,' Frederika said to Maija one morning.

Her mother pushed back her hair from her forehead. 'Yes,' she said. 'Yes, I believe it is.'

'School, school and school,' Dorotea muttered behind them.

A memory of a ring made of wind. Frederika felt calm and safe at the thought. 'I'll take Dorotea,' she said.

'So you no longer need to see Mr Lundgren on your own,' Frederika said as they walked. 'How come?'

'I don't know. Perhaps it is my feet,' Dorotea said.

'Why would it be your feet?'

'I don't think he likes what's happened to them. And then he said that Sara needed his time more than me.'

Frederika thought about what priests said happened if you didn't do well at the Catechetical hearing.

'But does this mean you don't need tutoring, or what?' she asked.

'Yes,' Dorotea said.

Mr Lundgren had said that Dorotea didn't have enough Bible knowledge. I'll have to ask him, Frederika thought. I'll have to make certain Dorotea doesn't get in trouble with the priest. Perhaps there were things they could practise at home?

'I'll come in with you today,' she said to Dorotea. 'There is something I need to ask Mr Lundgren.'

When they knocked, the teacher opened the door.

'We are still not ready, but you can wait inside,' he said.

They took off their woollens and left them in the hallway. Sara, Daniel's youngest daughter, was sitting beside the verger on the bench by the fire. Her shoulders were bent over the book in her lap, her feet hung straight down but didn't reach the floor.

Frederika walked to the window. The yard was still. The snow almost reached the roof at the back of the barn where nobody had shovelled. And then she realised: she could see. There was light. Light! Yes, a dawn, though weak. Spring was coming.

She put her hands on the window sill to press her cheek against the pane and try to see more. As she did so, her fingers touched a jaggedness.

There was a new carving in the wood of the window beside the other letters. 'S'.

Frederika turned to look at Sara. Had she done this? But she was younger than Frederika. She was Dorotea's age. How had she managed it without Mr Lundgren seeing? How had she dared? Frederika wanted to giggle.

The others arrived. They shuffled in the hallway to remove their outer garments.

'My father got it for me at the market,' one of the older boys said. He was showing another boy a knife. He put it back in its case.

Sara came to sit at the table. She was pale and red-eyed, her arms like sticks. The verger left the room to go outside.

One of the boys sat next to Dorotea, but rose again and walked around to sit at the other side. The boy who'd started to put his books on the table beside him gathered them up and followed him.

The older of the two boys leaned over the table. There were spots on his nose. 'Your mother is a heretic,' he said to Dorotea in a low voice.

'Says who?' asked Frederika.

The boy glanced up at her. 'Says my father, says my mother, says everyone on the mountain,' he said.

'You're just a child,' Frederika said. 'You have no idea what it is you're talking about.'

'She's not allowed to come to church any longer.'

'She's a sorceress,' the younger boy said. 'She brings misery on to us all.'

Frederika didn't answer.

'Your mother will be punished.'

'Perhaps she'll have to run the gauntlet. We'll all hit her. Boom, boom, boom.' The young boy's cheeks were flushed. He was banging his finger on the table.

'Awwww.' The older boy moaned and held himself as if hurt. He grinned. 'Besides, your feet smell,' he said and puckered his nose at Dorotea.

Dorotea looked up at Frederika.

Never before had Frederika felt such anger. White and hot, hatred pulsated in her ears. She squinted towards him. Burn, she thought. Burn.

The boy fell forward on to the kitchen table, hands flat beside his head.

Frederika took a step forward. Oh God, what have I done? I killed him, she thought. I killed him.

The verger came back in.

The boy sat up. 'Aaaaah,' he mocked. 'This is what she'll be like, your mother.'

Frederika's exhalation was uneven.

The boy stared at her, mouth open, waiting for her reaction. When there was none, he stuck his tongue out.

'Will you be staying with us today, Frederika?' Mr Lundgren asked and smiled.

'Yes,' Frederika said. 'Yes, today, I will.'

She had wanted to wound him, she thought later, after their evening meal. She was spinning wool, the greasy locks in her hands, twirling the fibres into thread with her fingers. No, it was worse than that. For the briefest of instants, Frederika had wanted the boy dead.

And after, she'd been so upset, she'd forgotten about asking Mr Lundgren about Dorotea.

I need to be careful. I need to grow up fast. When the day comes and these powers do what I ask of them, if I'm still unable to control my anger, then what?

The thought made her twirl the wool so hard, the thread became sharp enough to cut her index finger.

Dum. Tataradum.

When, she had thought. Not if.

She stopped the spinning wheel with her hand, stuck her finger in her mouth. It tasted salty. Her mother was sitting in front of the fire. She was mending a skirt with needle and thread, humming a little to herself as she did so. The boy had called her a heretic, Frederika thought. She should tell her mother that people on the mountain were talking about her, but she didn't want to. Her mother was already going to be punished by the church. Wasn't that enough?

She put her foot on the treadle and began to move the spinning wheel again.

Maija had to go out on the porch to see it. Faint, but it was there. A dawn. The sun hadn't yet mounted the horizon, but she sensed it there at the end of the world. Greylight would become longer and longer. Perhaps in a week sunlight would show. How long before nature produced something edible? Too long. But at least this gave hope. It was a while before she noticed him at the edge of the homestead. Fearless seemed to grow out of the earth. When he was certain she'd seen him, he approached. His skis made a hissing sound on the snow. He stopped beneath the porch.

'If you are here about me revealing what we found on Eriksson's grave, I am sorry,' she said. 'I didn't mean to get you into trouble with the bishop.'

He said nothing.

'It just slipped out,' she said.

'You said placing the antlers on Eriksson's grave was like a ritual.'

She shrugged.

'Then you said it was done to frighten and accused Nils.'

'Yes, well, I was wrong.'

'What if it was a ritual?'

Fearless wasn't looking at her when he said it, but into the air. As if he were thinking out loud.

'You said . . .' she began.

331

'Not our rituals,' he said, 'nor those of the Swedes, or the Finns.'

'The blood was sprinkled as if it might have been meant to resemble a cross.'

'Not the blood,' Fearless said, 'the skull.'

'Just tell me.'

'A Lapp from the east said there is this tradition, in south Russia. They burn the head of the animal they've slaughtered and are about to eat. They put the burned skull by the place of the elder.'

'Respect.'

He gave a nod.

'But who would have wanted to show Eriksson respect? And a Russian?'

Fearless shook his head. He looked into the air again.

'Don't be fooled,' he said. 'Spring is not here yet. It will still get colder.'

Maija, too, lifted her face towards the east. He was right. The wind held ice.

Frederika was in the barn. She was sitting astraddle the wooden bench, practising. At first, she tried to put a ring of wind around the goats to stop them from moving, but the goats weren't budging anyway, so she couldn't tell if it had worked. Then she tried seeing where Fearless was. She closed her eyes and focused hard, saw his face before her, but couldn't keep his features in her mind. It was almost as if a candle had been blown out. This happened again and again.

When Eriksson showed himself, she wasn't even surprised.

'Hello,' she said.

He didn't answer. He was standing up, chin raised, cold eyes not meeting hers.

'I am practising like you told me to,' she said.

He scoffed.

'What?' she asked.

'You ignored me the other night.'

'There was trouble down in the town,' she said. 'I needed some time to think it through. You understand, don't you?'

He still wasn't looking at her.

'I am sorry,' she said.

'I came to bring you a gift.'

'I am sorry,' she said again.

He sat down on the bench beside her. He supported himself

with his arms on his knees and wasn't looking at her, but at the goats.

'I still have no idea what I am doing,' she offered.

He hesitated, then nodded, sat up, and searched in his jacket pocket. 'Here.' He handed her something wrapped in a scarf.

It was a mirror, small and square with a twisted iron frame. It felt cold in her hand. Frederika turned it over. Its rear was made of black metal.

'Elin's,' Eriksson said. 'She used to be able to talk to what she called her helping spirits through it.'

'Is that how it works?'

'I don't know. I think there are many ways – but you need to find one that works for you.'

She knew he was right. The peace was temporary. When she thought about her protective circle of wind, she now also saw them: the wolves. Shadows in the storm, heads bent low, progressing slowly, but moving forward, on their way, in.

There was a rasping sound outside. Then there was a pause and so the sound of skis being placed to lean against the wall of the barn. Frederika tucked the mirror in her pocket. Another pause and the door opened. It was Antti. He bent his head in a greeting and came in.

Eriksson was gone. Antti took off his mittens and his hat. His black hair fell over his shoulders.

'I'm here with Fearless,' Antti said. 'He's gone to see your mother.'

'Fearless has gone to my mother? But why?'

'I don't know.'

Frederika felt a sting of jealousy. Fearless had chosen her mother, though Frederika was the one who was trying to walk in his footsteps.

Antti looked around, hesitated, then sat down on the bench where Eriksson had just been sitting.

'How are you?' he asked.

'Fine,' she said without thinking. 'Finer,' she corrected herself. 'I don't know,' she concluded.

They sat in silence.

His hand was on the bench beside hers. It was sinewy and broad, still summer brown. There were black hairs on his wrist. Frederika felt an ache in her stomach. Her own hand on the bench looked white and thin in comparison. She wondered what his skin would feel like.

She looked up and found him looking at her.

'I am wondering what your skin feels like,' she said.

He shook his head. 'Don't,' he said.

He stood up and she watched him put on his hat and leave. His movements were different from anyone else's. She was certain she'd recognise him from any distance. She sat still even after all had long gone silent and then her eyes became hot, and she rose. She'd felt as if she'd been weighed and found too light. She took out the mirror Eriksson had brought, and caught a glance of herself. It was her mother gazing back at her, the same white-blonde hair, the grey eyes. Then she saw the rest of her.

During the years, they had added length and breadth to her dress as necessary, season by season – inch by inch, flounce after flounce. And her hair . . . Untamed, untended, hanging down her back. She twirled it into a long string. She'd thought she was pretty. She'd given Antti the eye. She was unkempt, that's what she was.

Her eyes burned again and she closed them. She thought of Antti's hand, the tendons on its back. She imagined his face before her, his mouth coming closer to her. The feeling tore at the pit of her stomach. He probably desired one of his own, she thought. But it was she who felt the spirits. Not any of their women.

She stayed a long time in the barn. She held the mirror before her. 'Speak to me,' she demanded.

But all she saw was herself.

That night Frederika dreamed of black ants, their small bodies gleaming. They were in the school-house. At first there were just a few. She saw one. Then another one. Then she realised it was a trail of them making their way across the floor towards the fireplace. Outside, more were coming. They approached from south, west, north and east. They scaled the steps of the porch, clambering on top of each other in their fervour. The porch was full of them, seeking that tiny hole in the door that would let them in. Soon, inside, the floor was just one thick moving bulk, like flowing black treacle over wood.

The weeks passed. Yet again, like most days, the priest ended up sitting in his church. He had memorised the body nailed to the cross in front: the paltry legs, the hollow chest, the intense red drops painted on its side and in its hands, the tilted head with the large crown of thorns.

Once upon a time, there was a little bird . . .

Go and see Sofia, he told himself. Liven yourself up. He'd seen her horses and carriage enter the square two days earlier, coming back from another journey to the coast. He'd watched from his window as they unpacked the wagon. He had already decided to ask her to be his wife, but then he hadn't gone to greet her, and he had been relieved when she didn't come to see him.

He stared up at Jesus again. If he squinted, there was the halo. Jesus' head was hanging low on his chest. The priest couldn't tell if the figure's eyes were open. He hoped they were. Although Jesus was crucified. It was, of course, a bit much to ask.

You could try praying. The thought skulked through his head in stockinged feet.

His father used to pray. A pale shrimp of a man, mumbling into his clasped hands each morning, black holes on the sides of his head where once there were ears.

The King prayed, too. He lived according to the Word, went into his chamber and closed his door. Then, during sermon, when it was the priest's time to read the prayer, the King watched and nodded. As if the invocation was directed at him, not God. Which, in so many ways, it was. The King held the godly relationship. The Church agreed upon appropriate prayers with him.

If I did talk to you, he asked Jesus, what then would you say?

Strangely enough, it was Maija's face that came to him.

The large church door scraped open and he turned. Sofia pulled off her shawl and shook it to remove the snow.

Her footsteps echoed as she walked towards him. His heart sank.

'I was praying,' he said.

She stopped. 'I didn't mean to disturb you.'

'No, no. I had finished. Welcome back.'

He slid further in on the pew to leave her space. She sat down at the edge. She looked serious. There was a sheen on her upper lip. Was she ill?

'Is everything all right?' he asked.

'I don't know,' she said.

She inhaled and her nostrils flared. 'I met with Mårten Broman when I was in town,' she said. 'Of course, being the person he is . . . I don't know what I was thinking . . .'

She cleared her throat.

The priest felt cold. He waited.

'He's tried to find out more about you ever since you met at the market,' Sofia said. 'He wanted to know who you were. You were a court priest, but Mårten said you came from nowhere. Nobody has studied with you at the seminar, nobody has had you as a priest . . . Your life starts at the point when you emerge beside the King. We were wondering: how is it possible for a priest to have no past?'

Outside the church, hands grabbed at the priest's robe. He swirled around. It was the old man.

Oh, not now.

The man's lips were pale and cracked. He was hollow-eyed.

'Please,' he mumbled. 'Have mercy. I'll do anything. Take me off your list. Please . . .'

'But there is nothing I can do,' the priest said.

'Please.'

'It is not my decision,' the priest said. 'There is nowhere to go to appeal. Listen to me!'

He shouted the last words, just as the old man yelled, 'You must help me!'

They both breathed heavily.

'There is nothing I can do,' the priest said. 'It's God's will.'

The cold of April was different from that of January or February. While the cold early in the year was sharp and nervous, this chill was dull and slow but pounded your bones. Bodies were tired and worn by then. They hurt more. It was the day before Lady Day, which was supposed to be the first day of spring. If you ran with bare feet on Lady Day, you wouldn't injure your feet for the rest of the year. You wouldn't catch a cold that year, either. Although Frederika didn't think she would run around barefoot in a metre of snow. If the mirror worked, she ought to be able to tell how the year would turn out. She had practised with the mirror every day since Eriksson had given it to her, but she still couldn't see anything in it apart from herself.

Eriksson was trailing them, in among the trees. He kept himself far enough behind them, but every now and then she felt his eyes on her. Frederika had asked him to come to town, begged him when he said no. She didn't know why he had changed his mind. 'I need you there,' she'd said, though she knew he didn't care about what she needed. 'Maybe this is how I'll be able to help you. If everyone is in the same place at one time.'

Otherwise, she supposed she'd have to get used to the idea of having Eriksson around. Perhaps some folk carried the dead around all their lives, unable to find a way to send them onwards. No, that couldn't be. And she couldn't see Eriksson staying and not minding. He wasn't the kind of person who waited on anyone.

They were travelling on their own this time.

'No,' her mother had said, when Frederika asked her whether they were going with Daniel and Anna. There'd been a trace of regret in her voice. Frederika felt sad. She oughtn't to have asked. At Lady Day sermon, her mother's punishment would be meted out by the bishop. They had talked about it. What the girls would do if their mother was injured; what they would do if she had to spend time in the stock. It was clear they could have used some friends.

Her mother added another 'no'. Flat, this time. She pushed her hair back and raised her chin. Frederika softened. It wasn't her mother's fault.

They crossed the peak of the mountain and the town lay beneath them in the hole of the valley, hard in pink light. Around it, the white snow was untouched.

'Can I go out?' she asked her mother that afternoon, when they were installed in their cottage in Settler Town and the animals in their pen.

'Yes,' her mother said. 'Frederika . . .' There was a weakness by her mouth. 'Do you know where we put the skins?' she asked.

It wasn't what she had been about to ask, Frederika was certain. It was hard, because with each step, they walked further away from each other. I love you, she thought. I love you and I will always love you, but . . . they were different.

'Over there,' Frederika said, and pointed.

Her mother turned away.

The empty town was hoary: battered from winter. Snow-smoke

drifted along the street. Frederika bent her head and walked towards Lapp Town. The Lapps had not yet arrived. She had hoped Antti would have been there. She wanted to talk to him. Most of all, she wanted to sit on his lap, though she knew she was too old for that. She remembered what it had smelled like in his shelter: the smoke, sweat and something else. And then she felt stranger, because the thought of sitting on his lap and smelling him stirred her. Her cheeks felt hot. She glanced at Eriksson, but he didn't seem to notice.

At the market square, the large tree was thick and winter-furry. A few tradesmen had arrived. They opened the wooden shutters and slammed them against the walls, dull thuds, as if to try to wake up the town.

'Should we go and see the church?' Frederika asked.

Could Eriksson go close to it? She didn't know. She shouldn't have suggested it. After all, he was dead.

'Maybe we shouldn't,' Frederika said, and they remained standing.

Then she felt the mirror grow hot in her pocket. At first, it was pleasant: heat radiated through the wool and against her thigh. But the mirror grew hotter. She made a face and Eriksson looked at her. She put her hand in her pocket to remove the mirror and burned her fingers. She began to tear at the buttons of her coat to rid herself of the object that now scorched her thigh. Eriksson handed her his scarf and she used that instead to grab the mirror and throw it away from her, on the ground.

There was the sound of someone closing a door to one of the houses across the green. In the corner of her eye, she saw a man walking towards them.

Frederika approached the mirror. It still glowed, and the snow around it was beginning to melt. There was something in it. She leaned forward and saw Dorotea, sitting on somebody's

342

arm. No, she was wrong. This wasn't Dorotea. This child had red hair. The little body was white. She didn't have any clothes on. Why wouldn't she have clothes? The child had wrapped her arms around the adult's neck. So tight she almost lifted herself off the arm. Then whoever held her, rotated, and the child turned her head. The eyes, as they met Frederika's, were round, her mouth half open. The red, frizzy hair stood straight up around her face. It's Elin, Frederika thought. It's her when she was little. And then the child's face changed again, and instead there was another child. Blonde this time, but still naked, on somebody's arm, the same shock on her face.

'You've arrived early,' a voice said.

Frederika's heart was pounding in her chest. Her hands felt icy cold, yet she was sweating.

'Is something wrong?' Mr Lundgren asked. 'Frederika, you look unwell.'

The child in the mirror had been Sara, Daniel and Anna's youngest. Frederika's mouth was dry. Her legs were numb. If she moved now, she'd fall down.

'Frederika?' Mr Lundgren put his hand on her shoulder. He came close enough for her to feel his breath on her face. There was spit on his bottom lip.

'Why won't you teach Dorotea any longer?' she whispered.

He looked at her, those thick eyebrows raised in their perpetual question.

'Is it because of her feet?'

Their eyes locked.

'There is a new letter in your window sill,' Frederika said.

An 'S' for little Sara. But it wasn't children carving their initials, as she'd thought. It was a conqueror's list. She felt sick.

In the teacher's face: surprise. Then recognition.

'Stay here, Dorotea,' Maija said. Dorotea was lying down on one of the beds. 'Or do you want to come?'

'My feet look better and better, don't they, Mamma?' Dorotea said.

'Yes, baby, they do.'

'I am tired. I think I'll stay here.'

Maija walked outside. Twilight was turning night. She stopped outside. It had felt better when they were sharing a cottage with Daniel and Anna. But they would be living somewhere else this time. She leaned her head back towards the wall. It is me, she thought. I have driven everyone away from me.

Dorotea. Her baby wasn't tired. Her baby was in pain. What would they do? Maija pushed off the wall and began to walk down the street. Half of Dorotea's toes were already gone, and still there was more darkening of the flesh. Maija couldn't do the cutting that was needed.

'We don't always understand the ways of the Lord,' Jutta said beside her.

The flash of anger was so sharp, Maija had to stop.

'Don't you ever, ever talk to me about God's will,' she said.

Enough, she thought. They needed help. The priest might be in the church. He was their priest. Surely, if she begged him, he would know what to do and be compassionate.

The church hall was dark.

'Hello?' she called.

Nobody answered. She walked the stone floor towards the figure of Jesus on the cross and waited for a while beneath the yellow plaster body.

But his head was turned to one side: Jesus studying his own wounds.

She left the church and walked towards the Customs House. There was light on inside. The taxman had already arrived and installed himself. As Maija walked around the corner, she collided with someone. They crashed into each other so hard, both women called out and Maija grabbed the other woman's arm to prevent her from falling.

Blonde, curly hair, blue eyes. The widow of the former priest.

Sofia stared at her, mouth open. She closed her mouth, white teeth making a clapping sound as they came together.

'Maija,' she said, 'if I remember correctly.'

'Sorry,' Maija said. 'I was on my way to see the priest . . .'

Sofia looked at her as if evaluating something. At first, it seemed she decided Maija was not worth whatever effort she was considering. Her lip curled. Then, she changed her mind and that might have had nothing to do with Maija at all.

'I just spoke to someone about him,' she said.

Maija waited. Sofia was about to tell her something.

'We said it was interesting that there is no record of him anywhere.'

Why would they have asked about the priest? Maija thought. Then she realised what Sofia was saying.

'He was a court priest . . .' Maija said.

'It seems that is the first time anyone had ever met him.'

'Perhaps he studied abroad. Perhaps he lived and worked far away.'

Even as Maija said it, she knew it wasn't true. The world was small – that of the nobles, of those around the King, smaller. They had the same background, fathers and mothers who knew each other. No, someone would have known him in his earlier life.

'Something big', Anna had told her. Before Eriksson died, he had said he'd 'found out something big about someone big'.

'Why are you telling me this?' Maija asked.

Sofia looked tired. 'Yes, why am I?' she said. 'I really don't know.'

The blackest of nights, but cloudless. The priest pictured black spots welling down the lit snow of the mountain. He imagined the tramping of hundreds of feet. The settlers were coming. He strained, but could not see them.

Someone cleared their throat and he swirled around.

The night man? At his home? The priest felt cold.

'Something is hanging in the bell tower,' the night man said.

'What?'

'Someone.'

The blackest of nights. But cloudless. Stars. Plenty of stars. They were running. The body was visible from beneath the tower. It was hanging from the highest beam, back against the side of the bell, legs, from the knees down, slumped over the edge, swaying in free air. A small person. Neck at an impossible angle.

Jesus Christ. 'Get her down.'

Why he'd said 'her', he did not know.

The night man climbed the tower, past the shape of the bell, a black sprite. The priest grabbed the wood of the bell tower with both hands. He put his foot up on one of the beams and started the climb into that blackest of nights with plenty of stars. He hadn't climbed since he was a child. Then his father had called him agility itself. He might have been proud of that.

'Neck's in a noose,' the night man bellowed.

Then: 'Knot is too tight.'

'Hurry!'

The priest reached the top, put his feet on one of the beams and braced his back against another. He grabbed the legs and lifted.

But the legs bent at the knees. He let go and climbed higher, so that he came to stand with his head inside the bell. He leaned forward and grabbed the legs again. Stick legs.

'Higher,' the night man called.

The priest leaned his forehead against the metal of the bell and lifted.

'I have the knot now,' the night man said. 'When I say, let go . . . Now, let go.'

The priest opened his arms and let her fall. The body sighed down in the air before him and into the snow with a thud.

He lifted his head. Where his forehead had melted the frost, there was something on the inside of the bell. He stepped closer. With his mitten, he wiped the inside of the bell. It was an inscription. He rubbed further. It read: *Here lives a priest with dissonance in his soul.*

At first he didn't realise, and then he did: the bell-founder.

The night man had reached the ground. He was turning the body over on to its back.

'He's still alive.'

The blackest of nights and not a cloud. An abundance of stars. One moon, no larger than a nail clipping.

The priest threw his outerwear on to a chair. He washed his hands in the basin. The water was ice cold. He washed them again, scrubbed his hand with the nails of the other. But this dirt could not be washed off. It sat underneath his skin. He scrubbed until his hands hurt, and then he forced himself to stop and leaned with his hands supported on the basin, feeling the frail man's body in his arms as he had hugged him, the slight weight as he had carried him home. The pain as the old man's wife opened the door and screamed as she saw them. And all this for what?

Then he realised he was not alone and stood up straight. White-blonde hair by the window, slight figure. Why was he not astonished to find Maija inside his house?

She stepped out from the shadows. They stood looking at each other.

'I am not a priest,' he said.

'No,' she said. 'So what are you?' she asked.

'The son of a hangman.'

She gasped.

'I know. It is funny, isn't it? The lowest of the low. The furthest down you can get.'

'How?'

'I had a good head. The local priest taught me. I became a soldier.'

How could he explain it to her? That day with the air so thin, so high. That wild sunshine. That ecstatic frame of mind they were in after their victory, blood still on the cuffs and the fronts of their uniforms. How he'd begun to sing the psalm.

Who, then, could tell what he was or wasn't? Who cared?

The King on his horse inspecting his troops, stopping there to listen. The King's eagerness to forget where he'd found him. Perhaps the King had forgotten. Who else, then, would ask questions?

'Eriksson knew,' she said.

'He did,' Olaus said.

'How?' she asked.

'I don't know. Perhaps he made enquiries. Perhaps it was nothing more than a suspicion; he ventured a guess and I gave myself away. Had he lived, he would probably have made my life a misery. But I didn't kill him.'

She exhaled. The sound was as clear as a question: Why should I believe you? But the question she asked was: 'Why didn't you?'

It threw him.

'I'd acted the role of priest for so long, perhaps I believed I was one,' he said.

In some ways there was relief now that it was over. Although he had no idea what would be left of him once you removed the priest.

There were knocks on the door.

'Open.'

A child's muted voice.

'That's Frederika,' Maija said.

Olaus opened and Frederika fell in. There was a hump on her back. The hump rolled off her and sat up. It was her sister.

'It's Mr Lundgren.' Frederika was still on all fours.

'What?'

'He has done terrible things to the schoolchildren.'

Olaus's outbreath; so long and slow, it filled the hallway.

Maija's voice sounded from somewhere far away: 'No.'

'Not with Dorotea, Mamma,' Frederika said. 'But with others. Daniel's Sara, for one.'

When Olaus Arosander was ten years old, he was still Olof, the hangman's son.

His father hanged with confidence, he lit fires with speed, he beheaded with precision – in silence and with impossible poise. 'It isn't for us to judge,' he'd tell his son as they cleaned up afterwards and buried the bodies. 'God brought this man here to this place, and to us. God only knows his journey.'

One night, like so many other times, they were woken close to midnight by pounding on the door.

'Get up!' the voice outside bellowed. 'You're needed.'

It was the case of a father who'd abused his own daughter. He'd managed to escape and the hangman and his son passed time together with the members of the jury. There had been a strange companionship among those who waited. Hatred was permitted and cheered.

They'd caught the man, of course. 'This one we don't bury,' his father had said. 'This one we throw to the dogs.'

Olaus remembered it because it was the one time his father had had no mercy to show.

It might also be that he remembered the night because it was the one time he and his father had belonged.

He imagined it now: riders on horses, Lapps on skis. Johan Lundgren on the run. But before dawn they would have that devil.

Together with Maija and her children, Olaus had gone to Sofia in the vicarage. There were questions they wanted to ask her. Sofia's face was taut. She had pushed each hand inside the opposite sleeve, as if cold.

'Your husband said he'd seen evil when he visited Blackåsen,' Olaus said. 'He was travelling with the verger.'

'Perhaps he saw something,' Sofia said. 'Or one of the children told him . . .'

'How did you know?' Maija asked her daughter.

Her voice sounded flat. This had been a shock for her, too. From what Olaus understood, it could have been her daughter.

'There were carvings in the window sill in the school. One day there was a new one, an "S" for Sara . . . Dorotea said that maybe the verger didn't want to give her lessons because of her feet. I thought about how Lundgren once talked to me about flawlessness. It sort of fell into place,' Frederika said.

Sometimes that was how the most important insights came, in drips and drops. You took a step back and there it was: a waterway.

'What were the other carvings?' Olaus asked.

'There were so many,' she said.

Olaus steeled himself.

'There was a "B" and a "U".' Frederika frowned as she tried to remember.

Sofia put her hand in front of her mouth. When she spoke, her eyes were full of tears. 'The two children who disappeared on Blackåsen,' she said. 'Their names were Ulla and Beata. The first went missing not long after we and the verger had arrived here. We held wakes for them.'

'A "K", a "J",' Frederika said, 'and an "A".'

Olaus looked to Sofia, but she was shaking her head.

'I haven't known all the children by name,' she said.

Olaus thought about the old priest who was said to have died when about to mend the barn roof. It would have been easy. A frail man, a mild push. In the midst of the lambs, there had been a wolf.

When he turned, Maija was staring at the floor, her forehead wrinkled. Connecting the dots in that mind of hers, he was certain, assembling the picture none of them wanted to see, but one that she would spend time with until it was all crystal clear.

'On Eriksson's body, I found marjoram . . .' Maija said. 'Marjoram is said to kill the lust. Perhaps Lundgren was wearing an amulet with the herbs and Eriksson snatched it off before he was killed . . .'

They were silent.

'Someone needs to tell Daniel,' Sofia said.

The father. The bishop must be on his way to attend Lady Day sermon. Olaus could leave it to him to tell the father that a man of the Church had abused his position and their trust. No. He'd do it himself. This had happened under his watch. And then it would be his turn to face the bishop.

'We need to leave,' Maija said. She was looking at her younger daughter.

Dorotea's cheeks were red. Her mother was right; she shouldn't be hearing this. Olaus walked them out. The hallway was dark and quiet. Frederika opened the door and Olaus felt the chill from outside.

'Strange that the bishop didn't know about the verger,' Maija said. 'I can't help but think that at some stage he ought to have suspected . . . With the first child disappearing so soon after the verger's arrival . . . Well.' She nodded to him. 'Goodnight.'

He reached out and touched her arm.

Instead of stopping, she took a step towards him. She came to stand so close that he felt her against his chest. The top of her head was by his cheek. Olaus didn't dare to move. He realised he was trembling.

'The bishop will be here tomorrow,' he said in a low voice that turned into a whisper. 'In view of . . . You know . . . me and . . .'

Me and my past? Who I am? Who I am not?

He swallowed and felt her hair against his Adam's apple. 'I am certain the bishop won't punish you now. He will forgive anything he had against you. I'll speak with Daniel, but perhaps it's best if you talk to the bishop without me. Tell him he can find me in my home. I'll pack my things and I'll be waiting for him.'

She bent her head back to look him in the eye and reached up to put her hand on his cheek.

'You're my priest,' she said.

Their eyes locked.

'Mamma?'

One of her daughters called her from outside.

Maija held his gaze.

'I don't have anything to say to the bishop,' she said and pressed her hand to his cheek harder, as if to leave a mark.

Then the old church bell above them started swaying ringing in Lady Day. The dull clang tumbled from the bell tower, out of step, before finding its rhythm. Olaus stood chest to chest with Maija as the bell rang and rang, singing with its broken voice, heavier and heavier, making the air tremble long after it had stilled.

Maija could hear the news about the verger being spread in Settler Town. The whispers grew to the crackle of fire. The verger. The verger! Oh God, the verger! Then the town turned silent, and it was not silence as much as absence, awaiting what was to come. Morning arose and with it a ruddy, harsh light, which cut the corners of each house sharp, which turned every colour shrill, which revealed flaws and shortcomings without mercy. The mountains were spared by the light and in comparison with the town, they seemed at once soft and welcoming.

There they were: the sounds of runners crushing snow, whips lashing. The calls of men.

'You stay inside,' Maija said to Frederika and Dorotea.

'But Mamma,' Frederika said.

'You stay inside,' she repeated.

Maija followed the stream of people with tar torches flowing towards the church green. The carriages had stopped at the middle of the square. The horses were snorting, moving, adrenaline pumping. The men jumped off the sleighs. Inside one of them was the verger, clinging to its side. There was a murmur in the crowd around Maija. The men dragged the man down in the snow. The verger was shouting something. The mumble of the mob grew into a mutter, as it began to move forward.

The priest came running. 'Wait!' he called.

Apart from Maija, nobody else seemed to hear.

'Be careful,' she shouted to the priest and pushed to make her way towards him, but the mass of people moved as one man. They dragged and hauled the verger through the square and towards the gallows on the hill. On the hillside, the snow was deep. The snow and the cold should have brought the slow advancement to a halt, but even they could do nothing. The crowd advanced as if driven on by the Devil himself, faces black with hunger and hatred.

There was a shot. The priest stood on top of one of the sleighs, a raised shotgun in his hands.

Maija's chest ached from breathing the raw air. The square and the hill were still.

'Every man has the right to a trial,' the priest said. 'No matter how awful the crime. Every man must be allowed to speak and be heard.'

One of the men who stood by the verger let his hands fall. A woman beside Maija wiped her nose.

'I didn't do it,' the verger said. 'I didn't kill Eriksson.'

Oh no, no, Maija thought. Be quiet. But it was too late, the mob was growling.

'He will be sentenced,' the priest called. But people were no longer looking at him, they had turned back to the verger. 'There will be justice. For every sin he has inflicted upon one of our young ones, there shall be punishment.'

There was a second blast. Maija startled. The priest was craning his neck. He didn't shoot, she thought. He is trying to see who did. But the people had pulled together into a wall, protecting whoever had fired the shot.

When there was a gap in the crowd, she saw the verger lying face down in the snow.

★   ★   ★

The parishioners waited in the pews in the church. Lady Day Mass was two hours late by the time the priest walked in and, following him, the bishop. The bishop passed the priest and climbed the pulpit so forcefully the structure shook.

Maija tried to see the priest through the crowd, but couldn't.

'In view of the circumstances, it shall be me who gives today's sermon,' the bishop said. 'By the mercy of God, the evil doings of Johan Lundgren have been discovered. Olaus and I have spent time going through the events, but it is impossible for us to tell who pulled the trigger and no one has come forward. Perhaps it was, after all, an unfortunate accident.'

Maija moved closer to Dorotea, put her arm around her, and now she could see him. The priest stood underneath the pulpit, and though his face was drawn, his poise was assured and priestly. The bishop doesn't know, she thought and felt relief. It wasn't tenable, of course. Sooner or later, the priest's past would become known. Unless he stayed here, with them. Perhaps they could convince Sofia to leave things be . . .

The bishop kept talking, about how common man was not allowed to take justice into his own hands. The worshippers sat immovable. One of us shot Lundgren, Maija thought. Others among us saw. But no one will ever talk. Her eyes caught on Daniel and Anna, a couple of benches in front of her on the other side of the aisle. Their children weren't with them. Nobody sat beside them. It was as if their faces had been cut in stone. Maija's eyes filled. Thank you, God, she thought and felt guilt and gratitude mingle to something exceeding the space in her chest. She pulled Dorotea closer.

They had packed up, and it was time to leave for Blackåsen. Maija had made them late. First, she was convinced they had forgotten to pack the alcohol that she had bought to wash

357

Dorotea's feet, and they had to unpack the bag to find it. Then she wasn't certain whether there had been a key to the cottage and whether she ought to have locked it and returned it. As she closed the door behind them, she had to admit to herself that she had hoped the priest would come and say goodbye. How stupid; they were just members of a flock.

She grabbed the harness of Dorotea's sledge and tugged at it so that Dorotea squealed and had to struggle for balance.

'Do you want me to pull it?' Frederika asked.

'No,' Maija said.

They walked down the street in Settler Town, the last ones to leave. The church green, too, was almost empty. As they passed the priest's dwelling, she looked for him in each window. He was probably in the vicarage with Sofia.

At the end of the green, they followed the trail in the snow created by all those who had already left. When it was time to turn into the forest, Maija stopped.

Her daughters looked at her.

'Just . . . wait here,' she said.

She didn't say any more, but turned and hurried back along the path. She reached the empty square and began to run. She ran straight across it towards the church, snow whirling around her feet. She had to grab the handle with both hands in order to open the heavy door. She rushed through the vestibule and into the great hall.

When she entered, he was there, the priest, her priest, standing by his Jesus. He turned, and she froze. He waited. And then she ran down the aisle towards him; she couldn't run fast enough. He opened his arms and she threw herself into them, and they wrapped around her and lifted her and hugged her. The stubble on his chin grated her cheek.

There was a scraping sound from the church vestibule as

the door opened again and they let go of each other as if they had burned themselves.

The priest's mouth was half open, his breathing hard. His eyes locked on hers, and hers moved from his left eye to his right, trying to hold both in her gaze at the same time and, of course, she couldn't. She laughed. The priest smiled, too: a diagonal smile that was happy and sad, both at the same time.

The footsteps approached.

'Oh good,' the bishop said. 'So you've told Maija that her punishment has been made void.'

'Yes,' the priest said. His voice was hoarse.

'We forgot to make it clear in the upheaval,' the bishop said. 'Go now, my child, and don't sin again.'

Still, spring did not come.

Three days had passed since Lady Day, one travel day, and then two of the same low morning glow and slow afternoon light that brought on shadows too fast. The clouds looked grey, although she knew they were white.

Frederika waited and watched. She ought to have felt better, freed of all burdens, but the incessant thrum in the air was as strong as ever. She kept looking up to the top of the mountain. *We got him. Why are you not letting up?*

'I don't know how to thank you.' She put her hand on Eriksson's sleeve when he appeared. His arm felt hard and cold. 'If you hadn't kept me with Dorotea when she was getting her tuition . . .'

He didn't meet her gaze.

'I am so sorry,' she whispered and removed her hand. 'Did he get to one of yours? Was that what Elin found out that destroyed her?'

He didn't answer, but narrowed his eyes as if in pain.

After a while, he said, 'Elin should have known earlier. She could have known. She had lived the same thing when little, for God's sake! Jessika didn't say anything, but once I was gone, it didn't take Elin long to figure out what was wrong.'

Then the 'J' had been for Jessika, Frederika thought.

'Neither of you could imagine such evil,' she said.

They stood still and allowed the shadows from the trees to lengthen.

'Will you be leaving now?' she said.

Eriksson pressed his lips together. 'It's not over yet,' he said.

Frederika knew he was right. She didn't want to look at the protective circle of wind that she'd cast around herself and Dorotea, but could tell it was almost worn through. At night, she heard the wolves yelping. Their barks were growing more confident. Eager. She could try to throw another circle, but she wasn't certain it would work a second time.

Frederika was on the porch looking towards the top of the mountain, when, on day four, Fearless arrived leading a white reindeer on a rope.

'I've come to pick up the goats,' he said.

'Does that mean spring is coming?'

'In a while. We are getting ready to leave for the high mountains.'

'Thank you for the reindeer.' She took the rope.

When he had fetched his goats, he didn't leave, but stood and peered at her.

'I thought spring would have arrived by now,' she said. 'That after Lady Day, winter would let go.'

'I'm guessing she didn't bring the right things,' he said, 'Lady Day. Or maybe not all of it.'

Did he know what was missing? Frederika wondered if it was possible to have a vocation and then shut it off, or whether bits still leaked through: signs you couldn't avoid seeing. If you once thought you had the truth, could you ever leave it behind even if you rejected it, or would you carry it with you, that option of a different life?

They faced each other. Around them, the air began to pulse louder.

'You wouldn't have burned it,' she said and her voice sounded like that of somebody much older. 'Your drum. It's holy.'

'It belonged to the past.'

'You couldn't have. You wouldn't.'

He stepped backwards and broke the circle that had been drawn around the two of them.

She watched him leave, and then she turned to the creature. It looked more like a white cow than a deer. Its muzzle was round, its antlers slight. She hoped her mother wouldn't kill it, but knew they had to. If only Fearless had brought them an ugly beast. The animal was rooting in the snow beside her, but the lichen lay too deep.

She pulled on the rope and headed for the barn. She hesitated and instead tied the rope around one of the pillars by the building. She walked inside and took some of the goats' food and put it before the reindeer. She watched it eat and stroked its side.

She was right. Fearless would never have burned the drum. Even if he no longer believed, he wouldn't have destroyed it.

She thought about seeing inside someone, and of tracking the wolves' whereabouts from afar. Both times, she had used what Jutta had taught her. The only other thing she could remember Jutta teaching her was her litanies: 'The shrewdness of the fox, the wisdom of the owl, the strength of the bear . . .' Perhaps that, too, was something you could learn? To dip into the strengths of other beings?

But there was more than the old wisdoms. When she had called for her mother the night the wolves attacked – that summoning had come all by itself. And what the mirror had showed her; that, too, had happened on its own.

So it could be done without someone teaching you. And you didn't need a drum, because there were other ways. You just needed to open up to it. How much? Open everything. Not keep any reserve for yourself. Give it your all, saying, 'I am willing. Take me.' Even be prepared to die. And then . . . then what?

She didn't know. She couldn't know until she had tried it.

It was easier than she had thought. But also much more difficult. She would no longer be her own person. The spirits would make their demands and she would have to respond. In return, what she asked for would be given to her. But the sacrifice could be great. The spirits could ask for something that meant the world to her.

Footsteps in the snow.

'So he's been for his goats?' her mother asked.

'Yes.'

They watched the white animal.

'You know what,' her mother said. 'I think he brought us a cow.'

'I know,' Frederika said.

'No, really. I think this animal has milk.'

Her mother's eyes were scrunched up, as if she were laughing.

Olaus felt stripped without his pretences. He also felt fresh and, ah, it was true: he had never felt more peaceful. His future was a muddle, all things unclear, all things ripped up, destroyed. And still he was happy. The power of confession was immense, he thought. What a shame it wasn't a part of the Lutheran faith. Confessing all to another human being and still be –

He didn't dare to think the word.

He cleared the path outside his dwelling from snow. Then, gripped by an impulse, he walked across the green to shovel Sofia's, too. She was standing in the window and he waved to her. They'd have to talk. Soon, he thought.

He went to check on his animals. Their trays were full of food. He patted the flank of a cow.

As he took his evening meal, he thought of his father. He remembered the balding head, the slack chin and the full lips with what, for once, wasn't hatred. He didn't know what his father had done to be punished with the hangman's role. He'd never asked, and now he was gripped by the desire to understand. They'd parted in anger. He, impetuous and proud, unable to wait to leave his home, refusing to accept his lot. His father shouting to him as he walked out, 'You've rejected everything I stand for.'

'Stand for,' he had scoffed to himself as he walked away. But it had been true. His father had been principled and, despite his profession, he'd been a good man.

He wished his father could see him now. Forgive me, Father.

'We are what we are,' he whispered to himself, 'and I am grateful.'

He couldn't sleep and that wasn't because of his father, but because of Maija. He kept seeing her before him. That wiry figure. Those large eyes, her white-blonde hair.

'Strange that the bishop didn't know.' In his head, he mimicked her slow, sing-song accent.

He recalled Maija's hand against his cheek. Strong and dry. Warm. How close she'd been standing. So close, he ought to have felt her heart.

Oh, what was he doing?

He turned on his side. The sheet was swirled around his legs and he kicked at it, once, then several times. He swung his legs over the side of the bed and sat up.

'You're my priest,' she had said.

He sighed. A grunt that went all the way to his core. He placed his own hand on his cheek as if hers were still there for him to touch. He allowed his body to respond to the thought.

'Strange that the bishop didn't know,' she'd said.

Beata, Ulla, Sara . . . What other letters had Frederika mentioned? A 'K', an 'A' and a 'J'. Olaus suddenly remembered the entry in the Church Books: *K against the church*. Perhaps one of the girls had spoken to the old priest about what was happening on Blackåsen and . . .

Hold on . . . The family who had disappeared from Blackåsen overnight. What were their names? The Janssons?

The cold tore at Olaus as he crossed the yard. He unlocked the church, ran up the stairs to his room, found the Church Books first and lit the candle second. He turned the large pages. Births, deaths . . . *The Janssons.* His finger trembled as it followed the entries. *Arva Jansson. Born 1711.* 'A' as in Arva.

A young girl.

Olaus had to sit down. He felt sick.

If the *K against the church* had been the same 'K' whose initial had been carved in the window sill, that would mean one of the girls had told the old priest and he had dismissed the claim.

The old priest had been many things, but he had been conscientious. A claim like that – a man of the Church behaving inappropriately – even if the old priest had dismissed it, he would have told the bishop. He would have had to. It was too grave. And then there was what Mårten had said about a bishop who, the year before Olaus arrived, in secret, had sent away a young girl who was with child. That had been Arva and her family; the Janssons.

There was more . . . Something the housekeeper had said. South, he realised. Much later, just before he died, after returning from Blackåsen's Catechetical hearing, the old priest had asked his carriage to be prepared for him to travel south. Not east. Whatever it was the old priest had found out then, he had felt he couldn't tell the bishop and he'd prepared to take his tale south.

There was no question about it; the bishop had known.

Olaus hit the table with his hand. The swine, he thought, and didn't know whether he meant the verger who'd enacted the deeds, the old priest who, at first, hadn't listened to a girl in distress, or the bishop, who had known and not punished the culprit – or all three of them.

He had to knock for a long time before there was movement inside the vicarage. Then there were footsteps and Sofia opened the door, her head still in a night bonnet.

'You.' She smiled, voice thick with sleep.

'You too knew,' he said.

She stepped aside to let him in and closed the door behind him. 'Knew what?' she said, blinking.

'About Lundgren.'

When she realised what he was saying, she looked shocked. 'Heaven forbid,' she said.

He had to hand it to her; she was playing her part well.

'Your taxman helped the bishop arrange a trip south for a girl in trouble. On their own, the Janssons would never have got access to the bishop. It was you who convinced him to help.'

'I don't know of any trip. This is ridiculous,' she said.

He grabbed her arm. 'Don't lie to me.'

Her mouth opened and then closed again.

His grip around her arm tightened. 'What I cannot grasp is why; why would you protect someone like Lundgren? Tell me, or I shall persecute you myself. Do not think that the bishop or your mighty friends will be able to help you.'

She shook him off.

'After all I have done for you. For the mercy of God – I did not know. What monster could have known and kept silent? They are children!'

Well, that was that, Maija thought for the hundredth time. She brushed the floor of the cottage with the broom. Once all the dirt was cornered, she dampened a cloth, gathered it up and shook the rag over the fire. She felt hot, and took off her jumper. It fascinated her how eating this little for so long had changed her body. Her arms sticking out from inside the short-sleeved shirt were thin and straight, their veins large. She'd seen similar changes in the other settlers. Everyone was hungry. Even the priest had thinned. His body had been angular and . . .

She became cold, and put her jumper back on again. Her stomach hurt. Soon spring would come and they would eat. She would have fish, and meat grilled in butter, and . . .

Why hadn't she slaughtered the reindeer? There was meat for at least two weeks. It was just so beautiful.

She scoffed at herself. As if she could afford to be senti-mental. The goats gave milk; what they needed was meat. And so, she would take its life. Tomorrow. This evening she would speak with the girls, and they'd do it at dawn. They'd have to sharpen the knives. It was hard to kill a reindeer. It was a large animal and its pelt was tough.

What had she been thinking, implying Nils would have killed Fearless' reindeer? The head was severed. He wouldn't have had the spiritual resilience for it. And he had had no reason to show Eriksson respect.

She'd seen them in the morning: Nils, Daniel and Henrik transporting logs to the site they had chosen for the village by the lake. She thought of Daniel's and Anna's faces that last time in church. Poor Daniel. For so long, he had held fort against the evilness of his brother. And he'd been given no favours in return. He had lost Elin, a baby son, and now this had befallen his daughter. He would need to get it out of him. He'd probably try to use hard work as an outlet for his anger.

If Frederika hadn't stayed by her sister's side, it could have been Dorotea. Sara . . . *God*.

She began to wash the dishes in the basin and continued with the basin itself; scrubbed it until the unspoiled wood came up through the damaged, then ended up leaning against the basin, putting her thumb and fingers to her eyelids to keep them shut and her eyes empty. Her stomach pained her again and she pressed her fist into her side.

Anna had been wrong. There had been no good sides to Eriksson. To think he'd known about Lundgren and let it continue. Unless, of course, Eriksson had just found out and Lundgren killed him when he confronted him. No, that didn't work. Lundgren wouldn't have gone around carrying a rapier. And Eriksson would have been prepared for a reaction, wouldn't he? He would have come ready to defend himself.

Another thing that didn't feel right was the marjoram. If Lundgren had an amulet with marjoram around his neck, that implied he had tried to quell his lusts. Maija would have assumed that people who repeatedly committed the same wrong, with time surrendered to it completely.

Stop this, she told herself.

And why would Lundgren have put a reindeer's head on

Eriksson's grave after killing him? Or, perhaps the two events were not connected . . .

She thought about how Lundgren had shouted that he hadn't killed Eriksson. He would die, regardless, so what did it matter?

She threw the wet brush on the floor and hit her fist against her thigh several times. Stop this.

Paavo. Think about him. He would soon be home. Easter, perhaps. That was in one week's time. They would live. There were dues to pay. Poor Dorotea, her feet. Her life would never be what it could have been. But they would live.

It just didn't make sense, that was all.

A minute later, she was dressed and putting on her skis.

Anna's face fell when she opened the door.

Maija reached out, took her hand and squeezed it. Anna's hand was limp. Daniel was sitting by the kitchen table. They are not talking, Maija thought. They can't talk.

'I am so sorry,' Maija said. 'I am so, so sorry.'

Anna pulled her hand away.

Maija inhaled. 'Please forgive me for what I am about to do,' she said in the gentlest voice she had. She had thought about it all the way over. They had to go into the details even if it would cause Daniel and Anna more pain. If they weren't absolutely clear about what had happened, if they weren't certain they had got to the bottom of it all, then things might still be out there, small evil seeds just waiting to root and grow again.

'Please forgive me,' she said again, and inhaled. 'Do you think that Eriksson knew and kept silent?'

'Knew what?' Daniel asked.

'If Lundgren killed your brother . . .'

'If? You can't be serious. We know he did.'

Maija pressed on: 'It's the rapier. If the verger had brought a rapier with him to the forest to kill Eriksson, it couldn't have been their first conversation.'

Daniel's face was white. 'What right do you have to ask us this? Leave it, Maija. It's over. Go home. Be happy that it wasn't yours. Take care of your daughters.'

Anna had bent her head.

'We just need to be certain,' Maija said. 'It's for all of us, for our protection.'

Anna sighed. 'Eriksson was bad, but not that bad.'

Daniel moaned.

'His children too were in that school.'

'So if Eriksson didn't know what Lundgren was doing, then why would Lundgren kill him?' Maija asked.

Daniel roared. 'Haven't you done enough already, Maija? Our family is in pieces and still you won't stop. You won't stop until nobody on this mountain can trust anybody else!'

He stepped out from behind the table.

'We need to know,' Maija said, as Daniel pushed her towards the door. 'We must make certain.'

Dorotea was asleep when she came home. Maija and Frederika sat by the kitchen table and listened to her breaths. There was a rush of something – haziness or sickness – and Maija put her hands flat on the table before her.

'We'll slaughter the reindeer tomorrow,' she said.

Frederika bent her head, but nodded.

Maija's head stopped roaring. She felt better.

From over by the bed came Dorotea's cough. 'I feel hot,' Dorotea said.

Maija walked across the room and sat down on the bed beside her.

Her daughter's cheeks were swollen red. Maija stroked her forehead. It was warm; too warm. Fever.

Frederika brought her a cup of water. 'Here, drink,' she said to her sister.

Dorotea opened her eyes, took a sip.

'More,' Maija said.

Dorotea shook her head and lay back down on the pillow.

Maija removed the wraps around her daughter's feet. What was left of Dorotea's toes were black and blistered. The rot continued. But this time there was more: the angry red that had been close to the damaged toes had spread further up towards her ankles. Infection.

Not this. She touched the red ankles. They were burning. Maija felt Frederika's eyes, but couldn't meet them.

'We're going to have to cut into her feet,' Maija said in a low voice.

'No.'

'She'll die if we don't. It's spreading.'

'You can't decide this.'

'Your father isn't here, Frederika. We need—'

'There is still hope. We need to trust.'

'But trust what, Frederika? In God? Trust what?'

They stared at each other.

'There is more on this mountain than you know,' Frederika said.

Maija rose. Her heart was banging in her chest. Her stomach seemed to be falling far away from her head. 'I don't want to hear another word from you. Listen to yourself. Think, Frederika. Use your brain.'

'It's you who don't listen. You don't see. There is something the matter with you. Your decisions aren't good any more.'

Frederika's voice broke, and she ran out of the house.

'Frederika.'

Frederika sat up. Something had woken her.

'Frederika.'

Fearless' voice might as well have been in the same room.

Her fingers trawled the floorboards: trousers, blouse. In her mind, she hushed him. Be quiet, or you'll wake the others. They can't hear him, she thought then, but she still worried and buttoned the blouse wrong and had to start over. Then she realised that it didn't matter.

It was an overcast sky, with neither moon nor stars to give light. She walked across the yard holding her hands out in front of her in case she fell. The shape of the barn became clear, and when she drew closer, there was a glow from in between the timber slats.

Fearless waited for her in the barn, lantern lit. Without a word, he lifted a shape off the bale beside him. He unwrapped the reindeer skin and held the object towards her. She stepped closer. It was the drum. He nodded, and she took it.

'You will own or be owned,' he said.

There were brown paintings on the taut leather: reindeer, dogs, the sun, signs Frederika didn't recognise. With her finger, she caressed the surface. The skin was so soft, it felt downy against her fingertips.

'Listen to me,' he said. When he was certain he had her

eyes, he repeated: 'You will own or be owned. It depends on how strong you are. What animal are you seeing?'

'Wolf.'

'Wolf?' He stroked his chin. 'Almost impossible to tame. The drum will give you access to other worlds; to their world. That's where you'll have to conquer them.' He stepped closer to her and grabbed her arm. 'Use the gifts with great care, Frederika. Don't give in to evil. Don't give in to arrogance.' He sighed. 'The way you've chosen . . . You've set yourself up to be the carrier of justice.'

'Yes,' she said.

'No,' he said, shaking his head as if she didn't understand. 'It is not that easy to execute justice.'

He left, and she sat watching the drum.

She sat in the barn until morning. The drum seemed to pulsate in rhythm with the sound in the air. *Dum Tataradum.* It beckoned her to touch it.

Their cottage smelled hot and sour. Her mother was by the fire. She turned. Sideways, she was so thin the flames seemed visible through her. The knife blade glowed red from the heat of fire.

'No,' Frederika said.

'She is dying,' her mother said.

'I won't let you.'

'Look for yourself,' her mother said. 'Blood poisoning.'

Then her mother folded over. Her fingers clawed on to the side of the fireplace and she stood there, bent over, before standing up straight again with what looked like a huge effort.

When she spoke again, her voice was soft. 'Frederika, you can stay here and help me. I so need your help. Or you can leave and come back when it is done. But I am doing this now.'

'You need to wait. I am getting gifts. I shall heal Dorotea.'

'You've lost your reason. Frederika, listen to yourself.'

'You healed yourself when you were a child.'

'I have told you, that's not how it was.'

'You have to believe.'

Her mother started for the bed, for her sister. Frederika followed and her mother swirled around. There was a sting, like nettles burning her throat. When Frederika reached up, there was blood on her fingers.

She cut me, she thought, shocked. She cut me.

The knife was still between them and her mother took a step towards her. The glassy eyes, the twisted mouth: Frederika didn't recognise her.

'I told you,' her mother said and raised the point of the knife under Frederika's chin so she had to bend her head back so as not to be hurt.

Frederika felt a low churning in her stomach. Rage.

'I told you,' her mother said again.

Inside Frederika, this . . . black thing, swelled and grew. Her head felt light. She couldn't breathe. Her mother walked forward, knife still to her skin, and Frederika reversed.

You cut me, Frederika thought. She opened her mouth to scream the words.

With what seemed an impossible effort, she turned, found the door handle, opened it and fell out.

She ran towards the forest. The snow was deep. The wind strong. There was a muted scream behind her.

And then, between the tree trunks, black shapes: men. She recognised Nils, Daniel and Henrik. Somehow she knew they were coming for her mother.

Dawn was growing on the flat coastland. By the vast white that was the sea, the church stretched in its early light.

Snow from the horses' hooves had stopped spraying Olaus's face. Beneath them, the runners of the wagon sang, but it was more muffled now than when they had set out. They slid more often, too, and caught: the tracks were softer, the surface of the snow coated with mushy crystals. The air was warmer. Spring was not far away.

As they came closer to the coastal town, charred remnants sighed of war and the enemy across the waters.

Their horses galloped into the church yard and a boy ran out. He grabbed the reins and helped slow their animals. Olaus stepped off the cart, stiff after the long journey. He swept his cloak around him and walked towards the bishop's palace. Before he was on the porch, the door opened. A maid curtsied, took his cape and showed him into a room with a large fire. A bishop's world. Servants ready to serve the unexpected as well as the expected.

It wasn't long before the bishop entered.

'Olaus,' he said and clapped his hands together as if joyful. 'What a pleasant surprise.' He made a mock face of horror. 'No more ghastly revelations, I do hope.'

'You knew,' Olaus said.

'Knew what?'

'You knew what was happening to the children on Blackåsen.'

The bishop looked at him for a second. He walked two steps back to the door, opened it and said to someone outside, 'Bring us some wine. And bread – the white sort. Our visitor is hungry like a wolf after his very long journey.'

The bishop closed the door and walked to sit down in his chair. He gave a tweak to correct the drape of his cloak over his knee and indicated for Olaus to sit down. When Olaus didn't, the bishop tilted his head with a look of mild disappointment.

'And what is this?' he asked. 'A conscience?'

A conscience?

'Children,' Olaus said. 'They are children.'

'Yes, it was unfortunate,' the bishop said. He placed the fingertips of his hand against each other and nodded. 'Oh, trust me, I haven't known for that long, but when I found out, for a short while, it was necessary to let it be.'

Olaus's throat was thick. He couldn't speak.

'More important things have been under way.'

'Nothing can justify something like that.'

'Wake up, Olaus.' The bishop's voice rose. 'For once, look to something beyond yourself. Our country is torn asunder. Our people are dying. We can change that. But we needed more time. We had to prioritise. Some things had to wait.'

'What is it?' Olaus said. His brain was running away with him; he wasn't certain he wanted an answer. 'What is it you are doing?'

The bishop hesitated.

'It's something really bad, isn't it?' Olaus said. 'But what?'

The bishop spat out the words: 'The killing of the one who calls himself King.'

Unthinkable.

'The King is instated by God,' Olaus said.

'God?' The bishop gave a short laugh. 'You're not even a priest and you're talking of God? Ah, you seem surprised. But of course I knew. Always have done. I brought you here because, with your knowledge of the King's habits, I thought you might be of use. That was before I realised your infatuation with him was so great.'

The bishop leaned back in his chair.

'No, whatever mandate the King had from God, it is long gone,' he said.

'What is the link to Blackåsen?' Olaus asked.

'Killing a king is not difficult. I could perhaps even do it myself. Managing the aftermath is much more troublesome.' The bishop lowered his voice. 'A new constitution is already in the making which will give the power back to the people. With Kristina's link to the old gentry, we'll have the support of the two largest factions of the government's four: the Church and the aristocracy. Once the King is gone, the constitution will be voted through.'

Olaus thought about the entries in the Church Books. After the one stating Elin was being examined for acts of sorcery, the next entry reported the arrival of Nils and Kristina. That's what happened during the hearing, he thought. The bishop recognised Kristina and saw his chance, through her, to reach the gentry. Eriksson must have overheard the bishop and Kristina speaking about it. Or he had just guessed that there was some reason for the bishop suddenly losing interest in the hearing, and then he had opposed the bishop just to see how far the latter was willing to go.

Lundgren had moved to the region from the south, Olaus thought. If there had been a trial and they had begun to dig into his past, who knew how far the matter would go? And the last thing the bishop would have wanted was to attract attention to himself or to his region. Lundgren's death: what a convenient incident. No wonder the bishop had been willing to write that off as an 'accident'.

'Does Sofia know?' Olaus asked.

'Sofia?' The bishop laughed and shook his head. 'Sofia has nothing to do with this. She is one of those rare people who is precisely what she seems – an excellent priest-wife.'

Olaus wasn't certain he was telling the truth, but it hardly mattered.

'I will tell the King. I will warn him,' Olaus said.

'It is much too late. Besides, who do you think the King would believe? A bishop, or a priest who is no priest?'

There was a knock on the door.

'Enter,' the bishop called.

Both men stood in silence as only priests can, as the servant entered.

The King should never have sent him away, Olaus thought. He had loved him. He would have fought for him. He would have died for him.

'Put it on the table by the fire, please,' the bishop said.

The servant left. The door closed and they were back with each other.

'I will have no part of this,' Olaus said. 'Nobody can decide to take a life – no matter whose life it is. No matter what the cause.'

'That's not what you used to think, I believe.'

'You were willing to sacrifice the children. It matters. I am not like you.'

'That is true,' the bishop agreed. This seemed to amuse him. 'You are nothing like me. When did you ever do anything for anybody but yourself?'

Then the smile on his face disappeared. 'As I see it, you now have a choice, Olaus. Fight me, and, by God, I shall fight you. Or we forget about this. All of . . .' – he made a round movement with his fingers as if to make something dissolve into air – 'this.'

The bishop leaned back in his chair.

'After all, I am an old man, Olaus. I need to start thinking about who will replace me. As a bishop, and in the Privy Council.'

The bishop put his hands on the arms of the chair and rose. He walked to the door. 'Prepare a room for my guest,' he said.

The other settlers were already in Henrik and Lisbet's cottage when Maija was brought there. Anna and Lisbet were sitting at the kitchen table. Kristina stood by the window.

Maija had to get back home. Would Frederika know how to care for Dorotea? Yes. She would know.

If she had not run too far away.

She recalled the slight weight in her hand, the blade. How dull it had looked leaning against white skin, and then as it cut, sawed through tissue and bone, the foot becoming some-thing else, her hands turning red, her daughter screaming. She had tried to be fast, but the flesh had been tough.

At once, her stomach was in her mouth and she bent to vomit.

Beside her Daniel swore, and side-stepped.

She wiped her face on her sleeve.

'She's sick,' someone said.

'It's the Devil in her that's afraid.' That was Lisbet.

I cut my own daughter's toes off, she wanted to say, but nothing came out. And had my other daughter not fled, I might have killed her.

'Tie her, so she doesn't escape.'

Tie? Escape?

A chair was put forward and hands pressed her down on to it.

'We will have this out, here and now, once and for all.' Daniel was standing over her. His face was gaunt. He was no longer just his own. 'This is all linked to you. It ends here.'

'It happened before I came.' She looked Daniel straight in the eyes, but couldn't reach him.

'You can make barren cows give milk. You were one of the last people to see Elin before she slayed herself and her children.' His voice broke. 'You killed our unborn by the herbs you had Anna drink.'

Anna had bent her head. That's when it caught Maija. Fear.

'Daniel . . .' Maija said.

There was a knock on the door. Nobody reacted, but when Fearless opened the door, they still somehow jumped. Fearless looked small in the opening. He looked from one face to another, found the owner of the house.

'My people belong to this mountain, too. This concerns us, as well as you.'

Henrik glanced at Nils and at Daniel. Then he nodded.

'So be it,' Daniel said, 'but it is a settler matter, and so I ask you to be quiet.'

He turned back to Maija. His finger touched his knife in its sheath.

Maija looked past Daniel towards Henrik. 'Eriksson's killer is still loose,' she said.

Henrik hated fear as much as she did. He might listen. He might be the only one who would. And, apart from Daniel, he had been on the mountain the longest. He would have a say in what happened next. There was a wrinkle on his forehead and she spoke to that suggestion of uncertainty.

'Lundgren killed Eriksson,' Henrik said.

'No,' she said. 'Eriksson's children were in the school. He didn't know what Lundgren was up to. Had Eriksson found out, he wouldn't have confronted him on his own. Or, he would have come prepared. He wouldn't have been taken by surprise and let himself get killed.'

'He confronted each of us about our secrets on his own.'

'That's because he wanted something out of you and traded that for his silence. But what the verger did was too vile. Eriksson didn't know, and thus Lundgren didn't kill him.'

She looked around. No, it wasn't Lundgren, she thought, but one of you. She hesitated. Something was missing. What was it?

'You are not trustworthy, Maija.' It was Nils's voice. Kristina turned away from her husband and looked out the window.

The way Nils had said it. Slow. She met his gaze and he nodded. 'It's not only you who can ask questions about the past,' he said.

At once, Jutta was there, siding with Maija's accusers. Her bottom jaw with the under-bite was working.

'This is how it always is, with you, isn't it?' Nils said. 'You begin fixating on something and then your mind takes over.'

'What are you talking about?' Henrik sounded hesitant.

'Do you want to tell them yourself?' Nils asked Maija.

She was silent.

Nils turned to face the others, again. 'When Maija accused me of having killed Eriksson, I asked a fisherman I know to enquire in Ostrobothnia about Maija and Paavo's past. He returned saying that back where Maija comes from, it is widely believed that she killed her grandmother. There was an old story of fault involved, the villagers said, and Maija found out and became obsessed with it. She spent some time in a madhouse down south, her daughter meanwhile living with her great-grandmother. Then Maija was declared healthy, returned, and meted out the punishment she deemed right on an old woman.'

There were gasps.

It was nothing like that. Maija looked at Jutta and her eyes filled.

'The old lady suffocated to death. Nothing could be proven. Maija and Paavo stayed in the village, had a second daughter, but the other villagers were relieved when they left last spring.'

Maija tried to ignore what had just been said and focus on the clear lines before her; focus only on the picture of what had happened. Nils had a defence in the bishop. It hadn't been Daniel, she was certain. Henrik . . . No, Lisbet kept him so close. Gustav . . . She looked around.

Gustav was not there.

Deep in her mind, there was something someone had said. Elin. When he died, Eriksson had gone to see if the marsh could be harvested further out. But had she not also said he was going with someone? Hadn't she said he was going with Gustav? She thought of Gustav poking at the marsh with a stick. What was it with the marsh?

'Did Eriksson ever say anything about Gustav?' she asked and looked for Anna.

Anna didn't meet her gaze.

'Why would she know?' Daniel said.

'Anna?' Maija said. 'Please.'

'Don't answer her,' Daniel said to his wife.

'Please,' Maija said again. 'Anna, please.'

The other woman lifted her head. The room was quiet. She won't answer, Maija thought.

But Anna said, 'I think they were friends.'

Everybody was looking at Anna.

'Why do you say that?' Maija asked.

'I saw them once. Gustav and Eriksson. Gustav was on his knees.' Anna's voice went to incredulous as she remembered.

'It was like he was hugging Eriksson's legs and Eriksson was patting Gustav on his head . . . It was strange. I thought Gustav might be begging for mercy. And then Eriksson slapped him. Gustav fell down. And he just crawled back and hugged Eriksson's legs again.'

Gustav wouldn't have had any problems slaughtering Fearless' reindeer, Maija thought. He had that raw strength about him and he was a hunter. He was a soldier too. He might well have spent time in Russia, where he would have grown used to their customs, to their practices.

'Maija won't stop until she has destroyed all of us,' Daniel said

Not him. Don't let him distract you. Henrik. Speak to Henrik.

'Gustav returned from the wars a broken man,' Maija said. 'Eriksson knew how to recognise that which was damaged. God only knows what he did to this man.'

Henrik was frowning. Think about your wife, Maija sent the thought to him. Think about her having good reasons to remain fearful for the rest of her life. For the rest of your life.

'As long as you are not certain what happened,' she said, 'you'll doubt. You'll always be frightened.'

The settlers walked on the lake ice. It was to be the last run across, Maija thought. Already, at places, there was water. Spring was coming, but late. Fearless was studying the ice, too. Their eyes met. He knew.

Dorotea.

Maija sent the thought across the mountain. In her mind, she tried to see Frederika, but couldn't. See to your sister, she thought nevertheless. Please go and find her. I didn't have time to make sure she was all right.

There was something like a faint pulse in the air. Maija's ears felt blocked by pressure, like they did when she was on top of a high mountain.

'Can we come in?' Henrik asked, when Gustav opened the door.

Gustav hunched, stretched. 'Why?' he said. His scar pulled his mouth too large.

Henrik didn't answer. Gustav hesitated, then walked backwards and they followed him.

Henrik looked to Maija. She wished he would have asked Gustav questions. She was too blunt.

'Gustav,' she said. 'Tell them what you did.'

His back was working so much that a whining sound emerged from his throat. They were all watching him now with the pity or disgust you reserve for someone sick.

'You'll feel better if you do,' she said. 'It will be over. It wasn't your fault.'

And it really wasn't. Eriksson had played on Gustav's past as he had Elin's. He had used and mistreated a man who was already broken. At some point it had gone too far.

She shook her head to show she meant it. Gustav's shoulders fell a little, then more.

'I didn't mean it,' he said.

'I know.'

He moved forward and the others stepped away from him, but he didn't look at them, but at her.

'I didn't know.'

'I know,' she said again.

'And the fire got out of hand.'

Fire? What fire?

She shook her head, but he was staring at her, not letting go.

'I heard them scream. I tried to reach them, but the fire spread. I couldn't get to them.'

He searched with his eyes, took a step and fell on his knees on the wooden floor before Fearless. 'I had just arrived,' he whispered and looked up at the Lapp. 'I wanted to clear land for myself. I didn't know how fast it could spread. The fire was everywhere. And then, I didn't know what to do with their bodies, so I buried them in the marsh.'

The forest fire? Fearless' wife and child? But then what about Eriksson?

Fearless' eyes were black.

Sound no larger than the tapping of a fingernail against wood, but growing stronger.

Drum. Drum. Drum.

In town, a woman has washed, put on a new dress and braided her hair. As she crosses the green, there it is, that sun in the sky. Small, but impertinent, it reaches for her cheek. The woman mistakes the feeling for happiness. She sighs.

'I need to speak with the priest,' *she says, when she reaches the house across from her own and the door has opened.*

'I told him,' *the fleshy woman inside says, wringing her hands.* 'I told him, spring was coming and he risked being caught at the coast.'

Drum. Drum. Drum.

On the river and the lake, the snow begins to open. A spruce tree lets fall on the white below the seeds she has hidden in her cones.

Underneath the snow, on the ground, there are things; things long thought dead: flowers in knots, whole branches held in tight buds. They start to tingle and stir.

Drum. Drum. Drum.

North: a settler stands by the window. Daylight, he thinks. Would you have thought it? Daylight again, this year too. It has begun to drip from the roof and he stares at each clear drop as it grows and takes on colours, quakes and then falls.

Behind him, his woman coughs. He walks to put one hand underneath her frame and the other on her shoulder, feels her bones hard and thin as jail bars underneath her dress. He turns her on to her side.

He looks down at the shrivelled being in the bed. Has a sudden vision she'll survive him.

Drum. Drum. Drum.

In a clearing on the mountain's west side, the snow moves. It's being torn away from below. A paw breaks through and a litter of bear cubs peer out from their den.

There's a fluttering in the air. It's the small creatures that dare to return: tits and starlings. They dart through the air, hoping to find last year's nests still intact.

Drum. Drum. Drum.

South: a settler can't look at his youngest daughter. What could he possibly say?

In the corner of his eye, he sees her on a chair beside him, legs not quite reaching the floor.

'Stop staring,' he tells her.

She doesn't.

'I said, stop staring!'

He stands up and walks out.

He stands for some time outside the door. Then he steps off the porch. The surface of the snow breaks under his weight and he slips right through it down to his knee.

Drum. Drum. Drum.

Ice on all the branches, eyes on black twines. Underneath roof edges, close to the walls, the snow has become clear and is forming tall spears.

Water. Rippling, dripping, flowing. The sun turns the lake into a field of fallen stars.

Sounds: stirrings and awakenings. By the river, the white is covered in black spots. It is moving. Thousands of stoneflies crawling, looking for something to eat.

Drum. Drum. Drum.

The snow is leaving. The mounds sink and settle, pour out and down. It's already down to its first layers: coarse and grainy, so transparent the ground is almost visible right through.

The river tries to break through her lock. She groans. Down by her outflow, she begins to gnaw at the lake ice. Then she pushes through with a scream. Her whole centre starts slipping downwards, slowly at first, then tearing down.

In the lake, water warms up and rises.

Only the marsh is still frozen solid.

Drum. Drum. Drum.

Springwinter. Reindeer calving. Births of the new. The Lapps are hurrying to make it out. The high mountains await them.

Their leader is not with them.

Drum. Drum. Drum.

The days lengthen, going towards everlasting. The snow has gone and what has rotted underneath lies bare. There should be a foul smell, but there isn't. No, the air is unmoved. There's a whiff of something like plain wet earth.

Drum. Drum. Drum.

By the lake, a settler stands on his porch staring towards the water. By the shore, in the last remaining air pockets, perch and bream will be hovering, desperate for the ice to break. Yet he doesn't go fishing. Not much time now, he thinks. And: once spring breaks through, then all this will be over.

He goes inside. As he pulls his curtains shut, he relives how his screams echoed their every one. How, when he tried to carry them, they fell apart in his hands. He crumbles.

Drum. Drum. Drum.

And then, without warning, the water from the mountains breaks through . . . A tidal wave of the melted and dead.

The river scrambles its banks. The lake swallows its shores. Water gushes into the forest until the trees are knee-deep.

And now the marsh, too, begins to bubble as she thaws.

PART THREE

The church was white against the blue skies, the colour so bright it hurt his eyes to watch, the spire so tall it seemed it might just offer the physical tie between heaven and earth. Olaus imagined that was why they were built thus. To impress on to the peasants their divinity – the Church as all-knowing, all-seeing.

After his conversation with the bishop, Olaus had tried to return to the Lappmark. He hadn't got far. The thaw had set in. He had returned and spent the days on his knees in the barren room in the bishop's residence, in agony, facing choices, unable to pray, unable to do anything else, and it wasn't until towards the end of his stay that he had felt something, someone, and he wasn't going to say it had been the voice of God, he wasn't even going to say it had been a God, but he had felt compassion amid the pain. Finally the roads became passable and he had returned home two days ago.

A warm breeze brushed his hair and he tilted his head at an angle to catch it on his face. A flash of memory of another imprint there on the skin of his cheek, as warm and bright as the sun, followed by a sharp sting of pain. He didn't know how Maija was faring. He didn't know what, if anything, had happened on the mountain. He shook his head to himself. Reminded himself that it wasn't for him. She wasn't for him.

There was a rustling noise behind him on the square. Olaus's fingers flew up to touch his collar and he turned around to watch the horse and carriage arriving. The coachman halted the horse in front of the church and he walked to greet it.

'Welcome,' he said.

The horse snorted and the voice of the coachman calming it was that of a young girl. The war has taken all our men, Olaus thought.

The passenger stumbled as he stepped down from the carriage, tired after his journey. He was pale and had a slight figure. Blond. He bowed far down over Olaus's hand.

'My name is Laurentius,' he said as he rose. He bent his head back to take in the full sight of the church and his mouth opened. 'It is beautiful,' he said.

His first assignment, Olaus was certain.

'Isn't it just,' he said. He unfastened the key ring from his belt and gave it to the young man. 'For the church, the stables and your dwelling. Your farmhand and your housekeeper will show you around. You'll have to recruit a new verger. The former one . . . left us.'

Laurentius took the heavy ring and turned it around in his hand as if studying it. 'There is a lock on the church?'

So young, Olaus thought. 'It's the largest one,' he said and bent to lift up his pack.

Confusion on Laurentius' face. 'You're leaving? I thought we would have time. To talk about the church . . . its history, the parishioners . . .' As the knowledge that he was already left to his own devices dawned on the young man, his face weakened to that of a child.

'Don't worry,' Olaus said. 'The former priest's widow lives right there.' He turned Laurentius around and pointed. 'In the vicarage. She was her husband's right hand. Nowhere else have I heard of a woman who has contributed so much to the

396

service of the Lord. I recommend you make her acquaintance a matter of priority. Her year of grace is soon over.'

'But won't you introduce me to her?'

Olaus hesitated. 'No.' He threw his knapsack into the cart and climbed after it. 'But give her my regards.'

He was leaving. The pain throbbed so bad inside him, for a moment, he thought he'd never manage. He inhaled.

'The settlers on Blackåsen,' he said. 'Look after them.'

He left the new priest standing alone in the yard.

'As far south as you can take me,' Olaus said to the girl on the coachman's seat.

'I was supposed to take you to the bishop at the coast,' she said.

He shook his head. 'South,' he repeated.

As the coach set in motion, Olaus removed his collar and folded it up. He hesitated, then he took out the bundle of letters the bishop had given him for Maija from her husband. The bishop had promised to deliver them, but hadn't as he didn't know what the new stable boy would inadvertently divulge, about who had been in town at what time, or other things that would mean nothing to him, but might to somebody else.

Olaus wouldn't see Maija again. And Paavo was most likely already on his way back. He threw the letters and his collar into the forest.

The carriage bumped along the road and Olaus turned around. Not for the church or the old vicarage, no. Absolutely not to look at the mountains. No, he wanted to see the bell tower. One last time.

Maija was walking towards the top of Blackåsen Mountain. There were light green buds on the spruce trees. New grass already pushed up through what had mouldered: spiky, tall at once as if it had been before it even began. From the trees above her came the quickening song of a meadow pipit in flight. With every sign of spring, winter distanced itself. With every sound of the new, the past paled. She thought it would be the same for the other settlers, too, hoped even for Daniel and Anna and little Sara. This winter would be one they wouldn't talk about, that they would not be able to explain to someone who hadn't been there. It would be a winter they would choose to forget. Once Gustav had told Maija, Nils and the others about causing the forest fire that had set off so many things for Daniel, Daniel had released his grip around Maija's arm and walked out. With him gone, none of the others touched her.

Her quest to find Eriksson's killer had almost lost her everything. Now, in the light of spring, she couldn't understand what had taken her; why she hadn't been able to leave be. She guessed they would never know what really happened to Eriksson, but it was over.

Maija reached the summit and looked out over the verdant valley, towards the blue mountains on the horizon. She had to shade her eyes with her hand, so strong was the light. Winds from the west. A warm puff against her forehead. She breathed. She drank the fresh air. It was as if winter had lasted for a hundred years.

Paavo would be back any day now, she thought. She wasn't certain what to feel about it. She didn't want him to come, and yet she did. Together, they would make it better again. She wouldn't see the priest until the Catechetical hearing in September, and that was a good thing, although he was the one she missed so much, her heart could break. She would tell the priest that. Perhaps she would tell him all about herself. The priest was the kind of man you could talk to, and through meeting him, in a strange way, the past felt less present. Perhaps she could reconcile with it. The other day, she had thought about the gifts she used to have, and wondered whether they were lost to her for ever, or whether they were still there inside her.

Dorotea's feet were already healing. The toes were gone, but the scarring was white and neat. She would always have a limp. The thought had brushed by her, that perhaps Frederika had been right, and the cutting had been unnecessary. But that was a thought she couldn't allow to grow roots, so she sent it over the cliff and down into the valley.

She wanted her daughters. She turned and as she half ran down the path towards their homestead, a memory of Frederika as a baby came to her. Frederika had been in Jutta's arms. Maija had been sitting with them, fat and so tired, locked into her own head alone with all those thoughts . . . Someone had made a joke – she couldn't remember who or what was said, but she remembered laughing for the first time in months. And when she looked up, her baby was watching her and her little face was lit up, her mouth open. Her baby had been laughing because her mother laughed.

A movement to her left made Maija stop. She advanced, holding her breath, pushing the branches away.

In the midst of the trees, there was a small clearing. Six small, dark brown beings: biting each other, rolling around, nuzzling. Wolf puppies. At the far end of the opening, under a fallen silver tree trunk, lay the pale bitch. She was looking straight at Maija, her brows raised. Her jaw was open. She was smiling.

Maija watched the little ones play. But the rest of the pack wouldn't be far, ready to assimilate the new ones, love them as their own. She let go of the branches, stepped backwards and came face to face with Fearless.

Fearless' face was dirty, his silver hair dark grey. He had aged. She hadn't thought about him, and now she felt guilty.

'I am so sorry,' she said. 'I was wrong about . . . so many things.'

'And right,' he said.

The dirt on his face: vertical streaks on each cheek. As if he had cried mud.

He has lost a wife and child. Until she . . . until Gustav had told them, Fearless had had no idea what had happened to his family. Now he did.

'Tell your daughter I am back,' Fearless said, and took a step to the side to pass her.

Maija felt cold. 'What does that mean?'

She tried to meet his gaze, but he was looking far beyond her.

'What have you done?' she said.

'The customs of vengeance are older than both you and

me,' he said. The tone of his voice was the sort you used to comfort a child.

'What have you done?' she repeated, although in some corner of her mind, she already knew.

'I buried Gustav alive in the marsh. Facing them.'

Frederika leaned back against the warm wood of the barn. The sleeves on the dress her mother had woven had become too short, and her hands on the grass by her sides looked large. The air was soft and sweet. There had been the rich spirals of a nightingale's song – spring had indeed come, but now the yard was quiet.

Fearless was still on Blackåsen, although his footsteps were absenting themselves. That's good, she thought. Fearless could finally travel home to the high mountains. And not far from Blackåsen, in her mind's eye she could see Antti, motionless by the river, waiting for his elder.

Her mother's movements had ceased. Where there had been swells, there was now a mere flutter. Frederika wondered if her mother was crying. She had never seen her mother cry, and so she didn't know.

Frederika felt the other woman approaching, the one she was waiting for. Then came her footsteps: muted on the grass.

'Frederika?'

Her voice was jovial, but forced. Her blonde hair was tied up in a twist that had come loose. Her cheeks were red, her breathing awkward.

'I had such a strange dream.' Their eyes met and Kristina's smile disappeared. She nodded, efficient now. 'You called for me, and I came. How peculiar.'

'It was you who killed Eriksson,' Frederika said.

Kristina sighed.

'He deserved to die,' she said then.

'Perhaps. But that's not why you killed him.'

Kristina made a face. 'Ah, and so you know that too. My husband has a weakness. He likes children . . .'

Frederika nodded. 'This is why you send your daughters away,' she said.

Kristina hesitated. 'Yes,' she said.

'To be on the safe side,' Frederika said.

'To be on the safe side.'

'And why you wore an amulet with marjoram.'

'I do what I can.'

'So what happened?'

'When Nils helped restore the school-house, he and Lundgren must have discovered they had this in common. I watch my husband, Frederika. By God, I do. But I can't always be with him. I didn't know he had taken it up again until, two years ago, a girl became with child. I had to ask the bishop for help. After this, I was certain that Nils had learned his lesson, but no . . .'

Frederika felt the low churning in her stomach. Not one thought for the children. You're forgetting it could have been my sister, she thought.

'So what happened?' she asked.

'Whoever the young girl was this time, she told Eriksson. He came to our home to find Nils, knife in hand. I sent Eriksson to the King's Throne, said he'd find my husband there. As he left, I followed him.'

'Then the bishop lied when he said you and Nils were with him at the time of the murder . . .' Frederika said. 'Why is he helping you?'

'There are big things at stake. None of us is willing to risk that. Not now when we are so close.'

Frederika saw before her the man in the blue jacket and boots that reached his thighs, walking the trench. She remembered the faceless shadows following him. That was what Kristina was talking about. That's what she considered more important than the suffering of the children.

'Does Nils know it was you who killed Eriksson?' Frederika asked.

'I didn't lie about Nils being at the summit of the mountain. And I made certain Nils saw what I had to do for his sake. He was full of remorse, of course.'

'And then you sent him to us to talk of sorcery,' she said.

'We knew people would believe that. But then he got enamoured with the idea of a village. He just can't help it.' Kristina shook her head. 'I think he actually managed to forget what had happened and his own part in it. And the talk of a village, in turn, got your mother going.'

'And Lundgren?'

'That was Nils.' Kristina lowered the corners of her mouth and made a face as if, by shooting the verger, her husband had surprised her. 'Lundgren would have talked.'

They fell silent. Frederika saw the knife in Kristina's pocket. She saw the strong fingers gripping its shank.

'Join us, Frederika,' Kristina said. 'You are young, but if you have gifts like that . . . I'll teach you the ways of nobility and with the King dead, all roads will be open to you. You'd have all you could ever wish for.'

All I ever wish for, Frederika thought. She wanted to smile. She didn't need Kristina for that to happen. Her head felt light. She did smile and rose.

'You won't be able to stop what's in progress, you know,' Kristina said.

'I am not planning on trying.'

'So what will you do?'

Frederika brushed her hands off against her dress.

Then she said, 'Nothing.'

She looked towards the forest behind Kristina. At the four low shapes that she saw, but Kristina could not.

I will do nothing, she thought. But they will.

ACKNOWLEDGEMENTS

I would like to thank my much loved friend, Fergal Keane. Without you, I would neither have begun, nor finished, writing this book.

So many wonderful people have believed in this work. Their advice, editing and author aftercare have been priceless: thank you to my agents, Janelle Andrew, Rachel Mills and her team at Peters, Fraser & Dunlop – you are the wisest people I know; Amanda Murray and her colleagues at Weinstein Books in the USA; Sara Nyström at Wahlström and Widstrand, Sweden; Jennifer Lambert at HarperCollins, Canada; and Martina Wielenberg at Droemer Knaur in Germany. A special thank you to Kate Parkin at Hodder & Stoughton, UK, for being so supportive and encouraging, and making me laugh even in editing round three.

Thank you to my dear writer friends, Mary Chamberlain, Vivien Graveson, Haroon Hassan, Susanna Jones, Laura McClelland, Lorna Read, Alex Ruczaj, Saskia Sarginson, Lauren Trimble, for reading the many drafts over many years and following the evolution of this work. Your honesty, creativity and tireless feedback – even when it was difficult to hear – have helped me greatly.

I'd like to finish with the comment my husband sent to me in an email after reading my first draft acknowledgements, where the final thank you was to him, my mother and our twin daughters:

'I don't think you should dedicate this book to us. It's nice, but quite common – and you're not. Of course you love us and we feel part of your journey, but in reality it's what you created and the support you built around yourself that made this happen. All we did was give you some space.'

For that kind of love, Dave, – and the space, I am so deeply grateful.

FIND OUT MORE ABOUT THE WORLD OF *WOLF WINTER* . . .

- Q & A with Cecilia Ekbäck

- Reading Group Guide to *Wolf Winter*

- *Wolf* – a brief essay

- Author's Note

❄ ❄ ❄

Q&A
WITH CECILIA EKBÄCK

❧   Does Blackåsen Mountain actually exist?

Not as a physical place, but its nature is something I remember from my childhood: a combination of the places and memories I have from Hudiksvall, where I grew up, Knaften and Vormsele, the two small villages in Lapland where my grandparents lived, and Sånfjället, a mountain close to the Norwegian border, where our family had a cabin.

Blackåsen is the embodiment of what I felt like growing up in the north of Sweden. It represents the fear, the doubts, the religious fervour, the loneliness and the need to fit in and to belong.

❧   Why did you write *Wolf Winter*?

My father was my best friend. The period preceding and just after his death was my Wolf Winter. As he lay dying, I interviewed him about his life. He died and I continued speaking, with my grandmother, her sister, their friends, my mother . . . *Wolf Winter* came out of those conversations.

❧   What made you set out to write an historical novel?

I don't see this as an 'historical novel' as such. I wrote the book four times. The first time it was set in 2005 and was a family saga, then it was set in 1930, then in 1865 and finally the book found its true home in 1717.

So I didn't set out consciously to write a book set in the past. I have a bad memory, and little patience for detail, but this story seemed to set itself in 1717 and that was that. I read everything I could find on the period, and talked to people much more knowledgeable than myself, but while I hope that it does reflect its time and place, the writing is mine and ultimately I will always prefer a fascinating tale to the obsessively accurate.

🍁 Where does the title *Wolf Winter* come from?

The expression 'Wolf Winter' – in Swedish '*Vargavinter*' – refers to an unusually bitter and long winter, but it is also used to describe the darkest of times in a human being's life – the kind of period that imprints on you that you are mortal and, at the end of the day, always alone. The old Nordic religions talked about '*fimbulvetr*', 'the large winter,' that preceded the destruction of the world. *Fimbulvetr* took place when Fenrisulven, the 'wolf of the wolves', had eaten the sun . . .

🍁 Your book contains strong elements of faith, Shamanism and magic. Are you a believer?

I was raised in the Pentecostal faith and have found it difficult to rid myself of it. In principle I don't want to believe in a God I haven't chosen, but the beliefs seem to be braided in with my very backbone. Wrangling with 'faith' is a big part of who I am.

🍁 What are the goals of the characters in your book?

I think Maija and the priest are both desperate to 'make things right', to get a second chance. Unfortunately they are what they are. It will be hard for them not to repeat the same mistakes again. Frederika is still being formed – and this story is a large part of what forms her.

🍁 There are some very unfortunate mistakes made by characters in *Wolf Winter* . . .

Yes, but there are also some moments of grace.

Is thinking about death a Scandinavian trait?

Darkness does inspire dark thoughts, and our winters are long. Solitude does, too. But the summers are all light and seemingly never-ending.

Why do you write?

All my characters are flawed. I love flaws in other people, always have, both psychological and physical. I hate them in myself. One of the main reasons I write are because of these flaws of mine. I wish I was as wise as my mother, as loyal as my husband. I wish I was calm and composed, unselfish, reliable, disciplined . . . The list goes on.

The arrival of our twin daughters changed my view on nurture versus nature. I used to be heavily weighted towards the former, but each girl arrived with her own personality from day one. There are so many things we never choose, but that are just there in us, inherited from generations and generations. It doesn't absolve us from responsibility and, of course, all our actions have consequences, but the thought gives me some comfort. I think the reason I write is to explore that.

Who is your favourite character in the book?

The priest and Maija, equally.

Not Frederika?

No, with my background, and the struggles I have had with questions around 'faith' and 'callings' since I was young, she feels a bit too close to home. Writing her, I wanted to shout at her to leave it, to tell her she is too young to take on such responsibility, too immature. But she kept saying: there is nobody else . . .

When writing *Wolf Winter*, you had a full time job and twins. When did you write?

Between four and eight in the morning, and any other free moment I could find. Sometimes after the girls had gone to bed. But it has taken me four years to write this book.

❧ Why have you included interludes in the book?

In the old days when there were no roads in Lapland, there were periods when the snow did not carry the weight of a man, either because it had just fallen or because it was melting, and the settlers were confined to their homesteads. I liked that idea, because it forces a solitude onto the characters in which they cannot take any action, but can only reflect on what has happened and worry about what is to come. Ultimately, before the elements, they are powerless.

In this book, I wanted 'place' – the mountain – to be almost a character in its own right. It felt right to give it a voice in the interludes. Blackåsen Mountain watches the settlers. It doesn't care. It is dispassionate. It has already seen many of them come and go and it will see many more come and go after them.

❧ Was writing *Wolf Winter* a very different process from being a professional with a career?

Yes, in all ways. Writing is an internal life, as opposed to an external which is what I was used to. Writing is lots of solitary time, thinking. As I wrote a lot when I was younger, this time on my own and in my head, is something I have missed, but that I also find difficult to go back to. I am not patient. I have always worked towards deadlines. I am used to multitasking and working with continuous interruptions. I like to see the end result quickly. Writing demands a different working style and at times it is so painful, I feel I just had to leave, get out, see people, anything to take me away from the desk.

On the other hand, my work discipline helps me to be very disciplined in my writing – I rarely do leave . . .

❧ Why did you decide to use three voices to tell the story?

Society in those days was compartmentalised. Lapland was isolated. I wanted several people to tell the story from their perspective. I didn't want anyone of them to have the whole truth. I didn't want us to know if we could trust them.

I chose the priest for three reasons: because he is Swedish, because he is a man and because he is educated and therefore has access to the higher echelons of society. Maija is there because of her Finnish heritage, because she is a settler, and a woman who is very rational and progressive for her time. I chose Frederika because she is a child who is still developing and because she is spiritual. These three very different points of view provide a counterpoint and allow for different interpretations of the subject matter

Was it difficult to write from a male perspective?
Strangely enough, the priest was always the one who was most clear to me. I didn't find it difficult to write him. However, in the beginning he was even more vain and selfish. I loved him, but as time went I had to tone him down, make him nicer, for other readers to give him a chance.

Is the ending meant to be tragic or hopeful?
I want to leave that with the reader. Some of the characters find themselves in a very tragic aftermath, but, as people do, surely they will start all over again . . .

What other writers do you like?
I love Hilary Mantel, I love the Norwegian writer Aksel Sandemose, Philip Roth, Graham Greene, Ali Smith, Siri Hustvedt, Hannah Kent, Eowyn Ivey . . .

There is one book I keep on my book shelf and that will perhaps always only be half-read. It's Saul Bellow's *Herzog*. Every time I start reading it, I think to myself that, surely, this is the most brilliant book ever written and then I can't continue reading. What if I will never find anything better? And thus I put it back on the shelf.

What language do you find it easier to write in, Swedish or English?
I left Sweden when I was 20 years old, so my Swedish is still that of

a young adult in the 1990s. It has taken me a long time to be able to write in English, but now it is easier for me to write in English than Swedish. I still make a lot of grammatical errors and find that some Swedish expressions do not translate well. Sometimes I use them nevertheless, and poorly translated, because they demonstrate a way of thinking or they impart a wisdom.

I fixate on words and use them to death – but this is me being obsessive, and not linked to writing in a second language. In my first version of *Wolf Winter*, I had several hundred 'doors' and several hundred 'eyes.'

Since the birth of my daughters I use Swedish much more as I speak to them in Swedish. It used to be that I thought in a different language depending on the topic, but now I find my mind is fully Swedish. I worry about what this will do to my writing.

I write slowly. I need to use both dictionary and thesaurus. I need other people to help me proof read.

🍁 Is it challenging, writing about a country in which you no longer live?

In *Wolf Winter* I don't try to say something about Sweden. I do try and say something about myself.

🍁 Do you write about what you know?

Yes and no. I think it is easier to have unique insights into something you are familiar with; it also means you do not have to do the same amount of research, but ultimately it is probably about knowing about what you write.

The most important thing to me has been to write every day ('without hope, without despair'). It allows you to live in your writing and keep your head firmly lodged inside it.

🍁 Will your next book follow the lives of the same characters?

No, I think we have to leave them there. I, too, would so like to know what happens to the priest – I think he might be destined for something big. As for Frederika, Fearless and Maija, towards the end of *Wolf Winter*, they are all approaching the Spirits – I think this might become very troublesome for them. However, I think a sequel would run the risk of becoming too similar to the first.

Would you consider writing a book that didn't have a Swedish background?
Yes. I have lived half of my life abroad and feel very at home in a number of cultures, but right now I am homesick for Sweden so it will be a while before that happens.

Do you have a favourite Scandinavian writer?
I read the writings of a number of Swedish thinkers: Ylva Eggehorn, Olof Wikström, Tomas Sjödin.

As for novels, amongst the translated ones, I really like Finnish Sofi Oksanen and Swedish Torgny Lindgren, Icelandic Yrsa Sigurðardóttir. I love crime writer Åsa Larsson from Sweden, Henning Mankell and Jo Nesbø.

A READING GROUP GUIDE

TOPICS FOR DISCUSSION

- To what extent does landscape affect the behaviour of the characters in *Wolf Winter*?

- There are three narrators in this story: Maija, Frederika and the priest. How do their narrative styles differ?

- Women are at the centre of this story. Given the period in which the books is set, their agency is limited. How easy is it for a modern reader to accept this?

- How would you characterise the relationship between Maija and Frederika?

- Jutta, Maija's grandmother, appears to her. What role does she play?

- Why is Maija so hostile to Frederika's gifts?

- What role do animals – real and imagined – play in this story?

- Other, older, belief systems lies very close to the surface of people's lives on Blackåsen Mountain. How does the Church attempt to control and manipulate them for its own end?

- Cecila Ekbäck has described a 'Wolf Winter' as a moment in our lives when we confront our very darkest thoughts. How do the three main characters emerge from their Wolf Winters?

- What do you imagine lies in store for the priest?

- When Maija's husband returns (we may assume he does), how might their relationship have changed?

- Each of the settlers has brought with them to their new homes on Blackåsen Mountain the burdens of their pasts. How do the events in the book impact on them?

- What lies behind Elin Eriksson's actions?

- The Lapps lead their lives largely in parallel to the settlers. What happens when the two communities come together?

- Why does Maija persist in her enquiries?

- Do you think the priest is a moral, immoral or amoral agent in the story?

- Why do you think the other settlers regard Maija as a threat?

WOLF

I have never seen wolf in nature, only in captivity. But as a little girl, when I visited my grandmother, we would hear them at night howling higher up on the mountain – eerie, lingering wails. I would get out of bed and go downstairs to find my grandmother standing by the kitchen window staring out into the dark.

'Maybe Kenneth's dogs,' she would say to me, face grim.

We both knew these were not dogs.

My grandmother was afraid even though we were inside. It was clear wolf was not just a wild animal, but more. Wolf was part of the night. And wolf could, obviously, pass through closed doors.

In daylight, it felt different. She'd point out their dens. We'd study their tracks in the snow.

'This is the cliff they stand on when they howl,' she'd say and show me a big stone.

In the daytime we were Christian and we were not afraid.

Poor wolves. Seen as evil, or as a tool for evil since the beginning of times. In the 13th century, the Catholic church said that wolves were put on the earth by God to punish mankind for their sins. And in Sweden people were scared to the extent that they wouldn't use the real name which in Old Norse was *ulv* in case it might attract the beast. Instead we used the noa-word *varg*, which means something like 'the one who commits violence'.

Later *varg* became standard and then we couldn't say that either. People began to say 'grey legs,' or 'the grey one.'

The Swedish expression *vargavinter* – 'wolf winter' – means a very long, cold winter. It was sometimes used to describe the bitterest winter with starvation. People feared that during such winters, wolf would come south and look for prey . . . The old Nordic religions talked about *fimbulvetr*, 'the large winter,' that preceded the destruction of the world. It took place when *Fenrisulven*, the 'wolf of the wolves', had eaten the sun. 'Wolf winter' is now also used to describe the darkest of times in a human being's life – the kind of period that imprints on you that you are mortal and, at the end of the day, always alone. And 'vargtimmen', or 'the wolf hour', is that time at dawn just before light returns. The one who can sleep has their worst nightmares; the one who cannot, is gripped by severe angst.

For many people, wolf is an important symbolic animal, or totem animal. As a spiritual animal it symbolises a strong connection with instinct. The wolf is a representation of the night – the lonesome and scary time. But wolf ventures far into the forest to find what he requires for sustenance and if we, similarly, face our deepest fears, we might discover important things about ourselves.

Wolf has always polarised the opinions in Sweden. It still does. Cattle owners feared it, wanted it dead. Hunters admired it and wanted to learn its skills. Today the debate is between those who want to permit hunting and limit the number of wolves in Sweden, and those who say they are a vital part of our fauna and must be protected. For an animal which isn't seen often, it commands a lot of emotion.

And it does. Seeing wolf in captivity, I felt incredibly sad, but also fearful. It was irrational, and yet. . .

'It's in a cage,' my husband pointed out.

'Doesn't mean a thing,' I said tersely.

This – this deep-rooted fear of the animal – the expression 'wolf winter' – the fact that the characters in my book are all forced to face their deepest fears – is why I selected wolf to be

Frederika's spirit animal. It is said that spirit wolves are too difficult to tame, but the girl is powerful. If anyone can do it, it is her.

And now, here in Calgary, we hear coyote howl at night. Doesn't bother me at all.

AUTHOR'S NOTE

For *Wolf Winter*, I wanted to find a period where my characters' world was changing, crumbling, creating additional uncertainties in their lives. In the warm dusty corridors of the London Library in St James's Square, I came across a series of colourful, descriptive history books called *Svenska Folkets Underbara Öden* [*The Swedish People's Wonderful Adventures* – author's translation of title], by Carl Grimberg, written in the early 20th century and published by Norstedt & Söners Förlag. As I read the volume covering the period 1709-1759, I thought – yes, this is when it all happens. This was a real Wolf Winter for Sweden. On the first page, the book has an inscription in capital letters: 'SWEDEN IS ATTACKED, WHILST THE KING IS AWAY IN FOREIGN COUNTRY'.

In 1717, Sweden found itself on the cusp of massive change. Its position as a great power, which began in the early 17th century and had bestowed on Sweden control over much of the Baltic region, was looking increasingly uncertain. At this point Sweden was fighting in the Great Northern War against Denmark, Poland, Saxony, Hanover, Prussia and Russia. Apart from short periods, the country had been at war for over 150 years. These wars took their toll, both on state finances and, of course, on individuals. Sweden's population in 1700 was around 1.5 million. It is not known how many men died in active service, but the number often cited is close to half a million. The villages were depleted of able menfolk with, in additional to the personal costs, consequences for farming. To finance the wars, the king imposed higher taxes, higher customs fees, and – for as long as it was possible – borrowed abroad. Add to this a few years of crop failure and the plague that returned in 1710 and the times would have felt very dark indeed.

For most of his adult life, King Charles XII warred abroad. Crowned at only fifteen, he was a remarkable warrior who commanded fierce loyalty not only from his troops, but also from his subjects. Courageous, he displayed the kind of confidence that comes with the conviction that you are God's envoy. He abstained from alcohol and women and, by all accounts, seemed most comfortable at war, amongst his men, dressed like one of them. He was killed in 1718, during an attempt to invade Norway, shot through the head, in a trench at Fredrikshald. Theories suggest that he was in fact either murdered on the instructions of his sister's husband – later crowned Frederik I – or was the victim of an aristocratic plot. In an attempt to clear up the mystery, his body has been exhumed three times, in 1746, 1859 and 1917. Whoever was responsible, his death marked the end of autocratic kingship in Sweden.

The nobility had every reason to resent the king. The balance of power inside Sweden shifted during Charles XII's reign to rest even more firmly in the monarch's hands. Parliament was forbidden to convene in his absence: the king ruled Sweden from the battlefield. Furthermore, in a bid to appropriate some of the nobles' money (and to some extent control their power), in the mid-17th century the crown initiated a *reduction*, in which it took back some of the fiefs it had granted, sometimes accompanied by large fines or payments. This had a significant effect on the economy and on the status of the nobility in Sweden. In 1710, desperately worried by the collapsing economy, the starvation and the threat of loss of territory, the royal council convened the parliament despite the king's command, for the first time since 1697. In 1713, the council convened the parliament again and sent a letter to the king begging him to seek peace, explaining that they could no longer muster the people or money to defend Sweden. While they were still gathered, they received a letter from the king sent five months earlier after he had first heard rumours of a possible assembly. It simply forbade them to convene.

All the key characters in *Wolf Winter* are fictional. (Although the noble Magnus Gabriel De la Gardie, did indeed exist, as far as I know he did not have a granddaughter named Kristina.) I wanted one of them to have direct links to what was going on in a broad national context and the priest Olaus Arosander is thus someone who has been close to the king. Olaus would have been very influential in his local community. Priests taught, preached, punished, conducted national registrations (from 1686 priests were required to conduct yearly catechetical hearings and keep records of births, marriages and deaths in church books) and also played a vital propaganda role. They had to explain the necessity of the wars to their parishioners and draw links between the parishioners' sins and poor war performance, and vice versa. The wars would later come to have another consequence for the church. Pietist tendencies were reinforced by Swedish soldiers who returned after having been prisoners-of-war in Russia with a more personal kind of faith, enjoying meeting at home, leading each other in worship and Bible study. In response, the *Konvetikelplakatet,* a law forbidding 'unofficial' religious gatherings was passed, with fierce punishments for those who dared to defy it.

Lapland spans four countries: Norway, Sweden, Finland and Russia. For historical details I turned to local books, such as *Om Tider som Svunnit* [*About Times Past* – author's translation of title], by Wolmar Söderholm, 1973, produced locally in the town of Lycksele to celebrate its 300th anniversary. For details on the living conditions, the food, and the clothing, I spoke to my grandmother, her sister, and their friends. My grandparents came from two villages outside Lycksele. My maternal grandmother began working when she was eight years old. She desperately wanted to become a teacher (like Frederika), but instead, her father asked the priest to release her early from school so that she could begin contributing to the family. The priest, on the occasion of according this request, lectured my grandmother about pride. When my grandparents met, my grandmother worked cooking food to men who were charcoal stacking. My grandfather, who'd become an orphan at the age of twelve – owning nothing but the clothes he wore and a silver spoon – was one of those men. It is their personal stories and those of their friends that inspired the basics for the lives Maija and her daughters lead. Industrialisation reached Lapland very late. My grandmother used to say that there was no 'in between'. They lived like people always had and then, overnight, they went from home-made shoes, to high heels.

As part of its nation-building in Lapland in the early 17th century, Sweden encouraged colonialisation and a lot of land that had previously been used by the indigenous people, the Sami, (referred to as 'Lapps' throughout *Wolf Winter*, as that was the name used at the time) was distributed to new settlers. At the same time, the church began missionary work amongst the Sami. The Sami religion, which comprised animism (all natural objects have a soul), polytheism (a multitude of spirits and gods) and shamanism, came increasingly under attack and was ultimately condemned. As in much of Europe, fear of 'sorcery' was strong: witch trials in Sweden took place 1667-1676 and from the 1680s onwards the church worked hard to eradicate Sami 'paganism'. The drums, which were used by Sami shamans to reach a state of ecstasy and access the world of the spirits, were burned. Few of them still exist, although there is one in the British Museum in London. As very little has been written down about Sami religion, I based Frederika's emerging spirituality on shamanistic journeying, on my imagination and in the belief that all religions are ultimately very much the same. The Sami main character in *Wolf Winter* has borrowed his name 'Fearless' from my own Sami ancestors.